Praise for the Stage Dive series

"This book rocked my world!! *Lick* is an addictive blend of heart-warming passion and light-hearted fun. It's a story you can lose yourself in. The perfect rock-star romance!"

—*Aestas Book Blog*

"Pure rocker perfection in every single way . . . *Play* is a splendid marriage of romance and comedy, a possibly even better book than its stellar prequel, and I would recommend it to anyone who likes their love stories with a side of giggles." —*Natasha Is a Book Junkie*

"The stuff my rock-star dreams are made of. A thrill-ride. I felt every stomach-dip in the process. And I want to turn right around and ride it again. Every girl that's ever had a rock-star crush, this would be the ultimate fantasy."

—*Maryse's Book Blog*

"*Lick* is a breath of fresh air with a unique storyline, think *Hangover* meets Contemporary Romance."

—*The Rock Stars of Romance*

"Kylie Scott is quickly becoming one of my favorite authors at combining funny with sexy, and I can't wait to read more from her. *Play* is a definite must-read book!"

—*The Smut Book Club*

"Mal is taking us all by storm . . . go buy this book. Seriously. You won't regret it." —*Fiction Vixen*

Lead
& Deep

Kylie Scott

St. Martin's Paperbacks

This is a work of fiction. All of the characters, organizations, and events portrayed in this novel are either products of the author's imagination or are used fictitiously.

LEAD & DEEP

Copyright © 2016 Kylie Scott.

All rights reserved.

For information address St. Martin's Press, 175 Fifth Avenue, New York, NY 10010.

ISBN: 978-1-250-10372-7

Our books may be purchased in bulk for promotional, educational, or business use. Please contact your local bookseller or the Macmillan Corporate and Premium Sales Department at 1-800-221-7945, ext. 5442, or by e-mail at MacmillanSpecialMarkets@macmillan.com.

Printed in the United States of America

"Lead" St. Martin's Griffin trade paperback edition / November 2014
"Deep" St. Martin's Griffin trade paperback edition / March 2015
St. Martin's Paperbacks edition / December 2016

St. Martin's Paperbacks are published by St. Martin's Press, 175 Fifth Avenue, New York, NY 10010.

10 9 8 7 6 5 4 3 2

Lead

With special thanks to
Jo Wylde, Sali Pow, and Natasha Tomic.

Dedicated to
the Australian Romance Readers Association.

ACKNOWLEDGMENTS

With thanks to my husband and family for yet again enduring the madness of another deadline. Their love and grace under pressure is astounding. I couldn't do it without their wholehearted support and willingness to eat microwave meals.

Big thanks to everyone at St. Martin's Press and Pan Macmillan Australia and the UK. Special thanks to my wonderfully supportive editor, Rose Hilliard, Haylee, and Catherine. Thanks to my lovely agent, Amy Tannenbaum at the Jane Rotrosen Agency, for her unflagging belief in me and excellent advice. Also to Chasity Jenkins from Rock Star PR & Literary Services for her friendship and assistance and to By Hang Le for the awesome graphics and love.

An extra special thanks to the ladies in Groupies. You guys rock.

Book blogging is an act of love. I don't think you could pay someone enough for the around-the-clock single-minded dedication to reading, reviewing, and keeping the romance community informed of breaking news and new releases, etc. (As always, I know I'm going to forget important people so please excuse me . . .) *Natasha is a Book*

Junkie, The Rock Stars of Romance, Maryse's Book Blog, Smut Book Club, Totally Booked Blog, Aestas Book Blog, Give Me Books, Love N. Books, Angie's Dreamy Reads, Globug and Hootie Need a Book, The Autumn Review, About That Story, The BookPushers, Wicked Little Pixie, Heroes and Heartbreakers, Hopeless Romantic, Smexy Books, Under the Covers Book Blog, Book Thingo, Shh Moms Reading, Hook Me Up Book Blog, Ana's Attic Book Blog, Kaetrin, Nelle, Jodie and Jess from *Indie Author's Down Under, Sassy Mum,* the ladies from *Fictionally Yours, Melbourne,* Angie, Mel and the *Triple M Bookclub, The Book Bellas, Random Hot Guy of the Day, VeRnA LoVeS bOoKs, Valley of the Book Doll, Up All Night Book Blog, Lit Slave, Three Chicks and Their Books, Love Between the Sheets, Rude Girl, Joyfully Reviewed, Night Owl Reviews,* Crystal, Cath, *Dear Author, Twinsie Talk Book Reviews, A Love Affair with Books, Harlequin Junkie,* Sahara, Kati, *Martini Times Romance, booktopia, Rosemary's Romance Books,* and many, many more. If you took the time to read and review one of my books, then thank you.

PROLOGUE

TWO MONTHS AGO . . .

The man's mouth kept moving but I'd long since tuned out.

They weren't paying me enough for this. Impossible. Day two on the job and I was ready to throw myself out a window. The music biz will be fun, they said. It'll be glamorous, they said. They lied.

". . . is that so hard to understand? Am I getting through to you? An éclair is a long, chocolate-frosted donut with custard in the middle. Not this, this . . . round thing you've bought me. AGAIN," the idiot thundered, jowls shaking.

Over at her desk, his P.A. slunk further down in her seat, just in case he decided to make her the next target, no doubt. Fair enough. She probably wasn't getting paid enough either. Only a masochist would enjoy this for under a hundred bucks an hour. Usually I tried to get temp jobs that lasted a couple of months or so. Long enough to make some money, short enough to avoid getting caught up in any drama.

Usually.

"Are you listening to me?" Fake-tanned flesh turned from orange to a startling shade of burgundy as his anger grew. If he had a heart attack, I wasn't giving him mouth-to-mouth. Some other brave soul could make the sacrifice.

"Miss . . . whatever your name is," he said. "Go back to the shop and get me what I asked for this time!"

"Morrissey. My name is Lena Morrissey." I passed him a napkin, taking care not to touch him because a true professional always kept her distance. Also, the guy was just that repugnant. "And this is for you."

"What is it?"

"It's a message from the duty manager at the donut shop apologizing for the lack of long, tasty, phallic-shaped éclairs. Apparently they don't get baked until later in the day," I said. "Since you failed to believe me when I explained this to you yesterday. I thought you might be more inclined to believe it if it came from a higher authority in the donut world."

The poor perplexed darling looked from me to the napkin and back again.

"His name was Pete. He seemed nice, you should call him if you need further verification. You'll see I got him to write his number down there at the bottom." I tried to point to the digits in question but Adrian snatched his hand back, scrunching the napkin into a ball of rubbish. Oh well, I tried.

Sort of.

Laughter burst forth from the corner of his office. A good-looking guy with long blond hair grinned at me. Glad Blondie was amused. I on the other hand was probably definitely about to get fired.

Wait, was that Mal Ericson from Stage Dive?

Fuck a duck, it was.

So the three other men must be the rest of the band members. I tried to avert my eyes, but my eyes had other ideas. Famous people. Huh. At least I'd managed to see some up close before getting my ass canned. They didn't seem particularly different from us normal human beings, just a little prettier, perhaps. Even with having sworn off men, their wow factor couldn't be denied. The two guys with dark hair and fair faces were huddled together, flicking through some documents. They'd be David and Jimmy Ferris, the brothers. Ben Nicholson, the bass player and largest of them all, was stretched out, hands behind his head, fast asleep. Kudos to him. Not a bad method for getting through a meeting.

Mal gave me a finger wave. "Lena Morrissey, huh?"

"Yes."

"I like you. You're funny."

"Thanks," I replied drily.

"Mal, buddy." Adrian butted in. "Let me just get rid of this . . . woman. And we can finish up our business."

The corporate monster turned his beady little eyes back to me. "You're fired. Get out of here."

And there you had it. Big sigh.

"Not so fast." Mal rose to his feet and just kind of swaggered on over. Talk about snake hips. "So you do admin-type shit here?"

"I did. Yes."

He gave me an easy smile. "You don't seem very impressed by me, Lena. Am I not impressive to you?"

"Sure you are. I guess I'm just a bit busy getting fired right now to fully appreciate the magnitude of the moment." Hands on hips, I looked him in the eye. He was cute and I bet that smile of his worked on lots and lots of women. But it wouldn't be working on me. "Rest assured, later I'm going to freak right out."

He leaned against the doorframe. "I've got your word on that?"

"Absolutely."

"I'm trusting you here."

"And I appreciate that, Mr. Ericson. I won't let you down."

He gave me a huge grin. "You're a bit of a smart ass. I like that."

"Thanks."

"You're welcome." Cocking his head, he tapped a finger against his lips. "You single, Lena?"

"And you want to know, why?"

"Just curious. Judging by the frown, I think the answer there is yes. And shame on my brothers everywhere for overlooking such a fine girl as yourself."

Quite a number of his "brothers" hadn't overlooked me. They'd chosen to screw me over instead, hence the frown. But no way in hell was I telling him that.

"Uh, Mal?" Adrian tugged on the thick gold chain around his neck as if it were a collar.

"Just a sec, Adrian." Mal gave me a slow looking over from top to toe, eyes lingering on the swell of my breasts. Big boobs, a lack of height, and childbearing hips ran in the family. My mom was exactly the same so there was really very little I could do about it. The lack of luck in love seemed more exclusive to me, however. Mom and Dad had been married nearly thirty years and my sister was about to be wed, not that I'd be attending. Long story. Or a short and shitty one, you pick.

Either way, I was just fine and dandy as I was, flying solo.

"I really think you could be the one, Lena," the drummer said, pulling me from my thoughts.

I blinked. "That so?"

"It is. I mean, look at you, you're so cute and cuddly. But what I especially love is how you're giving me that go-fuck-yourself look from behind your foxy glasses."

"You like that, do you?" My smile was all teeth.

"Oh, yeah. Big time. But you're not for me."

"No?"

"Sadly, not." He shook his head.

"Damn."

"Yeah, I know. You're really missing out." He sighed, slipping his hair back behind his ears. Then he looked over his shoulder. "Gentlemen, that problem we were talking about earlier. I believe I may have found a solution."

David Ferris looked from Mal to me and back again, his forehead creasing. "You serious?"

"A hundred and ten percent."

"You heard her, she's a secretary." The elder Ferris brother, Jimmy, didn't even look up from the papers. His voice was smooth, deep, yet deeply disinterested. "She's got no qualifications."

Mal snorted. "Because all the ones with the fancy degrees have done such a fucking bang-up job. How many have you fired or run off now? Time to come at the problem from a new perspective, dude. Open your mind to the wonder that is Miss Lena Morrissey."

"What are you talking about?" I asked, mystified.

"Guys, guys." The asshat, Adrian, started flapping his hands about in a panic. "You can't be serious. Let's stop and think about this."

"Give us a minute, Adrian," said David. "He isn't easy to live with. Think she can handle it?"

Jimmy snorted.

"Yeah, I do," said Mal, bouncing on the balls of his feet all excited like. He put up his dukes, as if for fighting. "Show me what you got, Lena. Knock me out. Come on, champ. You can do it. Put me against the ropes!"

What a nutter. I swatted his teasing fist away from my face. "Mr. Ericson, you have approximately five seconds to start making sense or I'm out of here."

David Ferris gave me a small smile. Of approval, perhaps? I don't know and it didn't matter. This circus had gone on long enough. I had explanations to go make to the temp agency. Given this wasn't the first time I'd butted heads with a jerk at a job, my hopes for forgiveness were low. I might have been asked to moderate my attitude a time or two. But really, life was too short to take shit. Let people walk all over you and you got what you deserved. I'd learned that the hard way.

Shoulders slumping in disappointment, Mal sighed. "Okay, okay. Don't play with me. See if I care."

He and David shared a look. Then David nudged his brother with an elbow. "Might be worth thinking about."

"She gives Adrian shit and suddenly she's the one?" asked Jimmy. "Seriously?"

"Mal's right, she's different."

Adrian made a small sound of despair. Petty or not, my heart thrilled to hear it. Perhaps today wasn't a complete write-off after all.

"Tell me, Lena," said Mal, his grin splitting his face. "How do you feel about Portland?"

"Doesn't it rain there constantly?" I asked. In all honesty, the idea of heading quite that far up into the Pacific North West did not appeal.

Mal groaned. "I know, lovely Lena, I know. Trust me, I've tried to get them to move back to LA, but they won't budge. Portland's where the Ferris bros be hanging these days. Even Benny boy's settled in up there."

Ben, the bass player, opened one eye and gave us both a tired look. Then he closed it and went back to sleep.

"C'mon, Jimbo," said Mal, bouncing about on the spot again. "Help me convince her Portland doesn't completely suck ass."

Finally, at long last, Jimmy sighed and looked up at me.

What Mal couldn't do to me, this one did with ease. Everything paused, apart from my pulse, beating loud behind my ears. The man was beautiful in much the same way as the stars. I could only look upon him with longing, he was so far out of my reach. Still, moments like these are meant to be momentous. Fate shifting beneath your feet should feel big. But instead of mood lighting and dramatic music, I got a cranky cold blue stare from a guy in a razor-sharp suit. Dark hair fell over his face and collar, framing the cheekbones of an angel but the jaw of a stubborn child. Every other discernible inch of him appeared to be fully grown male. The way he held his jaw, however . . . well.

And the man might be pretty, but he sure as hell wasn't nice. I'd met enough not-nice men to know. Trust me to find him attractive.

So I frowned straight back at him.

His glare went up a notch.

I matched it.

"Why, you two are getting along like a house on fire already! It's like you've known each other for years. I think she'll make you a wonderful live-in assistant," said Mal. "Tell him, Lena."

"A live-in assistant?" I parroted, clueless.

"Since when did I need an assistant?" Jimmy looked me over from top to toe, lips tight with obvious disapproval.

"Since you can't seem to keep a sobriety companion." His brother returned calmly, a little coldly even. "But it's your call. If you don't want to give her a go, the record company'll find you another companion. Someone suitable."

Jimmy cringed and the broad shoulders filling his suit curved inward. I almost felt bad for him. The guy might not have the sunniest of dispositions, but it wouldn't hurt his brother to show a little support. Siblings. What could you do?

"They gotta luck out and get someone you can stand being around eventually, right?" asked David. "You're doing great, but we can't afford for you to get off track now."

"I'm not going to get off track."

"We go on the road soon and your routine'll be shot to shit. Sort of situation where you could fall back into old habits easily. You heard what that latest therapist said."

"All right, Dave. All right. Christ." Despite his brother talking, Jimmy's ice-cold gaze never left me.

I stared back, unperturbed. It wasn't my style to back down from a challenge.

"I'll hire her," he said.

I laughed. "Um, Mr. Ferris, I haven't agreed to anything yet."

"But there are conditions," Jimmy continued.

Beside me, Mal thrust his fists in the air, making muted crowd-type noises. My comment seemed to have been overlooked entirely.

"I don't want you getting in my face all the time," said Jimmy, staring me down.

"One moment, please. So, you're offering me a job as your live-in assistant?" I asked, just to be sure.

"No, I'm offering you a trial period as my live-in assistant. Let's say a month . . . if you last that long."

I could make it a month with him. Probably. The money would need to be good, however. "What does the position involve and what does it pay?"

"It involves you not getting in my face and it pays double what you make here."

"Double?" My brows crept skyward.

"You don't report back to anyone about what goes on with me unless I go into meltdown," he said. "Then you only talk to one of the guys in the band or our head of security. Got it?"

"What sort of meltdown, exactly, are we talking about?"

"Trust me, if it happens, you'll recognize it. What was your name again?"

"Lena."

"Tina?"

"No. Lena. L-E-N-A."

Adrian made a faint gargling noise like someone was choking him. But it didn't matter. The only thing that mattered was the way Jimmy Ferris's forehead smoothed out. The anger or tension or whatever it was disappeared from his face and he gave me a thoughtful look. He didn't smile. Didn't even come close to it. But for just a moment, I wondered what it would take to make him.

Curiosity was a killer.

"Le-na," he rolled my name off his tongue like he was trying it on for size. "Okay. Stay the fuck out of my way and we'll see what happens."

CHAPTER ONE

Jimmy was losing it.

The hotel room door shuddered, something smashing loud against the other side. Inside, voices were raised, but the words were indistinct. Maybe I'd just hang out in the hallway for a while. It was tempting. All of this was my own damn fault, I should have been dust weeks ago. The facts were, despite the great money, me and this job didn't mesh. Every time I opened my mouth to tell him I quit, however, the words disappeared.

I couldn't explain it.

"Hey." Ev wandered toward me in a simple black dress, her fingers twining nervously. Her blonde hair had been pulled back into an elegant chignon.

"Hi."

"David's in talking to him."

"Right." I probably should have worn a dress too, gone traditional. The last thing I wanted was to publicly embarrass Jimmy on a day like today. Only November in North Idaho could be butt-chapping cold. For a native of warmer climates, they didn't make tights thick enough to combat this sort of weather.

The band and their entourage had been in Coeur

d'Alene for just over a week and Jimmy's mood had been black since our arrival. Worse even than normal. Mal's mom had passed four days ago, losing her battle with cancer. From what I could gather, Lori had been like a surrogate mom to the Ferris brothers. Their own had apparently been little more than an oxygen bandit, abandoning them early. I'd only met Lori a couple of times. No one could dispute she'd been a beautiful soul.

More muted shouting. Another thump.

"Guess I shouldn't have gone out for breakfast." Coffee, French toast, and far more maple syrup than one woman needed, churned inside my stomach. Comfort eating sucked. "Thought I'd beat him back from the gym."

"You can't watch him all the time."

"I'm paid to try." I shrugged. "God help me."

"And if you did, he'd fire you for getting in his face. Just like he did all the others. Giving him some breathing room is a good thing." Ev flinched, another almighty crash coming from within the room of doom. "Usually."

"Hmm."

Jimmy didn't fire all five of my predecessors, some he gently coaxed into quitting. Or at least, that's how he described it. But I didn't bother to correct her.

"David will calm him down," Ev said, her voice absolute.

It was sweet, the way she hero-worshipped her husband. I couldn't remember the last time I'd had such faith in a lover. David and Ev had gotten married one drunken night in Vegas six months back. It'd been splashed all over the media. Apparently, it was one hell of a story, though I hadn't managed to hear it all yet. Ev had asked me to go out with her and her friends a couple of times, but I always made excuses. Not that I didn't appreciate the gesture, it just didn't feel right with me working for her brother-in-law.

At any rate, dealing with Jimmy was my job. I gave Ev a small smile of apology and slid the room key through the lock. Time to don the hat of hard-assery which according to my ex, bless him, definitely fit.

Slowly, calmly, I pushed open the door. Four feet from my face a glass smashed against the wall, shocking the absolute shit out of me. I in turn hit the floor, my heart going manic inside my chest.

"Lena," Jimmy bellowed. "Get the fuck out of here!"

God damn mother-fucking rock stars.

Seriously.

Lucky I'd worn pants after all. Carpet burned knees would not have been nice. Also, the minute we got back to Portland, I was either finally quitting, demanding hazard pay, or both. No way was I making enough for this.

"Throw one more thing, Jimmy, and I'll shove my three-inch heel so far up your ass you'll need a surgical team to extract it." I glared up at him from behind my dark bangs. "Is that understood?"

He scowled.

I sneered.

Same old, same old.

"Are you all right?" David Ferris strode across the luxury suite, circumventing a broken side table and smashed lamp. He offered me his hand, helping me back up. Both Ferris brothers had looks, money, fame, and talent. Only one of them had any manners, however. Regardless of etiquette, my gaze stayed glued to the furious man on the other side of the room.

"Fine. Thanks." I straightened my skewed glasses.

"I don't think he's on anything," David said quietly. "Just having a bad day, you know?"

God, I hoped Jimmy hadn't taken anything. For both our sakes.

"It's a tough time for everyone, Lena."

"Yeah. I know."

Across from us, Jimmy paced back and forth, hands balled into fists. Normally, the man was a princess, a show pony, put together with perfection. Hair slicked back and designer everything. As eye candy went, his superior rock-god status made him ideal. I was safe to fantasize and indulge my libido while remaining well beneath his notice.

(Sadly, my sex drive hadn't died when I'd taken my vow of no men. How much simpler life would be if it had.)

Today, however, Jimmy seemed all too human, only half dressed with his dark hair falling over the sharp angles of his face and matching stubble lining his jaw. His usual airtight control was nowhere in evidence. The state of him and the room was shocking. Nothing seemed to have been left unharmed. I must have looked like one of those clowns at the fairs, the ones you where you lob a ball in their mouth to win a prize. My head kept turning this way and that, trying to take it all in.

"What a mess," I muttered.

"Want me to get Sam?" David asked, referring to the band's head of security.

"No, I got this. Thanks."

He narrowed his eyes. "I can't imagine him doing anything, but . . . he's pretty wound up. You sure?"

"Absolutely. We'll meet you downstairs." Confidence was everything. I held the door open and he slipped through, giving me worried looks all the while. My fake smile apparently failing to assuage.

"Maybe I'll hang around," he said. "Just in case."

"You hired me to deal with him. Don't worry. We'll be fine," I said, shutting the door on David and Ev's frowning faces.

Jimmy paced on, ignoring my presence.

I took one deep breath, and then another. Nice and

slow. Cool and calm. All of the usual pep talks whirled around and around inside my head. You didn't need to be perfect to get a job done, you just needed to be motivated. And think what I might of the man, his well-being was my job, my priority. I would do my best by him. Glass crunched beneath my heels as I carefully made my way across the room. Around the toppled sofa and over the broken lamp. I didn't want to guess what the bill for all this destruction would be. Security should have been up here already. Other guests must have heard the racket and complained by now, surely. Perhaps five grand a night bought some exceptional soundproofing.

Jimmy flashed me a dark look as I drew closer. His pupils seemed okay, normal size. He slammed his ass down on a dining room chair, displaying irritability and aggressiveness but excellent coordination. Maybe he hadn't taken anything.

"What's going on?" I asked, stopping in front of him.

No sign of blood though his knuckles were scratched and pink, tender looking. Legs apart, he braced his elbows on his knees and hung his head. "Get out, Lena. I want to be alone."

"I don't think that's a good idea."

He grunted.

"Isn't this a little clichéd, trashing your hotel room?"

"Fuck off."

I sighed.

All right, so aggravating him probably wasn't a good idea. I pushed my glasses further up the bridge of my nose, giving myself a chance to think. Time to try something new. The man only had on black suit pants, no shirt, no shoes. And as nice as his inked chest and shoulders were, he couldn't go like that to a funeral. Especially not in this weather.

"Jimmy, we're leaving soon. You need to finish getting

ready. You don't want to be late, do you? That would be disrespectful."

No response.

"Jimmy?"

"I hate when you use that voice," he said, still staring at the floor.

"What voice?"

"When you try and sound like my therapist. You're not, so cut the shit."

With there being no right answer, I kept my mouth shut.

Veins stood out in stark relief on the side of his neck and a sheen of sweat outlined the musculature of his back. Despite the anger, however, his pose was one of defeat. The man could be more than an occasional arrogant dick, but Jimmy Ferris was strong and proud. In the couple of months since I'd become his babysitter I'd seen him in all sorts of moods, the bulk of them bad. Never, though, had I seen him beaten. It hurt. And the pain was as unwelcome as it was surprising.

"I need something," he said, voice guttural.

"No!"

"Lena . . . shit. I can't—"

"You can."

"Just get me something," he snapped.

"I won't do that, Jimmy."

He surged to his feet, face tight with fury. Every survival instinct in me screamed to step back, to run and hide. Dad had always said I was too stubborn for my own good. Even in my heels Jimmy towered over me, and the man's favorite new pastimes were jogging and bench-pressing weights. The adrenaline surging through my system made sense, but Jimmy wouldn't hurt me.

At least, I was pretty sure he wouldn't.

"One fucking drink," he roared.

"Hey—"

"You have no god damn idea what this is like. I just need one fucking drink to get me through. Then I'll stop again. I promise."

"No."

"Pick up the phone and order it."

"You smashed the phone."

"Then get your ass downstairs and get me a drink."

I shook my head.

"You work for me! I pay your salary. You answer to me." He jabbed himself in the chest with a finger to emphasize the point. "Remember?"

"Yes. But I will not get you a drink. Make all the threats you like." My voice wavered but I didn't back down. "That is never going to happen. Never."

He growled.

"Jimmy, you need to calm down now."

His jaw tightened and his nostrils flared.

"I don't want to bring anyone else into this. But I'm reaching that point. So please calm down."

"Fuck!" The war he waged to control himself played out over his perfect face. With hands on hips, he stared down at me. For a long moment he said nothing, his harsh breathing the only sound in the room. "Please, Lena."

"No." Shit, I did not sound convincing. I balled my hands up against my stomach, summoning up some strength. "NO."

"Please," he pleaded again, eyes rimmed red. "No one needs to find out. It'll just be between you and me. I need something to take the edge off. Lori was . . . she was important to me."

"I know and I'm sorry you lost her. But drinking isn't going to help," I said, scrambling to remember all the wise words I'd read on the Internet. But my blood pounded making it impossible to think straight. I might not be

scared of him, but I was terrified for him. He couldn't fail.
I wouldn't let him. "Drinking is a temporary fix that'll
only make things harder in the long run. You know that.
You can get through today. You can."

"We're going to put her in the ground." His voice
cracked and he slumped back onto the chair. "She fed us,
Lena. When there was nothing at home, she sat Davie and
me down at her table and she fed us. Treated us like we
were her own."

"Oh, Jimmy . . ."

"I-I can't do this."

Apparently, neither could I. And to prove it, I stood
there utterly useless, my heart breaking for him. I'd wondered what had happened to make him so hard. Of course
I had. But I'd never imagined anything like this. "I'm so
sorry," I said, the words not even beginning to be enough.

Truth was, Jimmy needed a therapist or a counselor or
someone. Anyone but me, because I didn't have a fucking
clue how to handle this. The man was cracking before my
eyes and watching him come apart felt like torture. I'd
been so careful the last few years, sticking to the fringes
and keeping to myself. Now suddenly, his pain felt like my
own, tearing up my insides, leaving me raw. The room
swam blurrily in front of me.

What the hell was I still doing here?

When I took the job, my instructions had been scarily
simple. Glue myself to his side and never, on pain of death,
dismissal, and whatever else his lawyers could think to
throw at me, let him consume a drop of alcohol or an ounce
of drugs. Not a single pill could be popped. Given he'd
been clean of his own volition for almost half a year, it
hadn't seemed such a hard task.

Until now.

"I'm going to go find your shirt," I said, blinking like
crazy, doing my best to pull my shit together. Qualified or

not, I was all he had. "We need to finish getting you ready and then we're going to go."

He said nothing.

"We'll get through this, Jimmy. We'll get through today, then things will be better." The words tasted sour. I just hoped they weren't lies.

Still nothing.

"Okay?"

"Why did I say I'd talk at the funeral? What the fuck was I thinking?" He scowled. "The guys should have known this wouldn't work out, not to put me in this position. I'm in no god damn condition to do anything. But Dave is all like 'you say a few words, I'll read some poetry. It'll be fine.' What bullshit."

"You can do this."

"I can't." He scrubbed his face with his hands. "If I'm not going to fuck up the funeral of the best person I ever knew, then I need a drink. One drink, then I'll stop again."

"No." I faced him down. "They asked you to speak because as much as they'd probably hate to admit it, they knew you'd do it best. You're the front man. You don't need a drink. Shining in the spotlight is what you do. It's who you are."

He gave me a long look. So long, it got harder and harder to meet his eyes.

"You can do this, Jimmy. I know you can. There isn't a single doubt inside of me."

Nothing. He didn't even blink, just kept staring at me. The look wasn't unkind, I'm not sure what it was, apart from too much. I rubbed my clammy hands against the sides of my pants.

"All right," I said, needing to escape. "I'll get your clothes."

Strong arms suddenly wrapped around me, pulling me in. I stumbled forward, only to be stopped by the hot face pressing into my stomach. His grip was brutally tight as if he expected me to fight him, to reject him. But I just stood stunned. His whole body shook, the tremors passing into me, rattling my bones. He didn't make a sound, however. Something dampened the front of my shirt, making it cling.

It could have been sweat. I had the worst feeling it wasn't.

"Hey." None of the last two months had prepared me for this. He never needed me for shit. If anything, I inconvenienced him. We clashed. He tried to cut me down. I cracked a joke. The modus operandi had long since been established.

The man clinging to me was a stranger.

My hands hovered over his bare shoulders, panic bubbling up inside. I was most definitely not allowed to touch him. Not even a little. The one-hundred-and-twelve-page employment contract had been quite specific on the subject. Prior to this, he'd gone out of his way to avoid any and all contact, but now his arms tightened, fingers digging in. I'm pretty sure I heard my rib cage creak. Damn, he was strong. Just as well I came from sturdy stock, otherwise, he might have squeezed the life out of me.

"Jimmy, I can't breathe," I wheezed.

The grip eased a little and I stood there panting, my lungs working overtime. Thick arms remained around me. Clearly, I wasn't going anywhere.

"Maybe I should get Sam," I said in a stroke of genius once I'd caught my breath. Their head of security most closely resembled a thug in a suit. But I bet he gave great hugs.

"No."

Crap. "Or David. Do you want your brother to come back in?"

His face shifted against me, moving first left and then right. Another no. "You can't tell them."

"I won't. I promise."

Silence rang in my ears.

"I just need a minute," he said.

I stood rigid in his embrace, useless, a mannequin would have been as effective. Shit, I had to do something. Slowly, ever so slowly, my hands descended. The overwhelming need to comfort him far outweighed any threat of litigation. Heat kissed the palms of my hands. He felt feverish, perspiration slickening the hard contours of his shoulders and the thick column of his neck. My hands glided over him, doing their best to soothe.

It was disturbingly nice, being needed by him, being this close to him.

"It's okay." My fingers threaded into his thick dark hair. So soft. No wonder they hadn't wanted me touching him, now that I'd started, I couldn't seem to stop. I should have been ashamed of myself, feeling the poor man up at such a time. But he'd been the one to initiate contact. He'd grabbed hold of me seeking comfort and apparently, when it came to him, I had a scary amount to give.

"What am I gonna say?" he asked, voice muffled against me. "How can I make a fucking speech?"

"You say what she meant to you. They'll understand."

He snorted.

"No, really. Just talk from your heart."

He took a shuddering breath, resting his forehead against me. "To top it off, she called."

"She?" I gave the top of his head a sharp look. Damn it, he had seemed okay. Certainly not delusional. "Who called you?"

"Mom."

"Oh." This couldn't be good news. Better than him

imagining phone calls from the recently deceased, but still. "What'd she want?"

"Same fucking thing she always wants. Money." His voice was harsh and low. So low that I had to strain to hear him. "Warned her to stay away."

"She's in town?"

A nod. "Threatened to crash the funeral. Told her I'd have her fucking arrested if she did."

Hell, the woman sounded like a nightmare.

"Davie doesn't know," he said. "That's the way it stays."

"All right." I don't know how wise that was, but it wasn't my choice to make. "I won't tell him."

His shoulders hitched beneath my hands, his misery surrounding us like an impenetrable shell. Nothing else existed.

"You're going to be okay." I bowed my head and hunched over, sheltering him with my body. My heart ached and emotional detachment was a dream. The compulsion to give to him was too strong. He was usually such a maddening man, so thoughtless and rude. Anger, however, made my job easier. When he behaved like an ass I could remain indifferent for the most part. These dangerous new feelings running through me, however, were soft and sappy, warm and weepy. No way could I afford to care this much.

Crap.

What the hell was happening to me?

He gripped my rounded hips and turned his face up to me, unguarded for once. All of his usual sharp edges were dulled by pain and if anything it just made his beauty more obvious. I licked my suddenly dry lips. Fingers tensed and tightened against me and his forehead bunched as he scowled at the damp patch on the front of my blouse. "Sorry 'bout that."

"Not a problem."

He let go and my legs wobbled, weak at the loss.

Intimacy fled and awkwardness rushed right in like a tidal wave. I could almost feel his walls slamming back into place. Mine were slower, weaker, damn them. Someone, somewhere along the line, had swapped my titanium for tinfoil, leaving me wide open and exposed. It was all his fault. For a moment, he'd actually stepped down from his self-imposed pedestal. He'd been real with me, shown me his fears, and I'd just sort of mumbled some vaguely comforting shit. Honestly, I couldn't even remember what anymore. Little wonder he'd closed up on me again.

Also, we were unnaturally close, positioned as we were. There were mere inches between us. Jimmy gave me a brief embarrassed look to enforce the fact, just in case I hadn't noticed. Obviously he regretted this. I mean, he'd cried on the hired help, for Christ's sake.

"I'll get your clothes," I said, grasping at the first useful idea to enter my head.

Blindly, I stumbled across the room. Thoughts and feelings were running rife through me, all of it a blur. I needed to talk to mom. Far as I knew, there was no history of heart ailments in the family. Leukemia took Uncle John. Grandma died due to smoking a pack a day. I think Great Aunt Valerie caught some strange fungal infection in her lungs, but don't quote me on that. Mom would know for sure. Whatever my heart was doing, it couldn't be good. I was only twenty-five, much too young to die. Probably about the right age to become a complete hypochondriac, however.

I grabbed a shirt and tie from out of his walk-in closet in the monster-sized main bedroom. My room, on the other side of the suite, wasn't bad. This room, however, put the Ritz to shame. Sheets, blankets, and pillows were strewn across the gigantic bed. Not from any crazy sex antics because as far as I could tell, the man was either asexual, abstaining, or both. Still, he obviously hadn't slept well. I could just picture him, tossing and turning, his big strong body thrashing about on that large, sturdy bed. Completely alone with all his bad memories. And I'd only been in the room across from him, also alone and not sleeping particularly well. Some nights my brain just wouldn't shut up or shut down, and last night had definitely been one of them.

I stood frozen, mesmerized by the tangle of sheets and blankets.

Again, my heart did something strange. Something totally out of context. What happened between my legs was best ignored. I'm certain something in the employment contract outlawed any and all wetness on my part, especially if it pertained to one James Dylan Ferris.

"Hey," he said, appearing at my side, startling the crap out of me.

"Hi." I hesitated, a bit breathless again for some reason. Perhaps I should have my lungs checked too just to be sure. "You need a quick cleanup. Come on."

He followed behind me like an obedient child. The lights in the white bathroom were blindingly bright after all the emotional turmoil, dazzling me. Okay, what next? Bottles and tubes were spread out over the counter. Still my beleaguered brain offered up nothing.

"We have to hurry," I muttered, mostly to myself.

I placed his shirt and tie on the counter, grabbed a facecloth and wet it. If I hadn't already done my makeup, I'd have splashed my face with the bitingly cold water, let it wake me up from all this weirdness. Meanwhile, Jimmy stared off into the distance, his mind obviously far away once again. When I held up the cloth he didn't react at all. Forget it, we didn't have time for this, I'd do the job myself. The cold damp cloth made contact and he reared back, nostrils flaring.

"Hold still," I said, and embarked upon my first ever

sponge bath. Basically, I scrubbed at him like a mad woman. I even washed behind his ears in my fervor.

"Christ," he mumbled, ducking to try and escape me.

"Keep still."

Next came his neck, then his shoulders. I wet the cloth again and moved on to his chest and back, rushing through the process. It was best not to think, just to see him as Jimmy, my boss. Better yet, the body beneath my hands was stone, not real in the least, despite the goose flesh erupting all over him. Base desires didn't matter when a job was at stake, surging hormones and emotions both could take a backseat. I could do this.

"Okay. Shirt." I picked up the thick rich cotton and held it open for him. He threaded his arms through, smooth skin brushing against the back of my fingers making tingles run up my arm. I fumbled my way through doing up the buttons. "We need cuff links. And I don't know how to do the tie."

"I'll do that."

"Okay." I passed him the neat strip of black silk. All good, I just needed some air, the colder the better.

Jimmy stepped around me, walking back into the bedroom. From the top of his dresser he collected a pair of silver cuff links and secured them to the sleeves of his shirt. Actually, they were probably platinum, knowing him. I could see tattoos peeking out from beneath the cuffs of his shirt and above the collar of his neck. There could be no disguising him as anything other than the rock star he was. He hadn't been made to hide or blend, the man was much too beautiful for that.

"Do you need anything else?" I asked, following him like a little lost puppy. My toes stretched and strained while my hands hung limp at my sides. No way did he need to know he'd made me jittery.

"I'm good." Socks and shoes waited at the end of the

bed. He sat down, getting busy. His suit jacket hung over the back of a chair, a long black woolen coat folded atop it. We were fine, everything set.

"You've got your speech?" I asked.

The frown increased. "Yeah. It's in my pocket."

"Great. I just need to get my bag and jacket."

His chin jerked and his gaze skittered over me. "You look nice, by the way."

"Ah, thank you."

"Just stating a fact. You look good." He turned away.

I, however, didn't move. At first I was stunned at the compliment, but then for some reason, leaving Jimmy alone didn't feel right. It niggled. What if he got upset again and I wasn't here to talk him down? His sobriety was too important to risk.

Lips fine, he studied the slowly drying patch on the front of my blouse. "You definitely won't tell anyone?"

"No. Never."

The air hissed out between his teeth and his expression calmed. "Okay . . ."

I nodded, giving him a small smile.

"Listen, Lena?"

"Hmm?"

He turned away. "There's nothing in here, no pills or booze. I haven't scored. I'll do a spit test if you need it, and you can search the room . . ."

"No, I know," I said, perplexed. "If there was, you wouldn't have wanted me to get you something and we'd currently be having an entirely different conversation. Either that or you'd be back in rehab and I'd be out of a job."

"True."

Neither of us said anything for a moment. I crossed my arms over my chest, my face stiff, tight with tension.

"You can leave me on my own," he said. "It's fine, go get your stuff. Do whatever so we can leave."

"Right!" One of those false embarrassed little laughs startled out of me. Crap. I'd completely forgotten. "Yes, okay. I'll get my stuff."

"Great." He pushed a hand through his hair the same as he'd done maybe a dozen times a day since I'd come to work for him. It was nothing new. Immediately, however, my heart did the drop-and-squeeze thing again.

No. NO.

It couldn't be connected to him, I refused to believe it.

"Are you going?" His face skewed with annoyance and thank God for that. His open irritation relieved me no end, we were back to normal.

"Yes, Jimmy. I'm going."

"Now?"

"Right now." I strode out, slamming the bedroom door shut behind me.

I did not have feelings for Jimmy Ferris. What a ridiculous thought. He was a former addict. And while I admired and respected him for taking charge of his life and fighting that battle, I did not need to get involved with someone who'd barely been dry half a year. Also, Jimmy was not a particularly nice guy the bulk of the time. A general lack of interest in, and consideration for, everyone else inhabiting the planet was his go-to setting.

But worst of all, the man was my boss.

I didn't have feelings for him. I couldn't, no way. I'd fallen for unsuitable, unstable, and outright criminal assholes in the past, but I was done with that. Especially the asshole and unstable portion. There's no way I had feelings for him. I'd really grown as a person and shit, right?

I slumped against the nearest wall. "Fuck."

I took a deep breath, focused on the funeral.

Things would get better.

CHAPTER TWO

Things didn't get better.

Mal's mom had apparently loved lilies. My head swam with the sweet rich scent. Seats had been saved for us down in the front with the family, which was fortunate, because the church was packed. It felt all kinds of awkward sitting with the Ericsons given I barely knew them, but that was where Jimmy wanted me. Security stood out front, putting the kibosh on any uninvited guests. A group of fans stood outside despite them and the weather. They'd called out to Jimmy, waving T-shirts and other shit to be signed when we walked in. I'd wanted to growl abuse at them, tell them to get a clue. Jimmy hadn't given them the time of day. You'd have thought in the guy's hometown, there'd be more respect for his privacy, especially at a time like this. Some people just didn't think or it didn't suit them to think. What they wanted was more important and screw everyone else.

God, I hated people like that.

Up front, the organ player pounded out a hymn and people sang along as best they could. Jimmy would talk next. His face still seemed paler than normal, a little gray even. The man might not be clinging to me, but he clearly wasn't all right. I grabbed his hand, holding on even when he flinched back from the contact. The look he gave our joined hands was distinctly bewildered.

"It's okay," I said.

He gave up trying to free himself of me and started fussing with the knot in his tie.

"Jimmy, you're going to be great."

The song wound down. Mal turned to us and god, the man's face. He looked devastated, eyes stark with loss. Anne, the drummer's girlfriend, stood at his side, her arm wrapped tight around Mal's waist. There'd been a hiccup with their great love affair a week or two back. It was good to see them together again, especially today.

Mal nodded to Jimmy, giving him the signal, and it might have started out with me holding onto him, but now the situation had definitely been reversed. Fingers clutched mine, bruisingly tight, but he made no other move. He'd frozen.

On my other side, David leaned forward, frowning. "Jim?"

There was murmuring in the hall, the crowd growing restless. Up in the pulpit, the preacher stepped forward, craning his neck and looking out expectantly.

Someone had to do something.

"Let's go." I put my hand to his back and pushed. Hard.

He blinked ever so slowly, like I'd woken him from a deep sleep.

"Time to go, Jimmy. You're on," I whispered. "Walk."

Steps painfully slow, he moved out into the aisle. I followed, the weight of all those stares making the hair on the back of my neck stand on end. No matter. We walked side by side, my hand guiding him, never leaving his back. Up the steps and then on to the podium. I fished in his coat pocket for the speech, laying it out flat in front of him.

There was whispering out in the crowd about our odd behavior. Screw them. Nothing mattered but getting him through today intact.

"You got this?" I asked.

He scowled. "Yeah."

I stepped to the side.

For a moment his gaze searched the crowd, moving over David and Ev, Ben the freakishly tall bass player, and then Mal and Anne. Next he turned to me, his mouth a grim line but his eyes asking for something. I gave him a little smile, a discreet thumbs up. No part of me doubted he could do this. Whatever else he might be, Jimmy Ferris was special and complicated, beautiful and beastly, all rolled into one. A natural-born performer.

His chin dipped infinitesimally in response and I let out a breath. He could do it, and he would.

Still, I swear I could feel his pain bearing down on me, threatening to snap me in two. Some sort of empathy overload had begun back in the hotel room and now I couldn't separate my feelings from his. Worse, I didn't want to. He'd let me in whether he meant to or not and I couldn't leave him alone with all this.

Tomorrow I'd take a nice big safe step back. Today he needed a friend.

"Hi," he said, his deep strong voice carrying perfectly. "My name is Jimmy Ferris. I first met Lori Ericson when she let us start practicing in their garage. I was about sixteen at the time. Mr. Ericson wasn't too happy with having us play there at first, but Lori talked him around. No one else would have us. To be fair, we made a hell of a racket. Barely a fucking . . . sorry, we barely had a clue what we were doing.

"In summer she'd bring us out these big jugs of Kool-Aid. People that know me won't be surprised to hear I used to dump about a quarter out, fill it up with this cheap vodka I'd talk one of the guys down at the liquor store into getting me." He looked to his brother and David gave him a tight smile.

"Anyway," he said, clearing his throat. "This one time she came back in, busted me doing it. Didn't matter that I was bigger than her. She grabbed me by the ear, nearly tore it off my head. Then she marched me outside and ripped me a new one. I was about an inch tall by the time she was done. Nice or not, Lori knew how to cut you down to size. And once she was done doing that, she calmed down and she talked to me. Just about general stuff. All sorts of things, really. But every time I went there from then on, she made time to talk to me, even if it was just for two minutes. Our own mom had taken off by then, so it wasn't something I got at home. Now, I wasn't Lori's kid. I probably wasn't even a kid she wanted around her kid. Still, she always made a point of giving that to me. She kept an eye on me and Dave, made sure we were clothed and fed, that we had what we needed. She cared when no one else gave a shit." He grimaced, cleared his throat. "She cared when no one else *did*."

His fingers stretched then curled tight as he took a moment. "I'd like to tell you how I stopped drinking in Lori's garage after that. That's how the story should finish. But some part of me was an addict, I guess, even back then. I did stop for a couple of days, and I was real sneaky about it afterward. I couldn't bear the thought of disappointing her. Maybe that makes it sound like she didn't do that much, that she didn't have much of an effect. But what she did was enormous. She was the first person I'd ever met who made me wish I was better. Was a good person. Could make more of myself. And that's a power, right there. If you can get even a guy like me to want to be a better man, then you're something special."

Jimmy carefully picked up the piece of paper in front of him, folding it back up. It didn't matter, he didn't need it. The poetry was in him, in the way he was baring his heart to these people. He stood tall, facing the crowd. His truth might not be pretty, but there was strength in his stance, pride. Warmth bloomed in my chest at the sight. A sense of satisfaction I hadn't experienced in the longest time. Not that I'd made the eulogy, I know, but still . . .

"This might seem a weird story to tell you," he said, his voice measured and calm. "It certainly doesn't make me look good. But I think it goes a long way toward explaining to you why Lori was so important. What made her so amazing was . . . she cared. She genuinely cared about people. And that's as rare as it is beautiful. It's why she'll be so badly missed."

I scrubbed a tear off my face with the heel of my hand before Jimmy could catch me crying. Sadly, not fast enough. At least it wasn't like I was the only one in a similar condition. Lucky the hall hadn't flooded.

He turned to me, face bereft of emotion. "Let's go."

I sniffed. "Yep."

We walked back down to our seats, his hand at the small of my back this time, guiding me forward. Before we could reach them, Mal stepped out. Wordlessly, he put his arms around Jimmy. He gripped him tight, giving him a thump on the back in the way men do. It took Jimmy a moment to respond and thump him back. The organ player started up again and everyone rose to their feet around us. Voices filled the hall.

I slid into the pew and retook my seat. Jimmy deposited himself next to me, the leg of his suit pants brushing against mine. I waited for him to grouse at me to move over, not that there was any room to be had due to of the sudden appearance of some woman's handbag. But he didn't.

Honestly, after all the drama and emotional upheaval, sticking close seemed a good idea.

For him, of course. I was fine.

His gaze dropped briefly to where we connected before moving away. "You okay?"

"Yes. You?"

He made a noise. It sounded agreeable enough.

"Good." I settled my hands in my lap.

Up in the pulpit the preacher started talking. Jimmy's leg leaned a little more firmly against mine. He looked straight ahead, however, apparently unaware of what his thigh was doing. Nothing showed on his face. Maybe it was his way of acknowledging me, of saying thank you. Or maybe the man had a cramp. Whatever. A small smile curved my lips, my shoulders sagging with relief.

We'd done it. We'd made it through.

CHAPTER THREE

Huckleberry pie was the devil's work.

It had taken me two thin servings to be certain. But now I knew.

I sat in the corner of the Ericsons' living room, Ev on one side and Anne on the other. Empty plates sat in all our laps. The wake had been something else. Something involving food, good music, and almost everyone the Ericsons knew. A sad vibe had prevailed at first. Of course it had. But talking and quiet laughter had slowly permeated the space until it became more of a celebration of Lori's life than a mourning of her passing. Now, five hours later, the crowd had begun to thin out. I smothered a yawn, blinking tired eyes. It'd been one hell of a day with all the emotional highs and lows.

Mal knelt at Anne's feet. His lush lips were understandably turned down at the edges. Not that I made a habit of checking out other women's men's mouths. Sometimes, however, these things were kind of hard not to notice.

"Hey," Anne said softly, placing her hand against his cheek.

"I need a happy."

"What can I do for you?"

"Tell me you love me." He leaned in and she met him halfway, placing a gentle kiss on his lips.

"I love you, Mal," she said.

"No you don't. You're just saying that to make conversation. That's a horrible thing to lie to me about, pumpkin. I don't know how you can sleep at night."

"I sleep very well, lying right next to you." She smiled and threaded her arms around his neck. For a long time they held each other tight, teasing and mumbling endearments.

"Where's Jimmy?" asked Ev, interrupting the show.

I guess we shouldn't be perving on the loved-up couple. Even if they were whispering sweet nothings and making out right in front of us. They were cute. Yes, I could admit to missing having someone special sometimes. Though the men I'd dated were more inclined to cause trouble than comfort. Hence my vow to stay sexless and single. I had to protect myself from my own shitty taste in men, even if I did find my own hugs somewhat lacking.

"Lena?" Ev laughed. "Hello?"

"Sorry. Ah, Jimmy . . . he's outside with Mr. Ericson. I think he was in need of some 'Lena free' time."

"He did a beautiful job with the eulogy."

"Yes, he did."

"And you did a great job of getting him through it."

"Thanks." I studied my empty plate.

"He hasn't had a lot of women around that he can depend upon," she said, her voice dropping volume. "Like he said, their mom took off early. Though I think that was probably a blessing. From what little David's told me, she wasn't someone you'd want around."

"Jimmy doesn't tend to talk about her. He doesn't tend to talk about anything much at all, usually." I frowned off into space again. I'd learned more about him in the last couple of hours than I had in the last couple of months. It was a lot to take in. The way I saw him was altering today in all sorts of ways.

"Yeah, Jimmy's not what you'd call chatty."

I snorted. "That's putting it mildly. If I can get two words out of him about his appointments I'm doing well."

"And yet you've survived the longest of them all." With a small sigh, Ev settled her hands over her tummy. She too had tried several of the desserts. "You're obviously doing something right."

"Huh. I wonder what?" I stared at the ceiling some more, thinking deep thoughts.

"I don't know. Maybe he likes you. Maybe he's lonely and just enjoys having you around."

"Yeah, right. We are talking about the same Jimmy Ferris here? The rock star?"

"Shame on you, Lena," she said, her smile belying her words. "You've been around long enough by now to know that being a rock star doesn't always mean what you think it does."

"Maybe . . ."

"If he's guarded, it's for a reason."

"He's talked to you about it?" I asked curiously.

She barked out a laugh. "Ha, I don't think so. I'm pretty much kept at a polite distance like everybody else. But you never know, ask him nicely, he might just talk to *you*."

I wrinkled my nose. Despite today's unprecedented events, the thought of Jimmy talking to me on a more regular basis as opposed to just barking out orders now and then seemed highly unlikely. "He might also just fire me for sticking my nose in his business."

"True. These are the risks we take when we care about people."

Something in the way she said that set me on edge. "Oh, no. Jimmy and I are strictly a business relationship."

"I know." Her smile? I didn't trust it.

With great thumping footsteps, David marched up to us. A small black-and-white pup squirmed in his hands, tail wagging madly. The man wasn't wearing his happy face. "The dog pissed on my shoe."

"Oops." Ev gave him a wry grin.

"It's not funny," grumped David, sounding so much like his brother for a moment they could have been twins. It was cute.

"Well done, Killer." Mal lifted the dog from David's hands. "I'm proud of you, son."

"He's not going to change the name?" asked Ev.

Anne shrugged, reaching out to scratch the puppy's head. "I've kind of gotten used to it now."

The pup had been a gift for Anne's birthday the week before, although Mal had already seen fit to bestow a name before gifting him. That Killer came with a luxury condo where pets were allowed probably took any possible sting out of the situation.

Sure as hell, I wouldn't complain.

A loud screech sounded from outside. Another promptly following fast. Only this time, the racket went on and on. It might have been an animal, except there were words contained within the furious caterwauling.

"Is that a woman?" I asked, cringing.

"What the hell?" Mal rushed to his feet, passing the puppy off to Anne.

Mal and David ran for the door, Ev and I close behind them. Outside, cold air slapped me in the face after the warmth of the house. It was the strangest, most disturbing damn scene. Beneath the limbs of a maple tree, a lone woman was busy shrieking at Jimmy.

What the hell, indeed.

David ran toward them. "Mom. What are you doing here?"

"You ungrateful fuck," the older woman cried, ignoring

her youngest son completely. "You think I won't tell them everything?"

Jimmy didn't even blink. "Go for it. I'm not giving you any more money. Already told you that this morning. What the hell did you think you were going to achieve showing up here?"

She had long dark hair and cheekbones you could cut yourself on. The family resemblance was obvious, only her skin was sunken and her hair hung in knotted strands down her back.

"Your threats don't scare me," she sneered.

"Mom, this is a funeral. Get out of here," said David, taking a stand beside his brother.

"Davie, you were always sweeter to me than he was. You'll help your poor old mom out, won't you?" Her voice was noxious, falsely sweet. "Just a loan, baby. I just need a little help getting back on my feet."

The man's shoulders straightened. "From what I hear Jim's loaned you more than enough money and you've flushed it all down the toilet. Haven't you?"

"I need my medicine."

"Your medicine, what bullshit," sneered Jimmy. "What you need is to get your ass out of here before we call the cops."

"Leave, Mom," said David. "This isn't right. We're here to say good-bye to Lori. Have a little respect, huh?"

People were gathering on the front doorstep behind us, watching the horrible scene with their eyes wide and faces curious. The bitch just carried right on with her banshee imitation, regardless. How any mother could be so mean was beyond me, but what this must be doing to Jimmy was the real concern. God, this was the last thing he should be dealing with today.

I quietly moved behind him, getting closer in case he

needed me. The moment I got a chance to put an end to this shit, I was taking it.

Their mother cackled. "What did that uptight judgmental cunt ever do but turn my boys against me, huh?"

"C'mon, Mom. Give yourself some credit," said Jimmy, his voice cutting. "You did that all on your own years before we ever met Lori."

The woman snarled at him, actually raising the side of her lip like a rabid animal. If she'd started frothing at the mouth it wouldn't have surprised me one bit. A potent mix of hate and lunacy filled her eyes. Little wonder Jimmy had his issues. I couldn't imagine being subjected to this from a young age.

"You are nothing but a user," he said, getting in her face, taunting her. "A scum-sucking nasty piece of shit that we have the very bad luck to be related to. Now get the hell out of here before we call the cops on you. Tell the media what you want because like fucking hell I'm giving you another dollar to buy drugs with. And if you think there's any chance I'm letting you try the same shit on Dave, you're out of whatever's left of your mind."

Her face turned purple like she was having a seizure.

"Get out of here."

Mouth contorted, she launched herself at him. Dirty nails raked his face, leaving raw jagged lines. Without thinking, I surged forward, jostling him. But Jimmy was too busy grabbing the woman's arms, trying to hold her back to bother with me. His brother just looked on, mouth agape. Insane with anger, the woman went at Jimmy again, teeth snapping.

Blood fell from Jimmy's face and I'd long since seen red. Anger thundered through me, heating me despite the cold.

The two brothers stood close together. Never mind.

I pushed forward, wedging my body between them. Then I shoved the bitch hard in the middle of her chest. Jimmy obviously hadn't been expecting it. His hold on her faltered and the woman went sprawling back onto the cold, hard ground. Her threadbare green coat fell open, revealing a faded summer dress. Her limbs were emaciated, littered with angry red sores. Good god, how was this woman even still alive?

"I'll sue you!" she howled at me. "That's assault. You think I don't know shit?"

Yeah, right. Little did she know, I didn't have anything worth suing for.

"Don't even try it, Mom." Jimmy ever so gently elbowed me back behind him. "I'm dripping blood here. Unprovoked attack. Lena just defended me. Cops'll laugh at you if you try."

"We'll see." The thin features of her face twisted with malice. Slowly, Mrs. Ferris climbed back up onto her feet, wrapping her coat tight around her body.

Neither of her sons said a thing.

"Stupid slut." She spat at me, then stumbled off across the lawn, onto the street. I'd never been so glad to see the back of someone before.

"So there's no chance I'm going to go to jail, right?" I asked, just curious. All right, maybe the tiniest bit scared of the mad woman's threats.

"'Course you're not." Jimmy looked back over his shoulder at me. Three bloody lines were etched into his cheek.

The sight brought the cold rushing back in. "We need to get your face cleaned up. Let's get inside."

"You knew she was in town? Last I heard she was still in LA." David watched the retreating form of his mother, her long dark hair flying wild in the wind.

"She tracked me down to the hotel, rang this morning."

David's lips flatlined. "Why didn't you say something?"

"Got enough going on without worrying about her," said Jimmy.

"Fuck's sake, man. She's my mother."

"Yeah, mine too."

His brother's forehead went all wrinkled. It must be a Ferris thing, they both did it at times of stress, bewilderment or just about any other emotion. Meanwhile, Jimmy hadn't moved an inch. He just stood there, bleeding.

"It's cold," said David.

Jimmy turned, giving their mom one last look. To all the world, his gaze must have looked bored, irritated. But the fingers fussing at the bottom of his jacket gave him away, to me at least. He wasn't nearly as unaffected as he'd wish everyone to believe. "What do you wanna do, put her in a shelter? She won't stay. Should we buy her some warmer clothes? She'll have them traded for booze and drugs in under a minute. It's all she cares about and all she wants."

"Yeah, but . . ."

"But what?" asked Jimmy, blood slowly dripping from his face.

"Shit." His brother shoved a hand through his shoulder length hair. They really were similar in so many ways. "Is it really that easy for you to just turn away?"

"I know it's cold, Davie. I know."

"Fuck man, you okay?" Mal asked.

Jimmy flinched as if receiving the wound anew. "Yeah. I'm real sorry about that, her turning up here and everything . . ."

"Boys, this was not your fault." Everyone should have a dad like Mal's. His voice was absolute, brooking no bullshit. Jimmy's mouth opened to protest and Mr. Ericson held up a hand. "No, son. That's enough. Why don't we all go back inside now, get out of this wind."

With the show over, the spectators on the front steps started moving back inside. Jimmy nodded and likewise did as he was told. I followed him and Mal into the downstairs bathroom, every part of me wound tight with agitation. I wasn't normally a violent person. What I wouldn't give to take another shot at the woman, however.

The bathroom was a narrow, cramped space. Apparently the Ericsons hadn't upgraded with the help of their son's money. The house was an older-model, wooden two-story, surrounded with now-dormant flower beds. Photos lined the hallway showing all the colors that grew there in the spring, however. My mom loved gardening. She always fussed on the weekends in winter, never quite knowing what to do with herself. Usually she took up some expensive intricate craft that got dumped the moment the ground thawed. A sudden wave of homesickness washed over me.

Which was silly.

No way did I want to go home yet. After my sister's farce of a wedding, once all of the fuss had died down? Fine. Then I'd spend some time with my parents, reconnect, and make things right. I'd catch up with my old friends and see what was left for me back home. It was a promise.

"Mom kept all the first aid stuff here." Mal riffled in the sink cupboard, pulling out a battered white box. "Ah, there you go."

"It's not that bad," said Jimmy. "I'll just wash it off."

"Definitely not," I said.

"And risk letting that handsome face get infected?" Mal tutted, interceding flawlessly. "Please, princess. For me?"

Jimmy gave him a faint smile and accepted the box.

"And I'm pretty sure you'd rather have Lena playing nurse. I'll leave you two kids to it."

I flattened myself against the wall and Mal squeezed

past, backing out into the hallway. "Yell if you need anything."

The lid on the old first aid box creaked mightily as Jimmy pulled it open. "Yeah."

"Thank you." I smiled at Mal.

He winked.

"Right. Sit on the edge of the bathtub," I instructed, taking charge.

Jimmy sat, inspecting the dark red stains on the front of his shirt. "This is ruined."

"You've got others."

"I had this made especially at Saville Road in London. You have any idea what something like that costs?"

Please. The man had more money than god. "You hitting me up for a loan?"

He snorted.

"Because honestly, I don't know if I like you enough for that."

"Wasn't aware you liked me at all," he said, smoothing down his shirt as if that would help matters. He was right, the thing deserved a one-way ticket to the ragbag.

"Hmm. You're not so bad. I've met much, much worse." And we didn't really need to get into that anytime this decade. I snapped my mouth shut and pushed up my glasses, got busy digging in the medicine chest. "What have we've got here."

"Listen, Lena, about today . . ."

I waited for him to finish. And waited. "What?"

He scowled at the wall, avoiding my eyes completely. "I just . . . I just wanted to say, ah . . ."

"Yes-s-s?"

"Well, that um, you were useful."

"I was useful?" My brows rose to dangerous heights, I could feel them. After everything we'd been through today, *useful* was as good as it got?

A shrug. "Yeah, mostly."

"Mostly? I was mostly useful." Slowly, I shook my head, biting back an incredulous grin. Lucky my sense of self-worth wasn't dependent on him or it'd be a sad, shriveled wreck hiding out in the corner by now. This man, he did my head in. It seemed only fair to repay the favor in kind. "I think that's just about the nicest thing anyone's ever said to me, Mr. Ferris. It was just beautiful, like poetry. I'll never think of the word useful the same way ever again."

He sniffed disdainfully, giving me a dour look. "Great. And it was *mostly* useful."

"Yes, sorry, mostly useful. Wow. I just don't know how to thank you."

"Less talk'd be a good start. Let's get this over with."

"Yes, sir. Right away, sir." I stopped short of saluting, but only just.

Down the hallway drifted various noises as the wake slowly started winding down. There was the clink of plates and cutlery being gathered. I could hear Mal saying good-bye to someone followed by the hair-raising bang of the front door. It must have been caught by the wind. Some old Bob Dylan tune played low beneath it all.

"You're welcome by the way," I said, softening my voice, cutting him a break. His day, after all, had been far worse than mine. Plus, it obviously wasn't easy for him to say thank you. Not that he'd exactly managed to. "I'm glad I was here to help."

He looked up at me, eyes unguarded. At least, they weren't cold and hard for a change.

"Me too," he said quietly.

For a moment, I actually forgot myself. We just stared at each other in near silence, like we were waiting for something or trying to figure something out. I don't know. It was weird.

Then he turned away.

"Lena, hello?" He pointed to his cheek. "I'm still bleeding here."

"Right," I ripped into a fresh pad of gauze, then got busy wrestling with the lid on the disinfectant. Stupid childproof locks. "Let's see if we can't fix you." When I sneaked a look he was staring off into infinity again, I'd apparently been tuned out.

"This'll sting," I said, liberally dousing the gauze. "Who knows how dirty her nails were. We need to clean it really well."

He wrinkled his nose at the smell. "Don't pretend you're not going to enjoy it."

"You wound me. As if I'd ever enjoy causing you mild pain or discomfort." I couldn't quite keep the smile off my face. Of course, I didn't quite bother. Verbally sparring with Jimmy was fast becoming more fun than I'd had with most other men naked. Which was sad.

Real sad.

Carefully, I started cleaning him up, wiping the blood from his cheek. I was trying not to overthink things but my mind refused to slow down. We'd now touched more in one day than I'd ever imagined possible. Judging by my ongoing heart condition, this was not good. I scrunched up my face, concentrating. This new heightened awareness of him was driving me insane. We hadn't connected, not really. It was just because of today being so overemotional and everything. There'd been more drama, highs and lows, than I'd experienced in ages and putting it all into perspective would take some time. Tomorrow we'd head back to Portland and things would revert to normal with Jimmy largely ignoring my existence. There was no need to freak out.

At any rate, I couldn't quit on the guy right now. Talk about kicking someone when they were down.

He winced. "Ouch."

"Don't be such a baby."

If only my stupid hands would stop trembling, giving me away. Happily, Jimmy didn't seem to notice. The more I tended to his face, the madder I got. Honestly, what an absolute shit of a day. Mal lost a wonderful mother while Jimmy and David suffered via their very alive and deeply crappy one. Where the hell was the justice in that?

Several packets of gauze and a sea of disinfectant later, we were done. If the bitch had scarred him I'd do worse than push her on her ass next time. Just to be safe, I smeared enough antibiotic cream on the ragged wounds to turn the side of his face snowman white.

"I wish I'd hit her harder," I said. "I'm sorry, I know she's your mother, but . . ."

"Don't pull that shit again," he said. "She's not rational, Lena. You could have gotten hurt."

"Ha. Then you'd have to listen to me bitch."

"Like hell."

"You wouldn't play Nurse Jimmy for me? How sad." I laughed softly. If I could just keep things light and easy everything would be okay. Or at least, as light and easy as things ever got between us. The air of misery around him, however, made it impossible to keep a distance.

"It wasn't your fault," I said.

He turned away, hands tight around the first aid kit making it creak again. "Finished?"

Carefully, I kept rubbing the cream in. The main problem with me is my mouth. In that I have one and use it far more than I probably should. It's especially irritating when it's hell-bent on bringing forth information that only serves to make me look dumb. "I dated this guy once who sold my car to score weed."

Jimmy leaned back, away from my fingers. "Lotta weed."

"Yeah." I braced my palms on my hips, keeping my greasy fingers away from my body. "Sometimes you have to cut people loose for your own good."

"You think I don't know that?" he asked in a deceptively calm voice.

"Out there, you couldn't bring yourself to hit her," I said. "But she needed to leave. Seemed the least I could do was give her a shove in the right direction. And I don't regret it."

"Next time, stay out of it."

"Is there going to be a next time?"

"I hope not." The pain in his eyes was heartbreaking. Oh my god, he was killing me. It had to stop.

"You're all good," I pronounced, turning to wash my hands at the basin. More than enough with the touching. It was feeding this ridiculous notion that Jimmy and I were close, like we were friends or something. We weren't, I needed to shake it off. History dictated once foolish enough to grow feelings for a guy, my heart stayed stuck till the bitter end. My collection of idiot exes was epic. When it came to mixing penises with emotions, I couldn't be trusted. He was my just my boss, no more, no less.

Jimmy stood and stretched behind me. "Bastard of a day."

"Yeah."

"Be glad when it's over and we can head home."

He studied himself in the mirror over my shoulder. "Lena, I can't go out there like this! Christ."

"There isn't a big enough bandage in the box to cover your cheek. I did the best I could with what I had."

"I look ridiculous."

"You look fine." I scoffed.

He mumbled expletives.

"Would you calm down?"

"Wasn't talking to you," he grumped.

He leaned in and I leaned forward, only there was no room, nowhere for me to go. Any contact between his front and my back must be avoided at all costs. It's basically impossible, however, to suck in your ass successfully. Trust me, I've tried. So I settled for grinding my hips into the edge of the bathroom cabinet, trying to stay out of his way. It was highly unlikely I managed to reduce myself any but a girl could always dream.

Behind me, he started prodding at his cheek, pulling weird faces.

"Stop it," I said. "You'll make it start bleeding again."

Icy blue eyes narrowed on me in the mirror.

"Why don't I go ask Mr. Ericson if he has a shirt you can borrow?"

He jerked his chin in agreement. Nine times out of ten this was Jimmy's preferred method of communication. So much more effective than wasting time on actual words.

"Um, Jimmy? If you could stop looking at yourself in the mirror for just one minute . . ."

"What?"

"It's a small space. Can you give me some room to move, please?"

His gaze raked over my back, down to the curve of my abundant ass and what had to be the hairsbreadth of room between us. Without comment, he stepped left, so I could go right.

"Thank you," I said.

"Ask if he's got a plain white shirt, yeah?"

"Sure."

"And hurry."

No please. No thank you. No nothing.

Typical.

I found Mr. Ericson standing at the kitchen sink, staring out the window. Music and chatter flowed in from the living room, but he remained apart, alone. No one could help him through this. There couldn't be many things as heartbreaking as losing your life partner, your other half.

What if this had been my mom or dad?

Shit. My throat tightened. I pushed the horrible thought away. They were both fine, I'd only talked to them the other day. Eventually, though, it had to happen, they were getting older. My aimless wandering had to come to an end. I needed to go back and see them sooner rather than later because if something ever happened I'd never forgive myself.

It didn't seem right to interrupt Mr. Ericson. Jimmy would just have to suck it up.

I stepped back, my elbow knocking a fruit bowl on the counter. The glass chimed noisily, alerting everyone within a twelve-mile radius to my presence. Mr. Ericson turned, staring in surprise. "Lena. It *is* Lena isn't it?"

"Yes, Mr. Ericson. I'm sorry to disturb you."

"Please, call me Neil. Is Jimmy all right?" The lines on his face multiplied.

"He's fine." I smiled. "But would it be okay if he borrowed a shirt? His got blood on it."

"Of course. Follow me." He led me up the carpeted staircase to the second floor and into a room covered in floral wallpaper. The scent of lilies lingered here too. On the dresser sat a wedding picture and beside it was a more informal shot of them from the '70s, I guess.

"Your wife rocked a pair of knee-high white boots," I said, crouching down to get a better look. Mal had obviously inherited his smile from her, the mischievous twinkle in his eye. Any money says Mrs. Ericson had gotten up to all sorts of things back in the day, really lived life to the fullest.

I hoped she had.

"She rocked everything, Lena." The depth of sadness in Mr. Ericson's voice was immeasurable. So too was the affection. "She was the most beautiful woman I ever met."

Tears stung my eyes.

"Which one do you think will be acceptable?" He

stood in front of the open wardrobe. Half of the space still contained Lori's clothes. Neat rows of skirts and slacks and blouses. A couple of dresses. How did you move on when half of your life was gone?

I grabbed the first shirt I saw, needing to be gone. "This'll be great. Thanks."

"Are you sure?" His brows rose.

"Yep. Jimmy'll love it. Thank you!"

I got out of there before I burst into tears and embarrassed us both. The man had enough to deal with without me turning on the waterworks. I barreled back down the stairs, breathing hard.

"Here." I held out the shirt to Jimmy.

He stopped, cocked his head. "You're fired."

"What?"

"Lena, look at it."

I did so. "Huh. Well, it's very bright and cheerful. No one will be looking at your face, that's for certain."

"Yeah. That's why you're fired."

"I think the clashing pink and red Christmas trees make quite a statement. And the frolicking deer are kind of cool . . . wait, is that one just jumping or has it actually mounted the little one beneath it?"

Angry fingers flew over the buttons of his ruined white shirt. He tore the last few, sending them pinging off into the four corners of the bathroom.

"Oh, goodness. There's even a threesome happening on the back. That shirt really has it all. But I think if anyone could pull it off, it's you." I should stop. I really should stop. But I just couldn't. "*The* Jimmy Ferris. I mean, whoa. You're basically the style king."

"I don't know why the fuck I put up with you."

I shrugged. "No, me neither. But you keep paying me so I keep hanging around."

"Awesome. Go away."

"You got it, boss."

I hovered in the doorway, trying not to laugh. "You're really going to put it on?"

He threw his stained shirt on the ground, jaw working. "I have to, don't I? Can't insult Neil."

"I'm sorry."

"Yeah. You'd be a shitload more believable if you weren't laughing."

True. Giggles poured out of me. It had to be all the stress from today. Though the look on Jimmy's poor face was hilarious. And the way he handled the shirt like it was something similar to dog shit, his mouth drawn wide with distaste just made it all the better.

"Am I really fired?" I asked, wiping my watery eyes. It would certainly solve a lot of my problems. Or just the main one—him. If I didn't have to see him every day, my unfortunate new feelings would dwindle and disappear, right? Right.

Well, probably.

"What's going on?" David ambled on down the hallway in his cool rocker way. I moved over to give him some room. "How's your face and what the fuck are you wearing?"

"Ask, Lena," Jimmy bit out.

"I can't. Your shirt's so ugly it made her cry."

I laughed even harder. Something tugged at the hem of my pants, next came growling. "Aw, Killer. What do you think of Uncle Jimmy's shirt, hmm?" I scooped up the gorgeous puppy before he could gnaw a hole in my hem. "It's magnificent, isn't it?"

"Hey." Mal crowded in behind David and I, peering over our shoulders. "What's this, a bathroom meeting? Do I need to find, Ben?"

Jimmy swore some more and put on his suit coat with great haste.

"Oh, you're wearing the fucking deer shirt," said Mal,

scratching Killer's head and generally stirring him up. "That's great, man. I got it for dad as a joke a few years back. But I think it's fantastic that you're secure enough with yourself and your masculinity to go there."

"I think it suits him." I grinned. "It reflects his inner beauty as few other shirts could."

"It does, it does." Mal smiled and this time, it was a little closer to his usual. Certainly the best attempt there'd been today. "I gotta take this guy back to his mama. He's due for crate time."

I handed the pup over. "Bye, Killer."

With the pup suspended high in one hand, Mal headed back down the hallway.

"You know, I'm sure Mal could've gotten you another shirt," I said.

"No." Jimmy stopped fiddling with the buttons on his coat and his face cleared. His anger seemed to have evaporated. "Least it was useful for something."

"You did good at the funeral." David crossed his arms over his chest, leaning against the doorframe. "Real good. It was a beautiful speech."

Jimmy rubbed at the back of his neck. "Think we can head back to the hotel yet? I wanna hit the gym."

Complete avoidance of his brother's words, which seemed to stem more from embarrassment, like praise had no place in Jimmy's world. Odd for a rock star. One would think he'd bask in any attention given how fussy he was with his appearance. The man was a walking contradiction.

No surprise at Jimmy's response registered on David's face. Instead, he smiled. "Sure. I'll find Ev and Ben."

"Good."

David paused. "Listen, earlier about mom. I didn't mean—"

"It's fine," cut in Jimmy. "Let it go."

"I just . . . I didn't give up on you. Seems harsh not to give her the same chance."

Jimmy inhaled sharply. "You were ready to give up on me. Hell, you threatened to, remember? You all did. But that's beside the point. I've given her every opportunity over the last few years. All she did was hit me up for more money every fucking chance she got. She doesn't want help. She's perfectly happy living in the gutter."

David winced.

I studied my feet and stayed silent. You couldn't have cut the air with a knife, it would have taken a chainsaw at the very least.

Awkward as hell.

If David hadn't been blocking the doorway I'd have made a swift exit, given them some privacy to sort this out. But I was stuck, forced to bear witness. I highly doubted Jimmy would appreciate me seeing quite so much of him in one day. Not him as in the physical, but him and his secrets, his past. Such information had a way of binding people and my boss was one of the least likely people to want such a thing. He made my efforts at staying separate and solo over the last few years seem like child's play. The strained relationship he had with his brother, whom he also worked with, was a prime example.

"Yeah," sighed David, turning to go. "Guess she doesn't."

I waited till Jimmy and I were alone to speak. For a long moment the only sound was the dripping of the tap. Time to break the silence.

"He's right," I said. "The speech was perfect."

Jimmy looked up at me from beneath his dark brows. His eyes were like ice storms, his jaw rigid.

"You did a brilliant job," I said, concentrating on the positive part of his talk with his brother. "Really fantastic. Just like I said you would."

The edge of his mouth twitched. Something inside of me lightened at the sight.

"You had to get that in there, didn't you?" he asked.

"Yes, I did."

He shook his head. "Great. Didn't I tell you to go away?"

"You're always telling me to go away. I'd be halfway to the Yukon by now if I actually ever listened to you." I yawned prettily. If he didn't make stirring him up so much fun, there was a decent chance I'd stop. Well, an even one. "You haven't told me if I'm really fired or not yet."

His brows arched, expectantly. "What do you think, Lena?"

"I think regardless of whatever comes out of your mouth, you keep paying me. And money talks."

He said nothing.

"I also think if I actually went away, you would miss me, Jimmy Ferris." For a brief moment, a messy, needy part of me yearned for him to agree, which was completely insane. I should cut the silly part out and cauterize it, excise it from my body. Without a doubt, it would be the sane thing for me to do. Any ridiculous longing after anything resembling a softer emotion from Jimmy was a big mistake. He either hadn't been made that way to begin with, or any softer parts had been ground out long ago by that epic bitch of a mother of his. Besides which, alone was best, I think we both knew it. Due to the situation, we just happened to be spending our alone time together these days. I guess it was better than being lonely.

"That so?" He gave me a cool look. "Why don't you go away and we'll find out?"

I smiled. "Okeydokey."

CHAPTER FOUR

TWO DAYS LATER . . .

"What?" asked Jimmy in a terse voice, never taking his eyes off the TV. On screen, a hockey game raged on, the someones against the someone else's. No, I honestly didn't care enough to figure out who was playing.

We'd been back in Portland for two days and had mostly returned to our usual routine with only one or two minor behavioral differences.

"Huh?" I asked, finger toying over the screen of my e-reader.

"You keep looking at me weird."

"No, I don't."

"Yeah, you do." He bristled, giving me impatient side eyes. "You been doing it all day."

"I have not. You're imagining things."

He wasn't imagining things. Ever since that day in Coeur d'Alene, things had been different. I'd been different. I couldn't seem to see, hear, or be near him without reacting in ways I sincerely wished I did not. Contrary to my hopes, the feelings had not dissipated. Instead, they seemed to have settled in for the duration, sinking further and further into my heart and mind. All of those glimpses into his psyche and his troubled past had changed things irrevocably. Both in how I looked at him, and how often. The truth was, this horrible idiotic crush, or whatever the hell it was, probably showed on my face every time I turned his way. It certainly felt like it did.

"I'm not gonna freak out again or anything, Lena," he said. "Relax."

A pause. "No, I know. I'm not worried about that."

"So stop looking at me already," he grouched.

"I'm not!" I protested, sneaking a look.

He slumped further down in the corner of the couch, a frown embedded into his handsome face. Jeans and a black Henley were Jimmy's casual home attire. I highly doubted a male model could have worn them as well. The man just had innate style and show. With my hair messily tied up on top of my head and glasses sitting on the end of my nose, I probably looked like an early candidate for a crazy cat lady. Give me a litter of kittens and I'd be set.

I put my e-reader aside, giving it up as a lost cause. With him in the room, I apparently had the concentration span of a four-year-old loaded up on sugar. But also, I had in fact come down here for a particular reason. "You didn't call your brother back."

"Hmm."

"He's called twice now."

A one-shoulder shrug.

Tiny rivers of rain trickled down the outside of the window and a streetlight shone in the distance. Typical cold wet weather for this time of year. Just the thought of what it would be like outside in it was enough to make me shiver.

"I could grab the phone for you if you like," I said. "I was just about to go get a drink."

He slicked back his hair with the palm of his hand. "Why are you down here? You normally hang out in your room at night."

"Is my being here a problem?"

"Didn't say that. Just wondering what's changed?"

Lots had changed. Lots and lots and then a bit more besides, the bulk of which I was still figuring out. No neat conclusions had yet presented themselves. I might have lied a smidgeon about not being worried about him. He did seem fine. Didn't mean it wasn't still my job to keep an eye on him. The funeral and his big blow-up still felt fresh.

"Nothing's changed," I lied. "Just got bored on my own, I guess."

I pulled my comfy big old green cardigan tighter around me, feeling self-conscious. Plus the headlights were on high beam for some reason. Let us not explore why. But my annoying him was a given, I could probably manage it simply by breathing, such was the glory of Jimmy's disposition. It'd never actually worried me before, however. I must be getting soft. Perhaps I shouldn't have come down. Maybe I should just abort the spend-time/check-up-on-him mission and retreat back to my room.

" 'kay," he said.

That was it. All of that inner turmoil and he couldn't even be bothered saying an entire word with regard to my presence. I guess he really didn't mind.

"You cold?" he asked.

"Pardon?"

His head lay against the back of the couch, slowly looking me over. Nothing changed in his face, but his eyes seemed to heat somehow. Or maybe I was just imaging things.

"You're all bundled up," he said. "Need me to turn up the thermostat?"

"No. Thanks." I might need to put some padding in my bra so my nipples were less obvious in their like for him. The room however was lovely and warm as the couch beneath my butt was beautifully comfortable. Jimmy didn't stint on life's luxuries. He wasn't cheap.

"I'm good," I said.

A chin tip.

"So, who's winning the hockey game?" I curled my skinny jean clad legs up beneath me.

"I'm not really that into it. You can pick something to watch if you want."

"Okay." I held out my hand for the remote.

A soft chuckle came out of him, a rare, delightful sound indeed. It tickled over my skin in the strangest yet nicest fashion. If he actually ever laughed out loud I'd be in trouble.

"Not a chance, Lena. Only I operate the remote. I'll flip through channels and you can tell me if anything appeals."

"Only you operate the remote?"

"Yup."

"Control freak."

"It's a state-of-the-art home entertainment system, Lena. I had it shipped from Germany, special." He waved the funky black remote around like it was his scepter. King Jimmy. He wished. "No way I'm risking it with you."

"What?" My mouth fell open. "What do you mean, you're not *risking* it with me?"

"The coffee machine." He grabbed a cushion and stuffed it behind his fat head, changing through to the first channel. A cooking show.

"Keep going." I liked food. I just didn't particularly want to be the one to have to make it. My mom had always done the cooking at home, suited me fine. "I barely touched the coffee machine. That was some weird random mechanical fault on the part of the universe."

"Whatever."

Next was some old '80s made-for-TV movie. You could tell by the hair, it was so high and dry looking. What wonders a keratin treatment would have done for those poor women. And the ginormous shoulder pads, yikes.

"Keep going, please," I said. An old episode of *Vampire Diaries* flickered on next. "Ooh, Ian, you're lovely. But I've already seen this one so keep going."

"Thank fuck." Jimmy punched the button and on came a nature documentary. Or at least I hoped that's what it was given a shiny black stallion mounting a slightly terrified-looking mare took up the screen.

"Hey, it's just like that shirt you borrowed off Mr. Ericson!" I clapped with joy and a slight amount of malice. "Horses humping, that's beautiful."

"You like that, do you?" his sly voice asked.

With the press of a button, miles and miles of bare and bouncy flesh filled the wide screen. With the exception of the woman in the man sandwich's boobs. Those puppies stayed eerily gravity-defying still. And unlike mine, they weren't the least bit pointy.

"That's so sweet," I sighed. "Nothing says true love like D.P."

Jimmy sniggered and changed the channel, cars roared around a racetrack.

"Why is it so many men have the sense of humor of a smelly, pimple-faced, barely pubescent little jerk?" I pondered aloud.

"You don't find that charming?" he asked, brow raised.

"Weird of me, I know." I snagged a cushion and cuddled it to my chest. "I had this boyfriend once who thought it was amusing to . . . actually, no. I don't want to tell that story. Ever."

"Go on."

"No. I'm happier pretending he never existed. Let's leave my shameful dating choices in the past."

"That's hardly fair," he said. "You know enough of my shit."

Before I could form a reply Formula One turned into *Downton Abbey* and I squeed with excitement. "Stop here. Stop!"

Jimmy winced, rubbing his ear. "For Christ's sake, use your inside voice."

"This is a great show." Two of the show's lovers were chatting, decked out in the usual glorious English-gentry-type gear. Awesome. "And particularly pertinent to our situation, I think."

"Huh?" Lip curled, he stared at the screen, distinctly unimpressed by the splendor. Plebeian.

"It's all about life in a turn-of-the-century noble house in England."

"Yeah. The castle and what they're wearing kind of gave it away."

"Aren't the dresses beautiful?" I hugged my cushion happily. I'd live and die in jeans, but it was nice to dream. "See, there are the wealthy lords and ladies who have everything and their servants, who have zilch and have to run around after the lords and ladies, catering to their every whim with barely a thank-you all day long. I mean, they're basically treated like second-class citizens and completely taken for granted by their bosses. Isn't that barbaric?"

My irony-laden comment garnered a lone grunt. Though to be fair, he could put a lot of emotion into a grunt, quite a variation of tone and character. The way Jimmy did it, it was almost a sentence, a story. He turned being a caveman into an art form.

"And that's Lady Mary." I pointed at the screen. "She says all sorts of horrible things that she doesn't mean, always hiding behind this snotty, rude persona. When really underneath she's got a tender warm heart and a conscience just like everyone else. Doesn't that sound similar to some-one we know?"

"You talk a lot." He yawned. "We watching this or what?"

"You'll watch this with me?"

"It's kind of nice having the company." He kept his eyes on the screen. I thought I detected a hint of somber to his voice. Perhaps Ev had been right and he was lonely. Often the guys were coming and going during the day, but with Mal spending some time in Idaho with his family, the band was on a break. Jimmy had been more fidgety than normal, at a loss for what to do with himself. Even normally, however, nighttimes were quiet in the big house.

"Yeah, it is," I said.

We sat in silence for a while, both of us studying the screen. Well, with the exception of me occasionally slyly studying him. I'd be an expert in covert relations by the time I finally left Portland.

He'd shoved his hands back behind his head, face relaxed and eyes open. Interestingly enough, he apparently got caught up in the period drama. Went to show you shouldn't judge people. It was nice—companionable—sitting there with him as opposed to hanging alone in my room. I'd have to do it more often. For his sake of course.

"Sure you don't want to call David?" I asked.

The edge of his mouth turned downward. "I can put the game back on real easy if you like."

"None of my business, you're right. Let's just enjoy the show in silence, shall we?"

"Let's," he said in his deep voice.

FOUR DAYS LATER . . .

"Lena, you seen my old black Led Zep shirt?"

"Nope."

"You sure?" His brows became one dark cranky line. The scratches on his face were healing well, thank goodness. Though it didn't reduce my desire to throttle his mother on a daily basis.

"Yes. I haven't seen it."

"Can't find it anywhere . . ."

"And this is a surprise, how?" I slipped my hands into my back jeans pockets. "Jimmy, you own more clothing than Cher, Britney, and Elvis, put together. Things are bound to go missing."

"Sure you haven't seen it?"

"For goodness sake, what do you think, Jimmy? That I stole it to sleep in or something?" I laughed bitterly. Sure as hell, the truth deserved a good mocking. I'd sunk so despicably low.

I hadn't even meant to steal the stupid thing, but the shirt had been mixed up with my laundry a few days ago. It'd been the first top I laid my hand on after stepping out of the shower, ready to go to bed. Without thought, I'd put it on and it'd been so soft, the scent of him lingering beneath the laundry detergent. Every night since, I'd found myself in it come bedtime. My shame knew no limits. And no, I still hadn't quit. The words still hadn't come even close to leaving my mouth.

He frowned. "No."

"That I have some deep secret longing to feel close to you resulting in my stealing your shirt like some creepy perv?"

"'Course I don't fucking think that," he replied crankily, reaching up to grip the top of the doorframe. All of his bulging muscles stretched the arms of his white T-shirt in the nicest way. It was all I could do not to start drooling, my heartbeat taking up residence somewhere down between my thighs. And who could blame it? Not me. Maybe if I got laid, this would go away and things would return to normal. It'd seemed safer to avoid rubbing up against any men just in case I got carried away and started dating again. This new situation, however, changed everything.

"Well, of course not! That would be crazy." And wasn't that the god's honest truth? Cray-zeee. Lock me up and throw away the key because it wasn't like I didn't know better.

"Just can't figure out where the hell it could be."

Angels couldn't have smiled as innocently. They might have tried, but they would have failed, the dirty-mouthed, winged, little liars. "Jimmy, I don't know where it is. But I'll look around for it later, okay?"

"Yeah," he said, and then added as an afterthought, "and stop looking at me weird."

"I'm not!"

SIX DAYS LATER . . .

"No, c'mon," he cried. "I saw that. That was a look."

"What?"

"You looked at me." His pointy threatening finger sat beneath my nose.

I smacked it away. "I'm not allowed to look at you? Really? Is this like one of those strange directives you hear about famous people having? No one's allowed to talk to you or look at you, and there must be bowls of chocolate pudding everywhere you go from now on?"

His eyes narrowed.

I might have felt a smidgen of guilt deep down inside. But this was about survival, I had no choice.

"I'm not on anything and I'm not gonna flip out again," he muttered.

"I know that."

"Do you?"

"Yes."

"So then it's not me, it's you."

Sirens and alarm bells rang inside my head. "What are you even talking about?"

"Deny it all you want, but I'm right. Something's going on with you," he said in a low voice. "I don't know what the fuck it is. And I don't want to know. I just want it to stop. Got it?"

"Jimmy, seriously, nothing's going on." I wound up my long hair and tied it into a loose knot, keeping my hands busy lest their shakiness betray my guilt, the bastards. "And have you called David back yet? He called again. I'm getting tired of making excuses for you."

"I've been busy." He turned his back on me, staring out the window. "And I pay you to make excuses for me."

"I think I'm going to start charging you extra for lies. Someone needs to pay for the stain on my soul."

No reply. His broad shoulders seemed to be bent beneath some weight, his spine bowed. Not good. This was a mood I apparently couldn't joke him out of.

"You know you've been really tense lately," I said. "Why don't I book you a massage? Wouldn't that be nice? And then afterward, we could chill out and watch some TV."

He watched me over his shoulder, a muscle twitching in his jaw. "Sure, sounds good. I'm going for another jog."

"It's raining."

"I won't melt." Without further ado he left, disappearing into the hallway. He was right of course, something was going on with me. What was going on with him and his brother concerned me much more.

SEVEN DAYS LATER . . .

"You're doing it again!" Jimmy stopped mid push-up, sweat dripping off his handsome face. "I'm not imagining it. You're fucking doing it again."

"Hmm?" I replied calmly, sitting at the kitchen counter. Black-and-white Italian marble because only the best would do for Jimmy. His house was expensively, luxuriously austere to a fault. Three levels of stark gray walls on the outside and black-and-white décor within. It basically looked like a post-modernist had thrown up in here and the decorator decided to call it a day. As if a splash of color would kill anyone. I was half-tempted to start buying obnoxiously bright rainbow-colored accessories, cushions, and a vase or two, and leave them around the house in protest just to see what he'd do.

"You *are* looking at me weird all the time."

"No, I'm sorting your e-mail. A different thing entirely." I pried my gaze off his hot (in every sense of the word) body and returned it to the laptop. "Oh, look. Lingerie Girl has sent you another picture. A demi-bra this time, hot pink with tassels. I think the tassels are a nice touch. She's even attached a video of her making them swing. Such a thoughtful girl."

"Delete it."

"But what if she says something important?"

"She's a complete stranger sending me pictures of herself nearly naked dancing and bending over furniture."

I hummed. "Yes, today we have a washing machine. Very sexy in a domestic erotica sort of way. A powerful statement about feminism, I think. This woman is deep."

"Right." He resumed his exercising. "This woman is not gonna say anything I need to hear."

Outside, a bolt of lightning lit up the sky, making me jump. The crash of thunder came next.

"That was close." I watched him carry on regardless of nature's showing off. "Some of your fans are loco. Luckily, others are just delightful."

A grunt.

The problem with the push-up lay within the way it

pretty much mimicked the act of sex. (Lay. Heh.) All the sweating, straining, and up and down of the pelvic region. It was disgusting, shouldn't be allowed. Also, I really needed to get laid or find someone willing to hold hands with me at the very least. Maybe I'd reached the limits of physical depravation and I was touch starved. God, I hoped that was all. Him holding me before the funeral had awakened certain needs I sadly couldn't meet on my own. Nor was spending more time with him helping. We'd pretty much fallen into a habit of hanging out together each night, debating who got to choose what we'd watch.

It was nice. Too nice.

Last night when I'd wandered into the living room he'd actually almost smiled and shifted about in his corner of the couch. Like he'd been waiting on me or something, anticipating my arrival. I had to be reading the signals wrong. I'd given him a clumsy grin, sat down, and endured a quarter of football before my wits returned, I'd been so surprised. Even if I was wrong, it might just be time to break the ban on men, sex, and romance. Or at least with regard to the men and sex parts. I couldn't keep mooning after Jimmy like a smitten teenager. Problem was, time spent with him just soothed something in me. Some need for companionship or a yearning for the friends I'd left behind when I'd decided to head out into the big bad world a few years back. When everything had gone to shit.

If only he wasn't so nice to perv on. I crossed my legs, squeezing my thighs together. Sweat darkened the thin cotton of his shirt and the material stuck to him outlining each and every muscle. Man, he had a lot of them, his arms for instance . . .

"Lena!"

"What?"

"Stop it."

My mouth slammed shut.

"You're watching me all the time and it's fucking creepy. I can't take it anymore."

Oh God, he was right.

I watched him constantly, I couldn't help myself. And when I couldn't watch him, I thought about him. Mostly about how I didn't want to feel anything for him, but it still counted. I was losing it. Actually, I'd already lost it back in Coeur d'Alene to be brutally honest. My stupid heart stuttered as if to second the sentiment. All the sappy feelings for him in me were growing by the day, squeezing out every last vestige of common sense.

This couldn't continue.

I could not go through this again.

"I have to go," I muttered. The thought of leaving him was like having my heart dug out with a plastic spork, but what could I do?

He paused. "What?"

"I mean . . . I'm tired and I work very hard. You think dealing with your fan mail is easy?"

"No one asked you to deal with my fan mail. You took that job on yourself."

"Well, I can't just follow you around all day doing nothing. I need mental stimulation."

With an exasperated sound, Jimmy jumped up in an overly athletic fashion. Show off. I bet he was amazing in bed. No, forget that, he'd be a selfish lover, too busy staring at himself in the mirrored ceiling to see to the business at hand. Between my legs just needed to calm the hell down.

Little lines appeared between his brows. "Explain to me how checking out pictures of chicks dancing around in their underwear is mentally stimulating for you. I need to hear about this."

"They're not all like that. Some of them are quite nice and just want a signed picture of you or a 'thanks for contacting me, glad you liked the album.' You were ignoring them. It was rude."

"Management can deal with them. And if you're tired, go take a nap and get out of my face with your weirdness." He looked at me like I was dwelling on the wrong side of the insane asylum walls. Fair enough, really.

"Fine." I jabbed at the keyboard, shutting the laptop down. "I will."

"Christ, you're moody lately. Worse than me."

I barked out a laugh. "Jimmy, did you just actually make a joke at your own expense?"

The side of his mouth curled up the tiniest bit. Good god, was that a flash of dimple? My pulse rocketed like it was the Fourth of July. I fucking loved dimples. They were so lickable, so divine.

"Lena," he growled.

Instantly, I got wet. "Sorry. I just . . . what is that?"

I stopped and sniffed at the air. There was a strange smoky smell in the room lingering beneath the musk of Jimmy's sweat and the remnants of his cologne. I thought my imagination must be playing tricks on me, but no. My heart sunk to the depths of my chest. As signs went, this wasn't a good one.

"What's what?" he asked.

"The cigarette smell." I stood, wandering around the table. "It's coming from you."

He sat back on his haunches. "Don't know what you're talking about."

"It's also coming from your jacket."

His gaze jumped to the item of clothing in question, left hanging on the back of a kitchen chair. It was a gray all-weather one, nothing fancy though I bet it cost a bomb. Perfectly suitable for skulking about outside to have a smoke. He licked his lips, eyes suddenly cagey. "Lena . . ."

"You've started smoking again, haven't you?"

"Don't require your permission. I can do what I like."

"Then why have you been hiding it from me?"

He jumped to his feet, brushed off his hands. "'Cause it's none of your business."

"Guess again, bud. You and your health is exactly my business."

Hand extended, he reached for the jacket. Sadly, for him, I was well ahead of the game there. I clasped the coat to my chest, riffling through pockets one-handed. It couldn't have been going on for long. Still, I should have been paying more attention, been on it the minute it began.

"Give it to me," he said, tugging on a stray sleeve.

I liberated the gold cardboard box from a side pocket and held it behind me, out of his reach. "No more, Jimmy. You've worked so hard to get healthy, you are not losing ground now."

"You going to bitch at me about drinking coffee next?" He tossed the jacket aside, well riled up. His damp hair hung in his face, eyes flashing fury. "It's just the occasional fucking cigarette. I've given up everything else. Hand them over, Lena."

"You know you shouldn't be smoking. That's why you look so guilty."

"I do not look guilty," he said, voice terse and face guilty as all god damn hell. "I'm a grown man and I repeat, this is none of your business."

"I care about you." I quickly dashed back away from him, putting some room between me and the angry rock star. The nice big eight-seater kitchen table made a suitable barricade. Though ideally an electric fence would have been best given the look on his face. A cattle prod wouldn't hurt either.

"You gave these up for a reason," I said. "What was it?"

"Give them back." He held out his hand demandingly, mouth flat and unimpressed.

"You made the choice to stop using them months ago, didn't you? Why did you do that, Jimmy? Tell me."

He declined to answer. Instead, slowly he moved left. So I of course moved right, keeping the same distance and the bulk of the table between us. Safety mattered.

"Lena," he said in a low voice. "I don't feel like going out in this storm to buy another pack tonight so you are going to give those back to me. And then you're going to keep your pretty little nose out what doesn't concern you."

"No."

"That's an order, Lena."

Did he really still think orders worked with me? By the firm set of his jaw, I guessed yes. Crazy wishful thinking on his part.

"Let's compromise here," I said, pulling a chair out from beneath the table. "I think we should sit down and talk about this like adults. Discuss the pros and cons, and make sure you're making an informed decision."

His big body held preternaturally still, strong fingers grasping the back of the chair in front of him. "Sure. We can do that."

"Thank you. That's all I'm asking."

Slowly, he sat himself down in the chair. Then he cocked his head, waiting for me to do likewise. Veins in his neck and arms stood out against the skin. Please, as if he wasn't ready to pounce. The man must have thought I was an idiot. My breath quickened, breasts rising and falling beneath my shirt. For a moment his gaze stayed caught on them, color lighting his face. Boobs did make for an awesome distraction.

I might not be able to stop him smoking long term. I knew that. But I was sure as hell stopping him for tonight and then talking to him properly about it. Sadly, he sat between me and the garbage composter which would have made short work of destroying the things. I'd have to get inventive.

"Okay. I'm really glad we can be reasonable about this." I pretended to start lowering my curvy butt onto the chair. "Thanks for agreeing to talk it out with me, Jimmy."

Shiny sharp teeth filled in his handsome smile. "'Course, Lena. Anything for you."

"That's so sweet." I smiled.

And then I bolted.

Adrenaline surged through me and my legs were pumping for all I was worth. I'd flush the fuckers in the bathroom off the front hallway. Perfect. Lucky it wasn't that far because even with the head start, he was gaining fast. Given he liked jogging and I liked pie, this was to be expected.

The chiming of the front doorbell echoed through the house. It kept time with the pounding of my heart and the thumping of Jimmy's heavy footsteps behind me. I grabbed hold of the edge of the bathroom door, socked feet slipping on the slick marble floor. So close now. Jimmy's arm looped around my waist, drawing me back. But with his bare feet and my socked ones, neither of us had great traction. We did, however, have a lot of momentum. I flew forward, feet leaving the cold hard ground. If it wasn't for Jimmy's hold I'd have cracked open my chin on the hallway floor. As it was, my knees bore some of the impact, but he took the brunt. His palm smacked hard against the marble floor, breaking our fall and holding me up those few necessary inches to spare my face from meeting its doom. I lost my grip and the pack of cigarettes skittered across the floor, stopping.

Again the doorbell rang.

My hair had escaped its topknot, falling in my face in a dark tangle. I spied the pack a few yards out from the front door and scurried forward, clawing after the damn thing.

Jimmy put a halt to this by simply lowering his monstrous weight on top of me, trapping me belly down. Muscle made him approximately the same bulk as a baby elephant.

It turned out that when squished, I made a sound horribly close to "oomph-urgh."

Jimmy laughed most evilly.

"Get off me," I yelled, wriggling beneath him.

"Are you going to give this up?" His breath was warm against my ear, the length of his body pressed against my back. In any other situation, it'd be damn arousing. My ass accidentally rubbed against his groin and oh wow, holy hell. A hot flush swept straight through me.

Damn. So, it was arousing. "Never!"

"You're not going to win." Sweaty fingers wrapped around my wrist, holding it back from reaching the treasure. I could feel his cock firming, pressing against my rear. Hell, now he was enjoying it too much too. It had to be just a physical response on his part. "You're being ridiculous."

"Oh, and you're not?" I panted, nipples drilling holes into the marble flooring.

"Lena—"

Someone banged on the front door. Huh, that's right, we had a visitor outside waiting in the storm. All while we wrestled it out in a pseudosexual manner on the front entry floor. Excellent.

Keys jangled and the lock turned, then David Ferris came in along with a gust of bitingly cold wet air. A damp late-autumn leaf slapped me in the face. Jimmy carefully peeled it off before I could react. The wind cut off as David shut the door behind him. He stood frowning down at us.

"Guys," he said, eyes alight with laughter. "You taking up wrestling or what?"

"Why yes." I tapped my short fingernails against the floor, put my head in my hand. "It was too wet for Jimmy to go jogging, so . . . yeah. Had to improvise."

David's tongue played behind his cheek, his smile huge. "Right. Great."

On my back, Jimmy groaned. "She was acting nuts about something. Long story."

"I was doing my job and caring for your welfare," I said. "Will you get off me already?"

Then David noticed the pack of cigarettes at his feet. Shit. The wrinkles on his forehead were too numerous to count. With the toe of his combat boot, he kicked them toward us. Lightning quick, Jimmy snatched them. Dammit.

"You start smoking again, Jim?" His brother's voice expressed great displeasure and disappointment. Every inch of Jimmy tensed against my back.

"They're mine," I said.

"No, they're not." My boss's gargantuan mass disappeared off of me. Before I could return myself to an upright position, hands gripped me beneath the arms. I was lifted back up onto my feet like I weighed no more than a dandelion.

Jimmy cleared his throat. "Something else for you to disapprove of about me, right Dave?"

"That's not the way it is," his brother said, face somber. "I've been trying to call you all week."

"Yeah. Sorry, been busy."

"Right."

The two brothers just sort of stared at one another. This reunion was not going well at all. If Jimmy had his lips any more tightly pinned together they'd have disappeared from existence. Women everywhere would mourn their loss. Or at least I would.

The pain and regret in David's eyes was horrible to see. Surely Jimmy would forgive him. He was family. Mind you, I wasn't exactly the poster child for absolving siblings. But these two were different, they loved each other.

"It's good you came over," I said. "How's Ev?"

"Fine. Thanks." David nodded.

"We're just in the middle of something here, Dave." Fingers wrapped crushingly tight around the cigarette pack, Jimmy did his usual avoidance thing. He glared at the floor like it'd eaten the last Reese's minicup in the pack. Not that he ate chocolate, but you get what I mean.

"I'll catch you later," he said dismissively, not even looking at his brother.

My spirits dived. "Jimmy—"

"Later okay, Dave?" His firm voice echoed through the room. The silence that followed it was awful.

"Don't." I stepped closer to him, keeping my voice low. "You two should talk."

"It's okay, Lena." David scratched his head, gave me a mildly embarrassed look. Water dripped off his coat, forming puddles at his feet. "We'll talk when he's ready."

Jaw set, Jimmy stared down at me, saying nothing.

Without another word David turned and opened the door, heading back out into the storm. Jimmy swung the door shut. Plastic crinkled as he crushed the pack of cigarettes into nothing more than mangled rubbish.

"Go after him. Now." I jogged over to the hallway closet and threw open the door, grabbing the first jacket I found.

He hurled the mess of cardboard and tobacco onto the side table. The cigarettes had definitely met their end.

"Be quiet, Lena."

"No. You only have one brother and he's actually a pretty decent guy," I said, the words tumbling out of me in a rush. "He messed up saying what he did and siding with your mom in Idaho, and I know it hurt you. But, Jimmy, he knows it too and he regrets it. It's eating him up, you can see it in his eyes."

"We're not talking about this."

"I have one sibling and we hate each other's guts. It's basically split my family in two. Trust me, you do not want this situation escalating into that." I grabbed hold of his arm. "Jimmy?"

He shook me off. "Can we not do this?"

"Everyone screws up sometime. You of all people know that. But he's your brother and he loves you. Give him a chance to apologize."

"What, so you're on his side now, are you?" He glared down at me. "Davie always was the pretty boy with the soft heart. Girls love him. But you gotta know he's taken, Lena. He's not going to give you what you need."

"Oh, please." I shoved him hard in the chest with the coat, actually sending him rocking back a step. So damn frustrated I could have kicked him. "Are you for real? I am not interested in your brother. And I am on your side. Always."

The man did not look convinced.

"I am only worried about you and how wound up you've been the last week, worrying over this and missing him. David was wrong, but he knows it. I promise you."

For a moment he stared at me.

"Please, Jimmy."

He looked away, Adam's apple bobbing. Then, with a snarl, he twisted the door handle, dashing straight out into the pouring rain. The cold wind whipped up my hair and stung my face. I wrapped myself up in his forgotten jacket, hiding behind the partially open door. Jimmy ran across the front lawn and out to the black 4x4, sitting at the curb. The car door opened and David stepped out. At first they kept a good body length between them, David's arms crossed and Jimmy's on his hips. Then David reached out, clasping his brother's shoulder and giving it a shake as if imploring him. Jimmy seemed to loosen up after that, they moved closer. Soon enough their heads were together, obviously having some sort of conversation despite standing out in a storm. Good. That was good. I think David nodded. It was hard to see.

A couple of gold and brown leaves blew past me into the house.

Jimmy turned to come back and his brother grabbed his arm, pulling him in for a brief back-thumping hug.

Yes. Thank you, baby Jesus.

Finally, Jimmy ran back to the house, soaked to the ever-loving bone.

"Careful, don't slip with your wet feet." I offered him his jacket but he shook his head and stripped off his shirt. Water ran off his wet hair, down his face and neck. "I'll get a towel."

"Don't bother. I'm fucking freezing." He made for the bathroom and walked straight into the shower, turning on the hot water.

"Everything's okay with you two now?" I asked.

"Yeah." He pushed down his sweat pants, baring his black snug-fitting boxer briefs with quite the parcel up front. Holy shit, his thighs, his washboard chest, his everything. What with all of the sudden sex fantasies filling my head, I was surprised there's any room left in the building. My body went into shock, pulse rocketing. I could warm him. For certain, my face and other pertinent body parts felt on fire. Good god, I bet his skin tasted divine.

Jimmy raised a brow. "Lena?"

I blinked.

"What, you waiting to tell me you were right again?"

"Sure?"

"Consider it done." Jimmy stood, hands on hips, watching me. The look in his eyes, I couldn't decipher it. But his lips parted and it seemed he was almost on the verge of asking me something. Then changed his mind. "C'mon, what are you doing in here? Unless you're offering to scrub my back, you need to get out."

My eyes went wide, as wide could be. "What? Are you serious?"

Gently, he grabbed me by the upper arm and marched me out of the bathroom. "Get out, Lena."

"I was just trying to talk to you." I was so not trying to talk to him. But now, we very much needed to discuss his back scrubbing needs and how I, as employee of the month, could meet them.

"Talk to me later."

"But—"

And he slammed the door in my face.

Nice.

Jerk.

Disappointment was a nasty big beast and it was sitting right on my heart. I wrapped my arms around myself, guarding against the chill. It seemed that standing in the doorway, I'd gotten a bit damp myself from the mist and the encroaching rain. Mostly, however, it was about being thrown out of heaven, a.k.a., the ground-floor bathroom. How was that for gratitude? I gave the door the finger.

"You did good," he hollered from within.

I dropped my arm to my side. "Thanks."

"Dave and me are all fine again."

"Great," I shouted back.

"Yeah, you told me so."

I smiled. "I'm glad. Are you going to stop smoking?"

Muttered swearing. "Yeah, okay. And stop hanging around the door when I'm showering. That's creepy."

I rolled my eyes. It wasn't like I could see anything through the keyhole.

Let's pretend I didn't try.

Two-thirty in the morning was kind of a bitch as times went. It fell into the in-between nowhere land. Too late to get a really good night's sleep, but much too early to start the day.

I rolled over onto my back and stared at the ceiling. It remained every bit as entertaining and enlightening as it had for the last four hours. Over on my bedside table, my water glass was empty. This made sense since my bladder felt demandingly full. All of me was awkward, uncomfortable. I bet Jimmy paid top dollar for this mattress, kings and queens probably slept on the same. And yet, it still did me no good.

With a groan I threw back the covers and dragged my sorry ass into the bathroom. I took care of business and washed my hands. Since I was already up and grumpy, I might as well go in search of chocolate.

Don't question the logic. It made sense to my sleep-deprived mind and that's all that mattered.

I trudged down the stairs. A flickering light came from within the living room, shadows playing across the opposite wall. I'd abandoned Jimmy to a documentary on Phil Spector hours and hours ago. Mr. Spector might have been a musical genius but considering where he wound up, it was all a bit too macabre for my tastes. I'd bid the rock star good night.

Tigers were mutely roaring and roaming the golden savannah on the wide screen. Jimmy lay passed out on the couch, fast asleep. The lines of his beautiful face were no less determined and harsh in repose. Yet they seemed softer somehow without his piss and vinegar going on. His long dark lashes lay against his cheek and his lips were slightly apart. They looked so soft. A feeling, a sensation worked its way up from deep in my belly, spreading right through me until it tingled in my toes. It was all about him. It was hot and cold, forever and never all at once. It was physical, but it was also more, much more. I wanted to know him, every last little thing about him. And I wanted him to know me. I wanted to be a real part of his life, not just his employee. To be the person he confided even his darkest thoughts in, the person he trusted.

It was insane.

Ever notice how the world seems different in the wee hours of the morning, when you've been awake too long? Surreal somehow and yet clearer, quieter so you can hear the whispered truth of things you couldn't bring yourself to face in the light. My feelings for Jimmy weren't fading. I was a fool to imagine they would, living in his house and breathing the same air as him. They weren't leaving any-time soon.

And if they weren't, then I had to.

I couldn't take another broken heart. Especially not when I could see it coming a mile away as in the case of Jimmy Ferris. He needed me to be a helper and a friend, not a lovelorn little twerp making starry eyes at him. He already had those by the bucket load.

I drew a deep breath, let it go. If only it didn't feel like I was being slowly cut open at the thought of leaving him. Overly gruesomely dramatic, but true. But it was just the like the old ripping-off-the-Band-Aid analogy. Better a smallish pain now than heartbreak and ruin down the track.

Still, the next few weeks were going to be hard.

Afterward, once I had my replacement settled in, maybe I'd go sit on a beach somewhere and feel sorry for myself. Get out of the rain and into the sun for a while, order frothy drinks with little umbrellas and fruit in them.

I could wait out my sister's wedding and then sneak home while she was away on her honeymoon. Yes, I had a plan.

Jimmy's feet were bundled together, arms pressed against his chest. Poor, baby. He must be cold. Not good after his time out in the rain this afternoon. I grabbed a couple of throws from the cabinet, chucked one at his feet and spread the other out wide. The fine woolen material drifted down to cover him from shoulder to toe.

"Better," I whispered.

"Yeah," he whispered back, opening one eye to look me over. "Cute jammies."

"I'll have you know that flannel teddy bear print jammies are on the cutting edge of fashion." I sat down, slumping tiredly. "What are you doing here?"

"Fell asleep. You woke me stomping down the stairs." He sat up in slow motion, rubbing at his head. His dark hair stuck out every which way. The television cast shadows across his face. "What time is it?"

"Just past two-thirty."

"What are you doing up?"

I shrugged. "Couldn't sleep. Sometimes I just can't get my stupid head to turn off."

A nod and a yawn. "Pretty sure we can find something better than a nature documentary to watch."

"You don't have to keep me company. It's late. Or early," I amended. "Go on up to bed, I'll be fine."

He picked up the spare blanket and tossed it into my lap. "Once I'm awake I don't tend to get back to sleep so easy."

"Sorry I woke you. Pass me the remote?"

He chuckled darkly. "Lena, Lena. Shame on you. I'm half awake, not crazy."

"Boys and their toys." I wrapped the blanket around me, settling in.

He just gave me a half smile with the faintest trace of

dimple. Actually, it was more of a quarter grin with a dash of the devil. But he was getting better at smiling and that's what counted. It was going to be one of the regrets of my life that I'd never got to see the full thing. I bet it was lethal in all the ways.

We didn't talk much. It was nice just having the company.

The last thing I remembered was being spread out on my half of the big couch, watching some cool old black-and-white movie about gangsters in the '40s. I woke up in my own bed the next morning, carefully tucked in. So carefully, it was a struggle to get my arms out at first from beneath the blankets. Jimmy had obviously carried me up and put me to bed. When I tried to thank him, he just ignored me and changed the subject.

Same old, same old.

CHAPTER FIVE

"Lena!"

My head shot up, the mug of coffee jumping in my hands. Hot liquid scalded my fingers, stinging. "Shit."

Jimmy came pounding down the internal staircase. "Where are you?"

"In the kitchen." I snatched up a tea towel, dabbing at my pink skin.

"What the fuck?" he roared, striding into the kitchen, dripping with sweat.

I sighed as only the long-suffering can do and rubbed at the coffee stains on my green Henley. "What the fuck, what, Jimmy?"

Another set of heavy-assed footfalls followed behind the man in question. Ben the bass player came into view. Picture a sexy lumberjack with musical abilities and you'll pretty much have him down right. He was equally sweaty—fitting, considering they'd both just been for a run.

"Hey, Ben." I waved a hand and the big guy gave me his usual chin tip. But wait, was that a smirk lingering on his lips? He leaned against the wall and crossed his arms, obviously settling in for something.

Whatever was going on here, I already didn't like it.

Jimmy tossed his phone onto the kitchen counter in front of me. "Why the fuck do I have some . . ." He picked the cell back up again, squinting at the screen. ". . . Tom Moorecomb really looking forward to meeting with me about the new assistant position?"

My stomach fell. "Oh. That."

"Yeah. That."

"I've been waiting for the right time to tell you."

Brows drawn tight, Jimmy braced his hands on the counter. "Let's try now."

"Well, I've decided to leave your lovely employ," I said, holding my head high and speaking nice and clear in a friendly professional tone. Just liked I'd practiced over and over again in the shower, in bed, on the john. Pretty much anywhere and everywhere when I got a moment. No more excuses. "Not that I haven't valued the time we've spent together, but I feel I'm ready to move on to new challenges. Tom is who I would suggest you hire as my replacement. He has a background in counseling, but is—"

"You're quitting?"

It'd never been so hard to meet his eyes. "Yes, Jimmy. I am. It's time."

"You organized all this behind my back." Not a question, a statement, and a very angry one at that. His usual cool gaze fell to well below subzero. It was pure luck I didn't snap freeze on the spot.

Instead, I nodded, goose bumps breaking out all over my skin.

"When?"

"When did I organize it or when do I finish?"

He jerked his chin. I took it to mean "yes" on both counts.

"The last couple of weeks, and in a couple of weeks," I said. "Thought I'd spend a few days settling Tom in before I left, making sure everything was okay. Of course there were other candidates, it's your choice whether or not you hire him."

"Big of you."

"But you will need to find someone to replace me."

"When were you going to tell me, Lena?"

"Soon."

He raised a brow.

"This weekend . . . sometime, I was going to give notice. I mean, definitely well before Tom arrived for his interview with you on Monday. You would probably want a chance to prepare, so . . ." I gave him my most charming smile. No matter what, never actually admit to flailing. "Monday morning at the very latest."

Color suffused Jimmy's face.

I cleared my throat. "Back to Tom's previous experience, which I think it's important to note, unlike me, he actually has some in a relevant field—"

"No."

I blinked. "What?"

"No. You're not quitting."

"Ah, yes. I am."

He shook his head just the once, but it was a fierce shake, brutal even. I'm surprised he didn't give himself whiplash. And while I'd known he probably wouldn't embrace my decision, I hadn't expected this level of obstinacy. "I'm a secretary, Jimmy. Not an addiction counselor. Fact is, I never should have taken the job in the first place. I'm not qualified, nor am I particularly good at it."

"I think I'm in a better position to make that call. Hell, Lena. This is ridiculous, what is it you want me to say?"

I shrugged, surprised by his response. "Good-bye, I guess. And if you wouldn't mind, a letter of recommendation would be nice."

For a moment he said nothing, just let his head fall back so he could stare at the ceiling. The muscles in his neck were thick, veins stark beneath the skin. "What's the real issue here? You want more money?"

"No. To be honest, you're probably paying me too much as it is. Not that I'm volunteering for a decrease."

"Then what?" His gaze bored into me, eyes a lighter shade than his brother's. Jimmy's eyes were like a cloudless sky, the perfect blue. They were beautiful, but rarely serene. And god help me for even noticing, let alone getting poetic.

"Why do you want me to stay so badly?" I threw up my hands. "Most days you barely tolerate me. Last week you stopped speaking entirely and just grunted at me for three days. Suddenly you can't bear for us to be apart? Come on."

Ben chuckled. "She's got a point."

"Later, Benny," Jimmy said without taking his eyes off me.

"Right. Have fun, guys." The big man ambled on out, not particularly bothering to hide his smile.

"I just . . . I got a bit moody last week." He crossed his arms and said in a rush, "But it wasn't nothing to do with you."

"No, of course not. But I have to live with you. So when you get into these moods, it affects me."

Further scowling.

"Not that this is about us." I shook my head. "I mean, there is no *us*. I don't know why I even used the word. This decision is just about me. It's time for me to move on."

Jimmy's jaw clenched. "I don't like change."

"We'll make the handover as smooth as possible."

"I'm used to you being around. We get on okay. Why the fuck should I have to go through all the trouble of breaking in someone new just because you've got your panties in a twist over something that probably doesn't even matter?"

My mouth opened, but nothing came out. I was officially stupefied. Over the breaking-in or panties comments I couldn't quite say, though really, neither should have surprised me. This was Jimmy in all his glory, rude as fuck and not a single social nicety to him. At least I was willing to pretend to get along with people the bulk of the time.

"Well?" he barked. When I took too long to answer he tugged his red sweatshirt off over his head, using it to wipe down his face.

"My reasons, which are personal, do matter. Maybe not to you, but they matter to me."

He looked off to the side, his lips drawn wide in a truly aggrieved expression. Had any man ever been quite so badly treated? No, I think not, according to that face.

"I've made up my mind," I said.

"I'll pay you twenty percent more."

"Were you even listening? This is not about money."

"Fuck's sake. Fifty."

I screwed up my nose. "Jimmy—"

His hand sliced through the air. "Enough. I'll double it. You cut the shit and we don't talk about it again, understood? Now I got stuff to do."

"Stop!" I yelled.

He stared at me, unblinking. Hostility seemed to ooze from his very pores.

"I'm leaving."

"Why?" he asked, through gritted teeth. "C'mon, you at least owe me an explanation, Lena."

Outside, it started to rain, the heavy gray clouds finally giving it up. And still Jimmy waited. I squeezed my eyes shut against the sight of him. Oh god, I couldn't. I just couldn't. This wasn't going at all like I had planned.

"I know we're not best friends, but I thought we got along okay," he said.

"We do, basically."

"Well, then?"

"I'm not right for this job."

"Look at me."

I opened one eye, he actually looked reasonably calm. His big arms were crossed, sweaty shirt plastered to his buff chest, but otherwise, he didn't seem too angry. So I opened the other eye too. Brave of me, I know.

"Unlike the other sobriety companions, you don't completely piss me off," he said.

"I know. I'm mostly useful." I laughed. Not that it was particularly funny. "Gah! Why are you fighting me so hard on this?"

"Because the record company and Adrian would still like someone around to keep an eye on things. I happen to agree it's not a completely bad idea," he said. "I don't need you counseling me and messing with my head, giving me your version of whatever philosophical bullshit turns you on. I just need you to be here. How is that so hard?"

"It's not. But it doesn't explain why you're so hell-bent on that person being me."

"Look, you're basically the best out of the bunch, okay? Someone else might be far worse. I'm not going to risk it. You have to stay."

My nose wrinkled up, I could feel it.

"Hang on, is this about what happened before the funeral?" he asked.

My mouth opened but I had nothing. He didn't mean when he clung to me, but thanks to my guilty conscience, it was all I could think of.

"It is." His forehead furrowed. He shoved a hand into his hair and grabbed a fistful, tugging on it. "That was . . . there were extenuating circumstances. You were never in any physical danger from me, Lena. Not ever."

"I know."

"Do you? I get that I freaked you out," he said. "I know I trashed that room, but I would never—"

"It's not about that."

"So what's the problem?"

I turned away, mind scrambling for a plausible lie of an excuse. There must be something I could use, letting him think I was physically afraid of him wasn't tenable. He had more than enough issues to contend with.

"It is the problem." He groaned, rubbing his face with his hands. "Fuck."

"No. It's really not. I get that you were in a bad place that day."

"Then what? What do you need here, an apology?" Irritation filled his eyes. "Fuck's sake. I'm sorry, okay?"

My jaw fell slack. "Wow. You are breathtakingly bad at apologizing, aren't you?"

His cell buzzed on the counter. We both ignored it.

"Jimmy, for future reference, when you apologize to someone you might want to sound like you actually mean it. Consider not sneering or swearing at them, perhaps. Hmm?"

He kicked and scuffed his foot against the floor looking for all the world like a schoolboy being scolded. "Okay. Sorry . . . and stuff."

"Slightly better."

"So we done here? We good?" he asked, already moving toward the door.

"Can I tell Tom Monday suits you?"

"Lena! Shit." He made a noise of sheer exasperation. "Why?"

The words stuck in my throat. I could have choked on them which was probably a better fate than letting them out, all things considered. The tension coiled inside of me, huge and horrible. If only I could have disappeared into thin air.

"WHY?" The ass shouted, the sound reverberating around the room.

"Because I have feelings for you, all right! And don't yell at me."

Silence.

Absolute, pure, silence.

Little lines appeared beside his nose. "What did you say?"

"You heard me."

"You have *feelings* for me?" The way he drew out the word, rolling it over his tongue like the taste disgusted him and belittled us both. I might never recover.

"Yes."

"You're fucking with me."

"No," I said, my heart on my sleeve. Actually, forget the sleeve, my chest felt like it had been ripped wide open. I stood there completely exposed, everything on display. Quite gross really. But it didn't mean I had to like it. "Well?"

He just stared at me.

"Say something!"

The bastard burst out laughing.

Great big belly laughs filled the room, the sound circling me, battering at my head. I couldn't get away from it. There were knives on a rack on the kitchen wall, many shiny bright knives all in a row. It would be so easy just to throw the odd one at him and see what I could hit. I might not be in any physical danger from him, but him being in danger from me was a distinct possibility. I imagined him bloody and beaten on the floor. It kept me from immediate violence, despite my clenched fists.

"You see now the wisdom of my not wanting to tell you," I said, mostly for my own benefit. No way could he hear me over his insane cackling. The man stood hunched over, actually wiping tears from his eyes. I prayed fervently for god to strike him dead but nothing happened, Jimmy just kept on laughing.

"And the strongest feeling I have for you right now is hate," I said. "Just in case you were wondering."

Ever so gradually (about a century later) his laughing slowed and then eventually ceased. It wasn't an easy battle for him. He'd look at me, at the floor, out the window, the strain lining his face. All I could do was wait.

And make snarky comments.

"Okay, that's great," I said. "Glad you could get that out of your system."

"Sorry." He rubbed a hand across his mouth. It didn't hide the grin at all. "Christ, I just figured all those times you were looking at me funny, you either had some kind of attention disorder or you needed to get laid or something. I had no idea . . ."

"Excellent." I clapped my hands together, pasting on a smile. "So, back to our discussion. Clearly this crosses a professional line. Therefore, I'll be leaving."

"No, you're not. Don't be dumb, Lena."

"Are you happy there, Jimmy, living in denial? Is the weather nice this time of year?" I stared up at him. "You see I've had my heart broken by assorted asshats in the past and I swore never again. So I'm not doing the unrequited love thing with you. That just doesn't sound like my idea of a good time, sorry."

My smile might have been a touch brittle, but his was brilliant. That smile, it could move mountains. It could also break hearts. I could feel the organ fading away inside my chest. Rejection stung, not that I wanted him to throw his arms wide open to me, I wasn't any more impressed with my misplaced feelings than he was. But did he have to dissolve into hysterics?

Fancy falling for someone you didn't even particularly like half the damn time. Who did something so stupid?

I mean apart from me, obviously.

"What'll happen is this," he said, voice absolute and a bit bored, even. "You'll get over this dumb crush you've got on me and I'll do us both the immense favor of forgetting this ever happened, okay?"

"You're an idiot." God, he was. He truly was. I gave him a look that hopefully conveyed this fact tenfold. "Don't you think if I could just switch it off I would have done so by now? Do you think I want to feel this way about you?"

"It's not about me, Lena. It's the whole fame thing. Once you realize that, you can just get past it and move on."

"That's the problem. It *is* about you. And that's why I can't move on," I said, pointing in the general direction of my bosoms which were, incidentally, heaving on account of my being worked up.

Jimmy's gaze dropped to said cleavage before darting back to my face. His lips thinned in anger, like I'd tricked him into checking me out. As if.

"I happen to like this job," I said. "It paid well even before you started throwing more money at me. I get to live in your palace rent free and for the most part, the work is easy. It's all good. But the thing is, sometimes, when you're not being a jerk, I like you so much it hurts. I like the way your true self comes out when you think no one else is looking."

"Lena . . ."

"But it's the little things, really. Like the way you pretend not to remember whose turn it is to pick what we watch on TV so I get more turns than you. And the way you sit up with me sometimes when I can't sleep."

He grabbed at the back of his neck. "God, Lena. C'mon, that's crazy. That stuff's nothing."

"You're wrong. It's something. I know you don't take praise well, but you're not half as horrible as you make yourself out to be."

"Yeah, you're right. I'm a real misunderstood sweet-heart. Shit."

"I'm not saying you're perfect. We both know you're a long way from that, and hey, so am I. I'm just saying . . ." I searched for the words and frustratingly came up empty. Hell, what a conversation. "Gah! Again."

"So, what? You're worried your"—he made quotation marks with his fingers—" 'feelings' for me are going to interfere with you doing your job?"

"What if for some reason you flip out again and I can't go all hard-assed and say no to you because I'm too busy feeling bad for you? What if I give in? It's too big a risk."

"That's not going to happen." He wandered around the counter and past me, grabbing a glass out of a cupboard and filling it with water. Without pause he downed the entire glassful, his Adam's apple working overtime. The scent of his sweaty, buff self filled the air. Had I not needed to speak, I'd have been tempted to hold my breath. I didn't need the smell of him intoxicating me, things were difficult enough as is.

"It could," I said. "You're not taking this seriously. Also, you should go shower."

"This is my point."

"What?"

"You shouldn't make any rash choices until you figure out what you want. In the past five minutes you've admitted to having feelings for me, then said you hated me. You've told me I'm an idiot and now you say that I stink."

"Of course you stink. You're dripping sweat."

Amused gaze never leaving me, he leaned back against the counter. "Yeah, and if you were so overwhelmed by these supposed feelings of yours for me, you wouldn't care. You'd still want me all over you. In fact, most women would want me more."

My mind basically exploded, trying to encompass what

having him all over me might entail. No, no, no, bad thoughts, horrible, wrong carnal thoughts. "That so?"

"Yeah. Women that are into me, they don't mind a bit of sweat. What do you think happens after we've been in bed for hours? Sweat, that's what. And those other women, they don't make all those sarcastic comments like you do either. They sure as fuck don't insult me every two minutes." He gave me a slow looking over. It wasn't appreciative. "I mean, I thought all the weird looks were about what happened in Idaho. Always kind of figured you were into pussy. Thought it was a damn shame, frankly, so there you go."

How many years would I get for throttling him? That was the question. "Wait. Are you actually suggesting that any woman who doesn't kiss your ass must therefore be gay?"

He shrugged.

"And you wonder why I must insult you."

"You doing what needs to be done isn't a problem, Lena. You're not going to have any issues telling me no."

Oblivious to my incredulity, the man cracked his neck, giving me another bored look. "Whatever the real deal is here, sort it out. I get that you're embarrassed, but you'll just have to get over it. Okay?"

I made no promises. But then again, I couldn't do much of anything just then. If I opened my mouth to speak, I highly doubted I'd be able to form words.

"Okay. We're done," Jimmy said, strolling from the room like he didn't have a care in the world.

CHAPTER SIX

The knock came on my bedroom door just before midnight.

After our "talk," we'd pretty much gone back to normal. Jimmy exercised morning and afternoon, usually with at least one of the guys along. Because I wasn't much of a sobriety counselor, and being Jimmy's shadow got boring after a while, I'd taken on the role of being his assistant also. I'd check e-mails, occasionally reading aloud the parts he needed to know. I'd chat with Ev (David's wife and assistant), whoever the latest poor unfortunate in Adrian's, the band manager's, office happened to be, and the PR person. There's a lot involved in keeping a rock star organized. These days, I also liaised with the builders and techie types responsible for turning part of the basement into a state-of-the-art studio. With that project nearing completion the guys had started doing their practice and writing sessions here as opposed to at David's. More room.

All in all, we kept busy.

We inhabited the same house and often the same room, but didn't necessarily talk much. The silence wasn't uncomfortable but companionable, I'd long since gotten used to it. Usually, after a while, Jimmy would put on some music. Today on the stereo was The Dead Weather, which was fitting, because outside the weather grew steadily worse. Within, however, we were our own peaceful enough world. There'd been some curious side-eyes now and then, but I'd determinedly ignored them all.

He knocked again on my bedroom door. Then, not bothering to wait for permission, charged on in. "Been thinking."

"I didn't say you could enter." I studied him over the top of my reading glasses, lying in the middle of my big bed propped up by no less than three cushions. Comfort mattered.

"It's my house. Nice jammies. Ducks this time, huh? Cool." He cast an amused eye over my flannel ensemble, because of course, his highness still looked slick (designer jeans and a black long-sleeved T-shirt that fit him to perfection) no matter the hour. Sweaty from a run was as mussed as the man ever got. Even then, his dark damp hair appeared to have been styled by the wanton fingers of a lingerie model as opposed to the elements.

"You're just jealous of my awesome stylin'." I clutched my e-reader to my chest, doing my best to hide my happy nipples. "I bet you sleep in Armani or something, don't you? Prada, maybe?"

He chuckled.

"What do you want, Jimmy?"

"Never been in here before."

"You came in here the night you carried me up to bed after I'd crashed on the couch," I reminded him.

"It was nearly four in the morning. Didn't stop to look around." He took a slow tour of the room, casting an eye over my belongings. It could be said I have tidiness issues when it comes to my personal space; clothes lay abandoned on the chair, shoes beneath it. In my bathroom, makeup, hair junk, and feminine hygiene products decorated the gray marble countertop. I'd gotten overly comfortable since moving in here and expanded upon my belongings. The last couple of years, I'd lived a minimal existence. It fit in with all the moving around. The surplus of stuff would make my eventual packing up and moving on a pain.

Jimmy's brows bunched. "Don't you let the cleaners in?"

"Of course I do."

"They come twice a week, Lena. How the hell do you manage to make a mess again so fast?"

"It's a gift. I don't leave my things around the rest of the house. This is my personal space and therefore none of your business. Did you barge in here for a reason?"

He faced me, hands on hips. "Yeah, after our talk today, I wanted to know where you were at?"

"So you accept that ordering me to stay doesn't actually make it so?"

"Maybe." He meandered on over to my desk and casually started sifting through the debris. Half of the contents of my purse were scattered across the table, along with a couple of magazines. Oh no damn it, one of them lay open. Shit. I'd already had about enough embarrassment today to last me a decade. Please god don't let him see.

"Leave my stuff alone please, Jimmy."

"What's this?" He picked it up, of course he did. Then he began to read. "*Guide to getting over him.* Interesting."

"Well you didn't just expect me to turn tail and run without at least investigating alternatives, did you?"

He lifted one shoulder. "Pretty much."

"Great. Your faith in me is heartening. So what have you been thinking about?"

"Your feelings," he deadpanned, looking up from the magazine.

I took a breath. "Jimmy, I'm impressed. You almost managed to say it in a normal voice this time."

"I practiced downstairs for a while." He sat on the edge

of my bed, legs spread wide, making himself completely at home. Which I guess made sense to a degree.

"So what about my feelings?"

"You know this isn't half bad. Some of this advice is pretty sound." He kept on reading.

"You've suffered from unrequited passions yourself, I take it?"

He snorted. "'Course not. I always got whoever I wanted."

"Of course you did." I bowed my head, properly chided. Shame on me for thinking otherwise. Doubtless he'd left a trail of broken hearts behind him an ocean wide.

"Which was not always a good thing." The arrogance slipped from his face and he frowned, his jaw taut. He stared into the distance, remembering what, I wondered? When he realized I was watching him, he swallowed, gave the magazine a shake. "We should do this."

"What? Do what?"

"One. You need to get out and see other people." He winced. "You're obviously not so great at getting hookups, so don't worry, I'll help you out with that. Two. Try to focus on my flaws."

"You want me to follow the list to help me get over my crush on you?"

"Yeah, stop interrupting. This is important. Two. Focus on my flaws." He gave me a cursory glance. "I don't see you having any trouble with that one. Three. Stop feeling sorry for yourself, needy and or angry."

I pushed up my glasses. "I see."

"Yeah. Honestly, it's really unattractive, Lena. No one wants to see that shit."

"R-i-ght."

"Four. A bunch of them sort of rolled into one here, again. Go out with friends. Try something new. Get fit. Pamper yourself. Have fun. Enjoy life. Go on a trip. Paint

your toenails, whatever the fuck. Blah, blah, blah. You get
what I mean."

"Mm." I nodded.

"That's pretty much it."

"And I'm supposed to follow this?"

He gave me a long look. "You said you didn't really
wanna leave, that you liked the job. Prove it."

I laughed ever so slightly manically. The decision had
been made and it hadn't been an easy one. Backtracking
now did not seem wise. "Jimmy, please. It's just some stupid magazine article probably written by a bored intern on
their lunch break. This is not science. It's not going to fix
anything."

"Then why was it lying open at this page?"

Good question. Strands of black hair hung over his
forehead, hanging in his eyes. Without thought, he pushed
them back. My fingers itched to do just that, to brush back
his hair and sooth his fevered brow. Not that he seemed
particularly hot in the temperature sense.

And he thought some wisdom out of a magazine could
cure me.

"Never know, Lena. It just might work." He dropped the
magazine in my lap, gaze pinning me to the spot. "And I
think you owe it to me to try."

My chin went up. "I do, huh?"

"I gave you a chance. Gave you this job, and made every effort to accommodate you. Not fair you'd just take
off after not even two months without giving it your best
shot. You owe me."

"You hired me because you thought I'd be easier to
manipulate than another actual counselor and because
Mal and David harangued you. Let's not lose sight of the
truth here."

One thick shoulder rose and fell. "Does it matter? I

gave you the job, you said you like the job. Least you can do is give this a chance."

"I'll think about it."

"You do that." A ghost of a smile touched his lips. "I know all about addictions and wanting things that aren't good for you, Lena. End of the day, it's up to you to decide whether to take control and fight it or not."

Jimmy Ferris as an illegal, dangerous, controlled substance. Funnily enough, I could see it. The man affected me on all the levels no matter how much I tried to resist, damn it.

He headed for the door, closing it slowly behind him. "Night."

"Night."

A bang like a shotgun startled me from sleep. I shot up in bed, blinking into the semidarkness. What fresh hell was this? A blurry shadow stalked toward me.

"Wha—"

"Get up," ordered Jimmy. "We're going jogging."

"Have you lost your fucking mind?"

"Rise and shine. Day one of your intensive desensitization-to-me program is about to begin." He threw back the drapes, letting the weak sunlight seep in. "You got tennis shoes, right?"

I fumbled on the bedside table for my glasses and shoved them on my face. The world unblurred. "God, Jimmy. It's barely past dawn."

A black Nike flew in my direction. I only just managed to deflect it. "Hey!"

"C'mon. Move it."

Next came a set of baggy old gray sweats, chucked onto the end of my bed. His lordship was already decked out in all black designer running gear. Ready and raring to go.

"You got a sports bra in here somewhere? Girl your size, I'm thinking you'd need one."

"Get out of my drawer." I threw back my blankets and stalked over to him. "Do not go through my underwear, you asshole."

He ignored me and kept right on burrowing through the drawers. "In my line of work, it's nothing I haven't seen before. C'mon. You need to get ready."

"I repeat, are you insane?"

"Told you, I'm not breaking in another companion, so I'm going to help you help yourself. We're going to work our way through that little list of yours so you can get past these silly feelings of yours. If anyone can kill a crush, it's me."

"You know where you can shove the list. And if you need help, let me just fetch a rubber glove and some lube and I'll be right with you."

With a sigh, Jimmy straightened. He held his fisted hand high, slowly uncurling his fingers. Way up high over my head dangled a pretty pair of black silk panties. "Say you'll go jogging with me and I'll give them back."

"I'm so tempted to just punch you in the junk right now and be done with it. I mean, it has to happen sooner or later, right?"

He made no move to cover himself, showed no weakness. Instead, one side of his mouth curled upward and a dimple appeared. My stomach dropped. I'd been right, definitely at least one dimple. He gave the panties in his hand a jiggle. Given my lack of height and Jimmy's abundance of it, there was no way I could reach them.

"Do you actually expect me to jump around like an idiot?" I asked in a withering tone.

"It would amuse me."

"Don't make me kill you at this hour of the morning, Jimmy. It's not civilized."

The semismile disappeared and he dropped the panties into my waiting hand.

"Thank you."

"You give the list some thought?" Hands on hips, he stared down his nose at me.

I had, long and hard, in fact. While getting away from Jimmy might make sense, it also hurt. Guilt snuck in every time. Maybe he and my replacement wouldn't get along, I mean, Jimmy and I often didn't get along. But we did it in a way where he stayed sober and on track. So I guess in the main way that mattered, this lopsided partnership was a success.

"What do you want here, Lena?" He rubbed at his temple. "I know you've dealt with some dickheads in the past, but that's not the situation here. I'm not out to do any damage. I just want you to keep doing your job."

"I know."

"Man," he groaned. "Would it help if I said 'please'?"

"I'm not sure," I answered honestly. "Maybe. Do you even know how to say that word without attaching any undue sarcasm and irony to it?"

He is head fell back as if in a silent plea to heaven. "Please."

"Please, what?"

"Come jogging with me. Do the list. Stop this shit. Lena, please?"

He seemed sincere, and he was right, I didn't completely, one hundred percent want to leave. Also, it was important to reward good behavior.

"Okay, Jimmy. Let's give it a go."

"Oh good god, I hate you." I panted, dragging my sorry ass after the bastard to whom the sentiment belonged.

"See? It's working already." Jimmy hadn't even broken

a sweat yet. The athletic ass might as well have been out for a stroll. "Plus, you'll be healthier. Everyone wins."

"I'm healthy. I eat fruit."

"In pie doesn't count."

If only I had laser beams for eyes. Damn the lack of technology.

"Not saying there's anything wrong with you," he said, turning to face me. Still jogging, the fucking show-off. If only he'd fall on his ass, I'd enjoy that so much. His gaze flitted over me, lingering overly long, though not unappreciatively strangely enough, on my hips. "I like a little junk in the trunk."

I whispered expletives because there wasn't enough breath in me to actually say them out loud.

"We jog every day, slowly work up your distance, you can eat more pie. How does that sound?"

It sounded like he was a patronizing judgmental asshole. I flipped him the bird.

"Lena, look at me."

I stopped, I looked. Also, I slumped over and gasped for breath because multitasking is important for the modern woman.

"You're a pretty girl and your curves are cool," he said, still moving on the spot. "Getting a little healthier won't hurt, though. Raise your energy levels, stuff like that."

Jimmy thought I was pretty?

Of course, he could have just been being kind. Either way, it didn't matter, not really. So my belly should just stop swinging about all lunatic like and be still. Though the jibe about pie still pissed me off. People from a local restaurant stocked the fridge, there were salads, grilled meats, pasta, and yes, occasionally pie. Like I made them put it in there at gunpoint or something. What I ate was none of his business and his opinion shouldn't even matter.

It shouldn't and yet it did.

"I don't need to conform to your ideas of beauty," I said, once my breath had been located.

He'd been staring off at the oversized houses and fall trees around us, but now his gaze snapped back to me. "'Course you don't, never said you did."

"Not all of us are born looking perfect like you, Jimmy."

"You're pissed?" He stepped closer. "Lena, I've got a lot of flaws. We've been living in each other's pockets for a couple of months now so you of all people know that. Not liking the way you look isn't one of them. You want to chew me out over something, pick another topic, you're way off on this one."

Neither of us spoke for a moment. We faced each other, our breaths misting in the cold morning air.

"I might be slightly defensive about this," I admitted eventually.

"I might have noticed." He pushed his hair back from his face. "I probably also didn't say it right. Add it to my list of flaws, has trouble expressing himself."

"Especially in ways that are socially acceptable."

He gave me an amused look. "You think that matters, what everyone thinks?"

"Sometimes. To a degree."

He snorted. "You can't affect what people think, Lena. They wanna think the worst, they will. I'm not wasting energy trying to make everyone happy. I have enough on my hands just keeping my own shit together."

There was wisdom in his words, though they weren't entirely accurate.

"People judge you whatever," he said. "People fucking love their own opinions and are all too happy to throw 'em at you, whether you ask or not. You have to be happy with yourself."

"Yes. But you care what the guys think," I said.

"Sure." He started jogging again, more slowly this time, thank you, god in heaven.

Ever so reluctantly, I fell into step beside him. My poor calves and thighs burned. Without a doubt they hated me with a fiery passion and I didn't blame them at all. "And Ev and Anne. You care about them."

He grunted.

"And Mr. Ericson." Sadly, I struggled to keep up even at this lesser speed. "Though you do mangle your words occasionally, don't stop to think before you speak. But don't we all?"

"Let's move onto another flaw," he said.

"All right." I searched my besotted mind for ammunition. "How about . . ."

"I'm self-centered."

"Yeah. That's true. You're pretty arrogant and narcissistic."

A lady jogger bounced on by, clad head to toe in form fitting Lycra. She gave Jimmy a wide inviting do-me-on-the-spot smile. He nodded to her, then concentrated on the path once more.

"Not entirely without cause, granted. But you don't date," I said, stopping (he halted too, happily). Jogging and talking at the same time just didn't work for me. Of course, neither did jogging and breathing. "Why is that? You put all this effort into your looks, buff up your body, buy the best clothes. And hey, kudos to you, it works. But you don't go out unless it's business or something to do with the guys, you're basically a hermit."

"There a question in there somewhere?"

"Why?"

"Why do I take care of myself or why am I a hermit?"

"Let's start with the first one," I said.

He shrugged. "I'm vain. What are you gonna do about it?"

Huh. "So you're completely happy with yourself?"

"With how I look? Sure." He raised a brow. "My looks are the one thing that's always worked for me, always gotten me attention. If I'm pouting on the cover of some magazine, then that helps sell records. It's a fact. I'm not a poet like Davie or crazy talented on an instrument. I sing okay, sure. But what I have is this face, that's what I contribute. And in this business, you use every advantage at your disposal."

I frowned up at him, amazed. "You actually believe that."

He frowned back at me.

"Jimmy, you're more than just a pretty face. You've got a beautiful voice." And I should know. He sang me to sleep on my iPod most nights. "God, how many Grammys have you won?"

"That's a popularity contest as much as anything." He licked his lips. "Are you?"

"Am I what?"

"Are you happy with the way you look?"

For once, I took my own advice and actually thought before moving my lips. "Obviously not given our conversation of a moment ago. But I try to be. It's not always easy with all the media representations of beauty, blah, blah, blah. I'm never going to be six feet tall with legs up to my armpits, and as you said, I like pie. I'm not willing to rule out eating it for the next fifty years just to have less dimples on my thighs. Little pleasures matter."

"Yeah, they do." A ghost of a smile touched his lips. "My going-out-wise, I don't want to fall back into bad habits. Sex, drugs, alcohol, they all went together for me. If you're changing your life, stopping the destructive shit, then you have to know what your triggers are."

"You haven't had sex since you dried out?"

"No."

"Really?"

"Yep."

My eyes felt as wide as they could possibly be and then some. "Oh."

Wow, extreme, but it had obviously worked. The man had conviction. In truth, his openness and honesty stunned me. I guess he was serious about my deprogramming.

"You never drank or did drugs when you were alone?"

He flinched. "Yeah, I did. That's why you or one of the guys are usually around, just in case."

"We're not all the time. But you've still stuck to it," I pointed out. "I think it takes real courage to do what you've done, to turn your life around."

He scowled. "Don't make excuses for me, Lena. I am not a nice person. I fucked my brother's first girlfriend. Did you know that?"

I shook my head.

"Yeah, broke his heart. I was so jealous of him I could barely breathe. I lied. I cheated. I stole. I destroyed everything that meant anything to me and hurt everyone around me. I blacked out constantly, ODed twice, nearly died. What do you think that did to them . . . to the guys? Visiting me in the hospital, seeing me like that?" He looked everywhere but at me.

A cold wind blew between us.

"That's the truth, that's who I am. Don't make excuses for me. I'm still the same moody selfish fuck I ever was, sober or not." His breathing hastened even though we stood still. "Thing is, you're never going to have much of a life being at my beck and call. You're better off away from me, and I know that, and I still don't care. That, Lena, is who I am."

I had nothing.

Jimmy about-faced and headed for home.

CHAPTER SEVEN

Thanksgiving dinner for the band happened Thanksgiving Eve. I'd given mom many excuses about why I couldn't go home. Luckily she'd accepted them.

Everyone gathered at Mal and Anne's new condo, opposite David and Ev's old one. Old as in they'd lived there for six months or so. Both places were gorgeous with lots of shiny, expensive, and new, much as you'd expect. The balconies looked out over the Pearl District. Very nice.

A picture of Lori, Mal's mom, took up prime position on the mantelpiece. Jimmy had lingered over it when we first arrived, just taking a moment. His brother had approached after a time and they'd quietly talked. I don't think anyone's pain over losing her was going away anytime soon.

Apparently, Ben hadn't told a soul about my announcement to quit. I appreciated his discretion immensely. Jimmy had barely spoken since our talk yesterday. He had unfortunately hammered again on my door at dawn this morning and tossed tennis shoes at me, however. I dragged my sorry self around behind him, sweating all the way. Hard to say exactly how far we went, it all blended into pointless agony after the first few yards. Later in the day, a beautician-masseuse-type person arrived to pamper me, thus fulfilling another of the points on the list. I have to admit, those three hours of bliss paid for by Jimmy made up for a lot of jogging.

Not all of it. But a lot. It felt like a silent apology or perhaps encouragement on his part. Or maybe it was just another lure into convincing me to stay.

Now he sat opposite me, hair artfully in his face. Aesthetically, the man reigned supreme as king throughout the land. Whether I cared to pretend he was my type or not, it couldn't be denied. He always seemed so polished, so perfect, you could almost ignore the chaos and pain living inside of him. But the things he'd said to me kept turning around and around inside my head. God, he'd screwed over his own brother. No wonder things seemed strained between them sometimes.

Around me, dinner conversation went on. None of it fascinated me half as much as Jimmy. He was such a dichotomy of good and evil, beautiful and bad.

He'd ditched his black woolen jacket at the door, rolled up the sleeves of a vaguely patterned button-down shirt. My own style was more sedate, consisting of ankle boots, skinny jeans, and a long knit top. When it came to throwing an outfit together, he had me beat. He shifted, leaning an elbow on the table. Such thick wrists, I'd never noticed before but his hands must be strong. When we'd fought over the cigarette packet, though, he'd been gentle. As gentle as you could be rolling around on the floor with someone. The memory of his weight on top of me filled my mind. Thank god there'd been no more smoking. He'd given me his word and stuck to it. A mishmash of tattoos covered his right arm. There was a star, a heart, flames, and words. I'd love to get closer and study them, really take my time over them. I took a sip of water, my dry throat needing relief. Higher up, the top two buttons of his shirt lay undone and a few fine dark chest hairs peeked out.

Nice.

The jerk also wore seriously thick-soled boots. Something made apparent to me when one descended upon my innocent unsuspecting toes.

I yelped.

"Anne's talking to you, Lena," he said.

Shit. I'd been staring at him again. His fault. If he'd sat beside, instead of across from me, it never would have happened. I tried to kick him back but my foot swung aimlessly, coming into contact with nothing but thin air. Screw him and his long legs.

"Jimmy, did you just kick her?" asked Ev, mouth pursed.

"No," he lied.

Ev turned curious eyes to me as if I could be expected to tell the truth.

"That would be a petty and juvenile thing for him to do. But no, I just sat up a bit too fast," I said. "Guess I got overexcited."

"She does that sometimes," Jimmy confirmed. "A real excitable girl is our Lena."

I showed him my prettiest forced smile.

Down the other end of the table, Anne's mom, the guest of honor, frowned good and hard. Good impression gone. And everyone had been trying so hard not to swear, let alone act crazy. Well everyone apart from psycho puppy Killer who had long since been banished to his crate for some quiet time. Ben was likewise in disgrace for having stirred him up in the first place. He, however, got to stay at the table. The dog should complain about the double standard. It was in all honesty wildly unfair.

Jimmy cleared his throat, loudly, summoning all of the

table's attention. "Don't think I told you guys. Lena's been talking about leaving."

Boom! I'd been ambushed.

Whats, whys, and general sounds of displeasure filled the room. Far more than I'd ever anticipated. From the other side of the table, Jimmy gave me a smirk, followed by a well-what-the-fuck-did-you-expect look. I countered it with my you-asshole-that-was-an-unnecessary-and-shitty-thing-to-do-to-me gaze. It seemed we could communicate entirely without words.

Awesome.

"No-o-o," said Mal from the head of the table. "C'mon, Lena. Why would you quit? You're the only one that fit in with us and didn't annoy the living shit out of Jim. You have no idea how rare a species that makes you."

A sea of sad faces surrounded me. Well, apart from Anne's mom, she just played with her food. Even Anne's sister Lizzy seemed down at the news and we'd met twice, maybe? This level of attachment was as surprising as it was heartwarming.

Tears stung my eyes as loneliness sucker punched me. I hadn't even realized I'd been lonely, but the way these people cared caught me by surprise. They actually wanted me around.

"What the fuck did you do?" David bitched at his brother.

The smirk fell from Jimmy's face.

"Nothing," I said, my defensive mode instantly fully engaged on his behalf. "Jimmy didn't do anything. I just thought it might be time to move on. I haven't fully decided yet."

Cue the intense staring competition between the brothers. Apparently, Jimmy won because David turned away first, brow heavily furrowed. Emotive brows obviously run in the Ferris family.

"What is it you do, Lena?" asked Anne's mom. Jan, that was her name. She looked to be about fifty with faded strawberry blond hair.

"She's my sobriety companion and assistant," Jim said without hesitation. "She stops me drinking. Keeps me clean."

People quieted, looked elsewhere. Jan's mouth gaped like a goldfish but nothing was said. Given the few things I'd heard from Anne about her mom, Jan should be the last person judging anyone. She hadn't exactly won parent of the year anytime in the last twenty.

Normally, we didn't discuss Jimmy's problems in mixed company, or much at all for that matter. The whole world knew every sordid detail so there was no real need. When he'd gone into rehab, news of his downfall had been everywhere, but apparently somehow Jan had missed it.

The silence stretched out and opposite me Jimmy tensed seeming to distance himself. Arctic eyes stared off into nothing. Perhaps people were embarrassed by his history, as if everyone else was flawless. He'd fallen further than most, true, but he'd crawled his way back up again too. Strength came in many forms. I'd always assumed the subject of his addictions lay dormant due to his need for privacy. This silence, however, felt wrong, it rankled me.

Why the hell didn't someone say something? Someone like me perhaps.

"I've enjoyed working for Jimmy." I folded up my napkin, placed it on the table. "I still do. The issue is mine, not his."

His gaze warmed slightly, his still face returning to life.

"What is the issue?" asked David.

"It's personal. I'd rather not discuss it."

"She needs to get a life is the problem." Jimmy said, pushing back from the table, giving himself some space.

"She needs to mix things up a bit. Being with me all the time isn't necessarily the party you'd imagine."

David half smiled.

"She's bored?" Anne studied me from three seats down. "We can fix bored."

And all of this gave me a very bad feeling. "Guys, this is a personal decision, not a group project. Thank you for caring, but—"

"No, pumpkin." Mal studied me over the top of his glass of red wine. "I don't think she's bored so much as she needs a friend. A special friend, if you know what I mean."

"I swear, that's you guys' answer to everything." Ev laughed.

"Hey, now. Everyone needs someone special to fuck and cuddle. There is no shame in that," said Mal, ignoring the startled little gasp from Anne's mom. Anne didn't seem concerned either, interestingly enough. "And Lena needs someone who isn't Jimmy for obvious reasons."

Down the table, David sat up in his seat. "Why not Jim?"

"Because she works for me?" interjected my boss, tugging at the collar of his shirt. Seemed he didn't like being the topic of conversation as much as he enjoyed throwing me to the wolves. Too bad, buddy.

"Davie, please." Mal continued on as if Jimmy hadn't spoken. "Stop and think about this. Everyone he sleeps with ends up hating him."

"That's not true," said Jimmy.

"No? Name one woman you've banged that still talks to you."

Time crept on, but Jimmy did not respond, and no one else came to his rescue either.

"My point exactly. You do no aftercare and it shows." Mal turned back to David. "He doesn't even have the common courtesy to pretend to be interested in hooking up again. Doesn't take the phone number or anything. It's just plain rude."

"That's appalling," I said, enjoying myself immensely. It was only by the grace of god that I managed to avoid having Jimmy's boot connect with my toes a second time. He missed, hitting one of the legs of my chair instead. I mocked him greatly with my eyes.

"And you!" Mal pointed his finger at me. "You're always giving him shit. You can't help yourself. You two have your little tiffs now and it's all cute and funny and we can all laugh at you behind your backs about it. But, Davie, man. Imagine if they were actually playing hide the sausage. We'd be spending every holiday listening to them bicker and carry on at the table, making a scene. It's just not on."

My mouth hung open.

"Whatever happens, you two must not bump uglies. I want your word on this." Cue more finger pointing from Mal, this time with the added benefit of waggling. "It would make life impossible for us all."

Anne's mom fled the table.

"When did I ever say Lena and me were getting together?" With a long groan, Jimmy looked to the heavens for help. "Someone shut him up. Shoot him or something, anything."

Ben scratched at his head. "Lena and Jim do fight a lot."

David and Ev just looked mildly perplexed.

"So, hang on, should I be going or staying," I asked. "I can't keep up."

"Oh you can't go," continued Mal. "Anybody, when was the last time Jim even had a friend, outside of us, who wasn't either using with him or supplying him, hmm?"

After a moment, David shook his head. "Honestly can't remember."

"Back in school, maybe," said Ben. "That kid who played roadie for us senior year?"

"God, you're right," said Ev, eyes bright with some emotion. "Lena's his only friend. We can't let her leave."

"She's not my only friend." Color rose in Jimmy's cheeks.

"Quiet, Jimmy," ordered Mal. "The adults are talking."

"But I don't know if them getting together's a good idea either," said Ben.

"Or maybe you and Mal should mind your own business." David slipped an arm around Ev's shoulders.

"What couple doesn't fight?" asked Anne.

"But she baits him, pumpkin," said Mal. "I've seen her. She thinks it's funny to stir him up. Wonder what that says about her." His eyes glittered with curiosity.

I sat bolt upright in my chair. "Okay. I think this conversation has gone far enough."

"You know, there used to be this girl in second grade who would always pick on me. But every time we played catch and kiss she'd come after me with everything she had." He turned to Anne. "It's all right, pumpkin. I was fast, she never caught me."

"That's a relief." Anne smiled.

"I might have been a bit afraid of girl germs back then. But she reminds me of Lena with Jimmy. Did I tell you how Davie found them rolling around on the floor one day?"

"That was a professional intervention," I said.

"Jim, just out of curiosity, how many of Lena's interventions wind up getting physical? Do you find she often comes up with excuses to *handle* you, so to speak?"

"I do not," I said, voice climbing in volume.

"Look how riled up she got when I tried to find out more about her," said Mal. "That's why you're thinking about quitting, isn't it? Afraid you're getting too attached, maybe?"

"Mal, that's enough," said Anne. "Leave the poor girl alone."

Anger surged, running hot through me. One of my buttons had most definitely been pushed. I jumped to my feet, sending my chair sliding back. "You have no idea what you're talking about."

"Fuck's sake." Jimmy's stood and reached across the table, his hand snagging my wrist. "Calm down, Lena."

"But—"

"Calm down," Jimmy repeated. "He's being an idiot."

I huffed.

"Yeah," said Mal. "Keep your lady friend under control, Jimmy."

"Mal." Jimmy gave our host flinty eyes of great unhappiness. His thumb stroked soothingly against the inside of my wrist, back and forth, back and forth. I doubt he even realized he was doing it. "I'm serious. This is Thanksgiving, enough of this bullshit." He turned back to me. "Okay?"

The fight bled right out of me. Sad to say, it only annoyed me slightly that his petting worked. "Yes."

Mal said no more. But he did give Jimmy's grip on me a smug sort of smile. Damn, the drummer had been playing us.

Unfortunately, the attention made Jimmy also look down at his hand. The frown on his face when he found his fingers still wrapped around my wrist was almighty. Like the digits belonged to someone else. I tore myself out of his hold, beating him to the chase, and sat back down.

So many interesting things to look at in the room. The man across from me and whatever expression he might have on his perfect face didn't even matter. For example, Anne was busy rubbing at her temples. If my boyfriend was that insane, I would probably rub at my temples too. Meanwhile, Lizzy was busy checking her phone while their mother Jan had yet to return to the table. Ev, David, and Ben were still discussing the likelihood of Jimmy and I being a couple. Wonderful, this dinner was officially hell. No amount of pumpkin pie could compensate and it was all Jimmy's fault for raising the topic in the first damn place.

"Right. Shut up, all of you." Jimmy banged his fist on the table, interrupting the conversation and making the plates and cutlery rattle. "Lena is not leaving and we are not fucking or whatever so all of you just . . . stop."

No one spoke for about a moment.

Mal relaxed back in his chair, face unperturbed. "Then what's all the drama for, man?"

"Christ." Jimmy scrubbed at his face with his hands. "Look, Lena is thinking of leaving. But I've got an idea for how to get her to stay. Could use your guys help with it, actually. If we could all just act sane for one fucking minute of the day."

So much dread, I could have choked on it. "Jimmy."

"She does need to get out more. Meet some people," he said. "So . . . Benny, you'll take Lena out, won't you?"

"What?" I flatlined.

"That's a great idea," cried Ev, while David nodded in approval.

Ben gave me a big affable smile. "Sure, Jim. Love to."

"Good," said Jimmy, steadfastly refusing my attempts to get his attention. "Not tomorrow night, got plans for then. The night after."

"Works for me," said Ben.

"Cool. Where you thinking?"

"Hey." I snapped my fingers in Jimmy's direction. Rude but highly effective. "Stop it. I do not need you fixing me up with people."

"It's my pleasure, don't worry about it." He turned back to Ben.

"Jimmy," I growled warningly.

People looked back and forth between us, faces rapt. So much for a nice Thanksgiving, this was fast degenerating into a war.

"We doing this or not, Lena? You said you'd try. You going back on that now?"

Oh, the guilt. He was such a manipulative piece of shit.

"You're embarrassing me," I said quietly.

He leaned in and lowered his voice. "No, look again. These people are your friends. No one's judging you or thinking badly of you."

"I'm judging her," called out Mal. "Ouch, don't hit me, pumpkin. I'm just being honest. She shouldn't want to leave us—we're the best."

"Lena," said Ben, his dark eyes warm. "It's okay, really. I would love to take you out. What do you say?"

Jimmy watched me patiently (along with everyone else). There didn't seem to be any malice in him, just the usual will to get his way. I had agreed to this four-step plan, it was true. But as far as I could recall, being turned into the night's entertainment hadn't even once been mentioned. If I had to date, though, Ben Nicholson was a damn fine choice. Attractive, could carry a conversation, rich as the Queen of England. The man ticked a lot of boxes and apparently, he did want to go out with me.

Always a plus.

At worst, it would be a pleasant night out with a friend. At best, my feelings would somehow magically detach themselves from Jimmy and turn to someone who (shock horror) just might actually want them. A win all around.

"Maybe it is time I started dating again," I said, shoulders back and boobs out. No point in being half-hearted about it. Go big or go home and all that. "But I can organize this myself." I turned to the bass player. "Ben, how would you feel about going to dinner with me sometime?"

"Love to," he said with a grin.

"Great. Okay, then." That wasn't so hard.

"Right." Jimmy continued, his arrogant air dimmed somewhat. He scrunched up his napkin and threw it onto the table. "Where you taking her, Ben?"

Mouth open, the bass player gave it some thought. "Ah, how about the sport's bar? Allen's?"

"She doesn't like sports and don't be cheap. This is Lena, you gotta take her somewhere good. Relaxed, but good. Mood's important."

Sweet baby Jesus. I sank lower in my seat. "Thank you for your concern, Jimmy. But Ben and I can discuss this later. In private."

"It's all right. Let me think." Ben scratched at his short beard. "How about the Japanese place we go to sometimes?"

"No," said Jimmy. "Not quite right."

"Well, where would you suggest?" asked Ben, amusement lighting his eyes.

"Why don't I book you a table at a place I know downtown?"

"Done," said Ben. "Thanks, Jim. Lena, I'm looking forward to our date on Saturday. Pick you up at eight."

"Right." My smile wouldn't quite stick.

Lizzy likewise gave me a strained look. I knew the feeling. Turkey and cranberry sauce currently sat like lead in my belly.

"You're looking forward to it too. Aren't you, Lena?" Jimmy's smile seemed to waver slightly. Though it could have been my imagination.

My own felt oddly like it'd been pasted on. "Yeah. Absolutely."

"Catch."

A desert spoon was tossed into my lap. "Will you stop

throwing things at me? It's bad enough you feel the need to start the day that way."

Thanksgiving itself had been quiet, just the two of us hanging out around the house. I'd phoned mom and dad in the morning and had a nice long chat with them. Then Jimmy and I had gone to an AA meeting. Or rather Jimmy had. I'd sat outside in the hallway, sipping a hot cup of coffee. He'd come out calm and in an okay mood, always a good thing.

"You're a heavy sleeper. Got to wake you up somehow," said Jimmy. "You did a little better with the jogging this morning, by the way."

"Thank you," I grumbled, somewhat mollified. Praise from him didn't happen often. Though he'd said I was pretty the other day so perhaps it was on the rise.

"Yeah, you only hyperventilated twice. It's an improvement."

Or not. "Great. I appreciate the feedback."

"Move over, you're hogging the couch." He threw himself onto the sofa, crowding me. A bucket of ice cream and another spoon were in his hands.

"What are we doing?"

"Think of it as more aversion therapy. Here." He handed over the goodies. Half-baked chocolate chip cookie dough in French vanilla ice cream. Oh, hell yes. My mouth started watering.

"Yum. I don't see me loathing you anytime soon if you keep giving me ice cream."

He flicked on the TV. Birds flew over water and arty shots of sunlight and a long winding river appeared on screen. It was as familiar as it was unexpected.

"We're watching *The Notebook*?" I asked around a mouthful of heaven. "Really?"

"Talking about my flaws the other morning didn't go so well. Figured we'd try again." He settled back in the seat. "Article said you should spend time with your girls, watch sappy movies and eat ice cream, bitch about me, and shit. But I know my flaws better than anyone anyway. So, here we are."

He paused. "Would you rather I got some of the girls over to hang with you?"

"No, this is fine." I swallowed down some more dairy-and-dough heaven. Truth was, we'd been hanging out in front of the TV of a nighttime for a while now. It was comfortable. Plus, it seemed a bit disingenuous and or pathetic to suddenly start accepting Ev's offer of a night out now that Jimmy had announced my lack of a life to all and sundry. "You said you didn't play an instrument but I thought I heard a guitar earlier."

"Said I didn't play as well as the others. Not that I don't play."

"Do you write songs?" I asked.

"For the band? No. Davie does all the lyrics."

"For you?"

"Yes, Lena." His laughter was brittle. He tapped my spoon out of the way and dug in again. "I write myself love songs saying how hot I am. I'm that much of a narcissist."

I cocked my head, studying him. Well, I never. "It upset you. My saying that."

He scoffed. "I could give a fuck."

For a long moment, he stared at the TV and I stared at him. Things got to Jimmy, of course they did. I just didn't think my opinion of him was one of those things. It took a while for my mind to absorb the fact that he actually cared about something I'd said. There was intellectually knowing he had more emotions than a brick and then there was seeing them up close and personal. Until Lori's funeral, it simply didn't happen. Jimmy had been like Superman, bullets bounced off him so mere emotions never stood a chance. But these days . . .

I needed to be more careful. He wasn't as tough as he seemed.

"I'm sorry," I said.

He gave me a weird look. "About what?"

"Saying you're a narcissist."

"I repeat, I could give a fuck," he ever-so-clearly enunciated the words. "Straight out told you I was vain, didn't I?"

Right, he had no deeper emotions, my mistake. The man was so repressed he made my teeth ache. Though when you thought about it, it made definite sense. Not only had his mother done a job on him, but he'd been hiding his drinking and drug taking since the age of fourteen or fifteen. A secretive reclusive nature must stem naturally from that sort of situation. I didn't need to look up stuff on Google to figure that one out.

"I looked up what narcissist means," he said, nearly reading my mind. "And I don't think I'm in any danger of spending days mooning over myself in the mirror. I think you seeing nothing but flaws every time you look in one is more of an issue. Maybe me being a bit conceited isn't such a bad thing."

"I don't see anything but flaws."

"But you're not happy. That makes no sense to me."

I frowned.

The movie went on. Nothing was said.

I passed him the tub of ice cream before I ate the entire damn thing. "Though I'm not convinced you are a narcissist after all. I think I was way off about that."

He gave me a questioning look.

"I thought about what you said, about how your looks are like a tool to you. And I think your appearance is just an area of your life where you're used to exercising extreme control."

The man just shook his head. "Lena, no more pop psychology, okay? It's for your own good."

He might have a point there. It wasn't my strong suit. "All right then, let's change subjects. Tell me about the songs you write."

"Didn't say I wrote any."

"You didn't say you didn't, either."

"I'm just the singer, Lena. That's all."

"You play guitar. I heard you downstairs earlier."

"Christ, you're annoying." He dug around, excavating another chunk of chocolate chip goodness. "I've been teaching myself how to play, all right? No more. I don't want to talk about it."

"Does David know?"

"No." His eyes flashed. "And you're not telling him either."

"You have my word."

My immediate agreement seemed to soothe him. He pressed back into the couch, exhaled hard. A muscle in his jaw moved repeatedly like he was grinding his teeth. "We're supposed to be bitching about me or something."

I groaned. "Can't we just hang out instead? All of this constant jogging and deprogramming is tiring. You're not half as interesting to talk about as you think you are."

He gave me one of his not-quite-a-smile smiles. "Works for me."

I grabbed the ice cream back from him. So sue me. It was good.

"Do we really have to watch this?" His nose wrinkled with apparent disdain. It was cute.

"It was your bright idea." I smiled. "What other movies did you get?"

"*Titanic, Thelma and Louise,* and *Silver Linings Playbook.*"

"Interesting mix. Put *Thelma and Louise* on, I think you'll like it better. It's got a happy, uplifting ending."

"Done." He fussed with the remote and Brad Pitt's sexy

voice came on the giant screen. Such a great film. But Brad Pitt really was a superb specimen of manhood.

"Can you put it back to the beginning please, King of the Remote? This is about halfway through."

He did so.

"Blonds have more fun, everyone knows that," I said. "You ever thought of bleaching your hair?"

He gave me a snotty look.

"Maybe I should go blonde instead," I said.

"No, don't," he said shortly, face creased with concern. "I mean, you're fine as you are. I've been telling you that for days." He stole back the tub and hoed in. "You don't listen."

Huh.

"I guess I thought you were just being kind." Melted ice cream dripped off my spoon, onto my jeans. I scraped it up with a finger, licking it clean. This was why I couldn't have nice things.

I looked up to find Jimmy staring at my mouth. His own lips were slightly parted, his eyes hazy. I froze.

No way.

He wasn't having those sort of thoughts about me. Impossible, and yet the evidence in front of me told a distinctly different tale. A knot twisted and tightened deep in my belly, a thrilling sort of rush pouring through my veins. Just that easily, he'd flicked the switch, turning me on. I don't think he even realized what he was doing.

"Jimmy?"

His gaze jumped from my mouth to my eyes and the frown descended. "I'm not kind. And I don't say stuff I don't mean. Stop fishing for compliments if you're not going to believe them. It's a waste of my time."

A curiously snappy response, even for him.

"Thank you," I said. "That's really very sweet of you . . . in a strange way."

He watched the movie, giving me no response whatsoever.

"You know, if I do end up leaving," I said. "We can still hang out sometimes, do stuff together. I wouldn't just disappear on you."

He threw his spoon onto the coffee table where it landed with a violent clank.

"Jimmy?" I'd meant the words as a comfort. Clearly, they hadn't been received that way.

"To answer your question, I've been on the cover of probably hundreds of magazines. I don't know. Got a stack of platinum records and a current net worth of about sixty-two million," he said, voice flat and unfriendly. "Messed up some product endorsements and part of a tour with the drug use or it'd be more. I own this house and another in LA. That's where I keep my collection of cars. I also got a few paintings I took a liking to."

"Impressive. I have about four-grand in the bank in savings. My watch is a swatch. Probably not really worth anything." I dragged the sleeve of my sweater down over the poor unimpressive thing lest it get performance anxiety. "Why are you telling me all this?"

"Because, last time I ODed, Dave made it clear. Get clean or I'm out. Out of the band, out of his life. He'd had enough, they all had." He stretched out his arms along the back of the sofa, fingers kneading at the leather. It might look the pose of a man relaxed, but the reality was worlds away.

I'd gathered this from what had been said in Coeur d'Alene, but still, it was hard to hear. Those guys were his whole world, they meant everything to him. I couldn't imagine how he must have felt. No matter what he'd done, and I know he'd done a lot, I accepted that. It didn't change the facts. His mother had hurt him and left him, his father had failed him, his brother and best friends had threatened to throw him out of the band. And now I'd been talking about leaving. Whatever our relationship, for several months now I'd been a staple part of his life, one he apparently liked in his own way.

My wanting to leave was bound to get a reaction.

"So I got clean," he said. "Cut ties with everyone in LA, anyone who I had anything to do with before. I came up here and started over. They've all been real supportive, my brother, the band. And I understand why they'd be willing to turn their backs on me, I do. Can't say I don't get resentful now and then, but I'm the one that pushed them to it."

"Jimmy—"

"Just listen." His cold hard eyes never left my face. "You leave, I'm not going to fall apart and start using again. Know that. I'm not trying to blackmail you here, I'm just making something clear. The guys probably were right last night about you being my only friend apart from them. We don't always get along, but still, you feel like a friend."

Both of his hands moved from bullying the back of the couch to holding back his hair. He gave the dark strands a sharp tug. "You're a friend I just happen to pay to hang around, which is incredibly fucking pathetic and messed up, but there you have it."

"I can still be your friend. I would like to still be your friend."

Another sharp tug. "It won't be the same."

My mouth opened but I didn't know what to say. He was right, it wouldn't be the same. No more seeing him and talking to him every day, hanging out with him nearly every night. This part of my life, the time spent with him, would become a memory. The sadness inside me felt huge, overwhelming. I couldn't possibly contain it. Much more of this and I'd explode, decorating his pristine minimalist living room in messy emotional Lena.

Man, he'd be pissed.

My stupid tongue lay still for the longest time. "I don't know what to say."

"Did I ask for your opinion?" he snapped. "No."

"Hey," I growled warningly. "Watch it."

He turned his face away, his jaw shifting restlessly.

Stuff happened on screen, none of it mattered.

"Lena, the point I'm trying to make is, the list is important. And it won't work if you're not committed to making it work. So don't talk to me about us still being friends if you go, okay? Just . . . commit."

I took a deep breath, studying his fierce features. Everything in life was so damn complicated, so confusing when it came to the heart. I don't know when that happened exactly, probably sometime during the early teenage years when boys overtook my interest in ponies and glitter.

Resented the hell out of it some days.

"Fine, I'm committed," I said, the only answer I could give.

"Fine." He relaxed back, crossing his arms over his chest, satisfied apparently. But I already knew, the list wasn't working.

CHAPTER EIGHT

"Is that what you're wearing?" Jimmy leaned against the bottom of the balustrade watching me descend. He wore a black suit and white shirt, very classy, very expensive. I bet it cost more than I made in a month. The man was such a show pony, one that I just so happened to be hormonally susceptible to. Blame it all on my girl bits, sure why not?

"Yes, this is what I'm wearing," I said. "Why?"

"No reason."

First chance I had, I was writing to Santa and asking for the ability to read people's minds this Christmas. Or just one mind—Jimmy's. Though I doubt I'd like what I found in there. "What's wrong with this?"

He took in my frilly navy-and-white polka-dotted blouse, black leggings, and boots. "Nothing. Just . . . interesting choice."

"I like this choice."

"Sure, it's real nice. Just thought you might dress up more."

"We're only going out to dinner downtown. It's meant to be relaxed." I straightened my glasses. Black rims this time, fuck him, I'd even accessorized right. Plus, I'd painstakingly applied my makeup and straightened my brown hair. Long and thick, it was my one true pride and joy. But Jimmy seemed utterly unimpressed. Little wonder I had trouble believing his scant compliments when the very next day he looked down his nose at me.

"And you look relaxed." His car keys swung from a finger.

"Oh, shut up. Where are you off to?" I asked. "Thought you said you were staying in tonight."

"I'm driving you," he said. "Told Benny we'd meet him at the restaurant."

"What? Why?"

"No need for him to pick you up when I'm heading that way." He took my red coat, holding it open for me to slip into. Typical of the dichotomy in his behavior. He boggled my mind, insulting me one minute, then behaving the perfect yesteryear gentleman the next.

"Thanks," I said. "You're going to David and Ev's?"

"Mhmm."

"Well, that's good you'll have some company."

He nodded and led the way downstairs to the garage. The new, nearly finished studio sat at the front of the building, the big open middle area cluttered with exercise gear and musical instruments. At the back lay the garage with Jimmy's two cars. The chrome on the black 1971 Plymouth Barracuda gleamed in the low light. I'd always wanted to steal the keys from Jimmy and go for a spin. But as always, he headed for the latest model Mercedes. So sensible this time of year.

We drove in silence all the way there, a soft rain falling. Instead of pulling up out front of the restaurant, he drove around the corner and parked in the first available spot.

"You're not just dropping me off?" I asked, reaching for my umbrella.

"I'll see you in. Say hi to Ben."

"All right."

We huddled together, Jimmy's arm loosely around my back and his hand over mine, helping to hold the umbrella steady in the strong winds. The restaurant specialized in Asian-French fusion cuisine and was rather fancy. Lots of carved wooden chairs and tables, with swathes of red silk on the walls. An antique mirror showed off my now damp frizzy hair to perfection. Oh well, I'd tried. Jimmy's hipster up-do still looked perfect, of course. I doubt Mother Nature would dare mess with him even at her bravest. She'd put so much effort into getting him right, after all.

At a corner table, Ben stood and waved. Strangely enough, his smile only grew at the sight of his bandmate beside me. I nodded to the gorgeous tattooed blonde girl on the front desk and made my way through the maze of customers chowing down. There were no evening gowns in evidence, I was dressed fine.

"Hey, Jim. Didn't know you'd be joining us." Big Ben grinned down at me. "Lena, you look fantastic."

"Why, thank you, Ben," I said. "You look very lovely yourself."

He bent down obviously intending to kiss my cheek. And then he bent down some more while I craned my neck and went up on tippy toes (it's important to be helpful). Besides my being a little under average height, the guy just was that damn tall.

"Good to see you, Ben." Jimmy's hand shot into the rapidly dwindling space between Ben and me, knocking me off balance. Before I could stumble, Jimmy grabbed my elbow, holding me steady.

"Yeah, Jim." Ben gave his hand a hearty shake. "You too."

"He's just dropping me off and saying hi," I said. "Which he's now done."

"Actually, I've got time for a drink." Jimmy raised a

hand and a waiter hurried over. "Bottle of Coke for me and a gin and tonic for her. Thanks."

The waiter nodded and rushed off. A bottle of Bud already sat on the table in front of Ben.

I gave Jimmy a look as I sat. It was not a happy one.

"What? You didn't want that?" Without waiting for an answer, he dragged over an unoccupied chair from a nearby table. Not bothering to turn it to face ours, he sat on it back to front. His arms rested along the high back. The man looked ready for a fucking photo shoot. This way he had about him, a natural grace, annoyed the living shit out of me. If only he'd be more like us little people, clumsy and inept. But no. "I know that's what you drink sometimes, Lena," he said. "It's not a big deal."

"Water would have been fine." I smoothed the frown off my face with some effort. "How did you even know what I drink? I haven't drunk in front of you. Not ever."

What Jimmy was going through, beating his addictions, was hard enough without me being so thoughtless. Plus, there was respect, support, solidarity, things like that to consider.

"Dave and Ev's second wedding," he said. The pair had decided to tie the knot again for their six month anniversary. A very fancy do, much as you'd imagine. I'd been working for Jimmy a month or so then.

"I was talking to Ben out on the balcony for an hour or so, you were inside," he said. "I guess the waiter came over, cause a while later I saw you nursing a gin and tonic. It was gone by the time I came back in."

"How did you even notice, or remember?" I asked. "I don't know if I should be touched or worried."

"Don't be anything." He gave me the trademark jutting of the chin. "My name is Jimmy Ferris and I'm an alcoholic. I know what Ben drinks. I know what you drink.

I don't even know what the nine people sitting on the three tables around us look like. But I could tell you what every one of them is drinking."

"The hell you can," said Ben.

Jimmy smiled darkly and sat up in his seat, moving his face close to Ben's to show he didn't need to look around. "The table of girls to my left. Two tequila sunrises and one Long Island Iced Tea. And the poor sap with the plain OJ, guess she's the designated driver. The couple behind me is easy—the bottle's still sitting in front of them. Porters."

"The challenge is the gents to my right—one of them is knocking back a lager, so that's simple enough. But the other two? Spirits glasses. Amber liquid, but not straight. No fizz. No ice. The clue, little children, is the tall glasses of water. They're proper drinkers, just enough of a splash of water to bring out the taste in their scotch. Since I know from past experience the top shelf here finishes somewhere in the attic. I'm guessing Blue Label Johnnie Walker." He shrugged. "Unless they're single-malt aficionados in which case I have no fucking clue."

"Holy crap, man," said Ben, "You should be on TV."

"I am on the TV, you chump."

"I shouldn't have let you come in," I said. "You used to drink here. This place is a trigger for you."

He scoffed and spread his arms wide. "This whole world is a trigger for me."

"Jimmy, I'm serious. You should go."

"Not just yet."

"He doesn't trust me to behave with you," said Ben, sliding his cell onto the table.

I scowled. "That's ridiculous."

Jimmy just gave me a cool glance. "I love Ben like a brother, but I've known him a hell of a long time. No offense, right Ben?"

"None at all." Something pinged on Ben's cell and he slid a finger across the screen, bending closer to read the message.

Calm as can be, Jimmy reached over and smacked the back of his head like he was some recalcitrant child. "Don't be so fucking rude. You're out with Lena, put it away."

"Waiting for news on something, get out of my face." Ben took a swig of his beer and winked at me. "So, Lena. What should we talk about?"

"Christ," Jimmy groaned. "You're going to make her do all the work? Really?"

Kill me now.

"Seen any good movies lately?" Ben asked without missing a beat.

"Ah, yes. We watched *Thelma and Louise* last night. I'd seen it before, but it's always great."

"You and Jimmy watched it together?"

I nodded. "Yeah, we often watch TV at nighttime. Have you ever seen it?"

"Can't say I have."

"It doesn't end happily," said Jimmy. "I can tell you that much."

"Depends on your perspective," I countered with a smile.

The waiter delivered our drinks. His eyes widened at the sight of Jimmy, and then he did a double take of Ben. To his credit, he didn't make an issue out of who they were. I ordered a plain soda water and slid the gin to the side.

"You look smooth, Jim. Wish I'd thought to wear a suit." Ben had worn a red sweater and jeans. It suited him. God bless a scruffy man in a pair of fitted blue jeans. Yum. Jimmy with his suits and smooth ways had never been my type. This attraction to him basically went against the very laws of nature. I could beat it, I just had to try.

I shuffled forward in my seat, determined to renew my

efforts with my date. Who knew, maybe Ben and I would hit it off. For certain, as a couple, we made much more sense.

"You should have thought to get her flowers too," said Jimmy. "That would have been a good thing to do."

Ben smacked his forehead. "You're right. I should have."

"You shouldn't have. It's fine." I gave Jimmy a warning look. Red lights and sirens, danger ahead.

Of course, he ignored it. "Send some to the house tomorrow."

"You got it, Jim." The cell at Ben's elbow pinged again and he gave it surreptitious look. "Sorry, Lena. I just need to reply to this."

"Man—" Jimmy reached out again, but I caught his wrist before he could strike.

"That's fine, Ben," I said. "Take your time."

Jimmy narrowed his eyes. "Who is it, Benny?"

"No one." His finger got busy tapping against the screen.

"And this no one is more important than being polite to Lena, I take it?"

My fingernails dug into the palms of my hands. "Shouldn't you be heading to David and Ev's? We don't want to hold you up."

"It's fine. I didn't give them a time."

Great. "Jimmy, read between the lines. It's time for you to go."

He turned a truly pained look heavenward. "Can't a man finish his soda? Is that really too much to ask?"

"Yes. Please leave."

"You don't have a problem with me being here a bit longer do you, Ben?"

"Not at all, Jim. So . . . Lena." Ben finally put down his cell and picked up his beer, giving me an easy smile. "Catch the game last night?"

With a groan, Jimmy rubbed a hand across his face. "She just told you we watched a movie. Plus, she hates sports. You're boring her, this is a disaster."

One of the great things about this restaurant was the small tables. I could easily kick Jimmy in the shin, I hardly had to stretch at all.

"What the fuck was that for?" he griped, reaching down to inspect his pants leg. "This is a custom-made suit, Lena. Have a little respect."

"Oops. Sorry," I lied with a grimace, thus displaying my brilliant acting abilities. "Did I accidentally catch you with my boot?"

"No! You kicked me on purpose."

My lips pressed tight together. "Oh, you asshole. I lied and covered for you the other night at Ev's."

With movements sharp and angry, Jimmy snatched up a napkin and carefully brushed off his pants. Threats of revenge shone bright in his nasty, beautiful, beady little eyes.

Yeah, bring it on, baby.

"Why are you two always kicking each other?" Ben asked, interrupting the heated looks. "Just out of interest?"

Jimmy shrugged. "Everyone has their hobbies, Ben."

"Right." Amusement lit his face and fair enough really, this date was a farce. His phone pinged again. "Sorry."

"Seems you're pretty busy with whoever keeps messaging you. Maybe we should try this another night, unchaperoned, even." I gave Ben a sweet smile. The one I gave Jimmy was distinctly less so.

"No, Jim's right, I'm being rude. I'll put this away." He gave the cell one last longing look before placing it screen side down on the table. "Ah . . . what shall we order?"

With a flourish, he passed me a menu. "Anything catch your fancy?"

Jimmy sipped his Coke in silence. He may or may not have been pouting, I refused to check.

"Mm, everything looks good." It also looked wildly overpriced. I always went Dutch on dates, but this time, it might very well kill me. Trust Jimmy to pick the most expensive damn place in town. I was tempted to kick him once more, just for fun.

Ben's cell pinged again and Jimmy reached over, picking it up. His brows rose high as he checked out the screen. "Fucking hell, man. Do you have a death wish?"

"None of your business." Ben held out his hand.

Jimmy placed the cell back in it. "Right. Good luck with that, I'll make sure your funeral's real nice."

Ben did not reply.

"I might just have an entrée," I said, interrupting whatever was going on between them. "I'm not all that hungry."

"What's wrong? You don't know what to try?" asked Jimmy, stealing the menu from me. He took his time looking it over. "Why don't you have the ginger chicken, it's got a caramelized sauce. You like sweet stuff. And . . . vermicelli with Asian greens. That'll be good, I think you'll enjoy it."

"I can order for myself, thanks," I bit out. "I'm just not that hungry."

"You haven't eaten since lunch. Course you are." His face creased up in confusion. "C'mon, the chef here is great or I wouldn't have chosen the place."

"Just a soup or something, will do. Can I please have that back, please?"

"No."

"Jimmy."

He held the stupid thing out of reach. "Tell me what's wrong."

Ben said nothing and hid behind his own menu. Coward. We were through. I could never date a man who didn't stand beside me in the face of mindless oppression. Also, he was just too tall, I'd have constant neck aches trying to get high enough to kiss the guy.

"You are wrong," I said, face warming in anger. "You are behaving all sorts of wrong. You shouldn't even be here."

He cocked his head and studied me. Still didn't pass the damn menu. I swear I saw red, endless expanses of it. Though that might have been the scarlet silk lining the restaurant walls.

I clicked my fingers in demand. "Give it to me."

A moment later his features relaxed, and finally, at long damn last, he handed the stupid thing over. "You're worried about money."

I followed Ben's good example and hid behind the thick black folder.

"Lena?" Jimmy hooked a finger in the top of the menu, pulling it down so he could see me. "Me or Ben will pay. Why the hell are you worrying about that? Just enjoy yourself, eat what you want. That's why I brought you here."

I closed my eyes for a moment, searching for a calm happy place. It eluded me. "Jimmy, I pay Dutch when I go out on a date. It's my way and I expect you to respect that. Also, you didn't bring me here. Well, you did, but . . . never mind, I'm supposed to be here on a date with Ben. You are supposed to be somewhere else. Not sitting here, worrying about what I'm ordering for dinner or who's paying or what we're talking about."

"And if I was somewhere else you'd wind up eating soup you don't even want and going home hungry having been bored shitless while Benny played with his phone. So it's just as well I am here." He rested his chin atop the back of his chair. "Right, Ben?"

"Right, Jim." Ben rose to his feet. "Guys, I'm just going to use the bathroom. Won't be long."

"Sure," said Jim, eyes still on me.

With a brief smile, Ben turned to go. Then stopped, collecting his cell off the table. "Better take this with me. Seriously, I'm having a great time hanging with you two. We should definitely do this more often. See you soon."

I watched the big man wander into a hallway. The broad expanse of his back disappeared into the dimly lit tunnel. Going, going, gone.

"He's not coming back, is he?" I asked.

"Nope. He's probably out the back door already."

"I've never actually run off a guy on the first date before. What an achievement."

"Don't." Jimmy looked up from the menu, pinning me with his eyes. "It's Ben's loss. You're great."

My mind reeled and my insides turned to mush. "No, you see? This is the problem with you. For every thoughtless assholish move you make, you then turn around and do or say something wonderful and it just makes everything all right. I can never find my balance because I never know what's going to come next. You're impossible."

He gave me a long look. "You finished?"

"Yes."

He stood and returned his pilfered chair to a nearby table. The he sat in the one the bass player had so recently vacated. "I'm thinking the sugarcane prawn rolls, ginger chicken, BBQ pork buns, and a couple of the vegetable dishes. Sound good?"

"Sure."

"I don't know that you and Ben would be good together after all. Not sure what I was thinking there." He didn't seem particularly bothered by the failure. But then again, deep down where it mattered, neither was I. A big *meh* now sat where any upset regarding the situation should have been. With Jimmy sitting opposite me, watching me, happy hormones flooded my brain proving yet again just what an idiot I was when it came to him.

"Oh, well. It wouldn't have gone any better if I'd picked someone," I said with a smile. "I have the worst taste in men."

He said nothing.

"Sorry. No offense meant."

"None taken."

"My collection of past boyfriends is not something to be proud of."

"That bad, huh?"

"You have no idea. I have in my time dated a cheater, a thief, a repressed homosexual, a foot fetishist, and various men who just wanted a chance to meet my sister."

"Why's the foot fetishist so bad?"

"Always with the strappy high heels. My toes were killing me."

"Ah."

"Anyway, this is no longer a date." I needed to say it out loud, just put it out there for the universe to hear. Let's not explore why.

"No, of course not," he agreed immediately with great conviction. It only stung a little. "It's a business meeting between me and my assistant. I'm paying, order whatever you want."

I swallowed a mouthful of soda water. "Thank you. Did I damage your suit?"

"No, just needs cleaning. I'm pretty sure you bruised me though."

"You bruised my toes," I said.

"We're even then."

I set aside the menu and slumped back in my seat while Jimmy ordered dinner. Poor Ben. Also, how embarrassing, I hope he didn't tell the others. Though they all knew we'd been planning on going out so the story was bound to get around. They were going to laugh their collective asses off. Mal in particular would never let me live it down. Sometimes, having friends was a pain in the butt.

It was nothing less than the truth. They were important to me. Somehow, despite my best intentions to keep to myself, I'd failed miserably. For the first time in a long time I did have people I thought of as friends. People who came over to the house and hung out. People who invited me to things and genuinely wanted me to be there. As crap as I'd been at accepting invitations.

It was nice.

Before the waiter could slip away, I handed him my untouched gin. "I'm finished with that. Can you take it, please? Thank you."

Jimmy watched in his usual blasé manner, completely unruffled. "You could have drunk it. I wouldn't have minded."

"I could have," I said. "But it wouldn't have felt right. And while it's great that you have opinions on everything I think, wear, and do, I'm not going to do something that doesn't feel right just to please you, Jimmy."

"You're not drinking it because of me, so that actually makes no sense."

I shrugged, gave him a halfhearted smile. "Sometimes things that make the least sense are the most true. Such is the mystery of life."

He cocked an eyebrow at me, then looked down at his menu shaking his head. "You got that out of a fortune cookie, didn't you?"

"Maybe."

CHAPTER NINE

"You never said your sister was getting married soon."

"What are you doing in here and how do you know about that?" I asked, carefully applying a last coat of mascara. Hair done, heels and dress on, round two of dating other people was a go. Hopefully, with more success tonight because it could hardly be with less. Jimmy and I needed to have a stern talk about boundaries with possible butt kicking involved.

Our day had been normal mixed with bizarre on account of the sushi chef showing up to give me lessons before lunch. Another little surprise from Jimmy to cover point four on the list. It'd been fun, though I doubted I'd be moving into the hospitality and catering industries anytime soon. Jimmy had taken one look at my attempts at sashimi and announced he'd be having a protein shake for lunch. Mr. Nakimura had just given me a sad sigh. To be honest, the disappointment hadn't hit too hard, raw fish really wasn't my thing.

But back to Jimmy's latest bedroom invasion.

"This got mixed in with my stuff." He threw the glossy ivory invite onto my bathroom counter. Without my glasses on, he was just a sexy smudge in the mirror. "You dressed up this time."

He bent over, apparently checking out my legs or the knee-length hem of my skirt. Whatever. I refused to be lead astray by his false attentions. He wasn't interested in me, not in any way that counted toward my vagina or my heart getting what they wanted.

"Nice," he said. "Red looks good on you."

"Thanks. Now get out."

"Put these on. You need to see something."

My glasses came at me. Carefully, he positioned them on my nose. I had my usual reaction to seeing him, having him standing so close. A certain lightness in my head, fluttery feelings in my chest and loins, that sort of thing. I wasn't proud, but the warmth and pull of his body was undeniable to my girl parts. Then, from behind his back he produced a bouquet of flowers, arranged in a glass vase.

Oh my god.

"You bought me dahlias?" Color me stunned. My heart gave a hopeful overexcited throb. "They're beautiful."

He snorted. "'Course I didn't buy you fucking flowers. Read the card."

"'Sorry about taking off. Let's just be friends. Ben.'" I laughed at me, him, and the universe. It seemed the best possible response. "You told him to send me these, didn't you?"

"Hmm," he uttered cryptically. Then he placed them on the counter while I put the final fix on my attempt at putting my hair in a bun. He stood there and stared which was not helpful for the pre-date jitters. I did my best to ignore him. Hard given the way he watched me, his gaze doing a slow circuit of my body, no curve left unnoticed. The man was the king of mixed messages. I didn't know whether to kick him or jump him, this was ridiculous. All of a sudden, balancing in my high heels seemed a test of great dexterity and conviction. The man made me quiver.

"Jimmy?"

"Yeah?"

"You're staring."

He met my eyes, blinked. "How much time you going to need off for the wedding?"

"None," I said, searching his face for some sign, some acknowledgement of what he'd been doing. But he just gave me the scrunched-up face of disapproval, brows tight and eyes narrowed.

No, come on. He had to know he'd been looking me over like a sex thing. I mean, like I was a person he wanted to have sex with.

Yes.

God damn it, my heart and hormones. Both were being stressed right the fuck out.

"I'm not going," I said, concentrating on rearranging the clutter on the counter. If I could just have a moment to pull my shit together I'd be fine.

"Why not?"

"Next few months before the tour are going to be out. I'm too busy. You can't possibly do without me here."

"Bullshit. I can spare you for a few days."

"Ah, but they don't know that. Move, please." I tapped him on the nose with the tip of my finger.

He stepped back, frowning. "So you got family issues? I wondered when you didn't ask to go home for Thanksgiving. I take it this is about that sibling hate you mentioned when I was having issues with Dave?"

"Indeed it is. But I get on fine with the rest of my family. I call my mom a couple of times a week, chat with my dad too."

"What'd she do to you?"

"Why so curious?" I picked up my coat and purse,

switched off the light. "I thought the goings on of the little people didn't interest you, oh mighty Mr. Ferris."

I paused, waiting to see if he'd actually admit to it. But got nothing.

He followed me down the stairs. No suit tonight, instead, he wore black jeans and yet another fitted black T-shirt, hair unstyled, hanging around his face. Hard to say which was more potent, suited Jimmy or relaxed. They were both hot as hell.

"So, what do we know about this Reece character apart from the fact that he's a friend of Anne's?" The living room seemed a good place to await his arrival. I dumped my stuff and then myself onto the couch as every muscle from my hips to my toes screamed in agony. Stupid jogging. A long soak in a hot bath would have been the night's plans if not for the thou-shalt-date-other-people commandment from the rock god on high.

My hopes for the date were subdued, courtesy of the night before. If he stuck around for the main meal I'd call it a win.

"Owns a book shop or something. That's about it." Jimmy sat with his usual natural grace. Such was the nature of ballerinas, models, rock stars, and other preternaturally good-looking creatures. Though to be fair, Jimmy had collapsed rather dramatically several times in public back when. Pictures of him out cold on the ground had made the rounds at least once or twice. Guess when he'd gotten dry he'd put all of that behind him.

"Why are you frowning at me?" he groused.

"What were you like when you were using?"

His forehead went from calm to crumpled in an instant. That part of his face was basically a barometer. "Where the fuck did that come from?"

"I don't know. I just . . . I want to know things about you. Is that so wrong?"

The look in his eyes said yes. Hell yes. Also, I was in all likelihood mentally deficient on account of being dropped on my head repeatedly as a child.

"Never mind," I mumbled.

"Haven't we talked about this enough? I was a mess, Lena. A total asshole. I was angry and fucked up and not someone you'd want to know." His lips pressed together. "Now, I'm a bit calmer at least. I'm in control most of the time."

I nodded.

"What's going on with your sister's wedding?" he shot back at me.

My lips sealed tight.

"I answered your question. So answer mine."

He had a point, didn't mean I liked it. Admitting to any weakness in front of Jimmy seemed a dangerous thing and this particular chink in my armor still stung. "She's marrying my ex-boyfriend. He dumped me for her."

All expression fell from his face. "He's the cheater you talked about?"

"Yeah. Awkward, huh? My own sister and everything." I laughed, mostly at myself. Just my luck to have the only decent guy I'd ever dated run off with Alyce. "You can imagine my relief at not being asked to be a bridesmaid at that one."

"That's pretty fucking low."

My shoulders relaxed, descending to more normal territory. "I thought so at the time. Apparently they're happy together, so . . ."

"Beside the point." Jimmy scowled at the coffee table like he was thinking of taking an ax to it. "Wouldn't kill your sister to show some loyalty. It's no better than what I did to David and that was . . . that was bad. She shouldn't have done that to you, Lena."

"Thank you." My lips curled up of their own accord.

His opinion meant so much more to me than it should. The absolute conviction in his voice eased me. It was tempting to throw some of the things Brandon, my ex-boyfriend, had said out there. Let them be heard by someone other than me just for the joy of possibly listening to Jimmy shoot them down. How I was too hard and difficult, detached and unreachable. So he'd reached for my sister instead and bless her lack of sibling loyalties, she'd reached right back.

Screw them both.

But if Jimmy agreed with any of the vitriol my ex had spouted, it would hurt a part of me I wasn't certain could heal. For all his put-downs, deep inside of him, he seemed to think well of me. I valued that more than words could say.

"Anyway," I said. "Thank you for opening up to me about when you were using. About a lot of things lately. It's been good, talking to you more."

He shrugged. "Talking is supposed to help both of our situations."

"Does it help you?" I asked.

"No, not really. I've accepted responsibility for all the things that I've done, and I've tried to make amends. Time to move on." He flicked his hair back. "It helping you?"

I stared at him, transfixed. Love is a convoluted thing really, there is little simplicity to it deep down. It consists of layers of emotions, thoughts, and memories, coalescing into one overwhelming point. The knowledge that one person in this world means more to you than most anything. Sense and reason don't stand a chance. Sometime-bastard and messed-up man that he was, I adored him, all of him.

"No, it's not," I said. "Because your dark parts don't scare me, Jimmy. They never did."

"They should." He licked his lips, holding my gaze all the while.

Good god, his mouth, so beautiful. My stomach went into freefall. In his eyes, it almost seemed there was something real there. A tangible bond or emotion that went beyond our ordinary everyday interactions. I don't know, it's hard to explain. But as always, it lay just beyond reach.

I turned away first this time, self-protection had to kick in eventually. The doorbell rang and the moment shattered. Probably for the best.

"Remember, you promised not to interfere." I leapt to my feet.

Sadly, he was faster. "Not gonna interfere, just interested in meeting him."

"Jimmy—"

"Hey, you must be Reece." The door stood open and Jimmy's broad shoulders filled the space. I couldn't see past him.

"Jimmy Ferris, I take it," a friendly enough male voice said. They shook hands, then Jimmy stepped back. Reece was average height, lean, and nice looking in a hipster boy way, short dark hair and thick-rimmed glasses.

"Hi, I'm Lena." I waved.

We looked each other over. First dates and set-ups really were among the most torturous of social endeavors. Whoever had invented them deserved a nice slap upside the head. But Reece's smile of approval filled his face, it seemed I'd passed the test. Perhaps tonight showed promise after all.

"I'll just grab my coat," I said, sidestepping back into the living room with all due haste. God knows what Jimmy would say or do left alone with him for long. This date needed to last longer than fifteen minutes. My pride demanded it.

"So, where you taking her, Reece?" My boss's voice carried through the house just fine.

I grabbed my coat and purse, and rushed back, heels

clacking against the marble floor. The inquisition had to be halted at all costs before Jimmy ran him off. "Ready!"

"Thought we might head out to a movie, if that sounds okay with you, Lena?" Reece stuffed his hands in his pockets.

"Sounds great! Let's go." Already, my cheeks ached from smiling. If I was any perkier I'd need shooting.

Jimmy exhaled gustily and did not smile. "Great. So I'll expect her back, what . . . about three, four hours?"

"Ah, sure," said Reece, brows high.

"Ignore him." I did up the buttons on my coat with great haste. "Jimmy, I'll check in with you later. Have a nice night."

"Drive safe," he commanded, stern gaze never moving from my date's now troubled face. "Slow."

"Always do," said Reece, taking a few steps down the path, obviously eager to be gone.

I wrestled the door handle from Jimmy's grasp and pushed at his hard flat stomach. "Go inside, it's cold."

He stayed put. There was much angry gazing going on.

"What's your problem?" I whisper hissed.

"I don't like the look of him."

"He looks fine."

Icy eyes cast me more doubting glances. "No, there's something about him."

"Jimmy."

"It's the glasses, I don't trust them. I think he's trying to hide something."

"I wear glasses."

He shrugged and gave me his well-there-you-have-it look. The idiot.

"He is not an ax murderer. He's a longtime friend of Anne's," I said, keeping my voice low. "You promised to behave."

"But what if—"

"You promised."

His mouth snapped shut. After one final glare at Reece, he relented, thank god. Few things had ever sounded as sweet as the click of the lock when I closed the front door.

"Okay," I breathed, giving my date a relieved grin. "We're good to go."

"He always like that?"

"No, well . . . he worries sometimes, I guess." I didn't know how to explain the recent emergence of Jimmy's proprietorial instincts. He didn't want me, therefore, he really needed to cut the crap.

"Anne told me a bit about you and the situation with Jimmy. How you work for him and all." Reece shuffled his feet. "I'm really not an ax murderer."

"Oh, you heard that. Good."

"No worries." He returned my inane smile with a laugh. "Let's get going."

Reece drove an older model hatchback, and he did indeed drive it slow and careful as directed to one of the movie theaters in town. The man immediately bought a large bucket of popcorn thus endearing himself to me immensely. To enjoy the importance of snacks was no small thing. We wandered through the lobby, checking out the movie posters and advertising paraphernalia. You couldn't rush deciding which film to sit through. Choose unwisely and you didn't get those two to three hours of your life back, let alone the money.

"There's stuff exploding in this one." I pointed to the latest Hollywood blockbuster. "And car chases."

"You don't want to see this?" He turned instead to this week's go-to dating film. A couple were laughing as they stood in the rain. How clichéd, I only barely held in my groan. It even starred Liv Anders, the latest in slinky blonde Hollywood starlets.

Kill me now.

"I don't know." I hedged.

"Anne said she thought you might enjoy it."

There was something in the way he said her name, something I chose to ignore for the time being. He had after all bought popcorn. This date had to go better, it just had to.

"I bet it all ends in tears," I joked. "The heroine probably catches a cold from standing in the rain and dies of pneumonia."

He blinked. "Anne said it had a happy ending. She thought we might like it."

Oh no, there it was again, the out and out reverence. Holy relics were spoken of with less awe than Reece speaking Anne's name. The sinking feeling came stronger this time, it swamped me. Politeness dictated I not ask outright if he'd agreed to date me tonight to make another woman happy. Suspicions, however, were strong.

"Anne suggested it?" I asked.

Smile in place, he nodded so fiercely I feared his neck might snap from the strain.

"Anne's really great." I shoveled popcorn into my mouth, watching him instead of the posters. And there it was, all the drama my night could ever need. I hadn't even had to buy a ticket to watch the wreckage of unrequited love played out in 3-D. Not a single vehicle was hurt or chased in the making.

"Yeah, she sure is." A dreamy faraway look came into his eyes. I sincerely hoped I didn't look like that when I thought about Jimmy. How embarrassing.

"You think she's happy with Mal?" he asked. "I mean, he seems to be treating her okay, right? They're not about to break up or anything are they?"

There could be no missing the distinct note of hope in his voice. A chill seeped into my bones despite our being indoors. My heart cried loud ugly tears. What a mess. To-night was a tragedy. When it came to love, a gypsy with a perverse sense of humor had cursed me at birth, of this I was certain. Because the only other thing all of these phe-nomenally bad dating choices had in common was me, and blaming myself did not appeal.

"I don't think so," I said gently. "They seem commit-ted. In love."

"Right." His mouth turned down at the corners. Kicked puppies looked less downtrodden.

"You're hung up on Anne."

"Yeah." His hands tightened around the bucket of popcorn. "How about you and Jimmy?"

"Ha. Yes. My affections are likewise unwanted and un-returned. Aren't we a pair?" I stared unseeing at the hus-tle and bustle of the people flocking through the theater doors. So many people just going about their lives, expe-riencing similar heartache and despair. We weren't unique in the least and yet the pain, it felt so damn big, like it con-sumed me. How perverse that it should be such a common, everyday occurrence.

Good god, love sucked.

"Why don't we just be friends?" I suggested.

Reece sighed, shuffled his feet. "Friends . . . yeah. Still feel like going into see a movie with me?"

"Sure. Why not?"

"The violent one?"

I managed a smile. "Sold."

Curtains swayed in the front window. Someone was snoop-ing. For a man of reasonable intelligence, Jimmy Ferris hadn't been acting particularly rational of late. Of course, my own actions where he was concerned were nothing to boast about.

Reece waited until I'd opened the front door to drive

away and I stood in the cold, watching until his taillights disappeared from view. Date two over and done. Go team Lena. We'd had a nice enough night, but we wouldn't be doing it again. Funnily enough, sharing tales of unrequited love and rebuffed offerings of one's heart did not lift the spirits. Ignoring such things worked better, I think. If ever I'd been tempted to throw my no-alcohol rule to the wind, tonight was the night. But I hadn't. I don't know, it sort of seemed as if I was on this journey with Jimmy and neither of us could afford to fail. Silly but true. Alcoholism was not my burden to bear, and symbolically, I couldn't lighten his load, I couldn't do shit.

"You can come out." I shut the door, put my coat and purse on the side table. "I know you're there . . . lurking."

"It's my house. I can lurk where I want." He appeared out of the darkness that was the living room, black clothes blending into the shadows. "And don't just dump your stuff there, take it up to your room."

"Yes, sir."

"How was your night?"

I smothered a yawn. "Okay. Yours?"

One shoulder rose and fell. "Watched some TV."

"Mm." I picked my belongings back up again. So ridiculous, only Jimmy would have furniture and not let people use it. Like a perfect appearance made more sense than actually utilizing something as per its designed purpose. The man was plain ludicrous. "I'll see you in the morning."

"That's it?"

With one foot on the step, I paused. "I arrived home in one piece thereby disproving the ax murderer theory and removing the need for you to replace me just yet. What else do you need from me?"

"Did you not have an okay time?"

"The movie was fun. Lots of explosions."

"Get along with him all right?"

"Sure, he's a nice guy. He's in love with Anne though so not prime dating material."

"Oh." Face contemplative, he came up beside me, leaning on the railing. He hadn't shaved today and the urge to run my fingers over the prickle of his stubble seemed insurmountable. My fingers dug deep into the leather of my purse, fighting for control. Everything about him called to me, the guarded but curious look in his eyes, his rarely seen softer side.

Maybe if his mom hadn't messed him up when he was a kid he'd have been different, less world weary and damaged, more open. Or maybe if I was more supermodel, less cute and cuddly. What would it take, how many changes would have to be made for him to see me differently? Because he stood less than two feet away from me but it felt like forever. My heart broke ever so slowly and I felt every piece of it shatter and fall.

Nothing I could do about it, not a single damn thing.

I fixed a tired smile to my face. "It was still an okay night."

"Does Anne know?" he asked.

"I doubt it or she wouldn't have suggested I go out with him."

"True."

"I don't really think we should say anything either."

His brows rose. "Why not? Wouldn't she want some warning?"

"He's harboring feelings for her, Jimmy, not planning a surprise attack. It's not our secret to share and it's not like it's going to change anything." I hugged my coat and bag to my chest. "Reece doesn't stand a chance. She's just not interested in him that way. He's been friend zoned and he knows it."

The poor schmuck.

"I don't know if I'd feel right not telling Mal," he said.

"I think it would only cause trouble. Though honestly Mal probably already knows. It's not like Reece is particularly effective at hiding it."

He stared over my shoulder at the wall. "Stupid of him, hanging onto a thing for Anne when he hasn't got a chance."

"Who ever said the heart was smart or that it followed directions?"

Jimmy just shook his head. "That's fucking dumb. He needs to wise up and get over it. It's pathetic, no wonder Anne doesn't want him."

And I just kind of needed to walk away before resorting to violence. This conversation was doing my head in. "Wow. Those are wise words indeed."

The man's eyes flashed in sudden understanding. "I don't mean that you . . . ah, well obviously you're not in the same category as him."

"No?"

"No, of course not." He put his hands on his hips, then changed his mind and linked them behind his head. All the while looking at me like I was just one small step away from the loony bin. At least we'd moved on from him laughing at my feelings.

"I mean, hello! Different situation entirely," he said.

"That's a relief."

"Yeah, you haven't realized yet that it would never work out between us." He looked up at me and I could almost see the cogs and wheels desperately working overtime in his head.

"Talk me through it, Jimmy."

I'm reasonably certain sweat broke out on his forehead. "Well, do I look like the kind of guy who takes relationships, seriously? No, I'm a player."

I cocked my head. "Except you're not, you don't have sex at all these days."

"True. But when I do, I'm not the kind that goes back for round two. Been there, done that. It's like they said at dinner, I don't pretend I'm interested in more." He wrapped his hands around the railing, holding on tight. "And they shouldn't be either. I'm a hell of a bad bet, Lena. Fucked up home life, reformed addict. I mean shit, my issues have issues. I don't want any of that. I just wanna be left alone, you know?"

"If you want to be left alone, then why don't you want me to leave?"

"This I can handle. We give each other shit, there's some give-and-take. It's good. But I can't do more. I just can't." His voice held such absolute heartbreaking certainty.

"How do you know if you've never tried?"

"No." He looked up at me from beneath dark brows, fingers white, he held onto the railing so tight. "There's too much to lose."

I just stared at him stunned. "I think that's probably the nicest thing anyone's ever said to me."

He pinned his lips shut, apparently not happy with the news.

So much information whirling around inside my head. I needed time to make sense of it all, to figure him out. Things were changing again, I could feel it, but I didn't quite understand how yet. The situation was as complicated as the man.

"Anyhoo, I don't think I'll keep dating people," I said, sucking in my stomach. "Let's just concentrate on the other stuff. If anything can convince me you're a monster, the jogging alone should do it."

"Lena, you need to keep dating." Little wrinkles appeared beside his eyes, his jaw tightened. "The next one'll be better. It'll be fun, I promise."

"I don't think god wants me to date. The signs have been quite clear."

"One more," he said, voice dropping to a highly persuasive rumble. "C'mon, just give it one more go then I'll drop it, I promise."

"I don't know . . ."

"Please? See, I used my manners."

"That's great."

"Lena . . ."

"All right, one more then that's it. And I do have a condition. Next date, you're banished to downstairs. You don't meet him and you sure as hell don't interrogate him. In fact, I don't even want to see you. I catch sight of you, it's home on the sofa all night watching TV. No excuses. No ifs, buts, or maybes. Do we have a deal?"

His jaw tensed, shifting beneath his skin. "All right. And the next date'll be better, you won't regret it."

I already did.

CHAPTER TEN

"Adrian sent through info about the first few venues and hotels booked etcetera." I passed Ev my iPad.

We were sitting on the steps, watching the guys work in the new basement recording studio setup. The finishing touches had been put on it the day before and Jimmy had gone all out. The walls alternated black soundproofing with floor-to-ceiling glass and lots of high-tech equipment sat shining within. The delight in his eyes when the guys made all the right sounds of approval was lovely. I had a feeling all the building and equipment was his way of trying to apologize to them for the past, his way of attempting to make amends.

Whatever way you looked at it, the studio was a very good thing.

"Looks like the publicity machine revs up after New Year's. There's not too much booked until then," I said. "A couple of interviews, that's about it."

"Good, they need a break."

"Yeah."

A scrawny Australian guy named Taylor and his gorgeous wife Pam, who had some Native American heritage, were waiting on the doorstep when we got back from jogging (swift stumbling/walking) this morning. Usually after I'd done my torture time, Jimmy would take off on his own for a "proper" run. Today, however, he'd acted mildly delighted to see these guests. The friendliest I'd ever witnessed him being previously was the small smiles Ev garnered for herself now and then. He'd even suffered through a quick hug from Pam, despite his limbs stiffening and his face screwing up. I don't think I'd ever met anyone so averse to letting people get close to them.

Taylor was apparently a longtime friend who also happened to be a roadie/sound tech/recording guru. His wife, Pam, was a photographer. She'd promptly pulled out a very cool-looking camera and started snapping the guys at work in the new studio. I'd followed her around, bugging her with questions.

Fortunately, she hadn't minded at all.

Pam said they were thinking of using the shots for the inside artwork of the next album. She'd even let me play with her camera, giving me tips and showing me which buttons to use. The play of light in the picture and the way it altered the mood was amazing. I'd never been around a real live professional photographer before. All day, whenever I got a chance, I tagged along behind her. It was fun and interesting, challenging in a way admin simply wasn't. Not for me at least. And playing with the camera got me out of my crappy mood.

"Hold it this way," Pam had said, repositioning my fingers around the Nikon.

I'd held it up to eye again, watching as the automatic focus zoomed in and out on various things. "It's amazing. The world looks so different. The detail and light and everything."

"Yes." Pam had smiled. "It really does."

"I don't want to know what one of these costs, do I?"

"No," she'd confirmed. "You really don't."

Jimmy offered Pam and Taylor one of the spare guest rooms for their stay but they'd declined, having already booked into a hotel in town. A pity because I'd have liked the chance to spend more time with her and her camera.

"Sooo . . ." Ev started. "Jimmy called late last night. Wants me to organize a girls' night out. Said something about you needing cheering up."

I cringed. Various factors had made me antsy and agitated all day and this line of conversation was highly unlikely to improve things. "He didn't need to do that."

"I heard about the date with Ben."

"That reminds me, I haven't thanked him for the flowers yet."

Ev shook her head. "Can't believe he ran out on you. Well, I can, I just wish he hadn't."

"The date with Reece wasn't a raving success either. He's a nice guy, but I don't know that I'm in a dating frame of mind."

"Jimmy manage to restrain himself this time?"

I seesawed my hand. "Mostly. It didn't matter, Reece is still hung up on Anne."

"O-kay. That'll do it." Ev handed me back the iPad. She turned her face away, fingers drumming on the wall. "So I'm just going to throw something out there and you can shoot me down or not as you please. I love Jimmy, he's family to me. But, Lena you do realize, he's been hurt in ways we're only just beginning to realize."

"Ev—"

"Please, let me finish." If the sincerity on her face had been an iota less, I'd have gotten up and walked away. My love life pained me enough without this.

"All right," I said.

She played with the end of the plait. "Has he said anything to you about their mother since she showed up in Idaho?"

"No, not really. It's still not something we tend to talk about." And what little he had said was in confidence.

"But he does talk to you. If it's even just a little bit, I don't think you realize what a miracle that is. David said he hardly even discussed their childhood when he had counseling. Just refused." Worry filled her eyes. "It's why you can't leave, if you care for him at all . . ."

"Of course I care for him."

"But you care too much, don't you? That's the problem."

I let my silence do the talking.

"I don't want to see either of you hurt. Jimmy's done a lot of work, just getting himself together in the past six months." She swallowed hard. "He was hell-bent on going through it alone until you. But has it occurred to you that he might not be up to handling these kinds of pressures yet? He was advised not to go into any serious relationships for the first year of his recovery."

"You think I would do something to hurt him?"

"Not on purpose, no."

And suddenly I was angry, I was actually quite pissed. "You know, you can't have it both ways. I'm supposed to care enough to stay and keep putting him first." I pushed to my feet, needing the space. "But I'm not allowed to feel too much and complicate things."

"Lena, wait."

"You think I don't know he's fragile?"

Ev picked up the tablet and rose to her feet also. "I think right now you both are."

And she probably had a point there. Also, I just might have overreacted something fierce.

"What's going on?" asked Jimmy, appearing at the bottom of the stairs looking anything but breakable, on the outside at least.

Awesome. Now David was there too, being all concerned. "Baby?"

"It's my fault," said Ev, climbing to her feet. "I said the wrong thing."

"Lena?" Jimmy started up the stairs toward me.

Down below, David drew Ev out of view, leaving me and Jimmy alone.

"No, I . . . shit." I slumped against the wall feeling ten types of stupid and hormonally washed up. "It's fine."

"No, it's not, don't lie to me. What's going on?" he asked, stopping the step below me. It put us at almost exactly the same height.

Fuck he was beautiful, inside and out, and he would never be mine. That information sat sure and safe inside of me, turning me to stone because it was utterly undeniable. But I was still expected to stay here, be with him, and support him, the job I both did and didn't want with all of my heart.

"I'm being wildly unprofessional again," I said.

He squinted. "That all?"

It was a throwaway question, but still, I gave it serious thought. Inside me, emotions were storming around, being in an uproar. My lack of professionalism definitely wasn't all.

"I need a hug," I said.

"What?"

"I need a hug." I nodded, warming to the idea. "Yes, that's what I need. I mean, don't even get me started on that farce of a date with Ben. But, you know, last night with Reece was pretty damn shitty."

His mouth opened but I kept right on.

"You're my closest friend, right now, Jimmy. With that position does come certain responsibilities."

Eyes wide open, he gave the ceiling a long pained questioning look. "Fuck's sake. Is it not enough that I make sure your favorite chocolate cream pie is in the fridge at this time of the month? Do I really have to put up with this too?"

"Yes. Apparently you do." It probably should have surprised me, but it didn't. We had been living together for several months now and for someone I'd once considered self-involved, Jimmy noticed the strangest things. My period having arrived mid-morning certainly explained my crap mood in the last twenty-four hours. "Though I do appreciate the pie."

"Great. I don't hug," he said.

"Everyone hugs."

"Not me, touching isn't my thing." He crossed and uncrossed his arms. "Unless fucking is involved and we're not doing that."

He was trying to scandalize me. I knew that about him by now. I wonder how scandalized he'd be if I offered. Instead, I said, "You've touched me no less than eighteen times in the past month. You're more of a toucher than you know."

His eyes widened, then narrowed. "You just pulled that figure out of your ass, didn't you?"

"You count drinks, I count touches."

"Hmm. I'm not doing it."

"What are you, a man or a mouse?" I asked, my voice challenging.

"Your boss."

Good answer. Still, in Coeur d'Alene, when he'd wanted comfort, he'd just grabbed hold of me. There'd been no debating, no negotiating. He'd sure as hell never asked what I wanted, he'd just taken what he needed. And what I needed right now was him, every last little molecule inside me knew it.

Fuck it. I launched myself at him.

Jimmy caught me with an "oomph," his hands grappling with my waist. My arms wrapped tight around his neck. I might have accidentally broken my nose on his collarbone but no matter. He was now obliged to console me, physically. The ache in the bridge of my nose could be ignored. The man stood petrified, I could almost smell his fear. But this, being so close to him, was nirvana.

Sheer, unadulterated bliss.

His breath hitched, but then his chest moved fast against me, ribs rising and falling. I waited for him to shrug me off, or, more likely, pry me off with a crowbar. Gradually, rock hard muscles eased against me. A tentative hand patted me on the back, out of rhythm. Apparently, years of musicianship and his innate natural talent had been lost due to my hug. Ah, the power, I would never let him go.

The combined sounds of our breathing echoed in the stairwell.

"Lena?"

"Shh, I'm concentrating." I clung on tighter, just in case he now decided to try and escape.

He smelled crazy good, some nice expensive cologne underlined with the sweat and scent of him. Thank god he'd forgotten about the shirt I'd stolen. The same smell was far fainter on it. Nothing like breathing deep straight from the source. And care of the questing tip of my sore nose, I had struck skin, the base of his neck, even. Wonderful.

"Your nose is cold," he bitched.

"Quiet. You're ruining the mood."

"There is no mood. You're acting crazy is all."

Downstairs people were talking, the muted beating of drums, but nothing mattered more than here and now.

"We done yet?" he asked.

"No."

"One more minute, then that's it, Lena."

"Two."

He exhaled hard. "I better not have to do this every month from now on."

Another timid pat or two. Then, ever so slowly, his

other arm wrapped lightly around me, hand slipping beneath my hair. Fingers stroked back and forth over the back of my neck. We stood there, my breasts mushed up against his hard chest. He rested his chin on the top of my head and I could feel his breaths faintly against my scalp, stirring my hair. Despite the differences in height, we fit together just right. His other hand started firmly smoothing up and down my spine, pressing me into him. Each time it went a bit further, fingers glancing over the small of my back and the beginning of the curve of my ass. My breathing faltered each time his hand went down, dying to know how far he'd go, wishing he'd do more.

My medicinal hug was fast turning X-rated.

"Sorry the dates sucked," he said.

I really didn't want to talk about the dates.

"Tonight's will be better."

Other men could get lost.

"Lena?"

God damn it. "What?"

His mouth was a tight line. "Did Ev really upset you?"

"No. We'll work it out between ourselves."

"You sure? I'll talk to her if you need me to."

"Would you really?"

"'Course."

"You're so dreamy, Jimmy Ferris," I happy sighed.

"Christ, now you're really weirding me out." His hands settled on my hips. "Okay?"

"Yes."

He gave me the makings of a hesitant smile while he straightened his shirt, setting himself to rights. Oddly, he seemed almost shy, looking down, avoiding my eyes.

"Right. I'm getting back to work." But he didn't move. Instead, he looked up at me like he was no longer entirely sure of who I was or what I was doing in his house. A shaking hand smoothed down the front of his shirt.

I smiled gently. "Thanks, Jimmy. I needed that."

He paused, as if he might say something, but then didn't. A distracted nod and he disappeared.

"Say one word about what I'm wearing and I will kick you." I told the man sitting on the bottom stair and I meant every word of it.

"I wouldn't dare. When's he arriving?" Jimmy looked up, checking out my jeans and tight black sweater. Lord knows I had the assets, might as well use them. Despite my ample bosom, his careful blank expression never altered. He'd been down in the gym, working out since everyone left an hour or so ago, sweat dampened his hair and the back of his gray T-shirt.

"He's not," I said. "I'm meeting him in town."

"You don't trust me not to give him shit."

"No, I don't."

"Why don't I drive you in?"

"Because I don't trust you not to give him shit, we just established that. Besides, I can drive myself," I said. "Us women are liberated these days. Why, next I bet we'll even get the vote!"

He raised his brows and gave me a dour look. "Right. You can't take your piece-of-shit car, it hasn't even been run in the last few months. I drive us everywhere."

"My piece-of-shit car will be fine. Thank you."

He let out a long-suffering sigh, as if admitting defeat. "Take the Mercedes. At least then I'll know you got there okay."

"You're sweet to worry about me."

A grunt.

"Can I take the 'Cuda?"

"Not a fucking chance."

I grinned. "You wound my soul, Jimmy Ferris."

He just watched me, fussing with my hair in the entry-way mirror.

"What are you doing tonight?" I asked.

His shoulders and arms flexed, straining the thin cotton of his T. "Haven't decided."

Something in his voice made me pause, a hint of lone-liness or a certain sadness I hadn't heard before. The man seemed almost verging upon despondent. Cranky and grumpy were normal, this was not.

"None of the guys are coming back?" I asked. "You didn't want to go hang out with them?"

"They've been here working all day. We'll be in each other's faces all the damn time on tour. No need to start now."

I didn't like it, but it did make sense. "No game on? I won't be here to complain about the unendurable monot-ony of it, for once."

"Not really in the mood for TV."

"What are you going to do, then?"

He groaned. "I'm a grown man, Lena. I can entertain myself."

"I know you can." I hugged my coat and bag in front of me. "But I'm trusting you to tell me if you need me around tonight."

"I do not need you around."

I hesitated while cold eyes watched me.

"Keys are in the car," he said.

The situation got me to thinking about what would happen to Jimmy if I did leave. No matter how many ici-cles he made with his gaze, he wasn't frozen inside, he just liked to pretend as much. But I'd seen his pain and his self-doubt. Perhaps what Ev said earlier had stuck with me. Allowances had to be made for keeping him on track. I needed to think ahead, see to his best interests. Love came in all sorts of shapes and sizes, but if it wasn't based upon doing what was right for the one you loved, then what was it worth, really?

Nothing.

And that's what my feelings for him were growing into, love. No matter how scary it was, there was a certain calm to be found in facing the truth. It might or might not have been fated, but it was fast becoming fact.

"I think you should date too," I said, the words small and tight. It's a wonder I could find them at all.

"What?"

"I think you need to start dating again for both our sakes. Just think about it."

He sniffed. "I'm doing fine as I am. It's a dumb idea."

"Holing up here, hiding from the world? That's not a long-term solution."

"No, you're right Lena." He slapped his hands together, rubbing them briskly. "I know, let's go to my favorite bar and hang out for a while. We'll do a couple of shots for old time's sake and then I can pick up a girl or two, bring them back here to play. Sounds fun, yeah? I think we'd all have a real good time."

I had nothing to offer on his suggestion.

"What, you don't like that idea?"

Change of plans. What I most wanted for Christmas was to wipe the stupid smirk off his face. No one else drove me this crazy. "If you're finished being an asshole, I'll explain what I meant," I said.

"Oh, please do."

"I think you need more," I said, my voice emphatic. "You need friends outside of me and the band."

"So I'd be dating to make you feel better?"

"No, Jimmy." I bundled my coat up against my chest like a shield. "You'd be dating because you're ready. Because you're a wonderful man who has a lot to offer a woman when you're not being a complete and utter bastard like now."

He gave me a slow clap. "That was beautiful, Lena. Like poetry. I think I almost cried."

"What even is it when you get like this? Are you scared? Is it your turn to PMS, what is it exactly? Do you need a hug?" I crossed the floor between us. "Because I'm trying to understand what motivates this shit with you. But at the end of the day, you're a grown man in control of himself and you're choosing to act like an absolute prick and you're pushing away people that care for you in the process. Explain that to me."

"It's a gift."

"Try again." I towered over his seated form in my heels, furious. The man was damn lucky there were no weapons at hand. Then slowly he stood, the solid length of him almost forcing me to take a step back. Except I refused to. "Well?"

The edge of his mouth curled up. "You never back down, do you?"

"Why the hell would I?"

There almost seemed to be a hint of gray in his eyes. Like he'd seen too much, like it had aged him in ways. His voice softened. "So fearless."

"No, I just refuse to be afraid of you," I said. "I think too many people over the years have gotten into the habit of scurrying off to do your bidding out of fear of being the target of your snide comments, or at the merest hint of that famous Ferris anger. It's bullshit. I will not be like that with you. You're not an overtired toddler throwing a tantrum, you are an adult. You can control yourself if you choose to. And it's about time you chose to."

His just stared at me, face expressionless.

"Well?"

He raised his hand and ever so carefully, lifted a strand

of my hair, tucking it behind my ear. Then he bent in close enough for his lips to brush my ear, his breath warm. "You're right, I was an asshole to you just now."

"I know," I whispered back.

The smile was in his eyes even if it was missing from his mouth. He studied my face, taking his time. "You never have to be afraid of me. I'd never hurt you."

"I know that too." Not on purpose he wouldn't. Never on purpose.

"Go on. Go on your date, Lena."

My chin rose. "Think about what I said."

He exhaled then gave me a begrudging nod. "Deal."

"That's the eleventh time you've checked your phone in the last half an hour. Something wrong?"

"God, I'm sorry," I said, slipping the stupid thing back into my bag. "You were explaining to me exactly what a sound technician does and I zoned out on you which was horribly rude."

My date gave me his crooked smile. Damn, he was cute. The problem with spending quality time with the godlike Stage Dive boys was, you lost touch with normality. They were the ideal that porny dreams were made of. Right here beside me, however, Dean Jennings was all that and then some. Brown hair fell to his shoulders and a silver ring pierced his lip, green eyes watched me with faint humor.

"I've worked with Jimmy on and off for the past six years," he said. "I know he can be a handful, so if you need to get back to him we can do this another night."

"That's good of you, but he's fine. He wanted me out of the house, so he's probably in need of some space."

Dean nodded. "I think it's great the way he's gotten clean and everything."

"Yes."

"Couldn't have been easy."

"No."

He picked at the label on his bottle of beer. Around us, the cool people partied in the underground dive bar. It was in Chinatown, a band and hangers-on favorite.

Maybe this bar was also the one Jimmy had referred to as his pick, though it wasn't the kind of place I could imagine anyone wearing a suit. Some of the women here were definite eye-catchers. There was a jukebox belting out indie classics, a couple of pinball machines, and a pool table. The place had a nice, dingy, sticky-floored vibe and they also did awesome chili fries. I popped one into my mouth and my taste buds wept with gratitude. Either that or I was drooling, they were just that good.

"Sorry. Guess you can't really talk about him," said Dean, summoning me back to the present once more.

I half covered my mouth with my hand. "No, not really."

"There's stuff in my contract about discussing them too, but since you're one of the in crowd . . ."

"It's a strange world we live in, isn't it? Being on the fringes of famous people's lives."

He laughed. "Yeah, it is. Some of the stuff I've seen over the years, back when all the guys were single and partying every night, it was pretty insane."

"Groupies and all that sleazy stuff?"

"All of it." He took another swig of beer.

Well, now this interested me. I sat forward, leaning my elbows on the table of the booth we were sharing. "You must tell me all. Leave out no details."

Dean barked out a laugh. "They'd kill me."

"If you're not willing to sacrifice yourself to sate my curiosity, what use are you?"

He shook his head, eyes shining. Such a pretty man,

not drop-dead gorgeous like Jimmy, but then, who was? I myself was no top model and yet Dean shuffled a little closer, his warm smile never fading. Now and then, his gaze dropped to the mounds of my breasts. I could forgive him that, in fact, I even kind of liked it. To be appreciated as an actual female was a fine sensation, one I hadn't had in quite this way for a while.

"I can tell you about the time he invited a couple of girls on stage in Rome about five years back. That one's pretty much public knowledge anyway," he said.

I gasped in true shock horror fashion. Gossip was the worst. "I remember hearing rumors about that."

"Jimmy'd been drinking heavily, they all did back then. At first it was cool, the girls were just hanging off him while he performed. But then during Dave's guitar solo the three of them start making out. One of the girls gets her hand down Jimmy's pants while the other's undoing his belt buckle and going for the zipper. Jim's laughing his ass off, doesn't care. Security went on stage and stopped them, but the cops shut the show down due to indecent exposure. Fined him a shitload of money over it."

"Wow."

"Lucky no one got a clear picture."

"Very."

Dean slowly shook his head, admiration shining in his eyes. "Jimmy was one hell of a guy back in the day."

I frowned. "He was out of control, hurting himself."

"Yeah. That too."

"I think I prefer the man he is today."

"Of course," Dean said quickly. "Absolutely."

"You were never tempted to pick up a guitar or some other instrument and get out on stage yourself?" I asked, changing the subject.

"I'm no Jimmy Ferris. Crowds scare the crap out of me.

All those people staring at you, gives me the chills." He mock-shivered in demonstration.

I laughed. "No, it doesn't really appeal to me either."

"Yeah. But those guys, they're made for it. Especially Jim. The man's a living legend."

I nodded in agreement. Then the most shitty, horrible thought descended upon me and I couldn't shake it. "Oh god, he isn't paying you to take me out tonight, is he?"

"What? Fuck no, of course not." Dean reared back. "Why would you even think that?"

My forehead met the table, dark hair falling around me in a curtain to hide my idiocy. "Sorry. I didn't mean to imply you'd prostitute yourself for my benefit."

"Lena?"

"I'm so sorry."

"Lena, look at me."

A hand gently applied pressure beneath my chin, encouraging me to rise. His eyes were so wonderfully green you almost had to wonder if they were contacts. Not that it mattered, I was just grateful they weren't ice blue. Also Dean's face was wider than Jimmy's, less sculpted. He wasn't as tall, but he was looking at me as if he liked what he saw, like I met his criteria, whatever that might be. No disdain, no impatience. It was refreshing.

"Hey," I murmured. "So, let's just forget that I asked that."

Ever so carefully, he tucked my hair back behind my ears, just like Jimmy had earlier. The contact was surprising, but I held still, letting Dean get closer, curious as to where this might go.

"I like to embarrass myself horribly now and then," I said. "It keeps life interesting."

"Right, I'll bear that in mind." He smiled. "I think what we have here is an opportunity to have some fun. So, with that in mind, you feel like going dancing with me, Miss Morrissey?"

My smile might have been slow, but it was wholly genuine. "I'd like that."

Dean walked me to my car close to midnight. By "my car," I meant Jimmy's, of course. Dean took one long look at the shiny overpriced vehicle and said a whole lot of nothing.

"Jimmy insisted I take it," I said, suddenly feeling self-conscious. "He worries about me driving in the rain. I tried to say no, but. . . ."

Dean just nodded.

"Yeah, anyway." I needed to shut up. Talk about protesting too much.

The sweat on the back of my neck from dancing gave me goose pimples out in the cold night air and my body felt pleasantly worn out, my brain ambling toward sleep. I'd have to wake up to drive home. If I put a scratch on his car, Jimmy would kill me.

"I had a really good night," I said, offering Dean my hand.

With a grin, he took it, tugging me gently in toward him. His lips touched mine. Warm lips, warm breath, warm everything, and his face was so close. I didn't close my eyes, I guess I was a little stunned. The moment had crept up on me, silly but true. Good god, his eyelashes were really long. Also, I'd never kissed anyone with a lip ring before. Metal pressed against the side of my mouth, it was a weird sensation.

He stepped back and smiled. "I'd like to do this again."

"I'd like that too." And I meant it, we'd had a great night.

He slid his hands into his jeans pockets.

"I'll see you later." I fossicked in my purse for the keys. " 'Night."

Once I was safely inside he leaned down, waved. I waved back. Then he stood on the pavement, waiting until I drove away smiling.

Tonight had been so much better, there was really no comparison. A date with a nice, intelligent man who surprised me with a soft kiss at the end. It was sweet. You didn't need to find someone who turned your world on its axis to be happy; inner body explosions and mini-heart attacks were not necessarily the answer to long-term joy. But this warmth, contentment, it was nice.

Jimmy would be pleased.

CHAPTER ELEVEN

We were halfway around the block the next morning when Jimmy pulled to a halt, his breath coming in harsh pants. No, all right, that was me. Jimmy wasn't even breathing heavy despite jogging having split me inside somehow. It couldn't be healthy. Though I'd made it farther before falling apart than yesterday. Progress was a slow, gradual, agonizing thing.

"You got in late last night." He bent at the waist, stretching.

"Yeah, we went dancing." No wonder my calves were being so unforgiving this morning.

Jimmy made some noise. I don't know what it meant.

When I'd called mid-date to check in on him, he'd said something about messing around with a guitar. The conversation had been curt. Basically he'd reported that he was fine, told me to get back to my date, and then hung up on me. A normal sort of phone conversation where he was concerned.

He straightened. "Thought about what you said, about me dating."

I tried to keep my surprise off my face. "And?"

Apparently the trees down the street were riveting because his gaze stayed glued to them. "Called an old friend. She, ah . . . she got sober recently too, went through rehab. We talked for a while. She's thinking of coming up from LA so we can catch up."

"Jimmy that's great." I tried to smile. Honest to goodness, I gave it my all, but my face felt stiff, wrong.

"Catch up" could mean so many things. To my twisted mind, catching up rock-star style had everything to do with copulation and nothing to do with cake and coffee with friends. This was, after all, Jimmy Ferris we were talking about. His abstinence had always surprised me. He was such a big moody animal prowling about the house, snapping and snarling. All too easily, my mind provided lurid images of him sinking his teeth into someone, tongue licking, nails scratching. Oh, god, now I was panting for an entirely different reason. My filthy mind was out of control.

He'd said he only touched when he fucked. I bet this old friend of his would have finger marks all over her inside of a day, lucky girl. And to think it had been my bright-ass idea.

God, I hated me.

"Great," I said, trying to conjure up mental images of Dean. So cute and sweet and stuff, so much more within my reach. He didn't have heartbreak written all over him the way Jimmy did. There was no need for a warning sign on his handsome forehead.

"Yeah." At long last he looked my way and I hid my misery as best I could. "Listen, Lena. I am sorry I was an asshole when you brought it up, guess you caught me off guard."

"You're apologizing to me?"

He did the chin jerk thing.

"Wow."

"Don't make a big deal out of it," he muttered.

"No. No, okay. Can you just say it one more time for me?"

He rolled his eyes. "I'm sorry."

"You're forgiven. Don't do it again or I'll kick your ass into next week."

"You're about half my size."

"Ah, but I'm highly motivated and own a fine selection of pointy-toed boots. Consider yourself warned."

"Right," he said, voice somewhere between wary and amused. Little did he know exactly how serious I was. Some of those boots could do real damage on the feet of a woman with a grudge.

Then he stepped closer, inspecting the general area of my mouth.

"What?" I asked, half tempted to cover my face with my hand.

"You've got a bit of beard rash."

"Oh." I scrubbed at my lips, not that it would do anything apart from making it worse. Guilty feelings slunk around inside me for some reason, like kissing on the first date was a crime. It had all happened so fast. Dean stepped into me and his lips were on mine and I let him. That was the truth of it, all feelings for Jimmy aside, I'd let Dean kiss me. He didn't make it to second base.

"How was it?" he asked, still standing much closer than necessary, still staring at my lips. Fear of the foreign look in his eyes held me immobile. Exactly what he was asking after, I didn't want to know. And if I didn't ask, I could pretend he meant the food last night or something equally harmless like the weather.

"It was . . . nice," I said.

"Nice," he said, voice low and mesmerizing. "You liked it."

I shrugged, committing in any other way felt dangerous somehow.

"How far did you let him go?" His gaze roamed over my neck, my chest, and everywhere he looked I lit up, sweaty, disheveled, and smelly as I was. When he looked at me that way, it didn't matter. It took all of my restraint not to cross my arms over my chest. I could only hope my sweatshirt was thick and baggy enough to hide any evidence of arousal. My nipples' ongoing infatuation with the man was a terrible, misguided thing.

"W-what?" I asked.

"Under your clothes or over?"

"I'm not telling you that."

"I'm thinking over," he mused. "You don't strike me as the type to give it away too soon."

I pushed back my shoulders, stood straight. "You're right, Jimmy, I'm a pure shining virgin. My ability to keep my knees locked tight is an inspiration to all. Now can we please stop talking about this?"

"You're uncomfortable?"

"Oh, like that's not your goal here."

The corner of his mouth twitched. "What can I say? You interest me, not many do."

"That's great and I feel all warm and tingly about it. But I'm still not telling you what goes on between me and another man." I got my legs moving again, the stumbling gait of what passed for me jogging. Such style. Such grace.

A moment later, he fell into step beside me. As always, his long legs and fitness levels made a mockery of my huffing and puffing.

"C'mon, Lena. You can't let me live a little vicariously through you?"

"Nope."

"Aren't you impressed I even know the word, a high school dropout like me?" He chuckled, but he didn't sound exactly happy about it.

"No."

He gave me a cynical smile. "Right."

"With everything you've accomplished in your life, you think I'd doubt your drive or intelligence?"

"All the drugs and shit you mean? Yeah, I accomplished a fuck load of that."

"You're a successful businessman and a seasoned, multi-award-winning, critically acclaimed musician," I countered. "Shock horror, you made some mistakes. Who the hell hasn't? You paid for them and moved on."

His eyes narrowed. "That what you really think of me?"

"Yes. You also have a sad tendency to be an occasional jerk but we're working on that. I have great hopes for your complete recovery."

The rigid set of his jaw let me know he wasn't convinced. Insecurity over his education obviously ran deep.

"It's not like I went to college," I said. "I didn't do well enough to get a scholarship. A friend's dad owned a business and he gave me a chance to try out as the receptionist, lucky for me. Otherwise, I'd probably be flipping burgers for the next fifty years."

He nodded. "Thanks."

"No problem."

We ran for a while in silence. But of course, he couldn't leave it alone, could he?

"So, tell me what constitutes a good first date, Lena? You know about this sort of shit. Teach me, how do you woo a girl, hmm?"

"Can't talk. Jogging."

He snorted.

Neither of us spoke for half a block and just as well. Conversation with Jimmy was hazardous to my health. The man really did need to come with a big red warning sticker on his forehead. Actually, the sticker should cover all of his face. If you only had to deal with his hot body you might stand a chance resisting. Oh, and his voice—good god, his voice—it was created to make a girl's sex parts sing. Not that I wanted to think about sex or singing or Jimmy, nor any lustful and passionate variation of all three combined.

My mind, however, was clearly against me.

"You know, I think I'm improving," I said eventually. My need to fill silences was a definite weakness. "I'm not getting winded so easily."

"Good. So you're going out with him again?"

"Are we still talking about this?"

"Yes. Why're you giving him a second date?"

I groaned. "Because he was nice."

"You're sure using that word a lot. Nice. He's *nice*. You had a *nice* time. I don't think any woman's ever used that word when it comes to me."

I peeled wet strands of hair from my cheek. "You can be nice when it suits you."

"I don't want to be nice, Lena." He chuckled. "But you using it to describe Dean makes me think that dating him is about as interesting as sitting through a business meeting with Adrian. Maybe you should date someone else."

"Hey, Dean was a lot of fun to be with. For one, he doesn't pester me with inappropriate personal questions like you do."

"You going to fuck him?"

"Jimmy!"

"What?" He barely hid back a smirk. "What's the problem?"

"I am certain there was something in the employment contract about never raising the subject of sex. Also, you're being rude."

"The employment contract?" A dimple flashed. "I think we're a bit beyond that, don't you?"

He had a point. "Probably, yes."

"If I cared about the employment contract I could have fired you day two."

"You could not have."

He gave me an amused glance.

"Well, maybe a little. But your life would have been the poorer for it."

"Right," he deadpanned. "What if he'd taken you to an expensive restaurant? Would you have let him feel you up then?"

"Are you suggesting I prostitute myself for a linen table cloth and a three-course meal?"

"Just wondering. You wouldn't be the first."

"Holy shit, you're serious." The man made my head spin in all the ways. We really did come from different worlds. "That's so . . . incredibly . . ."

"What?"

"Sad. Just sad. Jimmy, you need to aim a little higher. Try dating people that aren't going to fall onto their backs with their legs spread based on proof of your bank balance alone."

"It keeps life simple, easy."

"Ea-sy. Huh. You know, easy doesn't seem to have done you much good. In fact, easy made a mess of things for you from what I can see."

More eye rolling. If he kept that up he might just do himself damage.

"The right sort of complication might be just what you need, Jimmy."

"Waste of time." His voice was absolute. "If it isn't happening on the first date, why go back for more?"

"Hmm, I think you need to figure that one out for yourself." The world blurred for a moment and I blinked the sting of sweat out of my eyes. "Do you only hang out with a woman if you want to have sex with her?"

"Pretty much . . . apart from you." He pushed back his hair. Only just did I manage to keep my lusty sigh to myself. It was really quite sad how much I enjoyed such a simple thing.

"What about this girl who's coming to visit you?"

"What about her?"

"Well, is she just for sex or are you actually going to attempt to have some sort of relationship with her?"

"I dunno," he said. "Haven't given it any thought."

So many things I could say. None of them seemed quite right or unbiased, however.

"So what if it's just sex?" he said.

"Don't you want more?"

"Got everything I need. You said I should try going out more. That's what I'm doing. If I happen to be doing that with a girl I like to fuck, what's the big deal? I got you to talk to, I don't need *a relationship*, whatever you're thinking that is."

I rubbed at my eyes with the heels of my hands. Stupid sweat, so messy and inconvenient. Of all the human secretions to experience around him, he had to inflict this one upon me.

He just shook his head at my apparent foolishness. "So, what, you put out date three or four? There about?"

I stopped, staring at him with absolute wonder. "Do I ask you how often you jerk off, Jimmy?"

"Least once a day, lately." He threw the information out there like it didn't even matter. "My libido kind of disappeared there for a while but it's back with a vengeance now. You're probably right on with the dating idea because if I don't get something soon I'm gonna break my fucking wrist."

"Stop it!" I covered my ears, taking deep, even breaths. That was the key. Any lurid pictures of Jimmy fisting himself just could stay the hell right out of my mind, my dirty, smutty, way overly descriptive mind. "We're not the kind of friends that talk about this stuff."

"You take sex too seriously."

I stopped trying to block him out given I couldn't if I tried. "I do, huh?"

"Yes." And his smile, oh god his smile, I wanted to wipe it off his face with a pickaxe. I'd be gentle, you could trust me.

"While you don't take feelings seriously at all," I said. "They're a joke to you."

"They're not a joke to me. But the two don't have to go together. That's the mistake you make."

"Oh, god, Jimmy, this is so clichéd. You're the man whore and I'm the sensitive chick. And I'm not even particularly sensitive, for heaven's sake, it's just that compared to you . . ."

"Compared to me, what?"

"Well, you're so repressed. You don't let yourself feel anything until you're boiling over and out of control."

He shook his head, letting out a harsh breath. "Explain to me how the fuck me saying sex and emotions don't have to go together lead to this point. Because you're losing me."

"Look, what you said is true enough," I said. "Sex can be just a physical activity to make you feel good. I have no problem with that."

He scoffed. "You just condemned me for that."

"No. I just condemned you for insisting it could be nothing more than that. I just think you should have sex with people you actually like for a change. It might be refreshing for you."

One thick shoulder twitched, I guess it was a shrug.

"You think I should have just slept with Dean last night then—on the first date?"

"Not saying that." One of his tennis shoes pawed at the ground, big feral beast that he was. "I just think, talking about fucking or actually fucking shouldn't be a big deal. It's human nature, everyone does it."

"Except for us."

"Yeah, except for us. I had to clean the slate you know? Just strip everything back and start from scratch, get myself right," he said with a sigh. "Though giving up sex was nothing in comparison to cocaine. I felt like a god on that stuff, nothing could touch me. Stopping wasn't easy."

"No, I bet it wasn't."

He smiled at me, he actually double dimple smiled at me. Crap. Not only did my knees weaken but my toes curled it was so stunning, star shine and moonbeams couldn't compare. Unicorns could take a flying fuck.

"So, Lena, darling, tell me, for curiosity's sake. When *do* you put out?"

I stepped closer, going toe to toe with him. He got worried then, the dimples disappearing and his forehead creasing. So he fucking should.

"Jimmy, my love," I said, my voice soft and sweet. "I don't fuck a guy until he has the balls to actually man up and talk to me about his feelings."

Laughter followed me for the better part of the jog back home.

The doorbell rang out just after two in the afternoon. Downstairs, the band and crew were making sweet music following a lunch consisting of everything we'd had in the fridge. I'd already alerted our suppliers to the need for more, pronto. With the guys working here all the time, our usual order could easily be tripled and then some. Mal alone seemed to eat his weight in food at each meal. How he then managed to jump around and pound the drums, I had no idea. I'd spent the day making myself useful. When they were recording, it made sense to just pitch in and help where I could. If that meant I made coffee and fetched sodas then so be it. Dean had come into work with them today, a happy bonus.

I jogged up the stairs, every part of me jiggling. Kindly note, however, I did not lose my breath, the jogging was starting to pay off. Yay me!

Just in case there was some random paparazzi hanging around I loosened my ponytail to hide my face. The security camera screen showed one lone statuesque woman looking ten types of awkward on the other side of the door. Big black sunglasses hid her face. Hmm, interesting.

"Hello?" I stood back, opening the door just wide enough to get a good look at her. Then my whole world stopped.

Liv. Fucking. Anders.

The film star.

That's who Jimmy's old friend was and she had obviously wasted no time in getting to Portland to *catch up*. My heart gradually restarted, slow and painful was the way. Six feet worth of trim and tanned with white blonde hair looked back at me from atop her designer eyewear. I'd be the dumpy brunette in jeans and a long sleeve T-shirt then. Lovely, please just ignore my pale and pasty skin. She wore cute strappy sandals despite the cold wet weather and even her pedicure was immaculate. For the sake of my pride, couldn't the woman at least have a chipped nail or something? Surely, it wasn't too much to ask for.

My own fault really, I guess that's what you got for falling for a rock 'n' roll Adonis. His ex-girlfriends or fuck buddies or whatever Liv was, were bound to be flawless. Why, the care he took with his hair was evidence enough. As if he'd stick a body bit into anything less than the best.

"Hi," I said, in my smallest voice.

"Lena?" With a hand she lowered her glasses. "You are Lena aren't you? Jimmy told me about you, said you'd be here."

I blinked.

She held out her hand. "Hi."

My hand shook long before she started shaking it. Luckily, she seemed to write it off as my being starstruck. Let the lady think what she wanted. "Come in, please."

"Thanks." Her smile wavered a little at my odd behavior. Screw her, I was doing the best I could under the circumstances. Visions of Jimmy and Liv together filled my mind. Him with his dark hair and her with her sunny Californian good looks, such a dramatic contrast they'd make, the camera would just eat them up.

And I couldn't do it. I couldn't go down those stairs and see the expression on his face when he saw her. It would kill me. He smiled for me so rarely, even a flash of dimple made my day. If Liv Anders got an out-and-out grin I'd melt into a puddle of misery right there and then.

So instead, I kind of hooked my thumb in the general direction of the basement. "They're down there. Working. They, um . . . yeah. You should go down."

"All right." Her smile turned plastic, fixed in place. Guess her acting skills weren't so great after all. "Nice to meet you."

"Yeah."

"I'll see you later."

I had nothing.

With dainty steps, she descended. I wanted to hate her, it would have made life easier, but Liv actually seemed half decent, friendly even. If only she'd been a rampaging bitch. My intense dislike would have been so much more straightforward and reasonable.

"Hey." Dean wandered out of the kitchen. He'd turned up that morning with Taylor and been busy in the studio all day so we'd barely gotten a hello in. "I was thinking, maybe we could do something tonight?"

"Sounds good." I gave him the best smile I had in me.

Nice, normal Dean. The sight of him failed to soothe my heart however on account of it being the most clueless organ in existence. I should demand a transplant. "I'd like that."

"Great. Been trying to get a moment alone with you all day."

"Have you?"

"Yeah, but it's been busy down there." He moved closer. "I like your hair up like that."

"Thank you." Gratitude leached from my pores at his kind words, it was pathetic really. His grip slipped down my arm, fingers sliding over mine until we were holding hands. My muscles unwound, relaxed. I wasn't alone. My life wasn't over because Liv Anders had arrived, I would go on.

This was good.

For such a small intimacy hand-holding packed a punch. Sex was great, but sex wasn't everything and when it came to Dean, I just wasn't ready yet. Hand-holding worked. And it led to more kissing, a little necking maybe, some touching, followed eventually by a bit of rubbing in the right places. The steps leading up to sex should be enjoyed at a leisurely pace, the foreplay of dating and getting to know someone could only be done once so it should be done right.

And Dean was nice.

Jimmy could think what he liked about the word. Nice *was* nice. It had its place in the warm and fuzzy ways of beginning to feel for someone, and I wanted to feel for Dean. Feeling for him was pleasant, painless, and plausible. Three things I'd begun to appreciate more and more. The days of me throwing my heart and soul at Jimmy Ferris's feet were done.

A sliver of guilt existed over dating Dean when I had feelings for Jimmy. But if I didn't want those feelings, if I was willing to work at getting past them . . .

"What are you thinking about?" he asked.

"Work junk." It wasn't entirely a lie. "I should head back down."

"Me too," he said, giving me his lopsided grin.

Which was how we wound up walking hand in hand down the steps toward the recording studio. Right when the guys and company were pouring out of the place.

Jimmy's eyes latched onto our joined hands and his face hardened. It might have just been me, but I'm pretty sure the temperature in the room rocketed to lava levels.

"If she's here, she's working, Dean," he said, his voice flat and unfriendly.

What the hell?

"Right." Dean dropped my hand like it had been dipped in poison. "Sorry, Jim."

"Actually I was just on my break," I said, despite the fact I'd never actually had an official break since starting with him. He probably owed me quite a few by now.

A muscle jumped in Jimmy's jawline. "Lena, I asked you to get the info on the interview for next week."

"It's waiting for you in the office."

"I'm not in the office, Lena. I'm here."

"So I see. Just give me a moment and I'll fetch it for you."

"If it's not too much trouble."

"Not at all, Jimmy. Anything for you."

His jaw hardened. "And we can do without you carrying on with your boyfriend during business hours from now on," he said.

Carrying on? For fuck's sake. There was a lot I could say in response, but all of it came with the distinct possibility of putting Dean straight back in the firing line. "Duly noted."

"Great."

"Awesome."

He just glared at me.

Therefore, I got the last word in and I won. Take that, you god damn arrogant tyrannical shithead. I didn't know if he was jealous or what, but perhaps he'd snap and fire me this time. He certainly seemed angry enough, his eyes promising all sorts of damage. Part of me almost hoped he would, my heart hammering inside my chest. Do it, do it, do it.

"That's enough," he snapped.

"I didn't say anything."

"You didn't need to."

True enough. We could read each other far too well at times.

Everyone had frozen sometime during our verbal combat, all the better to watch the carry-on. Even Liv the movie star seemed discomforted by the scene. Her head turned this way and that, eyes wide with obvious confusion.

Then Mal let out a loud wailing noise. "I hate it when mommy and daddy fight!"

The crazed drummer barreled up the stairs in a dramatic exit. If Dean and I hadn't flattened ourselves against the wall we'd have been knocked over. David choked on a laugh, Ben at least had the good grace to turn his back before he cracked up, and behind them, Taylor and Pam said nothing. The movie star still had the oblivious thing going on. Then her hand crept beneath Jimmy's arm, her fingers wrapping around his strong bicep and squeezing before her fingers dropped away.

"Jimmy?"

He sort of started, the anger dropping from his face. "Yeah, Liv. Why don't we go out?"

I could see why the woman had made millions, her smile lit up the room. Fortunate for me and my sensibilities, Jimmy's face remained more reserved.

"Can I have a word with you first?" I asked him. We needed to clear the air about this hand-holding business. That, and I couldn't stand the thought of him leaving with her, of what might happen between them next. I just wasn't ready. Another minute or two maybe and I'd be fine, if we could just fix this latest fight.

"Not now," he said.

"But—"

"Not now." His voice was a whip and it cut through me sure and true.

The guys amusement cut off dramatically.

"Jim," said David, face serious.

"Stay out of it, Dave." Jimmy held out his hand to Liv and she took it. Apparently, the matter of me had been closed.

"We'll head off," said Ben, giving me worried looks as he passed me on the stairs.

I smiled back determinedly. "Later, guys."

God, did everyone know about my great unrequited love?

Or no, my boss's sweet words had gotten them worked up. Perhaps they thought I'd burst into tears. Like hell, it would take more than harsh words from Jimmy Ferris to do that. Dean now stood apart from me, concerned for his job no doubt, which was fair enough. We'd gone on one whole date, not enough to throw your career away over. When David went past, he reached out, grabbed my hand and squeezed it. I don't know how Jimmy reacted because I followed his brother straight up the stairs without looking back. Didn't mean I wouldn't make him regret the put-down later, however.

Liv said something down behind me and Jimmy answered in a suitably subdued voice. I didn't want to know what.

I'd asked for this, told Jimmy to date, pushed him into it even. But then he'd made me date too and then torn into me for daring to hold someone's hand. Rage boiled up inside of me, an inferno's worth. I didn't need to fetch shit. Jimmy was going out, he didn't really care about the interview info. Instead of doing my duty, I power walked my fine self up to the second floor. I didn't run, because to run would insinuate I was some sort of coward making an escape. I didn't slam my bedroom door shut either, calmly locking it instead.

Everything was fine.

I was okay.

And Jimmy Ferris could go fuck himself.

CHAPTER TWELVE

My bedroom door handle started rattling just after five, waking me from my afternoon slumber. Three hours I'd been holed up in my room. A lesser mortal might have cried themselves to sleep, but I'd had a nap with a slight amount of tear duct drama attached to its beginning.

Whatever.

I was over letting Jimmy Ferris turn me inside out. It was time to start acting like a grown woman and put the nonsense behind me.

"Lena." More rattling.

I raised my weary head off the pillow, rubbing at my sore eyes.

Some thumping. "Open the door."

"Have you come to apologize?" I asked.

"What the fuck do I have to apologize for?"

Slowly, I sat up. "Oh, I don't know. Try being a hypocrite, yelling at me, and embarrassing me in front of other people for starters."

A moment of silence. "Don't be ridiculous, open the door."

"No."

"Open. The. Door."

"We can discuss this tomorrow, Jimmy. Good night."
So I'd go to bed with no dinner. For once, my belly didn't
mind and my heart was too torn up to care.

At which point, Jimmy went off. "It's my fucking house
and you work for me. It is not okay for you to be carrying
on with him during business hours. Where the fuck is the
respect? You're on my time then and you damn well know
it. It's absolute bullshit. You're both completely out of line.
I pay you, you're my assistant, and he's got the fucking gall
to try something with you behind my back in my house. He
has no business touching you ever. I don't want to see that
shit happening again, he's to stay away from you. The pussy
didn't even stand up for you, Lena. Did you notice that? I
don't know what the hell you're thinking of having anything to do with the little dickhead."

I gaped at the door. Clearly, the man had lost his ever-
loving mind. He wasn't making a single lick of sense, but
he kept on keeping on. Apparently the fact that he'd set me
up with Dean in the first place had been completely forgotten. Amazing. I had to tune out for the sake of my sanity. I
crossed my legs and leaned back against the headboard,
waiting him out.

Eventually, the silence was deafening on both sides of the
door. I strained to hear something, anything.

Then the crashing began.

Boom!

The first bone-jarring noise made my whole body
jump. Second time around wasn't much better. My bedroom door smashed open and Jimmy strode in, seeming
twice as tall as normal, putting most mountains to shame.
Righteous indignation blazed in his eyes, red tinged his
skin. Maybe I should have been afraid, but I was too busy
being pissed.

"Did you just kick my door down?" I shrieked the obvious. "Are you out of your fucking mind?"

"My door, yeah." He marched on over to the bed, seeming ten foot tall. Then suddenly he stopped. "Have you been crying?"

"Nope. I'm all good. Thanks for asking. My door on the other hand, not so much!" I'm sure my most likely red-eyed, blotchy-skinned appearance told a different tale. But screw him. Such was the beauty of the ugly cry, its legacy lasted for hours no matter some beauty sleep. I probably looked like roadkill, slammed down by the semi-trailer that was rock 'n' roll legend Jimmy Ferris.

He sat on the edge of my bed. His broad shoulders seemed to have fallen by half a foot at least. "You have, you've been fucking crying. I don't believe you."

Give me strength, like it was some crime against him and I should be the one to apologize. "My eyes were allowed to do what they want, Jimmy. Nothing in the employment contract about that."

Meanwhile, the poor door was damaged beyond repair, he had actually kicked it in. Insane. How the hell this day had taken such a turn for the overly dramatic, crazy-town worse, I had no idea.

"Lena." His voice was a soft command. "Look at me."

I exhaled "What? What do you want me to say, Jimmy?"

He turned away, pinning his lips shut.

What a mess. I grabbed a pillow and hugged it to my chest.

There seemed no obvious telltale signs of his screwing around with Liv Anders, no bites on his neck or what have you. Not that it would be screwing around on me, it just felt like it. A faint headache from all the tears lingered behind my sore eyes. We'd started the day out laughing and teasing each other. How sad to have ended it this way.

Jimmy crawled onto the bed, sitting beside me with his

back against the headboard. The heating clicked on, just about the only noise in the entire house.

We sat side by side, saying nothing.

I studied him out of the corner of my eye, hands fidgeted in his lap, picking stray bits of lint off his black jeans, smoothing them down. Once he was done with his preening, he crossed his arms over his chest. But his fingers kept stretching out, then curling, over and over again.

"You hurt me," I said, because one of us needed to be brave and fess up.

His chin jerked upward.

"Don't do the chin thing, say something." I waited a moment. My patience was not rewarded. "Why'd you kick my door down?"

He turned toward me, eyes tortured.

"Jimmy?"

"I couldn't stand it, you locking me out." The words sounded dragged out of him, kicking and screaming. "You should have answered me. You shouldn't have . . . you shouldn't have done that."

"Why not?"

His eyes narrowed. "What the fuck do you mean why not?"

"Why should I open my door to you if you're yelling at me? If you've been acting like a complete bastard and hurt my feelings? Stop for just one minute, put yourself in my place and tell me, why should I let you in?"

He made some snarly noise.

"And don't give me any of the I'm-your-boss, it's-my-house, I-pay-you shit," I said. "Yes, it's all true. No, it doesn't actually matter in this circumstance, we're beyond that."

"But—"

"No."

His nostrils flared and emotion shone bright in his eyes. "You shouldn't have locked me out."

I just looked at him.

"I needed to . . ." A hand gestured aimlessly in front of him while he searched for words. "I needed to be able to talk to you, face to face, all right?"

For him, that was all. There was nothing else to it.

Words sat on my tongue, desperate to get out. It took me a moment to clear my head, form a coherent sentence. "You needed to talk to me so badly that you kicked my door down."

Nothing from him.

"Jimmy, does that sound like a normal friendship to you?"

"I know. I fucked up," he said, voice rough.

"What did you do?" Fear filled me. Apart from the paleness he seemed okay, pupils normal. Please god let him not have taken anything.

"You."

"Me?"

"You. Today. I fucked up. I'm sorry, Lena, I just . . . I'm sorry. Shit just came out my mouth and I knew it wasn't right." He winced. "I'm sorry."

"Honestly, Jimmy, the words just aren't cutting it for me right now."

"What do I do then? Tell me. I don't know how to do this stuff," he said. "React right."

"What did you mean to do?"

"I wanted to fix things, but I just broke them more." Eyes agitated, he gritted his teeth. "In the band, there was always the music to smooth things over if shit got out of hand. If the music's going right everything else just falls away. But there's nothing like that here with you. I don't know what to do when it gets messed up."

"You talk to me, Jimmy. You don't go crazy yelling and you don't get mean. You just come and you talk to me about it," I said. "It's that hard, and that simple."

He made no reply.

"Why did you flip out when you saw me holding Dean's hand?"

"I don't know." He gave a low growl and drew back, staring me in the face. "Just tell me what to do to apologize. What do you want? I'll buy you whatever."

"I don't want you to buy me anything."

"Well, what can I do?"

"Nothing," I said, because asking for him naked was probably out of the question. Begging him to never again have anything to do with Liv Anders probably ran a close second. "You can fix my door. That would be nice."

"Of course I'll fix the door, but you've gotta want more than that." He seemed so adamant, eyes alight with fervor for the idea of making reparations. Problem was, I couldn't have what I really wanted. We'd already established that.

"Fine," I said. "Let's go for a drive in the Barracuda to my favorite ice cream parlor."

He shrugged. "Sure."

"But." My pointy finger of doom hovered in front of his face. "I'm driving."

His mouth opened.

"Non-negotiable. You just asked how you can make it up to me and I'm telling you how. I'm driving the Barracuda and you're riding shotgun. You don't make comments about my driving and you act happy."

He gave me a snotty look. "Fine. But just to get ice cream."

"Absolutely, Jimmy."

"You think you're clever, don't you?"

I smiled and huddled in against his side, using him as

a buffer against the wind. His big hard body had to be useful for something. It was so damn cold, my teeth were chattering. "Who me?"

He raised a brow and licked at his waffle cone, topped with pistachio icy goodness. I didn't stare at his tongue. My gaze just so happened to wander in its general direction is all, not the least bit my fault.

"Isn't the salty ocean air bracing, Jimmy?"

"Yours is melting."

"Oh." I dealt with the triple caramel delight before it could drip off my fingers. "Mm, yum. Best ice cream ever. Didn't I tell you they had the best ice cream here?"

"Yes you did. Many, many times on the hour and a half drive out here."

"Hey, I could have taken us to Seattle." I shrugged down deeper into my coat. "Be thankful. I let you off easy."

"Right."

"You're having fun, aren't you?"

He gave me a look of much judgment.

"Admit it."

The faintest of smiles passed over his lips.

"Can we sit in the car already, I'm freezing?"

"No. You're not dripping ice cream in my car, Lena. That's all leather upholstery, a classic automobile, have some respect."

"I can't believe you care more about a thing than you do for my comfort." My cell buzzed silently in my pocket. "Three missed calls."

Jimmy leaned over, getting in my space. Pity I liked having him there so much. "You meant to be doing something with Dean tonight?"

"I forgot." I flicked through the voice to text messages. "Crap."

"He seems a bit pissed in the last one."

"Says the guy who kicked in my bedroom door." I texted Dean back a brief apology.

"Don't think he'll be pleased. That didn't sound very sorry."

"Yeah, well, you confused the hell out of that situation with your carrying on earlier. And it could have occurred to Dean that I might be just a little upset after that scene with you."

He stared out at the black expanse of the ocean. Waves crashed on the shore. "Said I'm sorry."

"Saying you're sorry isn't an immediate fix all, Jimmy. Actions have repercussions, you of all people should know that."

A pause. "You haven't asked about Liv."

My whole body tightened, I'd been trying damn hard not to think about Liv. Actually asking about her seemed plain suicidal. "Should I have? I guess I figured that was none of my business."

"I took her to a hotel and we talked for a while. I called just to check in with you." He wandered a few steps over to the trashbin, dumped his ice cream cone. The broad expanse of his back in the black woolen jacket a sharper shadow against the rest of the view.

"You did?" I asked, surprised.

"Yeah. You didn't answer."

"No, I was asleep."

He turned around, the wind blowing his hair in his face. With a hand he held it back. "I started worrying you'd gone. That you'd quit me and left like you were going to."

"I wouldn't do that without talking to you first."

"I wasn't sure." He avoided my eyes. "After the way I treated you, thought you might have just taken off."

"That's what got you so worked up?"

He sucked in his cheeks, nodded. All of a sudden, the ice cream lost its flavor for me too. I likewise chucked the rest of mine, licking my sticky fingers clean. Jimmy watched all the while, face wiped of expression. This conversation was a minefield. All I could do was to tell the truth, do my best by us both.

"I was jealous," I admitted, putting it all out there. "That's why I wanted to talk to you, to ask you not to leave with her. I just wasn't quite ready."

"Yeah, I know."

I nodded, put my hands in my pockets and waited. And then I waited some more.

Nothing.

I held in my groan, but only just. "Jimmy, now's your turn to admit that you were jealous when you saw me holding Dean's hand. Relationships are kind of a give-and-take thing, you know?"

He snorted. And then he scoffed. Then he kind of turned in a circle, his mouth wrinkling like he'd tasted something foul. I half expected him to bolt and run given all of the avoidance tactics previously displayed.

"Anytime you're ready," I said.

"I . . ."

"Yes?"

He winced. "I guess, I didn't think about what it'd be like if you really liked one of them."

"Even though that was the entire point to my dating other men? To like one of them more than I like you."

A shrug.

"You over it now?" I asked.

"Yeah." He chuckled. " 'Course, it's fine. Won't happen again."

Oh, the dubiousness, it filled me right up. But I couldn't make him admit to caring about me more than he liked. I couldn't make him do shit. "All right, one more go. I did enjoy going out with Dean and I was looking forward to seeing him again."

"Okay. Good."

"On one condition."

He gave me a wary look. "What?"

"You meet Tom."

The regal chin rose to unforeseen heights. "That replacement guy? No. Fuck no. We talked about this, you have to commit, Lena."

"This was always meant to be temporary gig. Given how much we push each other's buttons, I think it might be wise to have a backup plan in case I can't continue." I squared my shoulders, standing tall.

"I don't think we should do that."

"Jimmy—"

"If you just tried, Lena."

And this was about the point where realization struck home, tough love was tough on everyone involved. Sometimes, however, you just had to. "Jimmy, I'm not asking you. I'm telling you. You're going to talk to the man."

The surprise in his eyes, I wish I'd taken a picture. His jaw moved, face tensing. "Fuck, all right."

I held his car keys out to him, moonlight glinting off them. "Do you want to drive us home?"

He snatched them out of my hand. Something told me it was going to be a long and painful journey.

CHAPTER THIRTEEN

The next evening, Jimmy's attitude had not improved. His resistance to the very tall, thin, and polite Tom Moore-comb read plain as day in his body language. Should he turn any further in his seat, his back would be to the poor man completely.

"Tom was involved in couples counseling, Jimmy. Isn't that interesting?" I said, jaw aching from clenching so much. A tension headache was slowly but steadily brewing behind my eyes. "Jimmy?"

The jerk didn't even look up from his phone. It was like trying to deal with a toddler, a very cranky one. Sadly, he'd seated himself opposite the room from me, out of kicking range. I'd hate to have to smack him in the head with a pillow in front of Tom. Perhaps it could be left as my final die-hard option.

"Jimmy?"

He looked up at me from beneath his dark fringe. "What?"

The doorbell rang. Fortunate for him really.

"Let me just get that while you two talk." I gave the ignorant jerk a meaningful look.

He just blinked.

Before I could reach the door, Mal and Ben barreled on in.

"Lena, helloooo." Mal shook my hand so energetically I feared my shoulder would dislocate. "Looking foxy and strict in your business suit. I would totally take orders from you if my heart and soul were not spoken for."

"Thanks." I'd bought the navy suit in an attempt to make the right impression on Tom. Jimmy had just given my new outfit a weird look and told me double breasted didn't suit a girl with such assets. I'd been nervously fussing with the buttons on the jacket ever since.

"We in the living room?" asked Ben, already making his way into said location.

"Wait, we're—"

"Hi." David, Ev, and Anne followed close behind. Ev and Anne were dolled up, the first in jeans and a slinky top, the second in a smokin' hot green knit dress. Their awesome style however did not answer any of the questions pouring into my head.

"Hey," said Ev, kissing my cheek while David gave me the rock-star chin tip.

"I'm really looking forward to tonight," said Anne.

"Great." I smiled.

She stopped and studied me. "Shit, you have no idea what's going on, do you? Ev."

"What's up?" Ev about turned on her cool boots.

"Lena doesn't know anything about this."

Her face fell. "What?"

"Nope."

"Crap."

"Yep."

"Please," I said, getting a little desperate. "What's going on? Why are you all here?"

"Jimmy invited us over for dinner," said Ev.

"He did?"

And through the open door marched what I could only guess was a small army of butlers and one chef. So many black suits with one tall white puffy hat standing head and shoulders above the rest.

"We'll get set up," said the eldest of the butlers entering.

"Right," I murmured, turning back to Anne and Ev. "He's outplayed me."

"Sometimes," said Ev, throwing an arm around my neck. "You just have to follow Jimmy's lead."

"Are you insane? He'll lead me straight to hell."

"Perhaps. But he likes you, so I'm guessing he'll bring you back out safe and sound."

I narrowed my eyes on the insane woman. "We're interviewing my replacement. Right now."

Her face fell, yet again.

"We need to get in there," said Anne.

"So, Tom. Tom was your name, wasn't it?" Mal projected his voice so well. It positively rang through the marble halls of Jimmy's minipalace.

All three of us females bolted for the living room.

The drummer sat beside the poor innocent Tom. His muscular arms were stretched out along the back of the two-seater sofa.

"Yes, Mr. Ericson. It is." Tom's rather pronounced Adams apple bobbed.

Oh god help him, they were going to eat him alive. I leveled a death glare at Jimmy, a futile, wasted effort since he failed to notice.

"Tom, would you consider yourself, a rock 'n' roll man?" Mal asked.

My heart stopped when Tom visibly paused. "Ah, actually, I prefer classical music."

Ben huffed out a laugh. He was so off my Christmas card list. "Ah yeah, he'll fit in just great. Good call, Lena."

"He's here to discuss becoming Jimmy's sobriety companion," I said. "What music he listens to is irrelevant."

"Of course, of course," said Mal, soothingly. "Just curious."

Ev had perched on the arm of David's chair while Anne sat sandwiched between Ben and Jimmy on the couch opposite Tom and Mal. We had a full house. With all the seats taken, I chose to stand.

"Now, Jimmy likes to spend his free time working out," said Mal. "How do you feel about jogging and free lifting, Tom?"

By the look of him, I highly doubted Tom lifted anything heavier than a book.

"Mal, that's enough." I interceded, someone had to.

"You now go jogging with him, Lena. He's used to having company. Would you deny him that? We all just want what's best for Jim, don't we?"

The man in question had a hand covering his mouth, his face half turned away from me. So fucking glad he was amused.

"He still jogs on his own as well." I stood, hands on hips.

"Perhaps. Tom, Lena also spends all of her free time with Jim, watching TV or just generally hanging out with him. Will that be a problem?"

The man gave me a worried look. "Being a sobriety companion is a major commitment, of course. But . . . she doesn't have a life of her own at all?"

"Of course I have my own life," I said in a slightly shouty voice.

"Jimmy is her life, Tom. That man is everything to her." Mal crossed his legs and lazed back against the couch. "Are you willing to do as much?"

Tom blanched.

"Lena has also been working with Jim on breaking

down his boundaries regarding physical touch. A sort of hug therapy shall we say. I believe her next step in this delicate process will be sleeping with him nightly with advanced cuddling practices. Will that be a problem for you?"

Tom looked around in confusion.

"Right." I clapped my hands together, summoning the room's attention. "Jimmy, we're talking in the kitchen. Now."

He rose slowly from his chair, face calm as could be.

I turned to the drummer. "Mal, you say another word and I shoot you."

He drew back, aghast. "Threats of violence are not necessary. Tom, quick, counsel her, she's going over the edge!"

At which point, thank god, Anne stepped in and saved the day. She did this by sitting with her legs further apart. It was amazing really, almost as if Mal had some sort of extrasensory perception when it came to the girl and her sex. His gaze shot to the widening gap between her knees and all else fell away. The shadow beneath her skirt seemed to call to him on some mystical higher level. Or around the groin level, hard to say which exactly.

"What was I saying?" Mal muttered, leaning over, trying to get a better view up Anne's skirt.

"Nothing important," said Ben, playing on his phone.

"Something about how Tom seemed great for the job." Ev wound an arm around David's neck. "Not that we'd ever want to lose Lena."

"Right, right." Mal leaned a little further.

There were no ends on the two-seater Tom and Mal sat upon. And so, when Mal finally tipped over far enough in his attempt to see between Anne's thighs, he toppled straight off the end of the couch. David chuckled while Ev smiled. Big Ben didn't even notice, so taken was he with his texting. These people, I loved them as much as they drove me out of my god damn mind.

Anne just smiled. "Oops! You okay, babe?"

"All good." The man set himself to rights, still seated upon the ground. "But I need to tell you something in the bathroom."

"Do you?"

"Yep. Right now."

"Something good?" she asked, a certain lustful twinkle in her eyes.

"Yes, something good. It's a show-and-tell type thing, I think you'll really like it."

"Okay."

Mal sprung to his feet, hands in the air. "Hooray! Quick, let's go. Hurry, woman, no time to waste."

With much giggling, Mal carried Anne from the room. Ah, young love, all the feelings.

"After you," said Jimmy, standing beside me being all calm. It instantly brought my rage back to the forefront.

"Actually, let's make it the office," I said. "I forgot your dinner crew are busy in the kitchen."

"Sure, Lena."

I should have known he had something planned. For someone so resistant to the idea of my replacement, he'd gone all out dressing for the appointment. A black long-sleeved button-up shirt, black trousers, and shiny shoes adorned his fine self. His hair was carefully slicked back. Usually hanging around home warranted just jeans and T-shirts. The signs had all been there. But I could still salvage this situation damn it, right after I ripped Jimmy a new one.

Except it was too late. Tom got to his feet, his movements jerky. "I think I better go. You obviously have guests to entertain."

I stepped forward. "What? No. Tom—"

"That's a pity," Jimmy replied. "Nice to meet you Tom. See you around."

"Quiet." I turned to the counselor, hands outstretched. "Please, Tom. Just . . . if you could just give me a minute to talk to my employer. They're not usually like this."

"Don't lie to the man," said Jimmy. "This is exactly what me and my friends are like all the damn time."

I growled. "Way to throw him in the deep end."

"Honesty is the best policy."

"You're such an asshole."

"Language, Lena," he tutted. "Watch the fucking language."

Tom cleared his throat, straightening his already unbearably straight tie. "Mr. Ferris, I'm afraid I'm going to have to withdraw my interest in the position. And Lena, you seem like a nice girl, but this relationship you have with your employer isn't healthy."

"Hey," said Jimmy, looking down his nose at the man. "You don't know anything about it."

"Believe me, Tom, I'm aware," I said. The man obviously knew a train wreck when he saw one.

With one last nod, he strode out, taking with him my last hope of an easy exit. It had always been a pipe dream really, I should've known better. Nothing about Jimmy had ever been easy.

Speaking of which, I took the opportunity to smack him in the arm with the back of my hand.

"What was that for?" he bitched, rubbing at his arm as if I'd actually hurt him. Such a damn baby.

"Don't even start with me."

His scowl increased. "We talking in the office?"

"No, why bother? You've already managed to run him off," I said, folding my arms beneath the swell of my breasts. "Well done, Jimmy."

"You said I had to meet him. I met him."

"You take orders from her now?" Ben asked, putting down his phone for once. "When did this start?"

Jimmy didn't even spare him a glance. "Shut up, Ben."

"Yes, you met him," I said. "And then you terrified him. You probably just took ten years off his life."

"That wasn't me. That was Mal. Fuck, no one can control him."

I poked him in the chest. "*You* unleashed Mal upon that poor unsuspecting man. It was cruel, Jimmy."

"These people are my family, Lena. What, I'm supposed to hide them away, act like I'm ashamed of them? The guy was a judgmental dickhead with a stick up his ass. He would have lasted two seconds with me. Never would have worked."

"That is not true. You had your mind made up before he even walked in."

He cracked his jaw. "Look, just let it go, Lena. Everyone's here. Can we have dinner now?"

"I've got a date with Dean. Enjoy your dinner."

"What? You didn't tell me about that."

"You knew I was going to go out with him again."

Little lines sat alongside his lips and the story they told was not one of joy. "But not tonight. I organized this."

"Yes, behind my back. So sorry, I can't make it."

His chin rose and for a moment he said nothing, just looked at me. "You don't look sorry."

"Yeah? Well, I guess I'm mad at you right now," I said, my blood still rushing through me at a rate of knots. "And it's kind of hard to care about your feelings when you give so little thought to mine."

"That's not fair," he bit out.

"Oh, really?"

"You know I'm trying."

"Not today, you weren't," I said. "Today you just did

whatever the hell you wanted and fuck what matters to me."

Someone made a noise and I actually startled, spun on my heel, and gaped. I'd completely forgotten about the others. Entirely forgotten about our three-person audience, just sitting in the wings, watching the drama. David looked shell-shocked, his mouth hanging open. Ev was busy rubbing his shoulder, offering comfort. Meanwhile, the bass player's eyes were wide and white as moons.

"Huh," said Ben.

Down the hallway, Mal and Anne fell out of the ground floor bathroom, both laughing. They were still putting their clothes back to rights. It made for a perfectly timed distraction if I could just make a break for the door.

"That was fast," said Jimmy, voice cutting.

"But it was meaningful," cried Mal. "Shut up, Jimbo. What would you know about significant intimate relationships?"

"Seems Jim might know more about them than we realized." David gave his brother a speculative look.

Jimmy gritted his teeth. "Fuck off, Davie. She works for me. End of story."

It didn't hurt. It couldn't. Even my idiot heart had to accept the truth eventually. This particular harsh reality had been shoved in my face so many times I'd formed thick ugly scabs where the wounds would have been.

"Ah, I see," said Mal, still buttoning up his jeans. "Interesting. I'm going to tell you what I told Killer at puppy training today when he tried to mount a teacup poodle he'd only just met. If she means something to you, you gotta do the woo, son. You can't just be trying to stick it in."

"Fuck's sake." Jimmy scrubbed at his face with his hands. It would have been amusing if it hadn't been about me.

"And on that note, I'm out of here," I said, waving and walking backward. My hip of course caught the corner of the side table, a swift or smooth exit beyond me. "Shit, ouch. Have a nice night."

"You all right? Lena, c'mon. Blow him off." He swallowed hard. "Don't worry about that counselor guy."

"Tom. His name was Tom."

"I organized dinner to try and apologize to you about the door."

I shrugged into my coat. "Not necessary. I'd already forgiven you for that. Why don't you try apologizing for sabotaging the meeting with Tom instead?"

His lips thinned.

"Right. Well, why don't you give Liv a call, Jimmy? I'm sure she'd be delighted to get an invite. I'm meeting Dean in town soon so I have to go. 'Night." I jogged down the stairs. Right then, I just had to get away from him as fast as I could. A pity I'd be missing out a night with Ev and the guys. Despite the insanity they were beginning to feel more and more like family. Right now, I could have done with some of that.

The fake biker bar was hot and crowded and I most definitely wasn't having fun. If one more nice, clean, leather-clad cool person accidentally knocked into me I'd punch them in the face. This was, apparently, Dean's crowd. He seemed to know everyone here. Sure as hell, no self-respecting biker would step foot inside the place. You didn't have to be an expert in MC culture to know the place was a fraud. I'd more chance of tripping over a trust fund baby's leather loafer than a real live biker boot.

Bet they were having fun at Jimmy's dinner party.

Maybe I shouldn't have tried to force Tom on him. Crap, I no longer had a god damn clue what the right or wrong thing to do was regarding Jimmy Ferris. If I ever had to begin with. From day one I'd been out of my depth, wading in shark-infested waters. I wondered if he'd called Liv and invited her over as suggested. Jealousy slithered up my spine. Dating was the right thing for Jimmy, it was. My inability to find inner peace and harmony over it was my own damn problem.

Time to suck it up, baby.

Dean stood a few feet away from me, deep in conversation with some guy about the values of different soundboards. No one could blame him. Tonight, I'd officially been voted world's worst company. I played with the straw in my gin and tonic, pushing the slice of lime first to the left, then over to the right. Back and forth, back and forth. I'd yet to take an actual sip, it just felt wrong. Like I was cheating somehow, stupid but true.

Stage Dive blared out over the sound system and it was all I could do not to scream. Further proof of my predicament. My whole world was Jimmy Ferris and it was my own damn fault. For years I'd been drifting, getting over the betrayal of my delightful sister and her wonderful fiancé. It was time to start making plans again. If I could just figure out what I wanted.

Maybe I should talk to Pam again, ask about how she got into photography. There'd been something about lining up the shots, seeing the world through the lens that appealed to me. Bored, I pulled out my cell and started snapping off some pictures. The swaying dreads of one of the male bartenders as he shook up a cocktail. A crowd of patrons' hands, reaching across the bar, calling for service. A partial shot of a couple, the two women leaning in close, holding hands. This was fun. My night had been saved.

I lined up a view of some of the bottles behind the bar. The flat-screen beside them caught my eye and I lowered my camera. On screen was a face, an eerily familiar one. The marrow in my bones turned to ice.

"Oh, no."

They'd cleaned her up, but it was still definitely her, Jimmy and David's mother. Her normally pale sickly skin had been covered in garish makeup. She looked orange with coral pink slashes instead of lips. Still too thin with all sorts of nasty shit shining bright in her blue eyes, the bitch. Next a series of pictures of Jimmy flashed up, him walking into rehab and another of him obviously high on something. Then there was the snake herself, sitting on a couch, pouring her heart out to the camera if the dewy look in her eyes was any indication. Text ran along the bottom of the screen which was good. I couldn't hear a thing over the music.

"I'm homeless. I'm on the street while they live in mansions. They've turned their backs on me because they have money and fame. They're ashamed of the simple loving home that they came from. It's such a betrayal. My heart is broken, I don't know what else to say."

A big fat tear ran down her face, leaving a streak in her makeup. The equally tarted-up blonde interviewer reached across, clasping her hand, offering comfort. My stomach rolled queasily.

"Shit," I muttered.

"Lena?" Dean grabbed at my arm. "What's wrong?"

"I have to go. I'm sorry, I've got to go." I shook him off, not even looking back.

He called out something, but I didn't slow down. Bye-bye biker bar. Heels couldn't get me home fast enough, so they had to go too. I hopped along, tearing off first one then the other, dumping them both. The bitter cold of the concrete stung the soles of my feet, dirt and grit sticking to my skin. All that mattered was getting home.

Jimmy.

Please let him be okay. He wouldn't take this well, no one would, your own damn mother selling you out. The woman was pure evil. My heart pounded and sweat beaded on my forehead. People got out of my way, a good thing.

"Where's the damn keys?" I raged, searching through my bag, completely forgetting the Mercedes would open just because they were near. Thank fuck for technology.

I flung myself into the car, slamming the door shut behind me. Engine on and I was away, rushing through the nighttime traffic. Someone got in my way and I let loose with the horn. The guy flipped me the bird, as if I cared. Though if a cop saw me driving this way I was done for.

It seemed to take forever to get home and when I did, every light in the house was blazing like some ominous beacon standing in the mist. A horror movie couldn't have done it better. I pulled into the driveway, tires screeching. One of the butler dudes looked up from where he was packing stuff into the back of a white van, his face startled.

Into the house I ran. "Jimmy!"

Ev's face appeared at the top of the stairs. "Up here, Lena."

I might have busted a lung or two somewhere along the way because all I could do was pant. I'd gotten there, however, and that's all that mattered.

Everyone was loitering outside of Jimmy's bedroom door, including Liv. Had she been invited before or after I decided not to attend? It didn't matter.

Tension and pain lined David's face. "Lena, hey. He's refusing to talk to anyone, locked himself in. She did a real hatchet job on him, went after him with the worst."

"I can imagine." Given she'd focused her attack on him in Idaho, it made sense. "Can you give us a minute?"

Lots of worried looks. Mal and Ben both deferred to David, waiting on him to speak.

"Please," I said.

At long last, David nodded and slowly, the group headed down stairs, Anne nudging Liv along. No matter how many times Liv looked back, I wasn't meeting her eyes. One apocalypse at a time and all that. I waited for the last of them to go, the marble freezing my feet. Then I knocked on the door. "Jimmy?"

No answer.

"Jimmy, it's just me. Open the door please." I knocked again, then tried the handle. It was locked of course. "Jimmy."

Nothing.

I placed my palms flat against the smooth wood in entreaty. "I know you're upset and you want to be alone, but I'm not going away until we've talked. You need to let me in, I have to see that you're okay. Please open the door."

Silence filled the hall.

"Jimmy?"

Nada.

"One way or another I am coming in there." I rested my forehead against the door, frustration gnawing at my insides. There were no booms or crashes at least, just a scary sort of silence. The thought of where his head might be at terrified me. I hated feeling helpless. His hissy fit the other night when I'd locked him out now made perfect sense. Man, we were screwed up. Just his assistant my ass.

"James Dylan Ferris, open the god damn door." I smacked my palm against the door, waiting and hoping, though I didn't really expect him to answer. The stubborn jerk. "Fine. Don't say I didn't warn you."

If he could do it, so could I.

"You're not keeping me out."

And really, how hard could breaking down a door be? People did it all the time in the movies. I'd been jogging lately and was in better shape than I had been, despite the sweat currently coating my back. Sometimes, a girl just had to do what a girl had to do. And I had to get to Jimmy. He hadn't opened the door to his family so getting them to help didn't seem right. First, I'd try on my own. For all I knew, he could be crying again and if I let David and company see him in that condition it wouldn't be good. The man had his pride.

I took a few steps back, squared my arm, and rammed the bastard. Gave it all I had.

Bam!

And holy shit, ouch.

The door rattled and my arm stung from shoulder to elbow. My funny bone went beserk, making me wince. All right, so it was harder than it looked. Time to try something else.

I raised my leg and braced myself, taking a deep breath. There was no room for fear. Yes, I could and I would do this because I was woman, so hear me roar.

Instead, I howled.

My foot struck the door and pain reverberated up my leg, wave after endless wave of it.

"Motherfucker!" My ass hit the floor (which also hurt) and tears filled my eyes. "Ow."

The door opened. "Lena?"

"Hey." Care of watery eyes, the vision of Jimmy swam before me. "Hi."

"What the fuck did you do?"

"I was trying to kick your door down. It didn't work." My voice was not high, pathetic, and plaintive. I did not whimper. Instead, I held my sore ankle tight with both hands, swearing up a storm on the inside. "I think I might have sprained it."

Many footsteps pounded up the stairs.

"She all right?" That sounded like Ben.

"Get some ice," Jimmy directed, kneeling beside me. "Lena, what the hell did you think you were doing? You're not strong enough to kick in doors, for fuck's sake."

"Well, I didn't know," I hiccupped, blinking madly,

trying to stem the embarrassing stream of tears running down my face, rivers of the bastards. Luckily, Jimmy stayed between me and everyone else. Sometimes hiding really was the best response if you hoped to have any dignity left come morning.

"Let me see." He lifted my hands away, gingerly feeling up my ankle. "Wiggle your toes."

I did so.

"Probably not broken then."

"No."

With gentle fingers, he brushed off my sole. "Why are your feet all dirty?"

"News about the interview came up on a TV in the bar. Have you ever tried to run in heels?"

"Okay, calm down." Without warning, he slipped an arm beneath my knees. The other went behind my back and then up I went. Whoa, the man was strong. I heard no knees creaking or any complaints of lower back pain. All of the weight lifting he did must be paying off. He carried me in and placed me on his bed while I blinked the tears from my eyes. My ankle had apparently been replaced with a hot throbbing mess.

I'd never been in Jimmy's room before. He had a big-ass bed covered in supersoft black sheets—Egyptian cotton would be my guess. The walls were painted a soft gray and some dark wood furniture was carefully arranged. No wonder he'd been aghast at the lived-in appearance of my room. Apart from the smashed lamp on the floor in the corner, the place was immaculate. He saw me look at the broken light and said nothing. The shadows in his eyes were a horrible thing to see.

Damn the woman to hell for hurting him this way. Hadn't she done enough damage when they were little?

"I always figured you'd have mirrors on the ceiling," I

said, tipping my head back, trying to take his mind off the drama.

"I'll get right on that." He sat on the ginormous mattress beside me, placing my foot in his lap. "What the fuck was going through your head out there, huh?"

"Reciprocity. You destroy hotel rooms and kick stuff in, now I beat down doors. We have something in common, you know? It was going to be a beautiful moment, really bonding."

"Lena," he growled.

"I had to get to you." It was the simple unadorned truth. Didn't mean I needed to be looking at him when I said it, however. Ever so slowly, I flexed my ankle, turning it this way and that. It ached, but it wasn't the pass-out-and-die kind of pain any longer. Now it seemed closer to some mild form of torture. "Crap, ouch."

"Dave, call a doctor," he yelled to the hallway. "I need them here now."

"On it," he said.

Oh, great. Everyone was present to see me in my moment of triumph. I slipped a finger on either side beneath my glasses to wipe away any last remnants of tears. Two nights running I'd been reduced to this state. When had my life gotten so crazy? I shrugged out of my coat, got comfortable for the duration.

"Here." Ben rushed in, handing Jimmy a bundle of ice in a tea towel.

He held it against my heroic war wound, the chill giving me goose flesh. Though frankly, now that I could see clearly, Jimmy didn't appear to be all that impressed by my bravery and determination. Dark hair fell around his face as he frowned at my foot. There were a good five or six wrinkles on his forehead, a critical mass of creases. The man was seriously unhappy.

By now, everyone else had wandered on in, drawn by the drama. Liv didn't seem particularly enthralled by the goings on either. Though enthralled didn't quite fit and neither did confused. A mix of baffled and dismayed might best describe her expression.

"You need anything else?" asked Ben, hovering a few feet back.

"No," said Jimmy, staring at the French polish on my toes, compliments of the beautician he'd paid for. "We'll just wait for the Doc."

David slid an arm around Ev's neck. "All right, we'll hang downstairs until he arrives. Yell if you need anything."

Jimmy nodded, still holding the ice pack to my ankle. His other hand firmly braced the underside of my foot. As if I'd try to get away if he wanted to touch me, I was too far gone for such wisdom.

People shuffled on out.

"Jimmy?" Liv's voice had a slight tremor to it.

"Talk to you later, Liv."

Her hands moved restlessly at her sides. "I probably better get back to LA. I've got fittings starting in a few days."

"Right."

"Okay." Liv pasted on a pretty smile. Full marks to her, the woman was one hell of an actress after all. "Bye."

"Yeah." He didn't even look at her, the jerk. It was highly tempting to kick him with my good foot, make him be polite at the very least. But that would not only solve nothing, it would also be extremely hypocritical of me. Despite knowing Jimmy should date, seeing him with another woman hurt well beyond the current throbbing in my foot. It was just that the pain in her eyes was one I knew all too well, I couldn't help but relate.

Me and that pain, we were best buds on oh-so-many

levels. Jimmy Ferris was hell on a girl's heart (and occasionally on the ankles too).

Liv left.

For a few minutes we sat in silence, my slowly freezing foot resting atop his thigh.

"Jimmy?"

"Hmm?"

"Will you tell me what happened?"

His fingers tensed around my heel. "We were sitting at dinner and suddenly everyone's phones started going nuts. Apparently she only got fifteen grand for it, she should've held out for more. Adrian's got lawyers on it, but . . . I told him to let it go."

"Why?" I gasped.

"The stuff she told them, it's all true. Not like she signed a waiver when she gave birth, you know. Guess she's entitled to her slice of the cake."

"Like hell. She's entitled to exactly nothing."

A smile ghosted across his lips. I could only just see it through his mess of hair. When I'd left, it had been neatly slicked back. Now, his fingers had obviously staged some sort of revolt. The need to reach out and slide those strands back behind his ear so I could see him was huge.

"Did you see it?" he asked. "What she said?"

"Just the bit where she was saying she was homeless while you two live in mansions."

"Well you missed the best part." His chin almost touched his chest. "I did use to yell all sorts of shit at her, throw stuff. Only ever hit her once, though."

My throat tightened to the point of pain. "Why did you hit her, Jimmy?"

"I came home and she was cleaning the place out, ready to finally leave," he said. "I was fourteen. Dave was busy over at Mal's house, thank god. One of her stoner friends had a car loaded up in the yard with everything we had of value. Not that there was much, the TV, microwave, shit like that. She came walking out of the house carrying Dave's acoustic guitar. He worked his ass off mowing lawns all summer to pay for that thing. It was just a cheap one from the hockshop, nothing really. But he'd wanted one for so long, thought it was the shit."

"I bet he did."

"I told her to put it back, told her that it would break Dave's heart, but she didn't care. Said he was spoiled, that he could do with some toughening up. Like either of us were spoiled living in that house with her, holes in our clothes, miracle if we got fed." One side of his mouth drew up, but it wasn't in a smile. "She backhanded me, told me to get out of the way. She was wearing a ring." He pointed to a tiny star of a scar above his top lip, half hidden in stubble. "See?"

"I see."

"I slapped her, snatched the guitar right out of her hands. I wasn't that big yet, didn't get my growth spurt until I was fifteen, but I was big enough." He looked down at his palm. "Her cheek went bright red. It looked horrible, but she didn't do anything. Just kept looking at the guitar, stunned that I had it now and she didn't. Then her friend came, dragged her into the car and they were gone. Just like that, mom was a memory. Well, she came back eventually . . . unfortunately."

He looked up at me, face pale. "Everything she said, it's all true. No one needs to make shit up about me."

"Did you ever tell David about this?"

"No, just would have upset him. He still thought she'd sober up one day, get her shit together and be a real mom. He was a dreamer even back then."

"After everything she'd done?"

He didn't respond.

"You protected him for years, didn't you?"

"Someone had to. I'd tell him to go hide, soon as she started, didn't want him to see. He had to have heard though, because sometimes she'd scream at the top of her lungs. Mom was a mean drunk. Usually on dope she'd just drift off, leave us alone, but get a bottle of bourbon into her and the whole fucking neighborhood knew about it." He grabbed the back of his neck, face pained. "She'd slap me around. Couldn't have her doing that to Dave. He was always the sensitive one. No big deal. Besides, she could be pretty fucking funny stumbling around."

"Why didn't your father do anything about it?"

"She'd be better when he was home, mostly. But he just pretended it wasn't happening. Not like the signs weren't all there, our garbage can would be overflowing with bottles, no food in the fridge 'cause she'd spent all the money on booze and shit." He turned to me. "He loved her, Lena. Loved her so much that he chose her over us. That's what love does to you, it fucks you up."

"Not always. Look at David and Ev."

He inhaled. "They're happy for now. But one day, one of them will be like Mal's dad, like my dad's been since she left."

"So it's preferable to live your life alone and unhappy?"

"Better than winding up broken. Better than breaking someone."

I didn't know what to say.

"First pills I ever took were stolen from mom's stash. It was my great big fuck you to her." His laughter was bitter. "If she was going to tell me how like her I was all the time, then I figured I might as well live up to it. Look how well that turned out. I am just like her, Lena."

"No, you're not. You're clean now, you beat it."

"The shit I've done over the years." For a moment his eyes closed tight. Then he went back to studying my foot, reshuffling the cold wet ice pack. "All the things she said to me . . . she was right. I'll never be clean, not really. Always be an addict at heart."

"Jimmy, that's just not true. You know it's not. You did the work, you got clean." I knew a little about people saying stuff, wounding you with words. The scars lingered a long, long time.

His lips were thin and white.

"Have you ever told anyone?"

A sharp short shake of his head. "No."

"You can trust me, you know? I'm not going to turn on you or think less of you, that's never going to happen."

"Don't make promises you can't keep."

I cocked my head. "Did you just call me a liar?"

He pushed back his hair (finally), eyes wary. The man was in no rush to speak because he kept me waiting a long time.

"Well?" I prompted.

"This is one of those traps women use. No matter what I say you're gonna chew my ass out over it."

"I'm just asking for a little faith from you." I stared back at him every bit as carefully as he was at me. "Whatever that woman said to you is utter and complete bullshit, Jimmy. You know that. So why are you still letting it live inside of you?"

He gently rubbed the palm of his hand against the flat of my foot. "Break something badly enough, there's no point trying to fix it."

"That's what you tell yourself?"

"That's the truth."

"Hey, no. It isn't." I reached out, grabbing hold of his arm. Through the fine fabric of his shirt his muscles were strained, his skin hot. For over twenty years, he'd been carrying around all this pain and anger, self-hatred. The two people responsible for loving and caring for him when he was small and defenseless had failed him miserably.

Little wonder he was so defensive, he'd been taught to expect attack, to trust no one.

"You are a good person, Jimmy. You're a good man."

"Lena." He stared at my hand.

"She doesn't know who you are today. I do. So who are you going to believe?"

His mouth opened and I waited some more.

Yes, he was talking to me but I needed more, I needed an in with him. The pain he carried around had to end. Few deserved freedom from their past as much as Jimmy did. He'd worked so hard, turned his entire life around.

His jaw shifted and maybe, just maybe this time . . .

Someone rapped at the door, the same one I'd so utterly failed to break down. Of course they did, fuck the universe and all it entailed. Though honestly, what were the chances Jimmy would ever take that final step and trust me?

Unlikely.

No, I couldn't afford to think like that. I had to get through to him.

A neat middle-aged woman with short dark hair strode in, bag in hand. David followed behind her, gaze shifting between me and his brother with open curiosity. "This is Courtney. She's here to check out Lena's foot."

"That was fast." The doctor. Crap. My stupid ankle had ruined everything. I really needed to not try storming the castle by beating up innocent doors, in the future. But if I hadn't, if I'd just been content to sit outside, locked out, Jimmy wouldn't have told me as much as he had. I'm certain some distance had been covered. Exactly what it meant, I wasn't quite sure.

Jimmy lifted my leg off his lap, slipping out from underneath it. "She tried to kick the door down."

Dr. Courtney's eyes cut to me.

I shrugged. "I had something I had to say to him. He wouldn't open it."

She instantly turned judgey eyes onto Jimmy. Yay for the sisterhood!

"It wasn't my fault," he said, pouting.

"I've been called to lots of lovers' tiffs over the years, but this is a new one," the Doctor said.

"Oh, we're not involved," I said.

The good Doctor snorted and got busy feeling up my foot. Ever so not very carefully, she twisted and turned it, this way and that. I yowled and winced as needed. Finally, she pronounced the verdict of a sprained ankle. I declined any meds for the pain, not wanting them in the house. So, over-the-counter ibuprofen was diagnosed to stop the swelling and a highly fashionable boot thing would be arriving within the hour. At least this would get me out of jogging. Go silver lining on that gray cloud.

She informed Jimmy he'd be sent a bill and left.

"You're going to have to carry me up and down the stairs," I said, trying to keep the smile off my face. "You'll basically be my slave boy."

Jimmy sighed, handing me a glass of water so I could throw back two of the horse-sized pills. At least I seemed to have taken his mind off his mother. I would have preferred a method not involving me sustaining bodily damage, but there you go.

"I'll probably need a bell I can ring when I need you," I said.

"I don't fucking think so."

"You want me hollering through the house?"

"Seeing as you do that already, it's not like it'll be a big change," he said. "Guess you won't be leaving anytime soon. And you did it all to yourself."

I gave him a dirty look.

David wandered in and cleared his throat. "Hey. You two are obviously okay for now, so we'll all get out of your way."

"Right," said Jimmy. "Sorry about dinner . . ."

"Jim." His brother chided, grabbing hold of his shoulder then pulling him in for one of those back-thumping hugs. After a moment, Jimmy patted him stiffly in return a couple of times. A major move forward, frankly.

I couldn't help but smile with approval.

The two brothers spoke in muted voices for a moment and I did my best not to listen. Then David approached, laying a hand on my head in benediction or something. "Take it easy, Lena."

"Will do."

His smile was one of great warmth. "Look out for him."

"That's what I'm here for."

"I'll tell the others to catch up with you later. 'Night."

I got the distinct impression Jimmy and I were being left alone for reasons leading toward the romantic, by the youngest of the Ferris clan at least. His friends and family had perhaps gotten ideas about us. Oh well. The Stage Dive crew could think what they liked of the current status of Jimmy's and my overly complicated relationship. It was beyond my control.

On the other side of the room, Jimmy leaned against the wall, watching me through hooded eyes. "How'd Dean take you running out on him?"

"I don't know, probably not well." To be honest, I'd given it no thought, but the odds were, Dean and I were done. I lay back against Jimmy's bed, my foot propped on pillows. "Your bed's more comfortable than mine."

"Is it?"

"I'm just going to snooze here for a while." Wounded people were allowed to push their luck. Everyone knew that. "Wake me when the boot arrives, slave."

He said nothing, just watched as I made myself at home on his bed.

"This mattress is bigger than some small European

countries." I dragged my coat out from underneath me. A delicate procedure that involved much wiggling. My shirt rode up and I tugged it back down over my belly. "Say something, you're making me feel awkward."

"Why would you feel awkward, Lena? Just because you're rolling around on my bed."

"You could sit back down again and talk to me." I patted the mattress beside me in a friendly, inviting manner.

"We've talked enough for one night."

But he did flick off the light, leaving the glow of the bedside lamp on its lonesome. Then he walked around to the other side of the bed and sat down. He shucked off his shoes and, good god help me, lay down upon his back. Hands folded over his flat stomach he stared at the ceiling, giving it his usual frown of discontent.

Jimmy was on the bed with me.

I swear to you, my loins actually quivered.

This was better than my birthday and Christmas rolled into one, aching ankle or no. The most beautiful man I'd ever met lying close enough to almost touch. He was outright gorgeous. Ridiculously so. His face in profile, the curves of his lips and the perfect line of his nose. I didn't have words to describe him. I didn't have anything. My heart beat double time but I could ignore it.

"Are you okay?" I asked, voice little more than a whisper.

"Better than you."

He'd said he'd talked enough. So, in my infinite wisdom, I actually let it go for once.

"You really do need mirrors on your ceiling," I said.

He cut his eyes to the side and gave me an impatient look. "Where the fuck do you come up with these ideas?"

I laughed.

"Enough." He reached out, switching off the bedside

lamp. "Close your eyes and go to sleep. This day has been too damn long."

"What about the boot?"

"I'll get up when the boot comes."

"All right."

We didn't talk for a while. Then, out of nowhere, came a mumbled, "Thanks for coming home."

I searched for his free hand, grabbing hold once I found it. His fingers wrapped tight around mine

I smiled in the darkness. "Any time."

CHAPTER FOURTEEN

"Oh my god, this soufflé is amazing. It's like heaven in my mouth. Heaven, Jimmy, do you hear me?" I licked the last of the chocolate off my spoon then tried to find more. Stupid spoon for being empty. Better double-check just in case.

"I hear you." His gaze followed my tongue up the length of the spoon and he swallowed hard.

Huh.

The rock star in question sat across the table from me, his own breakfast long since eaten. He'd probably been up at the crack of dawn being all fit and energetic. In the basement gym, since paparazzi were lurking around outside given his mom's interview hitting the airwaves last night. A couple of security guys were out there, keeping an eye on things. So definitely no jogging for various reasons, but on account of my busted ankle I got to lie in bed anyways.

My own lesser bed sadly.

Once the boot had arrived the night before, he'd kicked me out of his room. Well, he'd helped me hobble into mine. At any rate, the end result was the same, I slept alone.

By the time I texted him to come help me down the stairs, he'd already showered and dressed in jeans and a plain black T-shirt. And now I tasted the abundant leftovers from his grand dinner party the night before. Screw cereal for breakfast, dessert was definitely the go-to. We'd be dining on leftovers for days, homemade pasta with wild mushrooms and pancetta, some exotic fish dish, and the best damn chocolate soufflé with berry coulis I'd tasted in my entire life.

Best. Breakfast. Ever.

"I want to have this soufflé's babies."

"Great," he said, watching me devour the innocent dessert with much zeal. The look on his face concerned me in so much as I couldn't read it. His eyes were guarded but there was something else there too, something more. An intensity I wasn't certain I could match at this hour of the morning.

"We need to talk," he said.

Were there any other words quite so dreaded in all of the human language? I didn't think I'd done anything, but still . . .

"About your mom?" I asked hopefully.

"No." His eyes shuttered. "Nothing to be done about that. She's played her card and I just want to forget about her now."

Which was more than fair. "All right. What then?"

"You made up your mind whether you're going out with Dean again or not?"

This wasn't so bad. I tapped the silver spoon against my lips, giving it some thought. Our first date had gone so well but then I had run out on him last night. Then there was the one that I forgot because I was out getting ice cream with Jimmy. Odds were, he had no interest in seeing me again.

"I think not," I said. "He's a great guy, but . . . maybe under different circumstances, you know? In another life."

"Whatever. We need to talk about point five on your list. Point four isn't working out, so let's give up on you dating."

"Hmm." I set the spoon down in my disappointingly still empty dish. "There wasn't a point five on my list. There were only four, date other people, focus on your flaws, don't be pathetic, and get a life, etcetera."

"Yeah, I made up number five. That list you found was complete and utter bullshit."

"I'm beginning to come to the same conclusion."

There was something different about him. A strange sort of tension running through him. He sat forward, elbows on the table, foot tapping out a beat beneath. I could hear it, the constant noise matching the overeager rhythm of my heart. Let's pretend the sugar rush from the soufflé stirred me up as opposed to the company I was keeping.

"So?" I prodded. "Are you going to tell me what this mysterious point five is?"

"We fuck."

Everything stopped.

Jimmy stared back at me, totally calm.

This couldn't be happening.

No. This wasn't right.

"Get out of here!" I laughed, sitting back in my chair. "God, you nearly had me there for a minute."

"I'm serious."

"Sure you are." I rolled my eyes, shook my head, still laughing.

"Think about it. All dating did was depress the hell out of both of us. And if I'm being entirely honest, I'm feeling a little sexually frustrated too these days. Not to give you TMI Lena, but I haven't jerked off this much since . . . ever."

I laughed.

And I laughed some more.

And then I stopped laughing because Jimmy's expression hadn't changed. Not one iota. He just sat there, sizing me up with his cool blue eyes, his mouth a straight, seemingly sincere, line.

"This is a joke," I croaked on account of my throat closing.

"No. No joke. I say we try fucking to get it out of our system."

"No joke?" But it had to be. Christ, I couldn't breathe. Air, I needed air immediately.

Jimmy pushed back his chair, the legs shrieking across the marble. He walked around the table and pulled me up, his hands beneath my arms. "Breathe, Lena. You're turning blue."

At his command my lungs kicked into high gear, filling with oxygen. Doing what they ought to. A strong hand rubbed up and down my spine, encouraging. He pushed my chair aside, the solid bulk of him standing directly behind me, warming me.

"You all right?" he asked, leaning over my shoulder.

I nodded.

He didn't move away. The hand rubbing my back didn't stop. Man, that felt nice.

"You, ah . . . you kind of surprised me," I said.

"Hmm."

"You're really . . . you want to . . ." I couldn't say it. The words tangled, making it impossible to get them out.

"Why not? I see it as a win-win situation. I get to release some of my frustration and you get to release any lingering feelings messing with your head. We fuck, we see we don't have chemistry, we move on. Or even better, everything falls apart like it normally does and you're happy just going back to being friends. What do you say?"

To have, or not to have, sex with Jimmy? A bit of a no brainer. "Sure, why not?"

He straightened, removing himself from view. His presence though could never be doubted. The man was magnetic, his heat and hard flesh pulling me in. The way he opened himself to me and told me his secrets, the way he gave me his trust, it all drew me closer. The temptation to lean back against him was almost overwhelming. Carefully, he undid my ponytail, spilling my dark hair across my shoulders.

He twirled a strand around his finger, rubbing his thumb back and forth across it. "Like your hair."

"Thank you."

Slowly, he unwound my hair from his finger. His hand slid to the base of my spine and then went lower, over my ass, down to the edge of my red jersey dress. Never had one limb's journey been so important. Goose flesh covered my back and it wasn't from any chill.

"And I like you in red," he said, brushing his lips against the tip of my ear.

"Do you?" I was just happy I wasn't in sweats. The too-sexy-for-words medical boot, bright blue with white straps across the front, was bad enough.

"Oh, yeah." His fingers skated right up the back of my bare leg, making me shiver. "Very much."

Jimmy Ferris did not mess around.

"You want to do it r-right now?" I stuttered.

"Might as well." His other hand slid around my front, stroking beneath the bulge of my breasts. He pressed his hard body against the length of me, grinding his erection against my ass cheek, making me ache. "Not inconveniencing you, am I, Lena?"

I sucked in a breath, my mind racing. "No. Not like I had anything else planned."

"Good." A finger traced the elastic of my panties around the top of my leg, sliding beneath to trace over my hipbone. It felt so fine my stomach pretty much turned itself inside out in elation.

To have him this close, the heat of him at my back, and the soap and subtle aftershave scenting the air, was bliss. Never in my wildest dreams had I imagined this, the chance to really be with him. My skin felt hot, feverish. And my heart had started beating somewhere between my legs. God, I needed him touching me there.

"Probably safer on your back," he said.

His words drifted right over me, meaningless noise. Right up until he reached around me and pushed aside the bowl and spoon. He turned me, picked me up, and placed me on top of the table.

"Lie back," he said. The look in his eyes, the tension, it was hunger for me. Amazing. Tightly leashed but there just the same. I'd never seen such a beautiful sight in all my life.

"Lie back, Lena." His hand on my shoulder guided me down until I was flat against the hard wood.

"We're really doing this?" All I could hear was my heavy breathing. So incredibly loud. It wouldn't have surprised me if the neighbors complained about the noise levels. "Jimmy?"

In lieu of a response, he slid his hands beneath my skirt and began divesting me of my sensible comfortable black cotton panties. Worn because the possibility of getting laid by my boss on the kitchen table hadn't really crossed my mind. Yet there they went, flying over his shoulder.

"I guess we are," I said.

He pulled a chair over and sat, hot eyes on me the entire time. A muscle jumped in his jaw repeatedly. Thank god I wasn't the only one wound up about this.

I went up on one elbow, nerves buzzing in my head. "What are you doing now?"

"What people do at tables." Strong hands held my legs apart. "Eating."

My stomach dipped. "Oh, god."

His head disappeared beneath my skirt.

Jimmy Ferris seriously did not mess around.

Warm breath hit my most secret female flesh. Okay, enough fancy talk, it was my vagina. Then he dragged his tongue up the length of my lips, sending lightning streaking straight up my spine. "Holy fuck."

Beneath my dress, he hummed. The sweetest sound in all of creation.

I wriggled, trying to get closer. "Jimmy."

His mouth attached to first one lip and then the other, sucking hard. Blood rushed through my veins at the speed of light, all of it heading straight to my pussy. It'd been so long since I'd had this, and never with someone so blatantly into the act. His mouth covered me, hot and hungry. Fingers sunk into my thighs and his tongue lapped at my labia, making me moan. I don't know when my back hit the table once more. Early on would be my guess. Same went for when my eyelids slid closed on the cold white ceiling, high above my head. What Jimmy was doing took my full, undivided attention, every wet sound and fierce sensation driving me wild. My hips jerked, head turning this way and that. It was too much and not enough. I never wanted it to end.

The knowledge that this was him pressed all of my buttons, bringing my love and longing roaring to the surface. So much emotion, I felt ready to combust. It was on the tip of my tongue to tell him all, to offer him anything. How incredibly foolish would that be? I bit down hard, the metallic taste of blood in my mouth.

He ate me like a man deprived, starved.

He ate me like I was his favorite meal.

Vaguely related, apparently singers had excellent tongue

control and strength. Bless them for that, many, many times over. In fact, the man excelled at oral beyond my wildest dreams. He worked his mouth between the lips of my sex, tongue diving deep, tasting me. Then he'd trail the tip up to my clit and tease me until I cried out. It was sublime. The muscles in my thighs drew tight. He gave me long, strong licks from just above my ass to my clit followed by sweet suckling kisses. My head spun, my senses reeling from overload. My sex had never been so spoiled.

And so it was that then, with all my elegant flailing, the chunky ass medical boot smacked him in the side of his head and we cried out together. In pain.

"Shit." He extricated himself from beneath my clothing, rubbing at his skull. "You okay?"

"Yes. You just have a really hard head."

He shook said head.

"Please don't stop." Pain didn't matter, only coming did. "Please?"

"Just a minute." Carefully, he draped my wounded leg over his shoulder. "There we go. You sure you're okay?"

"I'm fine," I said, panting.

"You sure?"

"You sure?"

"Jimmy!"

The smirking bastard. "Okay, Lena. Don't get all overexcited. Now, where was I?"

"You want me to hit you in the head again with the boot?" Desperation tightened my voice, murderous thoughts running through my brain. I was a sweaty horny mess and he needed to start taking me and my orgasm seriously. Now. "Do you? Really, Jimmy, is that what you're telling me?"

He chuckled.

And then he pushed up my skirt and got back to it, lucky for him. His ever-so-talented lips worked me up and up, to heights unheard of before. Up where the air was thin and the stars within reach. This was more than just great head. I felt so high, the rush of hot sweet emotions filling me had to be touching him too. The power of how he stirred me, driving me out of my mind was so intense.

He couldn't not feel it.

The tip of his tongue traced over my opening, making my muscles clench. So damn empty. Every inch of me drew tight, my legs shaking. My ass rubbed against the smooth surface of the table. He'd made me so impossibly wet, my pussy swollen and aching. I needed to come more than I needed to keep breathing. When his swift, clever tongue focused in on my clit, it was almost all over. A long, hard suck of it finished me off, tipping me straight over the edge. The freefall was magnificent. The world blurred to white and blood roared in my ears. It was basically an out of body experience. My mouth opened on a silent scream. Such pleasure, such joy.

It took me quite some time to come back down. When I did, Jimmy was standing, busy tearing open a condom wrapper with his teeth. He'd come prepared.

"We good?" he asked.

My breath . . . I'd lost it somewhere. No matter. I'd just lie there and glow, my pussy still pulsing with aftershocks. Perfect.

"Lena?" His hint of a smile was so cocky. There was a flash of dimple and everything. But honestly, he'd done such a superlative job on me. It was thoroughly well deserved.

I nodded, giving him proof of life. My mind was still drifting down from the heavens. God. Sex had never been quite that celestial before. All he'd done was put his mouth on me, I might not survive more.

Though I'd definitely die happy.

He stared down at me, hands busy rolling the condom over his cock. Before I could rise up on an elbow to get a look, he was positioning himself at my entrance. The slight pressure from the blunt head of his penis made sparkling little shocks break out anew. Baby fireworks. Shivers raced across my skin. He stroked over my tummy, setting his palm against the damp skin, up over the curves of my dimpled thighs, so white and big. All of my insecurities came running on home, despite the lust in his eyes. He was so big and beautiful standing over me.

"You're gorgeous," he whispered, voice ragged.

I couldn't talk, my throat dry as stone. So I just nodded. Surely he had all the permission he needed. I lay there decimated by him, wet and willing.

"It's been a while." A bead of perspiration ran down the side of his face. His shoulders rose and fell furiously, the struggle for control obvious in every part of him. "Want it to be good for you."

I swear my heart up and died at the doubt in his voice. Sometimes, we were more alike than I gave us credit for.

"Jimmy. I need you in me."

Something eased in his eyes and he nodded. "Yeah. You do."

I laughed in surprise.

Then I shut right the hell up. Capable hands held my legs apart and he started pushing in. And in. My pussy lips stretched around him to accommodate his size. Slowly but surely, the long hard length of him filled places I didn't even know existed. Honestly, it wasn't all that comfortable. It'd been a few months since last time, but this was ridiculous.

I wiggled and wrapped my good leg around him, trying to get into a better position. Really, I should have been wet enough after the phenomenal orgasm. "How big are you?"

"You can take me." His tongue ran over his lush bottom lip and his gaze stayed on where we were joined.

"That doesn't answer my question."

He gave me a quick look. "Not like I measure myself."

"That's still not an answer."

"Fuck's sake. Can we not argue when we're having sex? Please?"

"Fine." I stopped watching him over my still heaving breasts and stared at the ceiling. Despite his excessive skills with oral sex, it seemed we didn't match up down below. How sad. At least years from now, when I looked back on this, I'd know we'd tried.

His thumb toyed either side of my still supersensitive clit, making my back bow.

"Careful," I breathed.

He nodded, but didn't look up at me. Apparently our combined groins were just too fascinating. He drew back, before easing into me once more. Then again he slid out, withdrawing further this time, before sinking back in. Each time he did it, it felt better, and he did it over and over again, taking consummate care. The man moved like he was machine, no emotion, face set and eyes focused. Only his hands betrayed him, rubbing up and down my thighs, gripping tight and releasing hard enough to leave marks. They could not seem to stay still, too busy exploring my skin. He pressed my knees in hard against him, keeping us as close as could be. Sure enough, eventually tingles started in all of my favorite places, tension building low in my belly. I rarely if ever came twice in the same night. It just didn't happen. But having him inside of me was now a pleasure, not a pain.

"Jimmy," I gasped when he hit something particularly wonderful.

He didn't look up. "Yeah?"

"Do that again." My breasts felt heavy, hard nipples cruelly contained. Bad underwear. I needed to burn my bras.

"What . . . this?" His amazing dick did as told, striking me in exactly the right place, lighting me up like I was electric.

"God." My eyes rolled back into my head. "Yes, yes, yes."

"I think you like my cock." He laughed evilly, picking up pace, zeroing in on my happy spot, driving me out of my mind.

"I think I love your cock," I gasped, my butt grinding into the table.

"Damn, you feel good."

He hammered into me in a way that was pure art. Our bodies understood each other perfectly. The fit and feel of him marking me inside, making me whole. Each and every muscle in me drew taut until I was one mindless strung out mess. Jimmy thrust into me hard and fast while I moaned and groaned in appreciation.

Fuck, he could fuck.

I'd never known anyone like him. No way could I keep my eyes closed, I needed to watch. Skin slick with sweat and eyes squeezed tight, he pounded into me with absolute precision. He was so godlike and glorious it was scary. This had to be a dream. When he opened his eyes, the darkness of his pupil seemed to have swallowed the pale blue whole. He looked down on me, his heart and mind exposed.

He felt it. I know he did. It was so big, so all-consuming, how could he not?

This time when I came, the whole world blacked out. My entire body released in some orgy of mindless ecstasy. Sounds crazy, but it's true. My blood boiled and my brain blanked, every bit of me trembling. He'd turned me into some sex creature, wired just for him. And the payoff was sublime.

I heard a shout, then a warm weight settled on top of me.

We were both panting. The noise echoing, filling the room along with the frantic beat of my heart.

Slowly, I opened my eyes again. The world was still there, despite all internal bodily evidence to the contrary. Endorphins made merry with my whole being. How floaty and totally remarkable having sex with Jimmy was. Give me five minutes and I'd definitely go back for another round. Right now though, he'd earned a break.

"Hey." I stroked his beautiful black hair.

Immediately, he started righting himself. He lifted himself off of me, began dealing with the condom. He tied it off at the end and then tucked his cock back into his jeans, doing up the zipper and buttons. I missed the warmth of him instantly.

"Jimmy?"

He didn't look at me.

Between my legs was a wonderful wet mess. The delicious musky scent of sex lay thick in the air. Any money there was a loved-up dumb-ass smile on my face. I couldn't bring myself to care, let alone be embarrassed. He'd made me feel far too good.

"Jimmy?"

"Yeah?" He dumped the used condom and braced his hands beside the sink, staring out the kitchen window.

"Are you okay?"

"Sure. Yeah, no problem."

"Good."

He looked back over his shoulder at me, brows a worried line. "How are you?"

"Fine. Thank you." Man, this was all so very polite. Next we might have toast and tea, and talk about the weather.

Shoulders thick and strained, he said nothing for the longest time. I'd been locked out again. The walls were up. He studied me in silence and I could feel the distance seeping back in between us. First inches, then feet, until entire oceans separated where we were.

I couldn't stand it anymore, the silence was killing me. "What's wrong?"

"You shouldn't look at me like that."

Right. There you go.

My body cooled in an instant, all of the lax and lovely evaporating into thin air. I lay on the table, badly in need of another shower with my hair one giant tangle. The sex creature was gone, dismissed. I smoothed my dress back down over my ravished private parts before rising up. This most definitely wasn't the sort of conversation I wanted to have lying flat on my back with it all on display. Pride mattered.

"I want to fuck you every way I know how," he said. "But you can't look at me like that."

"I see."

"I, ah . . . I need some air." He strode to the kitchen door, no hesitation, he didn't look back. But instead he stepped straight out into the cold windy Portland morning without a jacket. He was going to freeze his ass off. And actually, I was okay with that just then.

My eyes itched though I wouldn't be crying. Stunned seemed the top response. I just . . . I couldn't believe he'd walked straight out on me after such magnificent sex. I hadn't clung to him, demanding a ring. There'd been no discussion of babies. All casual sex etiquette had been adhered to.

Like I could help how I looked at him.

I kicked my feet, the clunky med boot swinging back and forth below. There was no sign of him on the back patio. Fuck knew where he'd gone.

"You could have at least helped me get down, you asshole," I yelled, despite him being well out of hearing. "Mal was right, you do no aftercare."

Worst postcoital ever.

CHAPTER FIFTEEN

The next day the guys were back in the studio. It was a long day of all action stations, or as much action as I was capable of with the boot on. Ev took over the better part of the running around. Jimmy had made himself conspicuously absent the day after our fevered mating on the kitchen table. Whatever part of the house I was in, he was in the farthest point possible away, fuck him very much.

Like sex had been my bright idea.

Today, however, he'd apparently gotten over the episode and had been ready to resume life as per usual. Yeah, right, as if it would so simple after the way he'd behaved.

I ignored him in the morning. I ignored him in the afternoon.

I ignored him upstairs and downstairs too.

Apparently, he did not like this because much scowling ensued. I sure as hell didn't ask him for help with the stairs. With my boot, I could totter around well enough, slow and cumbersome as it was. Stupid Jimmy Ferris and his amazing mouth and penis. Who needed him? Not me, I could look after myself.

That's why god invented vibrators, thank you very

much. Masturbation was so much safer. My fingers never gave me this sort of trouble.

Yes, sometime in the past twenty-four hours, cold war had descended. A woman scorned and all that, or a woman denied further access to his dick. Either worked. If I'd been paying him any attention, I'd have seen him giving me odd looks all morning. But since he wasn't even on my radar, it went unnoticed. Mostly. Yep, I was so done with him I didn't even see him approaching once again out of the corner of my eye.

"Lena."

I did not reply.

"Here."

A parcel was shoved beneath my nose.

Ev and I had been sitting doing some work in the lovely comfortable chairs I'd had delivered for outside the recording studio. A brilliant turquoise blue, fuck him very much. Sitting on the stairs got old after a while and I had access to his credit cards so why not? I'd made another purchase yesterday afternoon he didn't know about yet.

But let's not go into that.

The interview with his mother had stirred things right up. With the paparazzi now out in force, camped out front, and the phone ringing off the hook, it hadn't been the greatest day in many ways. Jimmy had all the reasons to be stomping around all uptight and unhappy. I'd switched the phone to silent and concentrated on working my way through the latest buildup of e-mails. Earlier, I'd made the mistake of answering the door and been bombarded with cameras. They yelled questions at me, pushing and shoving so hard my heart raced, claustrophobia closing in. A couple of security guys had rushed in, driving them back, and helping me get the door closed. Last time I'd make that error. Within half an hour the shot of me looking startled with shitty hair was all over the Internet. An hour after that my mom phoned wanting to know if I was all right. And I was fine, just in need of some Photoshopping. It seemed a good enough time to distract her with the story of my sprained ankle. Only in this version, I'd accidentally tripped on a step. Yes, lying is a bad, bad thing. But no matter my age, I couldn't admit to my mom I'd tried to kick a guy's door down. It did momentarily delay her grilling me about my attendance at my sister's wedding, however. A blessing.

At any rate, I doubted they were getting a great amount of work done inside the recording studio. Everyone seemed distracted, acting either unnaturally chirpy or seriously subdued. Mal had just pounded on his drums for a while and everyone had left him to it. But it was nice they'd gathered around for Jimmy's sake. I'd have been a bastion of strength and support too, had he not insulted me and then abandoned me in the kitchen the day before. For the sake of the shit he was going through, I wanted to be all sweetness and light. Then I remembered him walking out on me not two minutes after having him inside me. He hadn't yet said sorry. Therefore, I could not yet forgive.

I'd spent some of the day in the studio taking photographs of everyone (except for Jimmy) with Pam's camera. Everyone loved the photos and Pam gave me lots of encouragement and helpful hints. She said some of them might even make it into the artwork for the next album.

Mine and Jimmy's falling-out hadn't been missed by a soul, certainly not Ev. She'd tried to broach the subject of her brother-in-law with me. I'd given her a grim smile and continued discussing logistics for the upcoming tour. Whatever was or wasn't going on between Jimmy and me was our own business.

I still didn't talk to him on account of cold war protocol.

"Lena, C'mon, take it," he said.

My hands stayed attached to my iPad.

He sighed. "Ev, will you tell her to take the fucking thing?"

"Jimmy, I know you are not dragging me into this fight with Lena because that would be wrong." With a steely smile, Ev crossed her legs. "Wouldn't it?"

Much muttered swearing.

"Ooh, pick me! I'll get dragged into it." Like the loon that he was, Mal jumped over the back of the gray suede couch and sat beside me. "What would you like me to communicate to Lena for you, Jim?"

"Forget it," he growled.

The parcel was retracted. Black ribbon and shredded glossy white wrapping paper started raining on my feet. I knew this due to still refusing to look up at him like the adult that I was. A camera was thrust in front of me, but not just any camera.

"Here," he said again.

"Jimmy said 'here,'" Mal reported beside me.

My eyes, they bulged. "That's the same as Pam's."

"Lena said 'that's the same as Pam's,'" Mal said.

Jimmy ignored him. "Yeah, a Nikon D4. She said that's what you'd need if you were thinking of getting serious."

Mal gave a low whistle. "Smooth move, Jim. I'm impressed. Nice work on the wooing."

I stared up at him, my mouth wide open. Google had told me exactly how much such a beautiful baby with all the accessories cost. Google had almost made me weep. "But that's thousands and thousands of dollars' worth right there. That's a really expensive camera."

One of his shoulders hitched. "It's for you."

"I can't accept it."

"Pam said if you came on tour with us you could tag along with her some of the time. It'd be like an apprenticeship."

Excitement at the possibilities boggled my mind. "Really?"

"Yeah." With another of his patented pained sighs, Jimmy handed the camera to Mal. Next, he grabbed me beneath the arms and gently pulled me to my feet. "Look, I need you to stop being pissed at me."

"So apologize. That's what you do when you hurt someone's feelings, Jimmy. You apologize."

"I just did."

"No, you just tried to buy me. It's quite different. Saying sorry and meaning it would be an apology," I said. "This is a bribe."

"This gets the job done faster."

My hands fidgeted at my sides. "I can't accept it. I can't allow myself to be bought by you."

"But you want the camera?"

"Of course I want the camera," I said. "But that's beside the point."

"No, Lena. It's exactly the point."

Hushed whispers surrounded us because of course we'd drawn a crowd. These people, being so overly involved in each other's lives couldn't be healthy. I also knew we were being watched on account of the way Jimmy's body tensed up. Beneath the long-sleeved black Henley, his shoulders seemed to thicken.

"Trust me. Nothing about this is easy for me." His gaze darted to either side of me. The hard line of his jaw shifted at what he saw. "Everyone's watching and I'm doing this anyway."

Ev rose to her feet. "Okay, everyone. Be elsewhere, give them a moment."

"I'm the drummer for Stage Dive." Mal set the crazily expensive camera on the seat beside him. "You can't order me around, child bride."

"It's so cute that you think that's still funny, calling me

child bride." From her back jean pocket, Ev pulled out her cell. "Am I calling Anne to tattle on you for refusing to give Jimmy and Lena some privacy or not?"

"You wouldn't dare."

Her finger moved across the screen. "Oh, I think I would."

David and Ben chuckled in their manly way, but did as told and went back into the recording studio. They clearly weren't messing with the girl.

A second later, Mal followed. "I do not like you women all being friends. This is not okay."

"And you should tell your girlfriend all about it when you see her tonight. I'd love to know what she says." With a final wave, Ev followed him back inside the mixing room or whatever it was called.

It didn't matter.

Jimmy and I stood almost toe-to-toe, watching each other warily.

"I bought it for you," he said. "You don't accept it I'm throwing it out. You wouldn't want that would you?"

"That's blackmail."

"Yeah. So sue me."

I crossed my arms. "Say you're sorry."

He groaned. "Lena."

"You had sex with me and then you were horrible and you hurt my feelings. That's no small thing. It's actually, in the scheme of things, pretty damn big." My fingers tightened around his strong wrist. "And two orgasms beforehand doesn't make up for it. Apologize and mean it."

"It just . . . wasn't what I expected."

"The sex?"

"Yes," he said.

"What did you expect?"

"I dunno." His forehead went all crinkly. "Something less good."

"It was only good? I thought it was great."

He rubbed at his face with his hand. "Fuck. Fine, yeah, it was great. Your pussy feels perfect and I can't think about anything else, all right?"

I had to smile. "Well, at least you're enamored of one part of me."

"That mean you forgive me?"

"No, not even close."

"Damn it, Lena." His arms went around me, pulling me in tight against him. My face was all mashed up against his chest. His hard, unyielding chest on account of the fact I'm reasonably certain he'd stopped breathing somewhere during this process. Thick steely arms froze into position around me.

"Jimmy, are you actually hugging me?"

A grunt.

"Okay, you're doing very well." I set my chin on his chest and looked up at him. "I'm proud of you."

"You'll stop ignoring me now, and we can go back to being . . . us?"

"Yes."

The air rushed out of him. "Good. That's good."

I wrapped my arms around him as tight as I could. He was my Romeo in black jeans and this story had just as much a chance of dying as tragic a death as the original. And still, all of the love I had for him in my heart spilled over, filling every part of me with those familiar warm fuzzy feelings. I'd been "in love" before, sure. The difference here was, I loved him, all of him, and there'd be no easy getting over it this time. Every part of me wanted him, I yearned for him on the cellular level. There could be no escaping emotions of this magnitude. His good and bad, dark and light, his nice parts and his nasty.

Everything he was, I loved, and it left me feeling utterly helpless.

Because if he knew it, if he ever suspected the entirety of the truth, that this wasn't just some passing fancy? Well, I'd be out on my ass so fast I wouldn't even hit the ground for three blocks. So I loved him in silence.

In return, he patted me on the head.

"Glad we got this sorted," he said, his arms falling back to his sides.

I squeezed him tighter.

"I should get back to it. The guys'll be waiting. But Lena, can you do me a favor?"

"What?"

"Keep the camera. Please. I want you to have it."

"But it's so expensive."

"It's just money, Lena. Relax. I've got more."

"Well, I'm finding it harder and harder to resist."

"Then don't."

I sighed deep, ever so surreptitiously rubbing my breasts against him (don't judge me). "Okay, but only because it would be terribly rude not to accept such a generous gift."

"It's nothing, really. With my kind of money, it's a drop in the bucket."

I studied his face and sure enough, his usual calm, no care demeanor had returned. "Oh."

"All right?" His feet shuffled, the connection between us suddenly severed. "We good?"

"Twenty G," said Ben's deep bass voice softly from somewhere behind me.

"I'm not taking your money again," answered Mal. "It's too easy."

"Fine, forty thousand says they're through by Christmas."

"Why are you always betting against true love, Benny? What's with that?"

"It's all bullshit," Ben muttered.

"Ben," said Jimmy. "Watch your fucking mouth."

"Sorry." Some grumbling from Ben. "Didn't realize they could hear us."

"Of course we can hear you, you idiot. We're not deaf. Enough of this." Jimmy stepped back, hands gently but firmly disentangling me from him. My grabby hands never stood a chance. He was just too strong, damn it. "Time to get back to work."

"Wait." I wrapped my hands around my sides, so they'd feel less bereft. "Did you mean it, what you said before about me maybe trying being Pam's apprentice on tour?"

"Yeah. She suggested it, so talk to her. She said you had a natural talent and could do with another pair of hands helping her out."

"But I thought you wanted me to keep working for you as your assistant?"

He drew his lips to one side, in query almost. "Figure you're gonna probably get sick of that eventually. You'll get bored. You work with Pam, then you can still work for me and do other stuff as well."

"So it'll be like a second job?"

"Sure. Why not."

"I'll give it some thought and have a talk with Pam."

"You do that, and then take the opportunity. It'll be a great experience for you."

"I'll think about it."

"What about sex?" he asked.

"What about it?"

"I want to have it again. With you." his voice dropped low. "What do you say?"

"Honestly, I don't know."

He stared into my face, saying nothing for a good long while. Agitated fingers started tap, tap, tapping against the small of my back. Eventually, he said, "We still haven't gotten each other out of our systems yet, have we? So the original reasons still hold."

My heart stopped. "We, huh?"

"Yeah." He paused, sighed. "It's the truth, isn't it?"

"I guess it is. It's nice to hear it."

"So, I think we should do it, try some different positions, and mess around a bit. Might fix things, you never know."

"You genuinely believe that giving scissors, the butterfly, or dragon a whirl is going to fix things between us?"

His eyes glazed. "Lena . . . ah, man."

"What?"

With the motion of his hand, he directed my attention downward. Huh, things were definitely happening in his pants.

"That's not my fault if you can't control it. It's not like it's attached to me."

He groaned. "Well, us having sex'll definitely fix one thing."

"True." Whoa, there really was a hell of a bulge behind his fly. And there went my panties. Cold thoughts. Boring thoughts. "But you didn't react well to good sex with me last time."

"That won't happen again. I promise."

"You do, huh?"

"Absolutely." He stepped closer. "Boy Scout pledge and all that."

"You don't strike me as someone who was in Boy Scouts."

"I wasn't. But I can still tie a hell of a knot."

My mouth opened, but yeah . . . nothing. Oh, the evil dirty thoughts dancing behind his eyes. I longed to hear all about them in detail.

He grinned. "That's about the first time I've ever seen you lost for words."

"Shut up." My face, it felt flambéed. I cleared my throat a few dozen times. "Anyway, I'd just like to take this opportunity to say how awful I personally feel that you enjoyed having sex with me. No really, Jimmy. I'm sincerely apologizing on behalf of my vagina, here."

"Yeah, okay." He turned his face away, trying to repress a smile. "Now you're enjoying this a little too much now."

"Impossible."

"And I know about the flowers you sent to Liv from me."

"You do?" My ecstatic fell back a few notches to something more subdued.

"She called, sounded pretty damn happy about them. How much did you spend exactly?"

I forced out some laughter. "You said money wasn't a big deal, you've got lots more."

He gripped my shoulders. The harsh line of his mouth suggested much crankiness in the immediate future.

"Hey, I did a nice thing for another human being to help her feel good about herself. I just happened to do it with your money. But Jimmy, you were not nice to her when she left, and I felt . . . you know, you invited her up here and then . . ."

He just looked at me.

"Can we go back to the part where I'm in the right and you're in the wrong? Personally, that was more fun for me."

Footsteps sounded, coming down the stairs behind me. Company would save me, hooray!

But Jimmy didn't seem to care if there was an audience to his throttling of me or not. Instead, he wrapped his hand around my ponytail, tugging gently until I tipped my head back.

"I don't care about the flowers," he said, leaning in and pressing his cheek against my forehead. Damn that felt good, I had no idea foreheads were so receptive to sensation. My body went weak, awash with good vibrations. It was basically like having one big happy spot smack bam on my face, mildly embarrassing but ever so rewarding. Imagine if he'd actually kissed me there, I'd probably have come.

"It was a nice idea," he said. "You did the right thing. Thanks."

"You're welcome."

"Don't care about the chairs either in case you're wondering."

I smiled and held perfectly still as he stroked his knuckles over my cheek. It was so nice being touched by him again, getting to be this close.

His gaze rose, going straight over my head to whoever stood beyond. "Hey, Dean."

"Jim," Dean answered, voice curt.

I stopped. The moment he'd touched me I'd entirely forgotten anyone was there, such was his power. And there he'd been, using me to make a point, showing Dean he'd won or some other such manly bullshit.

"Lena," Dean said.

With both hands, I pressed against Jimmy's stomach, forcing him back. "Hi, Dean."

His face was shuttered, his expression closed. "What happened to your foot?"

"She tried to kick my door down," said Jimmy, bless his helpful little heart. I'm sure there wasn't a trace of smugness to his voice at all, that would just be my imagination.

Dean wandered toward the studio. "Better get to work."

The door quietly closed.

"What was that?" I asked, voice deceptively calm.

"What?" he asked, shoulders already rising to protest his innocence.

"You did that on purpose just to get to Dean."

"Hang on, you do or you don't want me touching you?"

"Did you think I wouldn't tell him I couldn't see him anymore?"

He rolled his eyes, giving me his bored look. "I was just messing with him."

"No, you were being a jealous dickhead." I advised him as calmly as possible. "And it was insulting to me and assholish to Dean. The guy's worked with you for years. He deserves better."

He caught my hand. "You mad at me again?"

"Oh, you picked up on that did you?"

"Lena, c'mon."

I tugged my hand from his grip. "Fix it."

"What? How?"

"I'll give you a hint. Not by buying anything. You figure it out."

My private e-mail account had suddenly been bombarded by all sorts of messages. Mostly consisting of "oh hey, you know someone famous. Wanna hang out some time?" type sentiments. I guess people were easy come easy go on the twentysomething social scene. Most of my friends didn't appear to have greatly noted my absence when I bolted from home following my sister and my ex's engagement announcement. This renewed sudden interest on account of my being associated with a Ferris brother, I could do without.

"Hey."

I looked up from the laptop to find David Ferris hovering in the office doorway. Not someone I'd expect to come calling.

"Hi, David."

"Can we talk for a sec?" he asked, face serious.

"Sure."

He took two steps in, scanned the room. There was just the desk and a couple of chairs, some shelves holding various music awards and such. It was probably the simplest room in all of the house, the most utilitarian. He'd probably never even been in it before.

"Jim's busy in the booth, but we'll be finishing up soon," he said, lips drawn into an awkward sort of smile.

"Right. Is there something I can help you with?"

"I wanted to talk to you about him."

My guard rose a little higher. Again with the all of them being over involved in each other's lives. I kept my mouth shut.

"Glad you two made up. But, Lena, he'll keep fucking up. He can't help it."

"I don't think we should be—"

"In high school he could have any girl he wanted with a look. I swear, that's all it took, and they'd come running."

I bet they did.

"It's been the same ever since. He's never been the type to go back for seconds. None of them ever interested him that much."

I buried my hands in my lap, looked away. Wherever he was going with this, I didn't like it. Also, no matter how mixed up things were with Jimmy and me, I wasn't going to talk about him to his brother behind his back. "I've heard. David, I'm not comfortable with this."

"He's really into you. You walk into a room and he's all over it, Lena. Watching you on the sly, listening in to everything you say. I don't know if you realize . . ."

I blinked. "Um, no. I didn't."

"Jimmy's always been a hard case, closed off."

"He's not. He's just complicated." I leapt to his defense without thought. Those were the same damn things my idiot ex had accused me of being. Anything along those lines was still a big angry red button sitting inside of me, waiting to go off.

"Lena," David said. "Just let me explain. Please."

I nodded.

His gaze ran over the glittering trophies. He really was a very attractive man, but all I saw were the pieces of Jimmy in him, the shared genetics. Or maybe that was love, searching for traces of what your heart longed for everywhere you went. Perhaps I'd always be trying to see him from now on.

"Did you know it was his idea to start the band?" David asked.

"No, I didn't."

David nodded, half smiled. "Yeah, he likes to make out it was me, but it wasn't. Jim said if we were spending so much time fucking around with guitars and shit, we might as well try to make some money out of it. But that wasn't what it was about for him, not really."

Despite myself I edged forward in my chair, eager to know. "So why then?"

"Family, Lena. He wanted us all to stick together. I think . . . well, I know, even back then, he was starting to unravel. He was already drinking and smoking pot. Not just casually, but to excess. Then as the band got bigger, so did his troubles." His jaw shifted from side to side. "It was like, he didn't feel like he deserved success, so the more it came his way, the faster he ran."

"Why are you telling me this?"

"Because right now he's running from you. He's terrified of you, Lena."

I blinked.

"He's always keeping an eye out for you, and then the minute you're in his space he gets all agitated and wound up. It's like you're his new drug of choice. Only you're actually good for him." He squinted, forehead wrinkling. "Problem is, he just doesn't know how to deal with you. Doesn't feel worthy of the kind of love I have with Ev, or Mal has with Anne."

"I'm not sure what to do with that," I said, shifting my aching booted leg into a more comfortable position. My mind twirled in weary circles. It'd been a long day. "What are you saying here, David? What do you want from me?"

"Ah, I dunno." He laughed. "I guess I'm asking you to have patience, to not give up on him."

I just stared.

"Don't break his heart, Lena. Fuck, he barely even knows he has one, but he does. And it's actually a really good one. Just give him a chance to figure out what to do with it, please?"

"David . . ."

He held up his hand, forestalling my words, if I'd had any. "Just think about it."

"There's something I need you to think about too," I said. "Please."

"What's that?"

I breathed in deep, choosing my words with care. "After Idaho, when your mom showed up and you said those things. That hurt him. Badly."

His gaze darkened. "Lena."

"He protected you from her, much more than you know. I can't say . . ." I shrugged, my hands clasped in my lap. "It's not right for me to say more. But he needs you to be on his side when it comes to her. And what's more, he deserves it."

David gazed at the ground, then slowly nodded his head. "I know. And I will."

"Thank you."

He gave me a thoughtful look from beneath his brows. "I think we both love him, don't we?"

My lips parted to confirm it but I just couldn't say it. The words disappeared.

He smiled and walked out.

I sat there a long time, staring after him, thinking.

CHAPTER SIXTEEN

It was around midnight when he tiptoed on in. I almost smiled, the mental image of Jimmy sneaking into my room after lights out being so amusing. It was a lot like being sixteen again.

"Lena?" he whispered, crawling onto the bed. "You awake?"

After the fighting, making-up, fighting again, and then talking with David, I was wrung out. Over it. Emotionally, I just needed to be hung up to dry for a while, so I decided to fake sleep. I kind of also wanted to know what he'd do if I didn't answer.

He'd gone jogging with Ben after they'd finished up in the studio for the day. I'd fixed a plate of food and retreated to my room. Let me tell you, hauling my ass up the steps with a plate was no easy thing. Perhaps not the best idea I'd ever had. But there'd still been people around downstairs and honestly, I'd needed some quiet time, just me, fine food, and the new camera.

It was nice to slow down. Things had been intense lately.

Jimmy slid beneath the blanket, the mattress moving under his weight. I lay on my back my foot propped on a pillow. For a while, he seemed content just to lie near me. My ears strained, listening for every breath he took, every rustle of the sheets. What was he doing here? It had to be a booty call, surely. I frowned into the darkness awaiting revelation and getting absolutely nothing for my trouble. Never understanding seemed to be the theme of the year.

"I apologized to Dean," he said quietly.

"You did?"

"Yeah."

"Good. I'm glad." Then some fingers came seeking. They crept over my hip, stopped, and tugged at the material of my nightshirt, fingering one of the many small holes in the hem.

"That's my old shirt, isn't it?" He shifted closer. The mattress moved again as he reached across me and switched on the lamp on the bedside table. Little lights danced before my eyes. When they cleared, he hovered over me, a bit blurry on account of no glasses. "I fucking knew you took it."

"I have no idea how it got mixed up with my laundry."

"You're a lousy liar."

I bit back a smile. If he thought I was ever giving the shirt back, he was dreaming. "That's not a nice thing to say."

"You want nice," he asked, voice dropping in all the sexy ways. "I can be nice."

"I know you can be."

"I didn't think when I saw Dean. You were right, I get jealous." He quietly cursed, still toying with the hem of *my* shirt. His thumb tucked beneath the shirt and stroked over the bare skin of my belly. It was the sweetest, most ticklish of sensations. Booty call, just as I'd suspected, and shame on me for not minding. My momma should shout at me for being so easy.

I stopped breathing for a moment. When it came to him, I just was that silly.

"Talk to me," he said, voice soft.

"About what?" I asked, just as softly.

"Anything."

What to say? I turned to face him. His head lay on the next pillow over, neither too close nor too far away. The perfect distance for touch or talk. How great it would be to have him as the last thing I saw each night. To wake up to him every morning, lying by my side.

"Want me to go down on you again?" More fingertips traced over my stomach, making everything down low wake right the hell up. Much more of this and the state of my panties would be a disgrace. He went up on one elbow, a move I felt more than saw. "Lena? You still mad at me about Dean?"

"No, I'm not. Though I wish you hadn't felt the need to do that. We have to stop fighting all the time, it's wearing me out."

His hand grasped my hip. "You mean I need to stop fucking up."

"I mean we both need to figure out a way to not constantly be getting butt-hurt over everything the other does."

"Hmm." The flat of his hand glided over my hip, easing between me and the bed to grab at a cheek. So subtle. "I've got something that'll make your ass feel better."

"I highly doubt that given your size."

He snickered.

"I'm serious, Jimmy. We need to learn to live in some sort of peace and harmony before we accidentally on purpose kill each other one of these days." I reached out, touching his hair. As per the usual, he stiffened. But then he relaxed again, allowing it. It was like dealing with a wild animal, you never knew when the teeth might come out. Fingers kneaded my ass cheek, keeping up a firm grip.

"We've both got tempers," he said. "But I gotta say, you hold a mean grudge."

"You left me pantyless sitting on the kitchen table. Getting down from there with this stupid boot on was not easy."

"I'm sorry. That was an asshole thing for me to do." Straight out, no hesitation. Maybe there was hope for him yet.

"Thank you, you're forgiven. So, what?" I asked. "You just got bored in your room?"

"Something like that." The big shadow of him leaned over me.

"Or did you want something in particular?" My hand slid down to his neck, testing the hard muscles there. His skin felt so fine, smooth and warm. Maybe if I asked really nicely he'd take his T-shirt off? No, bad hand! Making me think all kinds of unwanted thoughts.

"I didn't want to go to sleep without talking to you," he said. "Shit was busy today. Then you went to bed early."

"You miss me?"

He huffed out a breath, gave a terse nod.

"That's good. A girl likes to be missed." The pad of my thumb trailed over the prickle of his stubbled jawline. He caught the digit between his teeth, nipping gently, surprising me. Jimmy wasn't someone I'd ever have pegged as being playful. His teeth did not release. I wiggled my hand, trying to get free.

"You're an animal." I laughed, finally tugging my thumb free. Enough of this nonsense, I wanted sex. Despite what my brain wanted, my tummy was wound tight and my thigh muscles clenched. I sat up and Jimmy shifted back, keeping the same distance between us.

"Kiss me," I said.

He gave my hip a squeeze. "Spread your legs, let me eat you out."

"First I want a kiss."

"I'll kiss your sweet pussy." Another squeeze, of my thigh this time. "C'mon, Lena, spread."

And I liked that idea, I really honest to god did because you'd have to be a certified idiot not to. But something more was going on here. My hand fumbled for my glasses on the bedside table.

"What's wrong?" he asked.

"You've never kissed me."

Jimmy laughed. He looked beautifully disheveled at the end of a long day, hair all messy. "We've only done it once."

"Most people kiss before they do it. It's actually kind of a tradition. You know, even this afternoon, when you were doing your manly statement thing to Dean you didn't kiss me. You just pressed your cheek to my forehead."

"The shirt looks damn good on you," he said, giving my perky nipples their due. Which was nice of him to notice but completely beside the point.

"You don't, do you?" I watched him look here there and everywhere, anywhere that wasn't me. "Touching you're sort of okay with it if I take it slow. But actual kissing is a definite issue."

He shook his head, withdrew his hand from my leg. "Lena—"

"I've got to say, diving head first beneath a girl's skirt is an excellent method of avoiding her mouth. Full marks, Jimmy, that's a genius plan."

The man actually had the good grace to look sheepish then.

"It's too personal, isn't it?"

He snorted. "That's fucking crazy, how can it be too personal? I'm happy to lick your pussy, so why I would be afraid of your face?"

"You tell me."

Apparently, he decided not to, for his lips stayed firmly shut.

"I want to kiss you, Jimmy. I've wanted to for forever. Kiss me?"

Brows drawn down, he gave me a frown instead.

"Come here, it's okay." I grabbed the front of his T-shirt, pulling him forward. "It's just me."

He gave a bare inch or two. "I'm just not that into it. It's not a big deal, everyone likes different shit, you know?"

"I know." I drew him a little closer. "I just, I need to know what your lips taste like."

"The other girls never cared. It's not like I left them wanting, I made sure they came."

"That's good." And a bit closer.

"I just . . . you know, I don't want to be getting in some-one's face, getting all up close to them. I don't like it. I've kissed girls before. I have done it, just never really got into it."

"Okay." Slowly, I dragged him in until our noses were close to bumping. Let me tell you, he was one unhappy camper. "We'll just kiss a little bit. It's not a big deal."

"No, I know." He pouted.

"And if you really don't like it, I'll stop."

A hesitant nod.

Sweetly, softly, I pressed my lips against the edge of his mouth. Both of us kept our eyes open the entire time. He licked his lips and let out a breath. When he made no immediate move to launch himself off of the bed and es-cape, I dared try again. A single kiss against his beautiful bottom lip. He flinched, but didn't retreat.

I tilted my head, kissing this point once more, giving him greater contact this time care of the angle.

"How was that?" I asked, feeling his breath warm my lips.

A shrug. "Not too bad. I didn't mind it."

"Did you want to try one more?"

"All right. One more."

"Will you open a little for me this time?"

His lips opened slightly and he held himself rigid,

letting me take the lead. The hesitant expression on his face calmed to curiosity, his eyes gradually closing.

"Thanks." I brushed my lips over his, taking it easy. "You have such a beautiful mouth, Jimmy, and your lips are so warm, soft."

He made a noise in his throat. I think it was good.

"I've been dying to kiss you."

Our noses bumped and I smiled, changed the tilt of my chin and went back for more. I opened my lips a little, kissing his top lip over and over. The feel of his breath against my face, his stubble against my skin. I wanted to sink straight into him, know him inside and out. I wanted to protect him and cherish him, encourage him and love him. Ever so slowly he leaned in, getting closer, meeting me halfway. When I flicked his bottom lip with the tip of my tongue he sucked in a breath, eyelids fluttering opening.

"Would you rather no tongue?" I asked.

"Tongue's okay." His eyes were dazed, pupils dilated.

"Open your mouth a little wider for me?"

He nodded, doing as told. His hand slid up my leg, strong fingers kneading my thigh. This time when I leaned in, he came toward me too. Hell yes, success! Sweet euphoria coursed through my veins. He wanted this. I canted my head and gently covered his mouth with mine, skirting my tongue over the edge of his teeth, exploring. He exhaled and I inhaled.

Timidly, his tongue reached for mine. A quick touch and it was gone again. I continued on, sliding over his teeth, toying with his lips, tempting him to go further. He tasted so damn good I couldn't say. Then again, his tongue touched mine, rubbing against it, making me moan. The kiss went deeper, harder, as Jimmy got more into it, our tongues tangling, time and again. When he finally broke it off, we both sat their panting, staring at the other.

"What do you think?" I asked.

His gaze stayed glued to my kiss-swollen lips. Cautiously, he touched his mouth. "Wasn't so bad with you."

"No?"

"One more." A hand slid around the back of my neck, drawing me in as his mouth met mine. Our lips, teeth, and tongue fought for dominance, but it was the sweetest of battles. We both won in the end.

Without hesitation, he reached for the hem of my shirt, pulling it up over my head and tossing it aside. Then his hands cupped my breasts, taking their weight. "I been needing to do this."

"Have you?" I panted.

"Oh, yeah. Your tits are amazing. Been needing to get my hands on them for a while." His thumbs stroked over my nipples, toying with them, making them tighten. My breasts felt swollen and heavy, things down low stirring up a whole lot more. It was mildly embarrassing how wet he made me. What a confidence boosting turn on it was, seeing how much he enjoyed my body. Fingers stroked over the curve of my hips and the round of my belly (alas, I liked food far too much for it to ever be flat). In his eyes there was no hesitation, only appreciation. Just having him this close, his hands on me drove every other thought out of my head. Only now mattered.

He pinched my nipples lightly and I gasped.

"Sensitive?" he asked.

"Yes."

"You want me to stop?"

"God, no."

"You're so fucking hot," he hummed. "You have no idea."

"Didn't realize you noticed me that way."

"I couldn't not notice you. And believe me, I tried. But

in Adrian's office. You were wearing that tight white shirt, glaring at me like you were ready to tear me apart. Nearly fucking killed me not to take a bite out of you."

"You remember what I was wearing when we first met?"

"Well, yeah. It's not a big deal."

I wasn't so sure about that. Or maybe that was just me getting my hopes up.

He laughed, low down and dirty. "And when we go jogging . . . shit. Never buy a better sports bra. I think I'd cry if I couldn't watch them bouncing around every morning."

"They're not that bad."

"No," he said. "They're that good."

"What else have you noticed, Mr. Ferris?"

His smile was so evil. I loved it. And all the while his hands kept playing with my breasts, molding them with his fingers, driving me out of my mind. My lungs struggled to keep up, I was so overexcited. There seemed to be an ecstatic line of nerves running riot between my nipples and sex. If he kept it up, I just might come.

"What?" I asked, breathing only slightly heavily. "What is that look about?"

"Your ass when you go up the stairs. Kills me to hold back and not grab you."

My lips parted. "That's why you always let me go first. You bastard, I thought you were just being polite."

"I know," he said. "On your back."

I lay down, every part of me tingling with excitement. His big hands covered me still, fingers playing with my tight nipples. Man, it felt good. I ached in the best possible, all-over-body way. Having him this close, feeling him touch me was its own reward, inside and out. I'm pretty certain I glowed every time he came near me. The man just had that effect.

His hands slid down my sides, tucking into the elastic of

my underwear. The heat in his eyes made my sex squeeze tight.

"Need you naked," he muttered, already dragging my panties down my legs.

And yes, it was a little nerve-racking, being totally bare in front of the man of my dreams. On the kitchen table I'd still been mostly covered by my dress. This time, however, I had nothing, not even my panties. It was all out there, on display. Jimmy Ferris, world-renowned, picture-perfect, singing virtuoso stared down at me. The butterflies in my stomach went batshit. But nothing in his eyes gave me pause. Pure lust filled his face. It made warmth spear straight through me. We really needed to get busy. Now.

"Jimmy?"

"Hmm?" Carefully he lifted my wounded leg, moving it out, taking the pillow too. He spread me open until there was enough room for him lay between my thighs.

"Take your clothes off too," I said. "I want to see all of you."

He climbed off the end of the bed, already ripping off his own T-shirt, tearing into the buttons on his jeans. Though he did pause to retrieve a condom from a pocket, throwing it onto the bed beside me.

No underwear.

Absolutely, not one single pair of boxers, briefs, or combination of same adorned him. Crap. So screwed. My breathing stopped and my heart went into palpitations. How the hell would I ever get any work done around him ever again knowing he was bare beneath only one layer of clothing? I knew my mind when it came to him, pure smut. I'd never be able to stop myself from looking for the out-line of his cock every time he moved.

I was doomed.

"What's wrong?" he asked, climbing back onto the bed, kneeling between my legs.

My mouth opened but no words came out. The hard heavy length of his dick was pointing straight at me and good god, did I want it. I melted for him, right there and then. My heart yearning to take him in, hold him tight. Someone in heaven had been truly inspired the day this man came forth. Penises had never struck me as being particularly graceful before. But Jimmy's seemed proportioned just right and swung slightly to the left. It was definitely a size or two bigger than it needed to be, so typical of him to take it a step too far. A bead of pre-cum formed atop the dark red head and my mouth watered. I watched, rapt, as he rolled on the condom.

"Lena, focus. What was the frown for?"

I stared at his cock, mesmerized. Even incased in rubber it remained a thing of true beauty. Had I any talent with a pen, I'd have written it poems. A haiku perhaps.

"Lena?"

I was hypnotized, helpless. Cock-struck.

Jimmy swore and suspended himself over me on his hands and knees. "Hey, my eyes are up here."

"W-what?" Obviously, my self-control and Jimmy's hard-on could not peacefully coexist in the same space.

"You zoned out on me," he said accusingly, his hair hanging in his face as he stared down at me.

"It's not my fault. You got naked."

"You liked that, huh?"

"Yes."

He half smiled and raised himself back up onto his knees.

"Don't go." My clingy hands reached for him, grabbing his wrist. "Please? Come down here, I want you on top of me."

"You want to do missionary position with me?" He put his hands on his hips, fingers resting atop those awesome lines leading down the groin that truly fit people have. "Really, that's your sex fantasy?"

"Yes. And next time, can we get one of those sheets with just the hole cut in it for our bits to join up in though, because I think they're a real turn-on too." I even gave him the fingers demonstration with one finger going through the hole made by the other hand. "You know the ones?"

The look in his eyes was less than amused. "We need a rule about no funny shit or fighting during sex."

"Okay. Sorry. That was my fault."

More head shaking. "Can we get back to the fucking now?"

"Yes, I just . . . come here. Please." I waved my arms around, beckoning him closer.

"Just this once," he said. "No one's even supposed to do missionary these days. It's considered boring."

"You're right, I know. I'm way out-of-date in my sexual repertoire and you're being very kind to indulge me."

The heat of him covered me. I quickly threw my good leg over his hip and wrapped my arms around his neck, just in case he tried to escape. His big hot body pressed me into the mattress and I was in sex heaven.

"Tell me if I'm squishing you," he said.

"You're not."

He took his weight on both arms just the same, my breasts pressing into his chest. Even the light dusting of hair across his pecs running down to his belly button was a sensory delight, teasing my skin and stirring me up. His hard-on lay heavy against my sex, ready and waiting. It pretty much made it impossible not to try to attempt some sort of frenzied squirming against him. I angled my hips trying for more contact without upsetting my bad ankle. Forehead furrowed and brows tight, he stared down at me. The expression in his eyes seemed curious, almost. Like he couldn't quite remember how I'd come to be there beneath him.

"Are you all right?" I asked.

"Yeah." He paused, like he was going to say more, but didn't. Instead, he angled his head and pressed his lips tentatively to mine. Once, twice, three times. How sweet. His tongue trailed across my bottom lip and a sigh slipped out of me.

"Okay?" he asked.

"Very." I opened my mouth and he took up the invitation, kissing me deep, turning my insides to goo. Kisswise, he might have been a late bloomer. The man showed every sign, however, of making up for lost time fast. He was a natural. We basically ate at each other's mouths. I'm not saying it was pretty but it was hot as hell. Tongues tangled and teeth chinked and we didn't bother coming up for air. Breathing was for pussies. I fumbled off my glasses, tossing them aside before they got broken.

His cock rubbed against the lips of my sex, turning me on even more and making my synapses sizzle. Everything down below was throbbing and wet, ready for the taking. The feel of him, smell of him, nothing about Jimmy didn't turn me on. I'd had hot sex before. But hot sex with someone your heart got dizzy over was another thing entirely. Once love was involved, it all changed into something entirely different.

At some stage he shifted his weight onto one arm, leaving the other free to reach down between us. The head of his cock nudged against my opening before slowly sinking inside.

"Oh god," I sighed straight into his mouth.

His hips moved against me, pushing his dick in deep. Perfection. Absolute utter fucking perfection, that's what having sex with Jimmy was like. In one smooth move he took me over, filling me up and igniting every last inch of me. I loved that he was more than big enough to make his presence felt. With him inside of me and over me, I got what sex was all about, what making love was for. Because every part of me was primed to take him in and turn us into a whole. Maybe David had been right about me being Jimmy's new drug. He was sure as hell mine.

We were one hot, surging entity seeking that high. Crazy but true.

Jimmy drove his cock into me, over and over. The more my fingers dug into his sweaty skin, the further I fell into oblivion. Hands sunk into my hair, gently tugging, as his mouth sought out mine. It was an unending battle for domination where we both won. The thick length of him surged into me harder and faster. A truly piteous mewling sort of sound escaped my throat.

I lacked the will to care. If I could just come . . .

His mouth traveled over my jaw, stubble scratching against my neck. Teeth nipped and my pussy squeezed tight. Jimmy groaned and went faster, pounding into me. There was every chance I'd be bruised from top to toe by the end of things, but good god was it worth it.

Lots of time passed, I have no idea how much. The turn on the kitchen table must have been a quick summary. On my back in a bed, he gave me the full story.

We were all about the frenzied fucking.

His hand held my thigh against him, keeping my good leg wrapped around his waist. The intensity of his gaze held me trapped, daring me to show him everything, exactly how much he was affecting me. In that moment, he was in control of my body, not me. The lines and angles of his face seemed etched in stone, a mask of concentration. All I could do was hold on tight, keeping him as close as possible. His pelvis slammed against mine, driving his cock in, sending me higher.

"Jimmy," I moaned.

Everything inside of me tingled and tensed, every muscle shaking, and that was before I started coming. His cock plunged deep, the base grinding against my clit and boom! Fireworks. A whole sky full of them. My body was one big exploding entity. Stars going supernova played it more subtly. My innermost muscles clenched down on his cock, fingernails digging into his back. If my throat hadn't closed, I'm quite sure I'd have screamed the house down.

When I came back to myself, Jimmy was carefully climbing off.

"Hey," I whispered.

Thud. His big body hit the mattress, making me bounce. Sweat covered me from top to toe and a sublime kind of lethargy crept through my veins. It seemed to take forever to catch my breath.

"Jimmy?"

He lay on his stomach, ribs working hard to give him back his breath. I'd done that to him, me and my vagina. Go team. Now and then a muscle spasmed in my thighs or lower belly, the last of the orgasmic repercussions. My legs were like jelly, wobbly and weak.

"You okay?" I asked, daring to reach out and touch. My fingers traced over the musculature of his arm, down to his hand.

"Yeah," he said, sliding his fingers between mine.

He rolled over onto his back, dealt with the condom. It was safely deposited into a tissue for throwing out later.

"Why don't we do this instead of jogging?" I asked.

He smiled.

"I think I prefer burning calories this way."

"We'll do both," he said, giving my fingers a squeeze.

"Okay." I breathed deep, shuffling a little closer toward the heat of his body. The scent of a room after we had sex was the best. In a perfect world I'd bottle it and carry it on me always.

"You mind if I crash here with you?"

"No. I'd like that." I pulled up the blankets, turned off the light. It felt so nice and normal. So right. He kept hold of my hand the entire time.

"Tired," he mumbled.

"Sleep," I said.

A nod.

And we slept. I had the most amazing dreams.

CHAPTER SEVENTEEN

"Lena, do something with your life." Jimmy teased.

"I am," I said, fiddling with my camera while sitting on his workout bench.

His fists pounded into the punching bag, smack, smack, smack. Little wonder my groin felt tender this morning given he had all that strength at his disposal. Vaguely related, my god, the view. He wore only a black pair of sweat pants and tennis shoes. Beneath the bright lighting, his skin gleamed godlike, all of his gorgeous muscles on display. The lines of his face so distinct, the determined set of his lips, I could have watched for years and never gotten bored.

"Watching me working with the bag isn't doing something." Hands stilled and he sucked in deep breaths.

"I'm taking pictures of you too." I held up the shiny new camera and clicked off a few in demonstration. "You don't mind me taking your picture, do you?"

"No."

"Excellent. Can you take all your clothes off for me please? I'd like to get some nude shots."

He gave me the look.

"It's for artistic purposes, I swear."

"I don't think so." He undid the straps on his glove

things. They weren't the full traditional boxing gloves, but less bulky.

"I'll make it worth your while." In a move that should have been beneath me, I toyed with the V in the neckline of my sweater.

"How?" His eyes darkened with interest.

Oh, the thrill of having some small amount of sexual power over this man. I got giddy on just the thought of it, my hormones rushing about like crazy. "All sorts of ways. I'll have you know, I can be very inventive when motivated. You just have to trust me."

He walked toward me, all slow and casual. But his eyes told a different story. "You playing with me, Lena?"

"No." I lowered the camera. "You let me lead last night. It wasn't so bad, was it?"

"When you kissed me?"

"Yes."

He bought his face close to mine. "When you made me lie on top of you?"

"That too."

"Thought you didn't like my sweat," he said, taunting me. "In fact, I distinctly remember you saying as much, and telling me to go shower."

"Do not hold that against me. I was trying to resist you at the time, it was a survival thing," I groaned in desperation, my mouth watering for the taste of him.

Then my cell started ringing over on the other side of the room. Jimmy jogged over and grabbed it, checking out the screen. "Who's Alyce?"

"My sister." I waved a hand dismissively. We'd barely talked in the last year or so, whatever she wanted could wait. Me kissing Jimmy, on the other hand, could not. "Let it go. I'll call her later."

With a sly smile he tapped the screen and put the phone to his ear. "Hello?"

No fucking way. My face fell, it plummeted.

"Yes, this is Jimmy Ferris her boss." He paused, listening. "That's right, I'm from Stage Dive." Another pause accompanied by a smug grin my way. "Thanks, didn't know you were a fan." Again he listened. "Lena has mentioned you to me, yeah. She actually told me a bit about how you fucked her boyfriend and now you two are getting married. How's that working out for you?"

"Jimmy. No." Shit, shit, shit. I put the camera aside and started the delicate process of getting my ass over to him, hobbling across the padded gym area floor. "None of your business."

The bastard took a step back, and then another, lengthening the distance between us. His face was serious now, mouth a harsh unimpressed line. Apparently whatever he was hearing did not please him.

He snorted. "I don't think so. Thing is Alyce, at the end of the day, you stole your sister's man. Unless you're calling to finally apologize to her, I don't really see what there is to talk about. I don't much give a shit if it was true love or whatever. You did wrong. You wanna know how I know that? Because I did a similar thing to my brother. It's a dick move made by insecure shits, but you know what, Alyce? At least I have a dick. What's your excuse?"

I mimed sliding a blade across his throat, still hopping toward him as fast as panic and a med boot would allow. When I got within snatching distance, Jimmy slid an arm around my waist, stopping me from reaching up. I stretched and strained but my mediocre height was firmly against me.

"You're not helping," I hissed. "Stop it."

"Yeah, I guess I am Lena's protector. Or maybe I'm just the only person prepared to call bullshit on this whole situation."

"Give me the phone." I tried to climb him to get closer,

but my fingers slid over his slippery sweaty shoulders. Damn his hot body.

My sister's voice sounded small, far away. I couldn't quite make out the words. Her tone however carried fine, all worked up and pissed beyond belief. You could just bet the perfect princess wasn't enjoying this conversation one little bit. Part of me kind of enjoyed that, but the larger part wanted to tear Jimmy to pieces for sticking his nose in where it did not belong. Despite everything, I did not need to go to war with my sister. And war was exactly where we'd be if he kept this shit up.

"Give it to me."

He ignored me.

"Jimmy!" Frustration bubbling over, I slapped his face (I know, I shouldn't have, but I did). It got an immediate reaction. He scowled down at me, then he slapped me good and hard on the ass in return. I yelped, my wobbling butt cheek on fire.

"Don't do that again, Lena," he said.

"Give me the phone." I grabbed at his arm, trying to force the far-too-damn-strong limb down.

"You are fucking kidding me," he said into the cell, voice incredulous. "Why on earth would you ever imagine your sister would be willing to step in and be one of your bridesmaids when you're marrying her ex? Why should she save your ass, huh? This friend of yours that dropped out, you fuck her man too?"

Much distraught shoutiness came from my cell.

"She wants me to do what?" I asked, confused. I must have heard him wrong. Alyce couldn't possibly ask me something so horrendous and tacky. Me standing up at the altar while she married my ex, the man she done stole, just as Jimmy said. "No way."

Rage made my blood hit boiling point. I could feel the steam pouring out my ears.

"You god damn thoughtless, insensitive, spoiled, fucking cow!" I screeched plenty loud enough for my beloved sister to hear.

Jimmy's brows jumped.

"I don't believe you, Alyce."

He handed me the phone.

I held it to my ear. "You seriously expect me to step in and be a fucking bridesmaid? I left. I did my best not to cause drama because everyone was so damn thrilled about your engagement. But how dare you think it mattered so little to me. You're supposed to be my sister! Does that mean nothing to you?"

"Lena," my sister said, sounding distinctly surprised. "Um . . ."

"You never even said sorry. God, Alyce, if you'd just once admitted that what you did was wrong I would have gotten over it, you know? I would have forgiven you." I leaned against Jimmy, borrowing his strength. "But you acted like he was your god-given right and fuck anyone who got cut in the process."

"I-I love him."

"Yeah? Well I loved him too. And it hurt. It really hurt, what you did to me. What you both did to me."

Jimmy's hand stroked up and down my back, his other arm holding me tight. I rested my cheek against his chest, feeling him breathe, hearing his heartbeat.

"I'm sorry," she said finally, breaking. "I . . . you're right. What we did to you was wrong and I'm sorry. I should have said it to you at the time."

Finally. All of the air left me in a great rush. My shoulders collapsed and I had the worst feeling a few tears had managed to escape my eyes. "Thank you."

"Will you please come back for the wedding? I'd like you to step in as bridesmaid since Tiffany took off on me.

But I'll understand if you say no. It just feels wrong for you to be missing. You're still my sister."

Oh, man. I didn't know if that was something I could do. The stupid joyous occasion was only in three days. Jimmy gave me a squeeze, just letting me know he was there. It helped.

"I don't know, Alyce. Let me think about it."

"Okay, I understand. Thanks, Lena." She hung up.

With my arm around his waist and my face pressed up against him, I stood there, taking a moment to get my bearings. "That was unexpected."

"Hmm."

"Don't answer my phone again."

"Don't slap me again."

"Sorry." I set my chin on his chest, gazing up into his flawless face. His hands settled on my shoulders and he frowned. Perhaps now he'd push me away, reclaim his personal space and stop all of this touchy feely nonsense. But he didn't.

"My butt stings," I said, just making conversation.

"Good. You going to your sister's wedding or not?"

"I honestly don't know. She seemed sincere, but . . ."

He crossed his arms, looking all kinds of big, strong, and drop-dead gorgeous. How protective he'd been of me with Alyce warmed the cockles of my heart.

"Would you come with me if I did?" I dared ask.

He pulled a face. "I don't know. I'm not so good with family stuff."

"Yeah, maybe it's for the best."

"If you brought me as your date, I'd have to meet your whole family, and that would be awkward considering the nature of our relationship"

I squinted up at him. "And what is the nature of our relationship Jimmy?"

"I'm your boss and occasional hookup partner," he said, giving me a jaunty wink.

"You are?" I said, my voice completely devoid of expression.

"Well, yeah. Though speaking of hookups, I heard wedding sex is supposed to be pretty hot, so maybe . . ."

"That's quite all right Jimmy, no need to overcomplicate our casual relationship. Now if you'll excuse me."

"Christ Lena, what did I say now?"

"Got work to do!" I gave him a wave on my way out. It was probably more than he deserved.

Jimmy was watching me. I could feel his eyes on me from the other side of the room. Despite it being pleasurable, another time would have suited things better. Sometime when we weren't surrounded by every last member of his extended family along with a few other people also.

The girls' night out he'd suggested Ev organize for me the night of that awful date with Reece had finally come to fruition. Except given the media onslaught caused by his mom's TV debut, we couldn't really hit the clubs to shake our booties. It seemed every camera in the country was pointed in the Ferris brothers' direction, particularly Jimmy's. Therefore, we were all hanging at David and Ev's. Music was playing and people were drinking, pretty much everyone except Jimmy and me. Couldn't help but wonder if that made him feel left out, apart. He lounged as only he could on a white sofa, Mal chattering on about something beside him. Anne sat on the drummer's knee, sucking back a Corona and playing with his hair. I stared in their general direction, just chillin'. David and Ben were somewhere nearby, no doubt messing with guitars.

I was just happy to be liberated from the dreaded med boot. My ankle still ached a little. I would, however, survive.

"Psst."

What the . . .?

"Psst, Lena." Ev's bestie, Lauren, threw a pecan into my cleavage. A nice enough girl, but lobbing nuts at me was unnecessary.

I fished it out and popped it in my mouth. "Something I can help you with there, Lauren?"

Ev and Anne's sister Lizzy also closed in on my neutral position near the balcony windows. The condo really had a gorgeous view out over the Pearl District. Plus, Jimmy.

"We come seeking information regarding you and Jimmy," said Ev.

"Bullshit," laughed Lauren. "She's already banged him. It's blazingly obvious."

I pushed my long dark hair back off my shoulders while perusing my would-be interrogators. "I don't know what you're talking about."

"Did you really bust your ankle trying to kick in his door?" asked Lizzy, sizing me up.

"Well, yes. That happened."

Her face went all dreamy. "I think that's really romantic."

"I think it's hilarious," said Ev. "Apart from the part where you got hurt, of course."

"Of course." I smiled.

"What's going on, Lena?" Ev leaned against the glass door, eyes curious.

"I do not know what you're talking about."

Her eyes narrowed. "Please, the way he's looking at you."

"How is he looking at me?"

"Like you invented . . . what, help me out here . . ." She turned to her friend.

"Blow jobs," supplied Lauren.

"Right." Ev crossed her arms. "Jimmy's looking at you like you invented blow jobs and you're still trying to play innocent with me? That won't fly. You and he are very, very involved."

I gave away nothing.

"Anne wouldn't tell me anything either. You girls are useless for gossip." Ev sighed. "You wouldn't hold out on me, would you Lizzy?"

"No, Ev. I wouldn't dare."

She gave me a side eyed glance. "Why do I not believe you?"

Lizzy laughed. "Okay, I'm going to go wrestle my sister away from her boyfriend for a few minutes. Later, ladies."

"Later," I said, doing a subtle look over my shoulder to check out the lay of the land. Jimmy was staring straight at me, eyes troubled. With Mal now busy talking to Lizzy and Anne, he had no distractions. I on the other hand had Ev and Lauren watching my every move.

"She's a goner," said Lauren.

"Yep," agreed Ev. "But I suspect he's rather smitten himself."

I ignored them both. Sort of. "How about instead of worrying about what romantic dramas I may or may not be going through, we wonder what's going on with their bitch mother? Any news on her?"

Ev winced. "Last David heard she'd taken the money and run."

"Jimmy acts like it doesn't affect him, but it must," I said, going back to staring at the object of my heart's desire in the reflections in the window.

His dark hair was slicked back and he wore a black dress shirt and a pair of blue jeans, shiny black boots. The sleeves were rolled back on his shirt, showing off his tattoos. I'd still never heard the story of those, what they meant to him. It was sad, the way there'd probably always be things left unfinished between us what with me only being his occasional hookup.

"Lena?" Ev moved closer, lowering her voice. "Are you okay?"

"Yeah. Sure." I gave her my best smile.

She didn't return it.

I let mine go since it was so completely unconvincing. "There's just a lot going on right now."

"You're not still thinking of leaving, are you?"

Lauren had wandered off to be with her boyfriend, Ev's brother, Nate. We were alone. Ev, me, and all my worries and doubts standing in the corner at the party, watching life go by.

"Some shit went down with my sister and my ex a while back. They got together behind my back and now they're getting married," I said, unloading it all. Something told me she not only could take it, but she wanted to. As much as I loved Jimmy, sometimes a girl just needed a female friend to talk things out with.

Ev's mouth formed a perfect *O*. "Crap."

"Yeah, pretty horrible. I think my confidence took a dive, you know?"

"I bet." She tugged on her elegant blonde plait, eyes thoughtful. "How are you and your sister getting along now?"

"She says she's sorry. She wants me to go home for the wedding and step in for a bridesmaid who bolted."

"Huh." Ev huffed out a breath. "That's a pretty big ask."

"Yes, it is." I laughed despite the situation being distinctly unfunny.

"You going?"

"I haven't decided yet. I don't want to leave Jimmy or subject myself to that, but weddings are a big deal. If I went, I'd be taking the high road. And all of the family will be there. I've stayed away for the last year or so, and they're all fired up for me to show my face at least. Though I think my actually ever being a bridesmaid is right out of the god damn question."

She didn't say anything at first, just looked at me. "Lena, is this wedding going to cut you? Or is it just going to be a shitty thing to sit through, have a few drinks, smile at the right people, and then get the hell out of there the minute you can?"

"The latter I think." I sighed. "I think I'll feel better in the end if I go. It'll give me some closure."

"Then go. Jimmy will be okay for a couple of days."

True, but the chances of me not getting all heart-down and despondent away from him weren't good. Not that it mattered.

Me and him sitting kissing in a tree wasn't what he wanted. Not in any permanent way anyhow.

I wasn't what he wanted. He'd said it so many times, in so many different ways. It seemed only now however that my heart was truly taking it in, letting go. Our time together would come to an end. I couldn't stop loving him, and he refused to start. That was the cold hard truth.

I needed to enjoy the here and now. Take what I could get, while I could get it.

Eventually, things would get problematic and I'd be leaving, just like I'd planned to right back at the start.

"Thanks, Ev."

She smiled. "You're one of us, Lena. Any time."

"Hey." The deep familiar voice came from directly behind me, making me jump.

I hadn't noticed him get up at all. "Jimmy. Hey."

"Lena, can I talk to you for a minute?"

"All right."

A speculative sort of look came into Ev's eyes. "I have to do something in the kitchen. Now."

"Right." I shook my head. The woman was as subtle as a sledgehammer.

"What would you like to talk about?"

"Not here. C'mon." Jimmy put a hand to my lower back, guiding me toward the bathroom.

I did as bid. But if he thought he was getting sex after his shitty hookup comments today, he was sadly mistaken.

He closed the door. It was a nice bathroom as these things went. Shiny gray stone surfaces, a huge well-lit mirror and lots of chrome.

"What's up?" I asked, taking a step back from him and crossing my arms.

"Been thinking about your sister's wedding and stuff."

I frowned. "And?"

"And I did some research." He pushed back his hair, smoothed down the front of his shirt. If I didn't know better I'd have said he was nervous. Only Jimmy didn't get nervous, certainly not because of me. "Your hometown doesn't have anywhere decent to stay, so all I could book you was a room at the motel. But I got you first class tickets there and back and a rental car, the same kind of Mercedes as I've got so you'll be comfortable driving it. That'll be waiting for you at the airport. But I can just as easily organize a chauffeur for you if you'd prefer. Wasn't sure what you'd want."

I pushed up my glasses, my mind blown. "You organized all that?"

"Yeah. And the girl at the motel, she said they have a small restaurant attached but I checked it out online and it looked like shit to me. I don't want you get food poisoning or something, so I'm gonna get the restaurant that does home to fly stuff in. Getting some decent sheets sent too. She said theirs were only poly-cotton." His curled lip expressed clearly what he thought of such a thing. Like sleeping on anything less than Egyptian cotton might mean be the death of me. Crap, he was cute.

"And I told Sam to organize security since we've still got some paparazzi hanging around. Just in case. They'll be discreet, I promise."

"Jimmy, I can't take security to my sister's wedding."

"You sure?"

"Yeah." I smiled.

"Fine. But it also occurred to me you might need a dress or stuff so my stylist is on top of that," he announced. "I described you and sent her your measurements. Don't worry, she'll send up a couple of things for you try."

"She will, huh?"

"A bit of a mix so you can choose for yourself. I told her not to forget shoes and shit too."

"You've thought of everything." I cocked my head. "But how did you know my measurements?"

He stopped. "Lena, I've had my hands all over you a couple of times now. I know your body. I'm not gonna forget it anytime soon."

"Oh."

"I'm not presuming, I swear," he said, eyes sincere. "If you decide not to go, that's fine. Not a problem. But I wanted everything in place for you just in case."

"You did all this? For me?"

One thick shoulder lifted.

"Just this afternoon?"

"Ev helped," he admitted. "I know you probably haven't seen your family for a while. As someone smart once said to me, family's important."

He leaned back against the bathroom counter, watching me. "Didn't mean to hurt your feelings. I know you think this is me trying to buy my way out of trouble, but it's not. I would have done this anyway. I just want the best for you, 'cause that's what you deserve."

My eyes went disturbingly liquid. I blinked repeatedly, sniffling ever so slightly.

He groaned. "Lena, do not cry. That's not okay."

"I'm not. I wouldn't dare."

"You think I don't care about you. But I do. If you still want me to come with you, then that's cool." He winced. "I mean, I'd like that. Whatever you want, okay?"

"Okay." I stared at him in wonder, staggered, my heart and mind struggling to keep up with it all. "Thank you, Jimmy."

He just watched me warily, unmoving. So I moved instead, straight into his arms. Without hesitation, he crushed me against his chest.

"Don't hate me, Lena," he whispered. "You want to be mad at me when I do dumb things, that's fine. But don't ever hate me. I couldn't take that, not from you."

I put my hand to his cheek, undone by the rawness of his voice, his apparent vulnerability. "Hey. I could never hate you."

"Promise."

"I promise." And it was true. He made me frustrated and angry all the damn time. There was no chance I could ever bring myself to hate him, however. I cradled his face in my hands. He was so precious to me, yet he sounded so alone, lost and scared like a child. "That will never happen."

Jimmy shut his eyes and exhaled hard. He rubbed his stubbled cheek against my hand, gently scratching the palm, making my skin tingle. I stretched up on tippy toes and he fit his firm lips to mine. His tongue slipped into my mouth, seeking out mine. Christ, he'd gotten good at this fast. The taste of him, the familiar feel of his body against mine, it was all so perfect.

He felt like home.

He kissed me slow and wet in what could only be

described as a full-out frontal sensual assault. His mouth conquered in the best possible way. All of his worry just fueled the hunger, I think, he seemed insatiable. His hands slid over me, stroking my face and neck, touching every part of me. My skin came alive beneath his fingers. No other man had ever made me feel this wanted, this adored. Sure as hell, none had ever called to me the way he did, body and soul.

"You forgive me?" he asked, trailing hot kisses down my neck.

"Yes. But don't do it again. And don't stop kissing me."

"Got it. Let me apologize to you properly. Let me kiss you between the legs." Strong hands cupped my ass, pressing me against his erection. "I wanna lick you, Lena."

"You like doing that, don't you?" I asked, a little amazed. Past boyfriends had not rated the experience highly.

"Fuck yes. I love having you squirming against my face, rubbing your pussy on me."

"God." The hard stiff length of him pressed into my abdomen, urging me on. But it was his words that made my blood surge.

"The smell of you, the taste of you, I love everything about eating you," he breathed.

"No more." I covered his mouth with my hand, squeezing my legs tight together. The state of my panties was a disgrace. He'd made me slick and needy without even touching me below the waist. The man was on a sexual rampage, out of control. Or I might be, it was hard to tell. Either way, he had to be stopped. "Someone might hear."

He escaped my hand, dimples flashing. "No one's hearing anything. This place has excellent soundproofing. How do you think Dave and Ev manage to fuck during parties? Thick walls. Don't worry."

"Just in case."

His eyes narrowed. "Are you wet for me, Lena? Is your pretty pussy getting ready for my mouth? I'm damn hungry. You're coming more than once for me tonight."

My face burned hotter than a grill and between my legs throbbed.

"I knew it. You like me talking dirty," he said, teeth nipping at my collarbone before his tongue lapped over it. The big animal.

"No I don't. You're making that up."

"You're practically vibrating with excitement. You love it." His laughter was diabolical, his breath hot on my skin. "Ah, Lena. Do I have some filthy things I need to say to you."

I hid my face in his neck, giving him my own love bite or two. Man, his skin tasted good. Salt and the warmth that was Jimmy. And he smelled even better. His fingers sunk into my ass, holding on tight. The seemingly ever-ready presence of his hard-on more than made itself known, poking into my stomach. If it got any harder he might hurt himself.

"Tell me, Lena. How wet are your panties?"

I would impart that knowledge over my dead body. Or a mild bit of erotic wrestling. Most likely the latter. But it should be noted, two could play at this game, and playing with him was about as fun as it got. He might be currently in the lead, but I wasn't so far behind.

"You feel so hard, Jimmy."

"Do I now?" he asked, tugging on my hair just a little. Enough to light up all of the nerve ending on my scalp.

I gasped.

"I love the noises you make," he said. "I wonder how you'll sound when I bite your sweet peach of an ass. It really is fucking magnificent, Lena. Of course, I'll finger your gorgeous pussy when I do it. Wouldn't want it to feel neglected."

"That's sweet of you." I slipped my hand between us, grasping his huge cock. "Would you like me to lick this, Jimmy? Of course I'm happy to suck it as well."

"Are you now?"

"We haven't done that yet."

He pressed his forehead against mine. "No, we haven't. And you do have a beautiful mouth."

I set my hands against his stomach and pushed, taking a step back. His arms fell from around me.

"Right now?" he asked.

"What could be more romantic?" I smiled.

He out and out grinned. "I don't know a shitload about romance. But I'd have to be a god damn idiot to turn down a blow job from you. But are you sure?"

"Yes."

Thick, fluffy white towels hung on the railing. I pulled one down, folded it and threw it at his feet.

His gaze moved between me and the towel. "You sure, you're sure?"

"Very." I pulled down another towel and tossed it on top of the first.

I got down on my knees.

His pupils seemed to have doubled in size almost. "Lena."

"Yeah?" My hand traveled up his legs, over his firm thighs. I undid his belt buckle, tore into the button and zipper of his jeans.

"Forgot what I was going to say . . ."

"Never mind. I like that you go commando." I took him in hand. Christ, he felt hot, so wonderfully warm. The skin was velvety soft, the broad head darkening to red. He filled my grip in a great way.

His hands fisted at his sides.

"And I really like your dick, Jimmy."

"Christ."

"I mean, seriously like it." My thumb smoothed over the eye of his penis, teasing just so. His thigh muscles twitched. "But I like you as a whole even more."

He tensed. "Thank you."

"Anytime." I smiled. "You want my glasses on or off for this?"

"On," he answered instantly.

"Okay, but no cum on the lenses, that's not cool. Understood?"

A muscle jumped in his jaw.

"All right, then."

I dragged the flat of my tongue across the head of his cock, collecting a bead of salty cum for my trouble. Yummy. Give me more. Normally, sperm didn't set my world on fire, but anything this man's body made for me was to be savored.

Such was the absolute lunacy of my love for him.

I wanted to make him feel as adored and wanted as he did me. To chase the doubt from his eyes and give him nothing but pleasure.

I took him into my mouth, sucking before laving the underside with my tongue. All due care was given to the sweet spot. I massaged it with the tip of my tongue until he swore quite profusely, his hips kicking forward. My spare hand cupped his balls, rolling them gently, the skin so soft and delicate. His hard flesh stretched my jaw, filled my mouth, and the musky scent of him was all I could smell. I took him in as deep as I could, working him with tongue, teeth, and lips. My hand stroked the rest of him, keeping all of him occupied. Careful of my teeth, I drew back, then forged forward again.

"Fuck, Lena." His heavy balls drew up closer to his body. "Feels so fucking nice."

And he'd used a word I just had to question. His dick came free of mouth with a faint popping sound.

"Nice?" I asked, curling my swollen lips into a smile.

He watched me through hooded lids. "Very nice."

I fit my lips around the head once more, sucking hard. His hips bucked in response. It was time to finish him off. The muscles in his stomach tensed, his legs went rigid. I sucked with all my might, hollowing my cheeks and taking him deep.

"God damn it, Lena." Various growling and snarling noises came above me. He was such an animal.

Hot bitter salty cum filled my mouth and throat. I swallowed fast, taking it all. It never even crossed my mind to spit . . . this was Jimmy. He came and he came as I worked him down gently, stroking his cock and rubbing his balls, cherishing him. His whole body slumped and he panted for air. My work here was done. The man was decimated.

"Help me up," I said, tugging on his jeans. His eyes slowly blinked open and he held out a hand to me. I took it, letting him doing the heaving lifting involved in pulling me back up onto my feet. "Thanks."

An arm shot out, wrapping around my neck, pulling me in against him. His whole body trembled.

"You okay?" I asked.

A nod.

"Feeling a little emotional, huh?" I petted his hair. "That's okay. It was an emotional blow job."

He snorted.

I gave him a squeeze. "I'm glad you enjoyed it."

"I'm clean, Lena," he said, face pressed into my neck. "Got tested, everything came up negative, okay?"

"Oh, yeah, I swallowed. Didn't even think about that."

The arms of steel around me didn't falter. "I liked that you swallowed."

Warm damp lips rubbed against my neck. Such affection from him, I'd never known the likes of it. My head swam with joy and the most disturbing words rose up and up inside of me until they stuck in my throat. And still they pushed and shoved their way out of me with such thoughtless dumb-ass intent. I tried to stop them because I knew better, I really did. But they spewed forth from my tortured lovelorn soul while my brain watched on in complete and utter horror.

"I love you, Jimmy."

Silence.

Absolute, dead silence.

The man in my arms snap froze, even his breathing faltered.

"I mean, not that it's a big deal or anything." My mouth, I wanted to kill it slowly and painfully in many and varied ways. We'd been in a good place, in the moment, and I had to go and wreck it, pressing for more. "You don't have to say anything. In fact you shouldn't, it would be better if you didn't, and we'll just carry on exactly as we were and pretend this never even happened, okay? Because we're doing great, just fine, and I really don't want anything to change."

Hands gripped my arms and forcibly removed me from him. Every instinct in me said duck and cover, run. Whatever happens, I should not look at his face. Because it was pale and drawn, and his eyes were vaguely terrified. "You love me?"

"Jimmy . . ."

He looked at me like I was foreign to him, unknown and unwanted in every way that mattered.

"Lena, I can't . . . I don't . . ."

"No, I know." Right then, I was dead in all the ways that mattered. My lungs just hadn't figured it out yet.

From down below came yipping and barking. Little nails scrabbled at my black stockings, shredding them beyond repair. He must have been snoozing under the counter and gotten woken up with Jimmy's yelling.

"Hey, Killer." I picked up the small bundle of black-and-white terror. He was the perfect distraction to my strung-out heart. "I didn't see you in here. Where were you hiding?"

"We better go back out." Jimmy studied the far wall with great ardor. I guess anything was better than looking at me and my messy, out-there emotions. Such an embarrassment.

"Yeah. I guess so." I led the way back out, same as I'd led him into my emotional blow job trap in the first place. Women were the worst. Killer's wet little nose rubbed at my chin.

"Son," Mal called to dog in greeting. He was still chatting with Anne and Lizzy on the sofa. "I was wondering where you'd gotten to."

"Found him snoozing in the bathroom." I handed the fur baby over to his daddy.

Mal's green eyes narrowed. "Your lips are unnaturally puffy and your lipstick is all worn away. What the hell were you two doing in the bathroom within sight of my firstborn child?"

"Nothing," I said, backing up a step. This was the last damn thing I needed.

He held the pup in front of his face. "Killer, tell daddy where the bad people touched you."

"We didn't do anything." I turned to Jimmy but he was still too busy being shell-shocked, the useless jerk.

"He's traumatized! Just look at him." Mal held up the puppy for all to see. Delighting in the attention, Killer waggled his tail and barked loudly twice.

"Here, give him to me." Anne wrestled the dog carefully from Mal's hands. "He's not traumatized. A little more experienced than he probably needed to be. But it's not like he hasn't been asleep in our bedroom while we've been otherwise occupied."

"Is it not bad enough that he has to grow up with the stigma of his parents being unwed?" Sadly, Mal shook his head. "My poor boy, he never stood a chance at a normal life."

"Hmm," said Anne, handing the dog over to her sister. At this rate, Killer's paws wouldn't touch the ground for years to come. He had to be the single most cosseted dog ever, talk about lifestyles of the rich and famous. And yes, worrying over the pampered pooch was much safer than turning to see if Jimmy had yet come out of his coma.

Anne climbed to her feet, and then knelt down on one knee before the blond drummer. "Will you marry me?"

All of the chatter around us fell silent.

"I'm the one that does funny shit," said Mal, brows drawn down. "Not you."

"I'm not being funny." Her hands found his and held on tight. "I love you and I want to marry you, Malcolm Ericson. What do you say?"

Mal's mouth opened and we all waited with bated breath. But he said nothing.

Eventually, Anne spoke again, "I'm not scared anymore. I know this is right and if you still want to do this, then I do too, with all my heart."

"Can we fly to Vegas and get married by a Santa Elvis for Christmas?" asked Mal, eyes suspiciously bright.

A single tear worked its way down Anne's cheek. "I'd really like that."

Pandemonium ensued as Mal jumped on Anne and the happy couple started rolling around on the floor. Everyone burst out into applause and screaming and god knows what else. Killer barked his head off at all the commotion. Only Jimmy and I stood apart, both still too stunned over my confession. I wanted to be happy for them. I really did, but I stood there with Jimmy's taste in my mouth and my broken heart floating around inside of me, razor sharp pieces cutting up my insides.

A hand touched my arm before falling away. "Let's go."

I looked up into his beautiful beloved face and gave him my grimmest of smiles. "Yeah."

Amidst all of the celebration and confusion, we slipped out to the elevator, taking the heady trip back down to ground level. Neither of us said a word. Outside a bitterly cold drizzly sort of rain was falling. I huddled deeper into my coat as Jimmy opened the passenger door of the Mercedes for me. A happy couple ran hand in hand across the road. The city lights blurred as spots of water smeared the lenses of my glasses.

You know those times on the edge of winter when the chill seeps so deep into you that it feels like you couldn't possibly ever be warm again? This was one of them.

"Lena," he said, still holding the car door open.

"Sorry." I climbed in to the leather-scented luxury of the Mercedes and Jimmy carefully closed the door behind me.

A moment later he was sliding into the driver's seat, wiping the rain from his face. Neither of us spoke. There wasn't really anything left to say. The trip back to his house passed uneventfully, the lights and buildings passing me by far too fast. Soon enough, the gloomy gray walls of his palace reared up before us. A few brave photographers daring the bad weather hovered out front, held back by the two stout security guards.

We drove around back, down into the bottom level. The big garage door closed behind us, shutting us in. I'd sat, stupidly stunned for so long, Jimmy opened my car door, offering me a hand.

"Thanks." I climbed out on my own. "I'm fine."

I wasn't the least bit fine. Unrequited love was a bitch.

Up the stairs we went, past the ground level, on to the second. My bedroom door was the second on the left. He paused by the entry and I switched on the light, turning it to low. It was a mood lighting sort of night.

"Lena." He swallowed, his eyes darkening. "Let me come in."

"I can't."

"But—"

"I can't," I repeated. "We need to stop."

"No, we don't."

"We do," I said. "This isn't working for me. I can't block it out. I can't pretend I don't feel things for you. I'm just not made that way."

"No, we're fine. I swear we're fine." His hands ran over my arms, my back, drawing me in. I wanted him, all of him, so desperately. His touch made it impossible to resist. "Everything's good."

"Jimmy . . ."

"Shh, it's okay. It's okay, it's just me." He pressed his lips to mine and the taste of him. God. Nothing tasted better, nothing ever could. And I couldn't hold back if I tried. I angled my face, opening my mouth to trace his lips with my tongue. He made a noise of pure hunger in his throat and hands gripped my hips, fingers fierce.

There'd be marks in the morning.

My hands wrapped around his neck, holding on tight. Right up until he tried to push my coat off my shoulders, then I had to let go. If he was the great love of my life, then it was only right that we went out with a bang. Nothing could fix things now the words had been said. I knew that. I felt it in every fiber of my being. This was good-bye.

We fumbled out of our clothes, stumbling in the general direction of the bed. The thing was, we got about halfway and Jimmy's hands smoothed up my thighs, pushing my skirt up to my waist. Thank god for thigh-high stockings. Our mouths were all over each other, tongues rubbing and teasing. He tore my panties down, pressing me against the nearest wall, and down he went.

The first feel of his mouth against me was ecstasy, the lashing of his tongue and sucking of his lips. All of the blood in me rushed straight to his command. I ground my pussy against his face and he groaned in approval. He was so hungry for me. If only that was enough.

"Oh god, Jimmy." My hands found his hair and his tongue found my clit and fuck . . . so good. My eyes rolled straight back into my head. Carefully, he lifted my leg onto his shoulder, opening me further to his ministrations. He worked me hard and fast up to climax, my whole body quaking. I was half primed from the oral earlier, despite the emotional turmoil. And thank goodness vaginas don't care for such heartbreak and pain. I didn't want to miss a moment of this, our last time together.

Two thick fingers slid into me, curved and pressed against a sweet spot inside. He'd said he knew my body and he hadn't been lying. I shouted out and came, blind-sided by the exquisite rush. My fingers knotted in his hair, pulling hard. But he didn't complain. My bones rattled and my mind emptied and it was beautiful. For one bright brilliant moment the whole world made sense. I was right where I belonged. Then reality and sadness came crashing back in. Eyes closed, his lips pressed against my pubic bone in a soft reverent kiss. It seemed almost an act of benediction. He pressed his forehead against my stomach, just taking a moment as if he'd been the one so recently turned inside out.

The silken strands of his hair sifted through my fingers. "Hey, are you all right?"

"Yeah."

Jimmy Ferris didn't mess around.

He got to his feet, tore down his zipper and reached for me. I'd yet to stop shaking from coming, but he didn't wait. He lifted me in his arms, winding my legs around his waist. I wished I was strong enough to hold on to him forever this way. The hard thick head of his cock pressed against my opening and slowly he sunk inside. He filled me in ways no one else ever could, and it had nothing to do with size.

"You're so fucking beautiful, Lena."

"God. Jimmy."

"Need you."

Teeth nipped at my ear lobe, the sweet sting stealing through me, making me gasp. He covered my face in kisses, hot lips moving over my skin, branding me as his. It seemed he couldn't get enough of me either. His hands, mouth, and cock were all determined to leave their mark on my body. My stupid heart beat hard and fast, feeling full to overflowing, but there was nothing I could do about that. I held him fast, letting him pound into me, imprinting himself in every pore. Nothing in me didn't belong to him, whether I wanted it or not.

Regardless of what made rational sense, my heart gave and gave until there was nothing left.

But isn't that the way of some loves? He came hard, cock jerking inside of me, teeth embedded in my neck. His head lay on my shoulder as he caught his breath, both of us sagging against the wall.

He carried me to the bed, collapsing onto the mattress at my side. I rolled onto my side, to face him. He looked wiped out, bone tired. Fair enough, I myself wanted to sleep for a thousand years. Dark hair fell over his face, hiding his eyes from me. The glare of the light was dazzling.

I should have turned it down more. Hell, I should have turned it off.

"I can't keep doing this," I said.

He didn't answer.

"We need to go back to being strictly business. It's for the best." I had no better words.

A shiver ran through him and he rolled onto his side, turning his back on me.

The most beautiful man I ever met crept out of my bed just before midnight and I let him go.

CHAPTER EIGHTEEN

I overslept. When I woke, the sounds of shouting and laughter already carried through the house.

Another busy day in the Stage Dive world.

In all honesty, I didn't know what came next. Since he'd run off Tom, I'd have to find him another replacement companion/assistant. Time would tell if I still got to do the apprenticeship with Pam. Perhaps I'd see about enrolling in an arts college or something, studying photography another way. I'd finally found what I just might want to do with the rest of my life. Something I could be passionate about. There was one almighty positive to come out of this screwed up situation.

"Hey," I said, wandering in to the kitchen, my hair still wet from the shower.

The guys were gathered around the table, throwing back coffee and various energy drinks. Mal was apparently practicing his wedding speech, ready for Vegas. He stood tall on a chair while the others jeered and threw wadded up balls of paper. Dean hung out in the corner, giving me a brief attempt at a smile. Even Taylor and Pam were here, standing with their arms around one another. Further proof of love everlasting and coupley happiness.

Next time I'd do the smart thing and be sure to fall for someone who wanted me as much as I wanted them. Next time.

"Lena, agrees with me. Don't you, Lena?" Mal called out upon my entering the room.

"Of course, Mal."

"You have no idea what you just agreed to," said Ben, smiling at me over the rim of his coffee cup.

"Shut up, Ben," said the mad drummer. "Every Vegas wedding needs a couple of burlesque dancers for effect, Lena gets that. She's more enlightened than you fools."

"Anne is going to shoot you down in flames," said Ben.

I shook my head and kept moving. No way was I getting sucked any further into that discussion.

I caught Jimmy out of the corner of my eye, dressed in his usual all black, leaning against the counter. If I didn't look at him directly maybe I could still get out of this with the one small, unbroken piece still intact. First things first, coffee. I headed for the pot, filling a mug to the brim. Forget sugar and milk, someone needed to pump caffeine directly into my bloodstream before anyone got hurt.

"Dave, get your fucking boots off the table," Jimmy grouched.

"You're a god damn delight today, Jim," said David. "Something happen to warrant the good mood?"

His brother didn't reply.

I sucked down some coffee, burning my tongue. No matter, it was a small pain, nothing really.

"I need that shit on the interview ready and the plans for the first leg of the tour, Lena. Now." Jimmy dumped his empty mug in the sink good and hard. I'm surprised it didn't break. "Try to be up on time and ready for work in the future, yeah?"

Slowly, I turned to face him, coffee still in hand.

He stared straight at me. "No more fucking around. Right, Lena?"

My cup started to shake. His message was pertinent on oh so many levels. So this was it, can't say it was unexpected. It almost came as a relief really, airing our grievances, casting it all out into the world. He might have waited until I no longer had his semen inside of me, just for politeness sake, though.

"Right," I agreed, my voice flat, strange. I didn't sound like myself at all.

Shadows lay beneath his cold pale eyes and the cut of his mouth and cheeks seemed harder, harsher than normal. I'd only gotten a little sleep, but it seemed Jimmy had gotten none at all. Every sharp line of him seemed wired, on edge.

All talk around the table stopped. Even Mal climbed down from his chair.

"You need a date for your sister's wedding you'll have to find someone else. I'm flying down to LA to see Liv." His hands gripped the counter behind him, the muscles in his arms flexing. "I'll be busy."

I nodded. My tear ducts were gearing up for something big, I could feel it.

"And when you get back, start looking for your own place."

I gasped, my stomach contracting. It actually felt like I'd been kicked and he'd caught a rib or two. So much hurt, inside and out. Foolish of me really, this messy ending had been written from the start. You didn't just fall out of love with a man like Jimmy Ferris.

"Don't need you in my face all the damn time," he said. "You work nine to five until we go on tour then as needed. Got it?"

David slowly stood. "Jim . . ."

"Stay out of it. This is between me and her." He turned back to me, his lips thinning in obvious hostility. "Understood, Lena?"

Ben cursed quietly.

"Understood. Will there be anything else, Mr. Ferris?" I asked, setting my coffee cup aside before I dropped it.

His voice cut through me like a sword. "None of your cute shit. We're strictly business. I don't want your opinion and I sure as fuck don't need your advice."

My throat was dust.

"You do your job from now on and that's it."

"Jimmy." David thumped his hands on the table. The one where Jimmy and I had made love. Fucked. Whatever.

"Stop this," said David, face lined with fury. "Don't talk to her like that."

"She is not your concern, Dave. She never was."

I stood there numb, but knowing what I had to do. "Fire me."

"What?"

Every eye in the room was on me, but I only looked at him. He'd wanted an audience and he'd gotten one. Fucked if I'd play into it any further. People would think what they liked and there was nothing I could do about it, he'd been right about that. We'd gone into freefall when I told him I loved him. It was time to hit the ground.

"Fire me," I said. "That's how this ends."

Jimmy's nostrils flared.

"That's how this was always going to end."

Fury flashed in his eyes.

"Go on."

"That's not what you want," he said, a shadow of doubt crossing his face for the first time.

"I can't have what I want, Jimmy. I never could. All you have to do is fire me and I'll go away. You won't have to think about it ever again. It'll be like it never happened. That's what you want, isn't it?"

Whoever said love and hate were the same knew what they were talking about. Because the way Jimmy was looking at me would have burned a lesser woman to the ground. Last night he'd loved me, or my body at least. Now, there should have only been ashes where I stood.

"I go away and everything's easy again, uncomplicated," I said. "You can go back to hiding from the world. I won't be here to stop you."

"Shut up."

"Fire me, Jimmy." My smile must have looked every bit as bitter as it tasted. "Send me away."

Someone said something but it passed right by me, unheard. There was only me and him.

"You know you want to," I said. "It'd be so much simpler if I wasn't here."

"Shut the fuck up, Lena."

"Go on," I urged, leaning forward. "No time like the present, right? Do it."

A muscle jumped in his jaw line.

"DO IT."

His chin jerked.

Done.

The breath rushed out of me and I shut my eyes tight. Tears escaped anyway, the cunning bastards. Talk about fucking drama. Enough.

"You promised you wouldn't relapse if I left. I'm holding you to that," I said, my voice cracking, the words coming so much harder now.

Another nod.

"Hang on," said Mal, rushing over. "Jim, man. C'mon, this is Lena. You can't fire her!"

"Lena, wait." David reached out a hand.

"It's okay," I said, wiping my face, forcing my way past the band.

I didn't want to see the others but of course my gaze went there, taking in the whole of the ugly pathetic scene. Plenty of shell-shocked faces and one vaguely embarrassed glance on Dean's part. Not like it really mattered, I'd never see any of them ever again. This part of my life was over.

An argument started up behind in the kitchen, numerous voices raised in anger and dismay. I didn't slow down, didn't turn back.

There's probably a lot of things I could say about the nature of love. Exactly what I did or didn't mean to Jimmy would never be known, perhaps not even to himself. Love was truly one of life's mysteries. That it could fuck you five ways to Sunday and still remain so utterly perplexing and unknown was kind of impressive. I guess it all depends on how you look at it. Right then, I was looking at the long lonely road home. My childhood home, that is. The home I'd shared with him was gone.

Tears flowed faster and I let them fall unchecked.

Somethings were meant to be felt to their fullest. Get it out, get it over with, and all the rest.

I liked to think he'd miss me, but the truth was, he'd be fine once I was gone. There'd be someone else to step into my shoes, someone to answer his e-mails and keep him sorted. Chances were, they'd do a better job than I ever had.

The end.

A massive white satin bow sat in pride of place on the front door. Christ, Alyce and her look-at-me bullshit. This wedding had clearly taken on gargantuan proportions in my absence. Maybe I should have holed up in a hotel room until all of this had blown over.

No. That was quitters talk.

I was made of tougher stuff.

After all, I'd already walked away from one life-altering, heart-shattering situation this week. To make it through my sister and ex's wedding would be no biggie. Eardrum piercing, girly squeals of glee could be heard coming from inside. It was the night before her nuptials, I guess she had all of her remaining three bridesmaids over. Britney Spears music suddenly pumped out, loud and proud.

Yeah, no, okay, I couldn't do it.

Not a fucking chance.

My weary body and mind had already been dragged halfway across the damn country. I'd left a lot of stuff behind in boxes with a message for Ev to please have it forwarded. All that mattered was getting the hell out of his house in one reasonable rational piece.

Pam drove me to the airport despite my protestations I could get a cab. Such a lovely woman, it was a pity I'd never get to be her apprentice. The rest of the band and company fortunately remained downstairs. To face any of them following Jimmy's and my drama-ridden breakup would have been more than I could bear. The $10,000 Nikon stayed behind on the piece of furniture formerly known as my bedside table.

Jimmy could do with it what he liked. No way was I taking it with me.

My immediate existence revolved around expunging every trace of him from my memory. I'd forget the sound of his voice and the smell of him covered in sweat. I'd never again think about the one hundred and one stupid little conversations we'd had, all the things we fought about. My broken heart had been taped and glued to perfection. And all of these things were gone.

They had to be gone so I could face the future and put him in the past.

There was no way, however, I could face whatever fresh

hell was happening inside my childhood home. Britney Spears. Give me strength. I about-faced, preparing to drag my full suitcase the two blocks back into town since my cab had already gone. So far as I knew, Toni still worked at the Burns Bed and Breakfast. If I slipped her twenty she'd keep my whereabouts secret for a couple of days.

But no, standing directly smack bam in the middle of my planned escape route stood my father. Time had made no major changes, he was still as stout and solid looking as he'd ever been. A bit more gray in his hair perhaps. In each hand was a bag filled to the brim with Kwong Chinese Restaurant containers. The best food to be had in my hometown, in my expert opinion.

"Lena?" He blinked at me in the violet and gray evening light. The weight around my heart lifted a little.

"Hey, Daddy."

He looked me over, face frozen in shock. "My girl's come home!"

"Yeah. I'm back." Gah. Instantly, I turned on the waterworks and my face was a mess. My emotions needed to calm the fuck down.

Dad took two big steps forward, giving me the best hug possible when laden down with takeout. The delicious scent of Honey Chicken made my mouth water and my tummy growl. It'd be too much to ask that I be one of those girls that actually loses weight when her love life goes to shit, apparently.

I cuddled in against him, taking comfort.

"Good to have you home, sweetheart," he said.

"Good to be home." And it was.

For a moment, we just stared at one another, smiling in wonder. It was nice to know some things couldn't be lost. The bond between me and my dad was one of those things.

"Was a bad business, what your sister did," he said. "Your mother and I gave her firm words over it."

"You did?" Huh, I'd always thought Alyce the Wonder Kid could do no wrong. There you go.

"Well of course we did. Though you were always too much of a handful for that idiot Brandon. He would never have made you happy." Dad looked down at me over the rim of his glasses. "And you're still not happy. What's wrong, sweetheart?"

"I got my heart broken again." I chuckled, shrugged. "Stupid me, huh?"

"Stupid him, more like it. My girl's a queen. Any boy that can't see that doesn't deserve to get within spitting distance." The man should be president. He said the nicest damn things.

"Thanks, Dad."

He just stared at me, waiting for more information.

"It really is a long story," I said.

A particularly high-pitched, ear-shattering scream communicating what I supposed was extreme delight came from within the house. I winced.

"It's going to be a long night," sighed Dad. "What do you say we go inside, get the greetings out of the way, and then go hide out down in the basement with my beer fridge?"

"Sounds like a plan."

"Your mother missed you, Lena." He dug into his coat pocket for the keys. An impossible process given his many tasty burdens.

"Here, let me help." I took one of the bags off his hands. "I missed her too. I just needed to get away for a while, find myself and stuff."

"And what'd you find?"

"I found that I still have no sense when it comes to choosing men. But you know what, Dad?"

"What, Lena?" he asked with a smile.

"I'm okay on my own."

His keys jingled as he fiddled about, searching for the right one. "Of course you are, you were always the strongest out of my girls. Your sister was always jealous of you, you know?"

"Get out of here." I laughed. The whole idea was ridiculous. "Shiny, perfect Alyce?"

"Try shiny, sassy Lena. Always ready with a clever comeback and able to talk to anyone." Dad smiled and pushed the front door open.

Light and noise assailed us along with many girls crying my name in surprise.

"Hi." I gave a finger wave.

Alyce gave me a tremulous smile. Five-foot-eight and willowy slender, with a glossy fall of mahogany hair. "Lena. Hey."

"Hi," I repeated, just proving exactly how excellent I was with conversation.

Dad squeezed past me, taking the food into the kitchen. Her bridesmaids watched on with big curious eyes, the damn gossips. News of my return would no doubt be texted all over town within minutes.

"Thanks for coming back," said my sister, looking all sorts of shy and uncertain. Her gaze wandered all over the place, unable to stay on me for long.

"Not a problem."

Then my pint-sized hurricane of a mother flew out of the kitchen and tackle-hugged me. Our ample bosoms slammed together with an "oomph!" Rock-and-roll wrestlers would have been on their asses. My glasses were most definitely askew.

"About time," she whispered. "Welcome back, honey."

"Thanks, Mom." I hugged her back until my arms ached. This had been the right thing to do, coming home.

I felt better already, lighter. I could put myself back together in peace here. Forget about rock stars and slick suits and all the rest.

Mom, Dad, and I piled our plates high with Sweet and Sour Pork and so on, then retreated downstairs. The feral female bridesmaid pack could run wild with their squeeing on the ground level. It seemed even mom was ready for an estrogen break.

We quickly outvoted dad and the game got turned off in favor of an old black-and-white movie that was on TV. It was nice, being home, being with my parents, all of it. Very nice.

"Another beer, Lena?" asked Dad from his seat in the corner.

"I take it that's your subtle way of asking me to go fetch you one?"

"I'm an old man. You have to look after your father."

"Ri-i-ight."

Mom just tittered. Lord knew how many white wines she'd sucked down before we came home. I didn't begrudge her, Alyce's wedding plans had obviously taken their toll.

The basement was Dad's man palace. A huge flat-screen TV, comfy couches, and of course, the aforementioned beer fridge in the corner. Framed pictures of football jerseys lined the walls. Sometimes I wondered if Dad regretted not having sons, but he'd never said or indicated anything of the like. My parents were good people. Any issues I had body wise or whatever were my own. And while it was seriously great to be back home, I didn't belong here long-term.

Forget the past, I was going to do my thing (whatever that was) and be happy. Decision made.

I grabbed my dad's beer, the second, however, I hovered over. I didn't have a drinking problem. Not drinking had been something I did in support of Jimmy.

"Fuck it," I mumbled, snatching another cold one from the fridge. I could kick back with my folks and enjoy a drink without it being a problem. Jimmy Ferris did not rule me in any way, shape, or form. Never had and never would. Not that he'd ever felt I needed to not drink, it'd been my show of solidarity and how far had that gotten me?

Whatever. It was time to kick back and relax. I was having a beer.

"Isn't that the man you were working for?" asked Mom.

I turned and there they were, spread out in full vibrant color, coming at me live from Hollywood. Jimmy and Liv on the red carpet at some event. He looked so damn good with his dark hair styled back and a black suit on. It was like a knife twisting inside of my chest. My whole body went into shock. The beer bottles slipped from my fingers, smashing upon the tiled floor. Glass glittered and foaming beer had splashed everywhere. I looked up and he was gone, the ad was over, the news had moved on. Our sweet old black-and-white movie returned to the screen.

Mom and Dad were already out of their chairs and rushing at me.

"I'm so sorry," I said, staring uselessly at the mess I'd created. My brain had stalled. Jimmy certainly however hadn't missed a beat. He'd smashed my heart, thrown me out, and moved on with being the rock 'n' roll bad boy.

"Fuck him," I whispered.

My sister dashed down the stairs. "What was that?"

"Your sister had an accident," said Mom, grabbing a towel out of the pile of laundry beside the dryer.

"I made a mistake," I agreed. "A really big one."

Dad blinked at me owlishly from behind his glasses. "Oh, sweetheart."

The tears started and they didn't stop for a long, long time. I think I finally cried myself dry.

CHAPTER NINETEEN

I'm pretty damn sure Dante meant to make weddings one of the levels of hell and just forgot.

I sat alone in the corner of the grand ballroom of the Long Oak Lodge as folk mingled and danced all around me. The room had been decked out in everything silver and white. Balloons, sashes, flowers, you name it. The overwhelming amount of blooms reminded me of Lori's funeral, the sashes, of Jimmy's silk ties. He'd said the entire world was a trigger for him when it came to addiction. I now understood exactly what he meant. My heroin was six-foot-one and as gorgeous as sin. It'd taken me higher than I'd ever been before, running riot through my veins. Then, not so surprisingly, it had indeed delivered me to the gutter.

You could say I had a bit of a self-pity thing going on in my party girl corner.

I took another sip of lemonade through my sparkly wedding straw.

Fun times. Brokenhearted people really did need to just be left the fuck alone. We're not suitable company for anyone.

Fairy lights and candles provided the moodiest of

lighting while up on the stage, a band belted out rock and pop love song classics. I'd borrowed a dress off an old friend (knee length silvery gray satin and lace—quite nice if a little tight in the chest area). Brandon had come near me once and I'd shown him my teeth. No, really I had. It was actually pretty damn funny how fast he ran away. He didn't try talking to me again. Apparently, I had issues forgiving people who said shitty things to me.

Now, it was near the midnight hour and the party was finally showing signs of winding down. Alyce and Brandon slow danced in the middle of the dance floor, giving each other loving looks. Despite their dubious beginning, I think they actually had a chance of making it and all the best to them. Mom and Dad danced alongside them, indulging in the occasional smooch. Everyone seemed to be having a great time.

Uncle Bob Lambada'd past and I gave him two thumbs up.

"That's great. You go, Uncle Bob," I said without a single touch of sarcasm because I'm awesome like that.

I slipped down my glasses, rubbing at the bridge of my nose. A headache had been brewing behind the back of my eyes for hours now thanks to the overly complicated updo I'd opted for. It looked gorgeous but it pulled like holy hell. And I didn't want to think about how long it was going to take me to pick out all the bobby pins.

I didn't notice the guy in the black suit at first. I was pretty damn busy feeling sorry for myself. He was just a shadow moving through the drifting figures of couples on the dance floor. When a scuffle broke out over the microphone, however, then he had my full attention.

"Back the fuck off," a gruff voice said over the loud speakers. It was strangely familiar.

Gasps were heard. Then faint voices argued on, only just audible over the airwaves.

"Yeah, I get it's a wedding," he said, nice and clear. "I've got the perfect song for the happy couple."

"No. It can't be." I sat forward, squinting, trying to see through all the candles and balloon strings hanging down from the ceiling. "That's not possible."

The softer voice fought back up front. People shuffled on the dance floor, the crowd growing restless. I don't think this wedding hijacking had been very well staged.

"Fine, what do you know how to play?" the strange man in the suit asked. More talking. "Yeah, okay, do that one."

The opening notes of a song began, some plucking of guitar strings. I knew the melody. It was Maroon 5's "She Will Be Loved." As pop songs went, it was pretty damn good, a bit of a favorite of mine.

Then the singing interloper opened his mouth. "Beauty queen of only . . ."

My knees trembled and all doubt fled.

What the ever loving fuck was he doing here?

Due to the delight of a cordless microphone, Jimmy jumped down from the stage and started searching through the crowd. Perhaps it was some bizarre coincidence and he'd decided to start performing at small events. He pushed through the sea of helium balloons, head turning this way and that. Still singing.

I didn't know what to do.

There was this weird warm expanding sensation in my chest. I could only assume I was having a heart attack of some type. The lyrics were not pertinent. Not in the least. I'll have you note, my smile was not broken, just a little quivery care of emotion. Also, he'd only had me three times, not "so" many times, and when I'd fallen after trying to kick in his door I landed on my ass on the floor, he did not catch me. All of this led me to the firm belief that the man was a god damn pop-singing liar.

Jimmy Ferris wove through the crowd, still searching. His voice was so suggestive and smooth, the sweetest thing I'd ever heard. Various women got flushed and fanned their faces as he passed on by, age was no discriminator. My own mother looked ready to swoon at his devilish good looks.

At the edge of the dance floor he stopped and craned his neck. Then he finally found his target. He looked straight at me, no longer bothering to sing the song. A murmur of disappointment went through the crowd.

"Lena?" his voice carried to every nook and cranny over the sound system. "What the fuck you doing sitting in the corner?"

My heart pounded hard. I just sat there being flustered. Honestly, I had no response.

Jimmy handed off the microphone to a passing waiter while the band played on regardless. His steps over to my table were measured, unhurried. I kind of wanted to shoot him for that. No way he didn't realize I was having a veritable meltdown while he slowly strutted his stuff. The man had donned one of his custom-made suits for the occasion. I suppose I should be grateful he'd go to such effort. Sadly, due to freaking out, I was a bit too busy right then.

"Hey," he said when he finally got close.

I raised a hand in greeting.

"You look beautiful."

"Thanks." Huh, I could speak, so there. I smoothed my hand over the skirt of the dress, fussed with the hem. Why the hell was I nervous? He should be nervous. Shit, the bastard should be in fear of his life.

"Guess you're wondering what I'm doing here."

I took a deep breath. "Just a little, yeah."

"I, um . . ." His gaze roved over my face, restless.

"What? You what?" I snapped eventually, losing all patience. Then I sat on my hands because this was awkward as all hell. My fingers itched to grab hold of him, to hurt or hang on to was still undecided. But it would be bad for me to kill him in public. Too many witnesses.

He grabbed the nearest seat and pulled it up, sitting down. I shuffled my butt back an inch or two, needing all the space I could get. It was really him. The oh-so-familiar lines of his face and guarded look in his eyes made me ache. I couldn't stop staring, I drank in the sight of him in like I'd been wandering lost for years.

"I did some thinking after you left," he said, leaning forward with his elbows on his knees. "About stuff."

The bullshit detector blared out loud and proud inside my head. "No you didn't. You went to some party with Liv Anders, don't lie to me."

"But—"

"No."

"Nothing happened, Lena. I swear. Please, let me explain." He rubbed at his much-aggrieved face with a hand. "I didn't know how to handle what you said. I just . . . if you felt that way about me, then the chances that I'd fuck up and you'd leave for good were too high."

"You did fuck up and I did leave."

"Yeah, you did."

I opened my eyes painfully wide. "So, what?"

"So, I need you to come back. I reacted wrong. Come back and we'll work something out."

"What exactly is it that you think we're going to work out, Jimmy?"

His forehead bunched up. The expression on his perfect face was so sincere, and yet so completely gut-wrenchingly clueless. "Well, I don't mind that you feel that way. It's all right. You come back with me and work for me again, and we can keep fucking. It can even be exclusive if that's what you want, okay?"

"No, it's not okay." I tried to smile, as if there was any

way to soften the blow for either of us. My hands twisted
and turned, lying in my lap. "You need to leave, Jimmy."

"What?"

It hurt to look at him. It hurt to love him even more.
"You need to leave. I'm not coming back. That's not going to happen."

"Lena." He grabbed my wrist, holding on tight. "You
don't mean that, you love me."

"Yeah, I really do you know." My throat hurt and my
eyes itched.

"Then why won't you come back?" he demanded,
keeping up his grip on me.

"Self-respect, self-preservation, both of these things.
And because you being willing to put up with my love is
not good enough. Not even remotely. I'm not going to be
your regular live-in fuck buddy, Jimmy, exclusive or not.
Your whole offer is soul destroying."

His eyes darkened. "I thought it would make you
happy."

"Well, it doesn't."

"I'm trying to give you what you want here, Lena."

"No, you're trying to give me what *you* want. That's
not how relationships work. You haven't learned anything,"
I said, my chin getting tight and quivery with emotion.
Damn annoying. "Wondering what I might want has yet
to even cross your mind."

"Fuck's sake, what do you want then, huh?" he bit out.

"I want you to love me." I pushed off his fingers. This
time, he let me go.

Frustration filled his face. "Ask for something else . . .
anything."

We were done. Slowly, I rose, standing tall.

Jimmy looked up at me, his jaw unyielding. "I can't."

"Then you shouldn't have come here. You should have
let me go."

He flew to his feet, violently shoving back his chair. "Wait."

"What?"

"She said no one would ever love me."

She being his bitch mother of course. I shook my head sadly. "She was wrong."

The room swam in my tear-filled eyes. Fuck love. God, I was so over this shit. I don't know how many times a girl could have her heart broken by one guy, but seriously, talk about being done. I needed to see if mom had a Kleenex.

Also, why was the band still playing that stupid song? As of now, I officially hated it. I determinedly walked on toward my destination, never say die and all that. Dad would drop me home. Only man a girl could depend upon was her father.

"Lena."

I stopped. Faces were staring, but none of them mattered.

"I'm sorry," he said, voice close behind me.

"Jimmy—"

"Just listen. Please. Just let me get this out."

My chin jerked.

"I need you to come back with me, please." His breath warmed my ear. The heat of his body beckoned against my back. "I can't stand not having you there, not knowing what you're thinking, what you're doing, not being able to tell you things and share them with you. It's just . . . nothing's the same. I hate waking up without you and I worry constantly that you're okay, that you've got everything you need. Look, the truth is, I'm all about you, Lena. You're my best friend. You're my girl."

I closed my eyes, just listening to his words.

"No one else has ever meant what you do to me. Please, just . . . just, come back with me and stay. For good."

My shoulders started trembling this time, my knees

apparently being worn out. Motherfucking rock stars.
Seriously. Strong hands slid over my shoulders, turning me
around.

"I'm sorry I fucked things up. I thought if we could just
stay the same, then everything would be all right and you'd
never want to leave. But I didn't give you what you needed
and it all went to shit." His beautiful blue eyes shone suspiciously bright. "I'm sorry. I don't want anybody else.
You're everything to me, Lena. I've never felt this way
about anyone. I need you to know that. You gotta understand that, okay?"

I just stared at him, transfixed.

"Say something," he urged.

"Jimmy, that's love."

His mouth opened, shut again. The look of surprise
would have been hilarious if my heart, soul, and future
happiness weren't at stake. I wasn't projecting, he really
had said all of those things. There was a chance at a happy
ending, there had to be. Because you didn't feel so damn
much for someone and then just walk away again. Not like
this.

"Love," he said, like he was testing the words, trying
them on for size. Hands sat on either side of my neck, his
thumbs stroking my jaw. "Shit. Okay. All right."

I waited.

His eyes seemed impossibly wide. "Yeah, you're right.
I love you."

"Are you sure?" I had to ask.

Slowly, he nodded. "Yeah. I am. I didn't think I could
do that, but . . ."

I grabbed two fistfuls of the bound-to-be-insanely
priced white shirt and buried my face against his chest. It
was all too much. His arms wrapped around me, holding
on tight. Honestly, I was half-tempted to kick him in the
shin for putting me through this.

"I'm sorry," he said, his face buried in my hair. "I'm so fucking sorry I hurt you. I love you, Lena. So damn much."

"I love you too," I sniffed, any chance at decorum long gone.

He shook and I shook, and I'm not even certain how we stayed upright and intact. We clung together, swaying on the dance floor while the band belted out a classic love song by none other than guess what band?

"Christ," he muttered. "We need to get out of here. That guy can't do me for shit."

At which point I lost it, laughing my ass off.

Life. What could you do?

Jimmy fit his mouth to mine and all humor fled, replaced by raw hunger. God, I'd missed him. It might have been only a couple of days but it felt like forever. The taste and feel of him, the scent of his skin. Each and every thing about him, both the good and the bad. His tongue slipped into my mouth and my eyes basically rolled back in my head. Heaven. We made out like we were alone and not being perved on by a hundred or so guests at a wedding. I kissed him good and hard until my lips lost all feeling and my brain turned dizzy oxygen starved circles inside my head.

"You really love me?" I asked again, as he rested his forehead against mine.

He grunted.

"Say it."

A rare smile. "I love you, Lena."

"About fucking time, Jimmy." I grinned.

He laughed, then kissed me some more.

And that's the story of how my sister married my idiot ex-boyfriend while I went home with the most beautiful man on the planet, Jimmy Ferris, the lead singer from Stage Dive.

EPILOGUE

What was meant to be an engagement party for Mal and
Anne had degenerated into some sort of bizarre hedo-
nistic musical bacchanalia. Instruments, gifts, vegetable
pizzas, and drinks were strewn here there and everywhere.
The happy couple had disappeared into one of David and
Ev's spare bedrooms a while back. Killer the puppy was
chasing Ben the bass player through the condo while Lizzy
lay on the couch laughing.

It was pretty funny given the size differences.

Jimmy and David were playing guitar while Jimmy
sang "Ain't No Sunshine," the sad old Bill Withers song. I
sat on the floor opposite, snapping off pictures of him on
the Nikon. My boyfriend, the most fascinating of subjects.
And god save my panties when he went into crooning
mode, because they never stood a chance.

He'd finally dared confide in his brother about learning to play guitar. David had been nothing but supportive,
helping him practice songs. They'd been talking about the
chances of Jimmy playing some rhythm guitar, back up his
brother during the upcoming tour. He seemed more con-
fident in his role, happier with having more to offer the
band.

"All good?" asked Ev, hanging out on the floor beside me.

"Very good. And you?"

She smiled. "Just swell, thank you for asking."

Over by the balcony doors, Nate and Lauren were slow dancing, lost in each other. Ah, love. So lovely and shit. The world was a glorious place.

"We going to be planning your and Jimmy's wedding next?" Ev sucked down some of her beer.

"Nah, I don't think so. We're good as is."

"We're what?" asked Jimmy, the song having finished. He held out a hand to me and I waddled over on my knees. All the grace.

"Ev asked if we were getting married next." I carefully placed my camera on the coffee table before climbing onto his lap. That he wanted me there, all over him, was both a duty and a privilege. Well, mostly a privilege.

"You wanna?" he asked, cocking his head.

"Someday."

"Sounds good."

"Jimmy." I leaned in close to whisper in his ear. "I think I just came."

One hand slid into my hair while the other grabbed hold of my hip. "Did you?"

"I mention a one day major commitment and you're cool with it. I feel like I can have whatever I want with you these days. It's starting to make me a little overexcited."

He turned his head, kissing me gently on the lips. "I like you overexcited. Keeps things interesting."

"I'll bear that in mind."

He nipped at my bottom lip.

I grinned, ducking back to evade his teasing teeth.

"Animal." I laughed.

"Yeah. I am. That a problem?"

My fingers slipped into his hair. "Nope. I like you as is."

"Love you, Lena," he said. He said it all the time to me these days. I never needed to doubt. My things had been moved directly into his bedroom upon our return and Jimmy had set about letting it be known far and wide that we were together. I didn't eavesdrop in on his conversation with Liv Anders when he broke the news to her. I trusted him. After the way he'd taken off from LA to get to my sister's wedding in time, she apparently hadn't been surprised.

She had my sympathy. I knew what it was like to love him and lose him.

But I wouldn't be giving him back.

Amidst much laughter and puppy barking, Mal and Anne finally emerged from the bedroom. Anne's face was flushed and Mal was still putting his rhinestone-covered, white satin, Elvis-style jacket back on. My mind was still coming to grips with exactly why he'd felt the need to wear it. Obviously the whole wedding in Vegas idea had been embraced wholeheartedly and then some.

"The king lives!" he cried, hands high above his head. "So, Benny boy."

The bass player collapsed on a chair in the corner, Killer still yapping at his heels. "Yo."

"Now that fair Lena has tamed the mighty Jim, you're the last of us swinging single."

Ben laughed. "And you can bet on me staying that way."

"Oh, come on." Ev climbed up onto the couch beside David, throwing an arm around him. "Look at all the deliriously happy couples in this room. You're not even tempted to settle down?"

"No," the man answered simply.

"No one special you want to tell us about, Benny?" inquired Mal, giving him curious looks.

"No." Ben crossed his arms over his barrel-like chest. "I'm happy doing my thing, having fun. Why limit yourself?"

The women booed him. All except Lizzy who suddenly popped up from her place on the couch.

"I have to get going. I had a big day." The girl threw an arm around Anne, giving her a squeeze. "Congratulations, again."

"Thank you. Again," laughed Anne. "I'll see you for breakfast tomorrow?"

"Sure thing." She gave the room a wave. " 'Night everyone!"

"Hang on, we'll catch a cab back with you," said Lauren, disentangling herself from an obviously amorous Nate. They'd both had a few drinks, neither were fit for driving. When Anne and Mal moved into the condo her sister had taken over her old apartment. Given Mal had paid the rent up for the next year, it would have been a shame to waste it. Lizzy had been only too happy to give up her small dorm room in favor of a rent-free, slightly larger apartment.

" 'Night," I said, waving to the party of three departing out the door.

Ben watched the group leave with a frown on his face. Curious.

But I was quickly distracted by Jimmy bussing his nose against my cheek. "You didn't tell me you love me, Lena."

"I love you, Jimmy." I smiled and kissed him on the lips.

Since discovering love, he'd set out to become somewhat of a connoisseur of the emotion. I have to admit, I was definitely reaping the benefits, sexually and emotionally.

The damage his mother had done was slowly being healed. His relationship with his brother was better than ever. He'd let me find him a new therapist and he was learning to trust and be open in all sorts of ways. Actually, I think we both were and it was a good thing. It wasn't always easy, but we both persevered because it was worth it to us. Our dedication to sticking together now was absolute.

"Take me home?" I asked.

Jimmy smiled, both dimples on show. It always made my stomach tumble and my sex melt. What happened to my heart couldn't be described.

"Whatever you want, Lena."

Deep

As always, for Hugh

ACKNOWLEDGMENTS

With thanks to all of the readers, reviewers, bloggers, crit-partners, beta readers, friends, family, publishers, editors, assistant editors, copy editors, formatters, artists, models, photographers, promotions people, receptionists, booksellers, sales assistants, mail workers, librarians, and any assorted pets any of you might have, for taking the Stage Dive journey with me. I couldn't have done it without you. You rock.

PROLOGUE

Positive.

I reread the instructions, doing my best to flatten out the creases in the piece of paper one-handed. Two lines meant positive. Two lines sat on the test. No, not possible. My gaze darted back and forth between the two, willing one of them to change. I shook the test and turned it this way and that. I stared and stared, but just like with the first one sitting rejected beside the sink, the answer remained the same.

Positive.

I was pregnant.

"Fuck."

The word echoed around and around the small bathroom, bouncing off the white-tiled walls and beating at my head. This shit shouldn't be happening to me. I didn't break laws or do drugs. Not since that blip after Dad left. I was studying hard for my degree in psychology and I behaved. Mostly. But those definite neat pink lines stood loud and proud in the pregnancy test's little window, taunting me, the evidence irrefutable even when I squinted or crossed my eyes.

"*Fuck.*"

Me as someone's mom. No.

What the hell was I going to do?

I sat on the edge of the bathtub in my plain black underwear, covered in goose bumps. Outside, a barren limb swayed in and out of view, buffeted by the wind. Beyond it lay the endless gray of a February Portland sky. Screw it all. All of my plans and dreams, my whole life, changed at the say of a stupid plastic stick. I was only twenty-one, for goodness sake, not even in a relationship.

Ben.

Ah, man. We'd barely talked in months, what with me doing my best to avoid any situation where he might be present. Things had been a little awkward ever since I threw him out of my hotel room in Vegas minus his pants. I'd been done with him. Finished. Kaput.

My uterus apparently did not agree.

We'd had sex once. *Once.* A secret that I'd long since decided to take to my grave. Him never telling anyone was a given. But still, his penis went in my vagina one time only, and I'd watched him roll the condom on, god damn it. Me lying spread out on the California king–size, trembling with excitement, and he'd just kind of smiled. There'd been this warmth in his eyes, a gentleness. Given the obvious tension running through his big body, it'd seemed so strange and yet wondrous. No one had ever looked at me that way, as if I meant everything.

An unwelcome warmth filled my chest at the memory. It'd been so long since I'd thought of him with anything other than *ugh*.

At any rate, apparently someone had diddled away their shift at the prophylactics factory and here we were. Pregnant. I stared unseeing at my skinny jeans, lying discarded on the floor. Sure, they'd fit. As in, I could wiggle up the zip halfway and the button was out of the question.

The pressure they inflicted upon my belly was a definite no go.

Things were changing so fast. I was changing.

Normally, I had more going on in the back than up front. But for the first time in my life, I actually had the makings of a rack. Not enough boobage to get me a job at Hooters or anything, but still. And as much as I'd like to believe that god had finally answered my teenage prayers, when you added up all the evidence, it wasn't likely. I had a person growing inside of me. A little baby bean-shaped thing made from equal parts of me and him.

Mind-boggling.

What I'd wear tonight was, however, the least of my worries. If only I could get out of going. He'd be there, all six foot five–worth of rugged rock star. Just the thought of seeing him turned me inside out, filling me with nerves. My stomach dived, nausea rolling through me. Puke rushed up, filling my throat and making me gag. I only just made it to the toilet in time to lose what little I'd had for lunch. Two Oreos and half a banana, going, going . . . gone in a hot rush.

Yuck.

I groaned loudly and wiped my mouth with the back of my hand, flushed the toilet and staggered over to the sink. Whoa. The girl in the mirror looked spectacularly crappy, face too pale and long blond hair hanging in straggly wet strands. What a hot mess. I couldn't even bring myself to meet my own eyes.

That I'd dropped the pregnancy test didn't even occur to me until I stood on it. My heel pressed down, grinding of its own accord. Plastic cracked and splintered, the noise strangely satisfying. I just stamped on it, over and over, trampling the bastard, pounding it into the scuffed wooden floor. God yeah, the good vibes just flowed. The first test soon met the same fate. I didn't stop until I was panting and only wreckage remained on the floor. That felt so much better.

So I'd been knocked up by a rock star.

Big deal.

Deep breath. Okay.

I would handle this like an adult, pull myself together and go talk to Ben. We'd been friends at one time. Sort of. I could still talk to him about stuff. Specifically, stuff relating to our progeny arriving in, oh . . . seven or so months.

Yes, I could, and I would.

Just as soon as I'd finished throwing my tantrum.

"You're late. Get in here," said my sister, Anne, grabbing my hand and dragging me through the doorway. Not that I'd been lurking outside, skulking and hesitating. Much.

"Sorry."

"I thought you were going to bail on me. Again." She gave me a quick, affectionate squeeze, then stole my coat off my shoulders. It got thrown onto a nearby chair already overflowing with other jackets. "Everyone else is already here."

"Great," I mumbled.

True enough, there was a goodly amount of noise happening within the multimillion-dollar Pearl District loft. Anne and I didn't come from money. Quite the contrary. If it hadn't been for her encouraging me to go for scholarships and supporting me financially by paying for books, etcetera, I'd never have made it to college. Last year, however, my normally sensible and subdued sister had somehow found herself shacked up with rock 'n' roll royalty.

I know, right? How it all happened still confused me, somewhat. Between the two of us, I'd always played the role of the bubbly one. Whenever Anne got down, I'd pick her back up again, fill the spaces in the conversations and keep right on smiling through the rain. Yet here she was, high on life and crazy in love, truly happy for the first time in just about forever. It was wonderful.

Details regarding their whirlwind romance ranged from vague to none. But just before Christmas, she and Malcolm Ericson, the drummer for Stage Dive (about the biggest rock band ever), had tied the knot. I was now counted as part of the band's extended entourage. To be fair, they'd embraced me wholeheartedly from the start. They were good people. It was just the thought of seeing *him* reducing me to a jittering, nervous wreck with super enhanced puking abilities.

"You'll never guess what happened." Anne linked her arm with mine, towing me toward the crowded dinner table.

Toward my doom.

A crowd of about seven sat around it with drinks in hand, laughing and chatting. I think it was The National playing quietly on the sound system. Candles flickered and small twinkling party lights hung overhead. My mouth watered despite my queasy stomach, what with all the delicious foodie scents filling the air. Wow, Anne and Mal had really gone all out for the occasion of their two-month wedding anniversary. Suddenly, my black tights and pale blue tunic (a loose-knit fabric which in no way hugged or hindered the waistline) seemed insufficient. Though it was hard to go for glamour with a plastic bag in your pocket just in case you needed to hurl.

"What happened?" I asked, dragging my feet ever so slightly.

She leaned in and whisper-hissed theatrically, "Ben brought a date."

Everything stopped. And I do mean everything. My lungs, my feet . . . everything.

A flicker of a frown crossed Anne's face. "Liz?"

I blinked, slowly coming back to life. "Yeah?"

"You okay?"

"Sure. So, um, Ben brought a date?"

"Can you believe it?"

"No." I really couldn't. My brain had stalled, same as everything else. There'd been no date in my plans for speaking with Ben tonight.

"I know. First time for everything I guess. Everyone's slightly weirded out, though she seems nice enough."

"But Ben doesn't date," I said, my voice sounding hollow somehow, as if it were an echo coming from far away. "He doesn't even believe in relationships."

Anne cocked her head, smiling ever so slightly. "Lizzy, you don't still have a crush on him, do you?"

"No." I barked out a laugh. As if. He'd disabused me of such idiotic notions, in Vegas. "So much no my cup is overflowing and the no is spilling onto the floor."

"Good." She sighed happily.

"Lizzy!" A booming loud voice rang out.

"Hey, Mal."

"Say hello to your Aunt Elizabeth, son." My new brother-in-law thrust a black-and-white puppy straight at me. A wet little tongue swiped my lips, and warm panting puppy breath, ripe with the scent of dog biscuits, filled my face. Not good.

"Whoa." I leaned way the hell back, trying to breathe through the urge to yet again heave. Pregnancy was the best. "Hi, Killer."

"Give him to me," said Anne. "Not everybody wants to French kiss the dog, Mal."

The blond, heavily tattooed man grinned, handing the fur baby over. "But he's a great kisser. I taught him myself."

"Unfortunately, that's true." Anne tucked the pup under an arm, giving him a scratch on the head. "How are you?

You said you'd been feeling sick, the other day on the phone."

"All better," I lied. Or partly lied. After all, I definitely wasn't sick.

"Did you go to the doctor?"

"No need."

"Why don't I make an appointment tomorrow, just in case?"

"Not necessary."

"But—"

"Anne, relax. I'm telling you I'm not sick." I gave her my brightest smile. "I promise, I'm fine."

"All right." She placed the pup on the ground and pulled out a chair in the middle of the table. "I saved you a place next to me."

"Thanks."

And so it was (with me trying not to barf while wiping dog spit off my face) that I saw him again. Ben, sitting opposite, staring straight at me. Those dark eyes . . . I immediately looked down. He didn't affect me. He didn't. I just wasn't ready to face up to this. Wherein this equaled him and me and that room and Vegas and the consequences that were currently growing in my belly.

I couldn't do it, not yet.

"Hey, Liz," he said, deep voice calm, casual.

"Hey."

Yeah. I was so over him. The date thing had thrown me, but now I was back on track. I just had to compartmentalize any unhelpful lingering feelings, file them away for never.

I took a step closer, daring a peek only to find him watching me warily. He threw back some beer then set the bottle down, swiping his thumb across his mouth to catch a stray drop. In Vegas, he'd first tasted of beer, lust, and need. The most dizzying mix. He had beautiful lips, perfectly framed by his short beard. His hair had grown out of the shaved on the sides and longish on top cool hipster cut, and honestly, he looked kind of shaggy, wild.

And big, though he always looked big.

A silver ring pierced one side of his nose and he had on a green plaid shirt, top button open to showcase his thick neck and the edge of a black rose tattoo. Any money blue jeans and black boots were below. Apart from Vegas at the wedding, and then later that night in my room, I'd never seen him out of jeans. Let me assure you, there's nothing bad about the man naked. Everything was as it should be and then some. In fact, he'd looked a lot like a dream come true.

My dream.

I swallowed hard, ignoring my perky nipples while firmly pushing the memory back down where it belonged. Buried among the Hannah Montana song lyrics, *Vampire Diary* character histories, and other useless and potentially damaging information collected over the years. None of it mattered anymore.

The room had gone quiet. How awkward.

Ben tugged at the collar of his shirt, shifting in his seat.

Why the hell was he staring at me? Maybe because I was still staring at him. Shit. My knees gave out and I collapsed into the chair with an ever so dainty thud. I kept my eyes cast down because down was safe. So long as I didn't look at him or this date of his, I'd be fine and dandy. Dinner couldn't last for more than three, four hours max. No worries.

I half raised a hand in greeting. "Hi, everyone."

Heys and hi's and variations of both floated back.

"How have you been, Liz?" asked Ev, from further down the table. She was seated beside her husband, David Ferris, Stage Dive's lead guitarist and songwriter.

"Great." Crap. "You?"

"Good."

I sucked in a deep breath and smiled. "Excellent."

"You been busy with school?" She pulled out a hair tie and bundled her blond hair up into a rough ponytail. God bless the girl. At least it wasn't just me keeping it casual. "We haven't seen you since Christmas."

"Yeah, busy." Puking and sleeping mostly. Gestating. "School and stuff, you know."

Normally I'd have an interesting story to tell from my psych studies. Today, nada.

"Right." Her husband slipped an arm around her shoulders and she turned to smile at him, eyes all lovelorn and our conversation forgotten.

Which worked for me.

I rubbed the toe of my boot back and forth against the floor, looking left and right and anywhere but straight ahead. I toyed with the hem of my tunic, winding a loose thread tight around my finger until it turned purple. Then I loosened it. It probably wasn't good for the bean, somehow. As of tomorrow, I needed to start studying up on this baby stuff. Get the facts, because getting rid of the bean . . . it just wasn't for me.

The date tittered at something he said and I felt a stab of pain inside. Probably gas.

"Here." Anne filled the glass in front of me with white wine.

"Oh. Thanks."

"Try it," she said with a smile. "It's sweet and kind of crisp. I think you'll like it."

My stomach tipped upside down just at the thought. "Later maybe. I drank some water right before I arrived. So . . . yeah, I'm not really thirsty just yet."

"All right." Her eyes narrowed as she gave me a that-was-weird smile. All too soon it morphed into a flat, unhappy line. "You look a little pale. Are you okay?"

"Absolutely!" I nodded, smiled, and turned to the woman on my other side before Anne could grill me further on the subject. "Hi, Lena."

"Lizzy. How you been?" The curvy brunette held hands with her partner, Jimmy Ferris, the lead singer of Stage Dive. He sat at the head of the table, resplendent in an undoubtedly handmade suit. When he saw me he gave me one of the chin tips the guys seemed to specialize in. It said it all. Or at least it said it all when all they wanted to say was *Hey*.

I nodded back at him. And all the while I could feel Anne hovering at my side, bottle of wine still in hand and big-sisterly concern growing by the moment, pawing at the ground and getting ready to pounce. I was so screwed. Anne had pretty much raised me from the age of fourteen, when our dad left and our mom checked out on us—one day just went to bed and didn't get up again. Now and then Anne's need to nurture still got a little out of control. What she'd have to say about the bean didn't bear thinking about. It wouldn't be pretty.

But one problem at a time.

"All good, Lena," I said. "You?"

Lena opened her mouth. Whatever she'd been about to say, however, was lost beneath the sudden thrashing of drums and insanely loud wailing of guitars. It basically sounded like hell was spilling forth all around us. Armageddon had come a-knocking.

"Babe," Anne hollered at her husband. "No death metal during dinner! We talked about this."

Said "babe," Malcolm Ericson, paused his head banging at the top of the table. "But, Pumpkin—"

"Please."

The drummer rolled his eyes and, with the flick of a finger, silenced the storm raging through the sound system.

My ears rang on in the quiet.

"Christ," muttered Jimmy. "Time and a place for shit like that. Try never when I'm around, yeah?"

Mal looked down the length of his nose at the dapper man. "Don't be so judgy, Jim. I think Hemorrhaging Otter would make a wonderful warm-up act."

"Are you fucking serious? That's their name?" asked David.

"Delightfully inventive, no?"

"One way to put it," said David, nose wrinkled in distaste. "And Ben already picked a warm-up act."

"I didn't even get a vote," grumped Mal.

"Dude." Ben shoved an irritated hand through his hair. "You'll all want to hang with your women. I'll need some people around after the show I can chill and have a beer with, so I went ahead and chose. Suck it up."

Bitter grumbling from Mal.

Ev just shook her head. "Wow. Hemorrhaging Otter. That's certainly unique."

"What do you think, babe?" Jimmy turned to Lena.

"That's disgusting. I think I'm going to throw up." The woman swallowed hard, her face going gray. "I mean, I think I really am."

Huh. And also, ugh, I knew that feeling.

"Shit." Jimmy started rubbing her back with frantic motions.

Without a word, I pressed my spare plastic puke bag into her hand. Solidarity among sisters, etcetera.

"Thanks," she said, happily too preoccupied to ask why I'd had it in my pocket in the first place.

"She had some stomach bug before Christmas." With his spare hand, Jimmy filled Lena's glass with water and passed it to her. "Keeps messing with her."

I froze.

"I thought it had gone," said Lena.

"You're going to have to go to the doctor. Enough excuses, we're not that busy." Jimmy planted a soft kiss on the side of her face. "Tomorrow, yeah?"

"Okay."

"Sounds wise," said Anne, patting my rigid shoulder. Holy hell.

"You've been sick too, Lizzy?" asked Lena.

"You should both try some green tea with ginger in it," a voice reported from the other side of the table.

Female.

Damn, it was her. His date.

"Ginger creates warmth and helps to settle an upset stomach. What other symptoms did you have?" she asked, causing me to immediately sink down in my seat.

Ben cleared his throat. "Sasha's a naturopath."

"I thought you said she was a dancer," said Anne, her face screwing up ever so slightly.

"A burlesque performer," the woman corrected. "I do both."

Yeah, I had nothing.

A chair scraped against the floor, and then Sasha was standing, peering down at me. Any hopes of avoiding and/or ignoring her presence fled the scene. Bettie Page hair done a vibrant blue, very cool. Christ, did she have to look like she actually had a clue? A bimbo I could handle, but not this. The woman was beautiful and smart, and I was just a dumb kid who'd gone and gotten herself knocked up. Cue the violins.

I smiled grimly. "Hi."

"Any other symptoms?" she repeated, gaze moving between me and Lena.

"She's been tired a lot too," said Jimmy. "Passes out in front of the TV all the time."

"True." Lena frowned.

"Lizzy, you said you'd missed some school, didn't you?" asked Anne.

"Some," I admitted, not liking the direction this grilling was taking. Time for a smooth segue. "Anyway, how are the plans for the tour going? You guys must all be so excited. I'd be excited. Have you started packing yet, Anne?"

My sister just blinked at me.

"No?" Maybe a sudden outburst of verbal diarrhea wasn't the answer.

"Hold up. Have you been sick, Liz?" Ben asked, his deep voice softening ever so slightly. Though maybe that was just my imagination.

"Um . . ."

"Maybe you got the same bug Lena's got," he said. "How much school have you missed?"

My throat closed tight. I couldn't do it. Not here and now in front of everyone. I should have fled for the Yukon rather than come here tonight. No way was I ready for this.

"Liz?"

"No, I'm fine," I wheezed. "All good."

"Um, hello," said Anne. "You said you'd been nauseous for the last few weeks. If I hadn't been away I'd have dragged you to the doctor's way back."

And thank god she'd been on her second honeymoon with Mal in Hawaii. To have found out about the bean with Anne in attendance would have been up there with watching the four horseman of the apocalypse riding into town. Terror, tears, chaos—all of these things and more. Definitely not my idea of a good time.

The date, Sasha, fixed her inquiring gaze to the ever so subtly still gagging Lena.

"Did anyone else get this?" she asked.

"I don't think so." Anne looked up and down the table,

taking in the various shaking of heads. "Just Lena and Lizzy."

"We've been fine," said Ev.

"Weird," said Anne. "Liz and Lena haven't been around each other since the wedding. That's over two months ago now."

Murmurs of agreement.

My heartbeat raced. Mine and the bean's both.

"Well, I think they should both take a pregnancy test," announced Sasha, retaking her seat.

A moment's stunned silence.

"What?" I spluttered, panic coursing through me. Not here, not now, and sure as fuck not this way. Bile burned my throat, but I swallowed it back down, fumbling for the second puke bag.

Ben's brow wrinkled and there were startled coughs and gasps from others.

But before anyone could comment, a strange screechy noise came from Lena.

"No," she cried, voice very high and very determined. "No, I am not. You take that back."

The back-rubbing by Jimmy went berserk. "Baby, calm down."

She didn't. Instead, she pointed a shaking finger at the now very unwelcome stranger in our midst. "You have no idea what the fuck you're talking about. I don't know, maybe you've taken a hit to the head from one of those big fancy dancing fans lately or something. Whatever. But you . . . you couldn't be more wrong."

"Okay, let's calm down a little." Ben raised his hands in protest.

Sasha kept quiet.

"Lizzy?" My sister's fingers dug into my shoulder, bruisingly tight. "There's no chance, right? I mean, you know better than that. You wouldn't be so stupid."

My mouth opened, but nothing came out.

Suddenly, Lena clutched at her belly. "Jimmy, in your car outside my sister's wedding. We didn't use anything."

"I know," he said quietly, perfect face white as snow. "Time we fucked against the door, night before you left. We forgot then too."

"Yeah."

"Your tits have been really sensitive." With one hand, Jimmy scrubbed at his mouth. "And you were complaining your dress wouldn't do up the other day."

"I thought it was just pie."

They both stared at one another while everyone looked on. I was pretty damn certain they'd long since forgotten they had an audience for all these intimate details. As dinner entertainment went, this had turned into one hell of a drama, and oh god, the horror of it. My head started to turn in dizzy circles.

"Lizzy?" Anne asked again.

Okay, this wasn't good. I really and truly shouldn't have come. But how the hell was I to know Ben would bring along a gynecological psychic? The edges of my vision blurred, my lungs working overtime. I couldn't get enough air. Not to sound paranoid, but I bet that Sasha bitch had stolen it all. Never mind. The important thing was not to panic.

Maybe I should jump out a window.

"Liz," a voice said. A different one this time, deep and strong.

However I'd imagined me and Ben having this talk, it was nothing like this. Not tonight, before I'd even processed it myself. Time to go.

"Lizzy?"

Also, wow, if this was the result of having great sex then I was so never going there again. Not even for mediocre sex. Nothing. I might even rule out masturbation, just in case. You couldn't be too careful. Random attack sperm could be anywhere, just waiting to get a girl into trouble.

I stumbled to my feet, sweaty hands on the table to steady myself. "I should go."

"Hey." A big hand cupped my chin. Lines had appeared between Ben's brows, beside his mouth. But you could only see the hint of them behind his beard, the implication. The man was not happy, and fair enough. "It's okay, Liz. We'll get this sorted—"

"I'm pregnant."

A pause. "What?"

"I'm pregnant, Ben."

The ensuing silence echoed in my ears, an endless gray noise like something out of a horror movie.

Ben stood bent over the table, breathing heavy. I guess I'd looked to him for strength, but now he seemed every bit as strung out as me.

"You're pregnant?" Anne's voice cut the silence. "Lizzy, look at me."

I did, though it wasn't easy. My chin didn't seem inclined to go in the desired direction, and who could blame it?

"Yes," I said. "I am."

She went horribly still.

"I'm sorry."

"How could you? Oh god." For a moment she squeezed her eyes shut, then opened them again. "And why were you telling *him*?"

"Good question." Ever so slowly, Mal rose from his seat and started walking down the other side of the table. "Why'd she tell you, Benny?"

"Liz and I need to talk." Ben's gaze skipped to Mal, his hand falling from my face. "Man."

"You didn't," said Mal, his voice low and lethal as the tension in the room took an entirely new turn for the worse.

"Calm down."

"Told you stay away from her. Didn't I? She's my girl's kid sister for Christ's sake."

Ben stood tall. "I can explain."

"Shit," muttered David.

"No. No, you can't, Benny. I fucking asked you to leave her alone, bro. You promised me she'd be off-limits."

Past Ben, David Ferris got to his feet, as did Jimmy at the end of the table. It was all happening so fast.

Ben's date, Sasha, the burlesque dancer with the blue hair, seemed to finally understand the shit storm she'd unleashed with her most excellent announcement. Perhaps she wasn't so psychic after all. "We should leave. Ben?"

He didn't even look at her, his gaze glued to Mal.

"You're like a brother to me, Benny. One of my closest friends. But she's my little sister now. Tell me you didn't go there."

"Mal, man—"

"Not after you gave me your word. You wouldn't do that, not to me."

"Dude, calm down," said David, moving up to try and get between the two. "Let's talk about this."

Ben was almost a head taller than Mal, definitely bigger, stronger. It didn't matter. With a battle cry, Mal launched himself at the man. They fell together onto the floor, rolling and wrestling, fists flying. It was a mess. I jumped to my feet, mouth hanging open. Someone screamed, a woman. The rich copper scent of blood hit the air and the urge to hurl was almost overwhelming, but there wasn't time for that.

"No!" I yelled. "Don't, please."

I'd done this, so it was up to me to fix it. I got a knee up on the table before hands grasped my arms, holding me back no matter how I fought.

"Mal, no!"

David and Jimmy tore Mal off of Ben, dragging the struggling man back across the room.

"I'm going to fucking kill you," Mal hollered, his face a mixture of reds from fury and blood. "Let me go!"

More blood dripped from beneath Ben's nose, trailing down his chin. But he made no move to stop it. Slowly, the big man got to his feet, and the look on his face tore me in two.

"You said you wouldn't chase after her."

"He didn't," I shouted, still standing on one foot with a knee on the table and Anne's hand on my arm. "He didn't want anything to do with me. I chased after him. It was all me. I'm sorry."

Silence fell and I was surrounded by stunned faces. And a couple of still-bleeding ones.

"I practically stalked him. He never stood a chance."

"What?" Mal scowled, one eyelid swelling at an alarming rate.

"It's my fault, not Ben's. I'm the one who did it."

"Liz." With a heavy sigh, Ben hung his head.

The fingers on my arm gave a small tug. I turned to face my sister.

"Explain this to me."

CHAPTER ONE

FOUR MONTHS AGO

Good girls don't fall for rock stars. It just isn't done.

"Pumpkin! PUUUMP-KIN!"

"Oh god." My sister, the aforementioned Pumpkin, giggled.

I just gaped. It seemed to be my go-to look of the day.

Lord knows, I'd been wearing it ever since letting myself into Anne's apartment this morning. Because I lived on campus, we'd starting doing brunch every Sunday morning since moving to Portland a few years back. It was our sisterly thing. But instead of standing ready to serve the bacon and eggs this morning, I'd found, Anne was fast asleep on top of a tattooed stud on the sofa. Both of them mostly clothed, thank god.

But, wow, what a revelation. I mean, I didn't even know Anne dated. I'd thought me dragging her along to the occasional party on campus was the sum total of her social life.

"C'mon, woman," said Mal, her brand-spanking-new boyfriend. "We can't be late to practice or Davie'll get his panties in a wad. You have no idea what drama queens guitarists can be. I swear, last week he threw a total hissy fit just 'cause he broke a string. Started screaming and throwing shit at people. True story."

"That is not a true story," admonished Anne, shaking her head. "David is a perfectly nice guy. Stop trying to scare Lizzy."

"No-o-o." Mal gave her big innocent puppy eyes, even going so far as to bat his eyelashes. "You think I would lie to Lizzy, my sweet little future sister-in-law?"

Anne just shook her head. "Are we going in or what?"

"Can't believe you doubted me, Pumpkin."

We followed the manic blond drummer into a big old building down by the river. As good a place for a loud rock band to practice as any. The only neighbors were industrial buildings, abandoned for the weekend. Inside wasn't any warmer, but at least we were out of the bone-chilling October wind. I stuffed my hands into the pockets of my gray woolen coat, nervous now that we were actually about to meet them. My sole interactions with the rich and famous started this morning with Mal. If the rest of the band was anything like him, I'd never keep up.

"As if anyone could doubt me. That hurt bad," he said. "Apologize."

"Sorry."

Mal smacked a noisy kiss on her cheek. "You're forgiven. Later."

Stretching his fingers and rotating his wrists, the man bounded off toward the stage assembled at one end. Instruments, amps, and other sound gear covered it and the surrounding area, with roadies and sound techs busy amid it all.

It was fascinating, this, him, and my whole damn morning. Mal and Anne seemed so in tune with each other. Perhaps Anne and I had been a touch too hasty in our dismissal of romantic love and affection. So it hadn't worked out for our parents. Hell, those two had pretty much made a mockery of commitment and marriage. Mal and Anne might yet make a far better case study.

Fascinating.

"He's borderline insane by the way," I said quietly. "So manic."

"Yeah. Isn't he great?" She grinned.

I nodded, because anyone who could make her smile so bright clearly must be. The light of hope in her eyes, the happiness, it was beautiful.

And the man in question? None other than Malcolm Ericson, drummer for worldwide renowned rock group Stage Dive, had somehow shacked up with my sister. My quiet, calm, color-within-the-lines-or-else sister. Anne was being vague about the details, but the facts remained the same. Her new boyfriend stunned me stupid. Perhaps someone had slipped something into my coffee back on campus. It would certainly explain all of the crazy.

"Can't believe you told him about me crushing on him when I was a kid." Ever so gently, Anne elbowed me in the side.

I grunted in pain.

"Thanks for that," she said.

"You're welcome. What else are sisters for?"

We wandered toward the couple of women sitting on storage boxes at the back of the hall. So cool, getting to see the band practice. Anne had truly been the psycho fan, plastering her bedroom wall with posters of Stage Dive. Mostly of Mal, making today's dating revelation all the more holy hell. But if anyone deserved some amazing, mind-blowing good to come their way, it was my sister. I couldn't begin to tell you how much she'd given up to get us this far.

The blond woman smiled in greeting as we got closer, but the curvy brunette just kept playing with her cell.

"Hello, fellow Stage Dive groupies and hanger-onners. How is your Sunday morning?" the blonde asked.

"Good," said Anne. "How are you feeling, Mrs. Ferris?"

"I am feeling very, very married, thank you for asking. How are you and Mal doing?"

"Ah, good. All good." Anne joined them, sitting on one of the boxes. "This is my sister, Lizzy. She goes to school at PSU. Lizzy this is Ev, David's wife, and Lena, Jimmy's . . ."

"Assistant. Hi." Lena gave me a small smile and chin tip.

"Hi." I waved.

"Nice to meet you," said Ev. "Anne, quickly before they start playing. Tell me the story of you and Malcolm. I still haven't heard how you got together, exactly. But Lauren mentioned he basically invaded your apartment."

Back at her apartment, I'd overheard an odd argument between her and Mal. Something about them having an "agreement." When I questioned her she'd basically told me to butt out, in her own sweet way. I could only take her word that all was well, and try not to worry. Still, the question and Anne's reaction to it interested me greatly. I ever so subtly shuffled a little closer.

The whites of Anne's eyes flashed. "Ah, well, we met at your place the other night and hit it off."

"That's it?" asked Ev.

"Yes, that's pretty much it." Anne's smile wavered only slightly. "What is this, Ev, a grilling?"

"Yes, this is a grilling. Give me more information, please?"

"He's really great and yes, he kind of moved himself in with me. But I love having him there. He's wonderful, you know?"

So they weren't going to get any more out of her than I had. No big surprise. Anne tended to be tight lipped, a private person.

The girls kept on talking.

Up on the stage only the band members now remained,

the rest moving off to the side to play with various bits of equipment. They stood gathered around Mal and his drum kit, deep in conversation. So this must be the band. Jeans and T-shirts seemed to be the go-to, scruffy cool hairdos and lots of tats. One of them stood a good half a head taller than the rest, and the rest were not tiny. This guy must be a giant. And it'll sound crazy, but there was just something about the way he stood, the solidity of him. Mountains had never seemed so strong and imposing. Big boots several feet apart and a hand wrapped high around the neck of his bass guitar as if he might swing it club style at any moment to subdue some stray bear. The thick width of his shoulders and the ink on his muscular arms made my fingers itch with the need to explore. It couldn't have been healthy, but I'm pretty damn sure my heart skipped a beat. Every inch of me vibrated with some sort of hyper, crazy sexual tension courtesy of his presence. Never before had just the sight of a man made me go so gaga.

I couldn't look away.

The band meeting broke apart and he took several steps backward. Someone counted them in and *boom!* The first deep, heavy notes of his bass guitar slammed into me, rattling my bones. It left no corner of me unaffected. The song he played was like a spell, sinking deep, taking me over. My belief in love or lust or whatever this feeling was suddenly became assured. The sense of connection seemed so real. I hadn't had many definites in my life. But him, us, whatever this was, it was one. It had to be.

Finally, he turned in my direction, his gaze on his instrument, a short beard hiding half his face. Wonder if he'd be willing to shave it? He wore a faded red tee and dark blue jeans, as per the band uniform. As he played he'd rock back and forth on his heels, nodding or smiling every now and then at the singer, guitarist, or whoever.

And I'm certain each and every one of them performed like the prime specimens of rock 'n' roll musicianship that they were. None of them mattered, though. Just him.

Of course, I knew who he was. Ben Nicholson, the bass player for Stage Dive. But his presence in music videos or Anne's extensive collection of posters had never affected me like this. To be here, seeing him in the flesh, was a different experience altogether. My blood ran hot and my mind emptied. My body, though—it was as if it went on red alert, tuned in to every little move he made.

The man was magic. He made me feel.

Maybe love, marriage, and commitment weren't all some archaic social construct designed to give our young the best chance of survival. Maybe there was more to it. I don't know. Whatever this emotion was, however, I wanted him more than I'd ever wanted anything.

The music went on and on, and I stood staring, lost.

Hours later they finally stopped playing. Roadies flooded the stage, relieving the guys of their instruments, slapping them on the back and chatting. Everyone knew their jobs to perfection and it was fascinating to watch. Soon the four men approached us, looking thoroughly bedraggled. Sweat dripped off their hair, running down their tired but smiling faces. My walking male fantasy had an energy drink attached to his lips, the liquid in the bottle disappearing at lightning speed as he chugged it down. The closer he got and the more I saw, the more my body wanted. The way his T-shirt clung to him, dark from perspiration, made me start panting. The salty scent of sweat coming from his body got me sky-high. I'd sincerely love to explore what else he enjoyed doing that involved getting overheated.

Hells yes, sign me up for some of that.

Up this close, I could see the start of little lines beside his dark eyes. So he was a bit older than me. He couldn't be more than thirty or so, surely, and what was ten years between soul mates? And yes, I knew I was getting a bit overexcited. I just couldn't help it; the way he made me feel didn't come in halves. There could be no moderation.

I didn't tune in to the talk, just him. The rest of the world could disappear for good. I'd happily stand and stare at Ben Nicholson for hours. Days. Weeks.

One of those big hands ran over his short hair and I swear my sex wept in gratitude at the sight. I was out of control. If he fondled his beard I might faint.

"I'm starving," he said, his deep voice in every way a perfect, wonderful thing. "We finding somewhere to eat and drink?"

"*Yes.*"

Dark eyes turned my way, looking down, noticing me for the first time. Oh lord, it was like an epiphany, being held in his gaze. It was starlight and moonbeams and all that fantastical ridiculous stuff I'd spent the last seven years mocking, care of my parent's example. This man's existence gave it all back to me—hope, love, things like that. He made me a true believer once more.

Then he gave me a slow looking over. I stood still, grinning, waiting, and inviting his perusal. Fair was fair, I'd been ogling him for hours. And while I might not be putting any supermodels out of a job anytime soon (average height, not much up front, but curvy in the back—just like my sister), he'd be hard pressed to find a girl who could beat me for open and eager enthusiasm. I might only come up to his shoulder, but god damn would I make bending down worth his while.

Slowly, a smile curved his lips, making my heart jump with glee. The man reduced me to the state of a starstruck teenager. Yes to anything and everything that might possibly cross his mind.

"Well, okay then," he said.

"Don't you have to get back to school, Liz?" someone asked. Anne. Right. Whatever.

Man, he was divine. Maybe god existed after all. There might be a few more topics besides love that I'd need to reassess. What a day of revelations.

"No, I'm fine."

"I thought you had an assignment to do?" My sister's voice tightened in a way which normally sent red sirens screaming through me. But try as she might, I would not be swayed.

"Nope."

"Lizzy," she grated out.

"Ladies, ladies," said Mal. "We got a problem here?"

There were no problems anywhere. Not so long as Ben's gaze stayed fixed on me, making my world turn round. My smile grew shaky as our lustful staring contest continued. Then the man smirked playfully and butterflies went berserk in my belly. Damn him, I would not look away. I could and would win.

But suddenly there was a distinct disturbance in the happy. Some woman was wound around Mal, giggling and cooing and carrying on. And the problem was, that woman was not my sister. Instead, Anne stood watching the scene with her face pale and her mouth set in a grim, resigned line.

Like fuck.

All thoughts of Ben faded from my mind like I was waking from a dream. Sisterly duties called to me loud and proud.

"Hey, Mal," I said, trying for happy-go-lucky and probably failing miserably. "Should we invite Anne's friend Reece along to eat? He often does stuff with us on Sundays."

Reece was her boss and sometime crush. At least until Mal had come along. I most certainly wasn't above using petty jealousy to further the cause.

Anne's brows drew tight. "I think Reece said he'd be busy."

I gave her my best guileless look. "No. Really? Why don't you give him a call and check, Anne?"

"Maybe another—"

"Fuck no, Lizzy. I mean, I don't think there'll be room." The moron rock star looked around, finally noticing the assorted embarrassed faces (his friends') and the outright murderous face (mine) of those assembled.

The ho batted her eyelashes at him. "Is something wrong?"

"It's cool," said Anne. "Why don't you go for a drink with your friend and catch up?"

"I thought we were gonna do something." And Mal might be beyond pretty, but he sure as hell wasn't the smartest drumstick.

"Yeah, but . . ."

"I'm sorry, you are?" the ho asked in her high girly voice.

Ev cleared her throat and announced in a no-nonsense manner, "Ainslie, this is Mal's new girlfriend, Anne. Anne, this is Ainslie."

"Girlfriend?" Ainslie laughed, and I pretty much definitely really now did want to kill her. Slowly. Painfully. You get the gist.

"I was just saying hi to a friend," said Mal, carrying on with the male obliviousness. "What's the big deal?"

"There isn't one. It's fine."

"Yeah, there obviously is or you wouldn't be looking at me like that."

"You need to not talk to me in that tone of voice," Anne bit out. "Especially not in front of other people. Go out with your friend, have a nice time. We can discuss this later."

"We can, huh?"

"Yes."

His mouth curled into a farce of a smile. "Fuck it."

Everyone kind of looked at everyone else, but Anne just stood there. Her fingers clenched and unclenched at her sides, same as mine. God damn it, this couldn't be happening, not to Anne, not now. Just for once let the world play fair.

Soon enough the angry crashing of drums filled the hall, however. It was over. Let the animal pound on his skins.

It seemed no one had anything more to say.

Almost.

"Crap, I forgot!" Rather dramatically, Ev grabbed at her head. "We women all have to go meet Lauren. Girls' night out."

Her husband, the guitarist, just gave her a blank look. "You do?"

"Yep. We're starting early."

And hallelujah.

Anything to get Anne out of this god-awful situation with some of her pride intact sounded good to me. I ignored any inner conflict. Yes, the thought of giving up my chance with Ben hurt. I'm pretty sure my heart and vagina would never forgive me. But Anne looked devastated, her hands trembling. I grabbed her arm and towed her toward the door. A muscle-bound dude done out in all black, who just had to be security, met us beside a shiny new Escalade. We all bundled in with minimal small talk. Everything inside was leather. Seriously, the car was one sweet ride. Not sweet enough to get the sour out of my mouth over Mal's defection, however.

"I don't understand." I turned to face Anne, sitting so eerily still in the backseat. Every inch of her was wound tight and inward, her shoulders rounded and hands clasped in her lap. It was like she was just waiting for another attack, for more hurt. I hated that. If Mal Ericson had kicked a puppy I couldn't be more pissed.

"This," I said, waving a hand at her. "He makes you happier than I've ever seen. It's like you're a different person. He looks at you like you invented whipped cream. Now this. I don't understand."

She shrugged. "Whirlwind romance. Easy come, easy go."

My mouth opened to call bullshit, but I couldn't. I knew Anne too well. We stared at each other for a long moment until the luxury car started rolling forward. The past seven years had bound us tightly together. Tighter than either of us might have liked, truth be told. Love and hope equaled pain. They fucked you over and left you high and dry.

Stupid to believe otherwise. Those were our home truths and we'd learned them the hard way when Dad up and left. Love sucked, and men . . . well, it seemed they were as dependable as they'd ever been.

Still, I couldn't get the memory of Ben out of my head. The way his dark brown eyes had fixed on mine and never wavered. In all honesty, it could have meant anything.

Nothing, or everything, or something in between.

I just didn't know.

"I do not need him," Anne announced from atop the coffee table, her chocolate martini held high in the air.

A round of applause from Lauren.

"I really don't!"

"Right on, sister. Amen."

"In fact, I don't need any man! I'm a . . . I'm a . . ." She clicked her fingers impatiently, face deep in thought. "What's the word I'm looking for?"

"You're a modern woman."

"Yes-s-s," my sister hissed. "Thank you. I'm a modern woman. And penises are just weird anyway. I mean seriously, who the fuck even thought that shit up?"

On the floor, Lauren started laughing so hard she had to clutch at her belly. Me, not so much. Why Anne couldn't give her speeches with her feet safely on the floor was beyond me.

"No, really. Think about it. They're fine when they're hard, but when they're soft . . ." With a faint frown, my sister crooked her pinkie finger and then wiggled it. "So wrinkly and weird looking. Vaginas make much more sense."

"Oh god." I squeezed my eyes shut for a moment.

We'd finally arrived at my sister's apartment late afternoon, due to Ev needing to make a couple of stops. First there was a liquor store. Next, Voodoo Doughnuts. And last but not least, a pizza shop in the Pearl. The big burly security guy driving us had taken it all in his stride. He'd lugged the myriad bags, boxes, and bottles required up the stairs into Anne's small two bedroom apartment. When it came to throwing an impromptu man-hate party, Evelyn Ferris clearly had all bases covered.

My rage toward the drummer in question, Malcolm Ericson, had dropped from boiling to a simmer. The precarious way Anne was swaying atop her high perch worried me more. "Please don't fall off the coffee table and break something."

"Ohmyfuckinggod." Dark liquid sloshed over the edge of her glass, splattering onto the scuffed wooden floor below, only narrowly missing a red-faced Lauren. "Stop being such an adult, Lizzy. I'm the older sister here. You're the kid. Act like it."

I opened my mouth to tell her what I thought of that bright idea, but a hand swiftly covered my lips.

"Do not engage," Ev whispered in my ear, her arm

draped over my shoulders and palm still silencing me. "She is drunk off her ever-loving ass and arguing with her will get you nowhere."

The hand withdrew, though the arm remained.

"That's what I'm worried about," I said.

It probably should have felt weird, being so friendly with her on Anne's impressively soft new velvet love seat. I'd only just met Ev. There was something about her, though. Her and Lauren both (I'd met Lauren once before, briefly). You had to appreciate women who exuded an air of no non-sense. Whatever happened with dickhead Mal, I hoped they stuck with Anne. She needed real friends, not the money-, time-, and energy-sucking leeches she'd attracted over the years with her momma bear ways.

"Tell me if I'm wrong, but I don't think your sister lets herself blow off steam very often. She might just need this."

I frowned. "Perhaps."

Up on the table, Anne hummed along with the music playing softly over the stereo. Lost in her own little world. At least the sad face was gone. I'd seen enough of it to last me a lifetime. Just the same, I made a mental note to beat Mal Ericson bloody if I ever saw him again. About the bil-lionth thought of its type for the day.

"Did you enjoy seeing them practice before it all went south?" asked Ev.

"Yeah. I really did." I gave the woman discreet side eyes. "The bass player . . . what was his name?"

"Ben?"

"Hmm." I nodded, feeling my way through the conver-sation ever so carefully. "He seemed interesting. Pity we didn't get to head out for a meal."

"It was a pity. Couldn't help but notice you noticing him at practice," said Ev, ending any charade of subtlety.

Awesome.

"Relax. I'm not going to say anything to your sister."
The woman sighed. "Ben, Ben, Ben. How to describe him?
He's a great guy, very laid back."

I said nothing.

"Be warned, though, he's not known for actually
dating."

I gave her side eyes.

She gave me a small grin. "Of course, neither was David until we got married. Anyhoo . . . Ben. How serious
are you about him?"

"Are you asking about my intentions?"

A startled laugh flew out of her. "Huh. Yeah, I guess
I am. I've got a man now, so I have to meddle and play
matchmaker. Apparently it's what women do. But seriously, it's not *him* getting hurt that I'm necessarily worried about."

"You going to tell me I'm too young for him?"

"That would be hypocritical of me, considering I got
hitched at twenty-one. And you're what?"

"Nearly twenty-one." I shifted in my seat.

"Well he's nearly twenty-nine, just so you know."

Eight years. Not so bad.

I stared into the murky dregs of my second martini as
if somewhere in the muck lay a clue. You need tea leaves,
though, to tell the future. Vodka, cream, and chocolate
liqueur didn't quite cut it. "I probably won't get to see him
again anyway, so . . ."

"You give up that easy?" she asked. "The way you were
looking at him, I thought you were more determined than
that."

"He's a rock star. Are you saying I should stalk him?"

She shrugged. "Rock stars are just people too. I don't
think standing outside his hotel in the rain would be a lot
of fun, though."

"No. Probably not." I could just see myself doing it,

however, sad but true. The idea wasn't entirely stupid. Maybe it would work. He'd definitely been interested. At least, I'm pretty sure he had been, what with the staring and vague smiling. . . .

Yeah, okay, I needed to find out. "Which hotel, just out of curiosity?"

A certain twinkle came into Ev's eyes.

"Yo," a voice hollered. It took about a year, but with movements painfully slow and deliberate, Lauren eventually got to her feet. "Let me grab you another drink there, kiddo."

"I'm fi—" My glass was torn from my hand and the night's self-appointed bartender stumbled off toward the kitchen.

"I better help her out with that or you'll be served straight vodka." Ev sat forward, withdrawing her cell phone from her back jeans pocket. Her fingers moved over the screen, then she tossed it onto the seat at her side, giving me a meaningful look. "I'll just leave that there. I'm sure I can trust you not to look up any bass player's number while I'm in the kitchen, right?"

"Absolutely. I have no intention of searching *N* for *Nicholson* in your contacts index."

"Try *B* for *Ben* instead." She winked at me.

"Thank you," I said quietly.

"No problem. I've seen that wide-eyed crazytown blown-away-by-a-rock-star look before." She climbed to her feet. "On my own face as it so happens. Use that number wisely."

"Oh, trust me. I will."

CHAPTER TWO

Lizzy: Hi, it's Lizzy. Anne's sister. We met at band practice the other day, remember?

Ben: Hey. I remember. How u doing?

Lizzy: Good. U?

Ben: Good. How'd u get my number?

Lizzy: Mutual acquaintance.

Ben: Ur sister & Mal don't want us being friends.

Lizzy: U've friend zoned me already? Ouch. I haven't even made a clumsy inappropriate pass at u yet.

Ben: Ha. U know what I mean. Didn't realize u were only 20 or connected to Mal. Us talking isn't a good idea.

Lizzy: Lucky we're only texting then.

Ben: Bye Liz

Ben: Did u just send me a pic of ur lunch?

Lizzy: No. It's an artistic representation rendered in fries and ketchup of my immense sadness over u ignoring my texts. See the face in the middle?

Ben: What's the green stuff?

Lizzy: Those are pickle tears. Stole them off a friend's burger.

Ben: Cute.

Lizzy: Are u moved?

Ben: Absolutely.

Lizzy: Are u going to talk to me now?

Lizzy: Haha. You're having pizza for lunch?

Ben: Does it look sad or happy?

Lizzy: It looks lewd. How dare you send such explicit pepperoni. I'm not that kind of girl.

Ben: Ha. Got to work. Later, sweetheart.

Ben: Got no one to jam with & your town's music scene is crap on Mondays.

Lizzy: Never. Try The Pigeon. A friend goes to their open sessions.

Ben: I'm there. :)

Lizzy: How'd you go last night?

Ben: Good. Thanks for the info. Not Nashville but not bad. Might head up to Seattle for a few days. Friend's playing up there. Anyway, TY

Lizzy: You're welcome. Busy day?

Ben: Mal's walked in. Can't talk.

Lizzy: Ok. Later.

Ben: Feel shit going behind his back.

Lizzy: Let's talk later.

Lizzy: Hi! How'd ur day go?

Ben: Busy right now.

Lizzy: Ok

Lizzy: I'm going to assume by radio silence that you're not comfortable with us being text buddies. Didn't mean to put u in a bad position with Mal. I'll delete ur number.

Ben: Don't.

Lizzy: ?

Ben: I want to know if u need something u can call me.

Lizzy; Thanks. But I don't want to complicate things for u.

Ben: Problem is I like talking to u. Maybe if we keep it on the down low?

Lizzy: Ok. I'd like that.

Ben: Me too.

Ben: Attached pic is sunset out at Red Rock.

Lizzy: Amazing. What are you doing out there?

Ben: Filling in on keyboard for a friend. His guy broke hand.

Lizzy: Crap. Didn't know you played piano.

Ben: Grandma taught me. But Dave wanted bass so I learned.

Lizzy: Wow. Play for me sometime?

Ben: How about now?

Lizzy: Over the phone? That would be awesome.

Ben: Calling.

Ben: In the studio in LA for a few. How u going?

Lizzy: Studying for a test. Wish me luck.

Ben: You got this, sweetheart. Won't distract u. Later.

Lizzy: :) Later

Lizzy: Roses are red, violets are blue, I like u Ben, do u like me to?

Ben: Ur a terrible poet.

Lizzy: True. I think I might stick w psychology. How's ur day going?

Ben: Slow. Had a business meeting. Boring as shit.

Lizzy: U just want to play music?

Ben: Got me on that. How u doing?

Lizzy: Had an awesome prac. Off to work at book store next. Then got an assignment due.

Ben: Work all u do?

Lizzy: Pretty much. But I enjoy it. Texting u just made my day, tho.

Ben: Fuck ur sweet. Tell me something bad about u. Make it easier for me to stay away.

Lizzy: I see no benefit to me in doing this . . .

Ben: Go on. I'm waiting.

Lizzy: I suck at sports and I'm messy.

Ben: Can't imagine you messy.

Lizzy: My apartment looks like a war zone. Anne always tidied. Gave me bad habits. What about u?

Ben: I flirt with girl's I'm not supposed to. Otherwise I'm perfect.

Lizzy: All that fame and fortune and not an ego in sight.

Ben: Exactly.

Lizzy: :)

Ben: Gotta go, Jim's waiting. Later sweetheart.

Lizzy: Later Ben

Ben: WTF is that pic?

Lizzy: U tell me.

Ben: A mash up of a lion, a beer, & a girl's eyes (yours?)

Lizzy: Right on all counts!

Ben: What's it mean?

Lizzy: I am using my psych studies to mess with your mind. Studies show association with fear encourages romantic thoughts.

Ben: Sly. U uncovered my fear of beer?

Lizzy: Haha. The fear is the lion.

Ben: Ok. So what's the beer?

Lizzy: You know the phenomenon of beer-goggles?

Ben: Chicks look hot when you're drunk?

Lizzy: Right. But turns out the beer-goggler doesn't need to be drunk. Just an association with beer will do. Even a picture.

Ben: Me looking at a pic of beer will make u seem hotter?

Lizzy: You can't argue with science. You poor hapless male. You never stood a chance.

Ben: Liz, I think ur gorgeous. Save the beer pics for someone who needs em.

Lizzy: Damn ur smooth

Ben: U like that?

Lizzy: Very much

Ben: Good. U poor hapless female. U never stood a chance.

Lizzy: :)

Ben: What do you think?

Lizzy: I think that's a pic of a banjo. Yours?

Ben: Deering Black Diamond. Thinking of buying it.

Lizzy: U play banjo too? Whoa.

Ben: Want to learn.

Lizzy: And I want to hear you play. You're a musical virtuoso. Do you sing?

Ben: Ha. U do not want to hear me sing. Trust me. Think I should buy it?

Lizzy: Do it. :)

Ben: Done. :)

Lizzy: ===v=^=={@}

Ben: This another psych test?

Lizzy: No. It's a rose. I worked on it all morning.

Lizzy: Well . . . a couple of minutes between classes.

Ben: Beautiful.

Lizzy: :) Why don't we have coffee?

Lizzy: Is the lack of a response a no or are u shy?

Ben: Shy of Mal shooting me. We better just stick 2 text.

Lizzy: Fair enough.

Ben: Been thinking about u. Talk to me.

Lizzy: I'd love to. Calling.

Ben: U ok? Haven't heard from u lately.

Lizzy: I didn't want to seem too obvious. The stalker handbook said play it cool.

Ben: I know ur not a stalker. Ur dangerous in another way.

Lizzy: I love that u said that.

Lizzy: So do u actually have real stalkers?

Lizzy: Apart from me, I mean.

Ben: You're not a real stalker. They camp across the street with binoculars.

Lizzy: That's crazy. U get a much better resolution with a telescope.

Ben: You're a goose.

Lizzy: Our honesty is beautiful.

Lizzy: Psychologically speaking, most relationships fail due to lack of constructive criticism. Obvious we're made for each other.

Ben: You're a total goose. Seriously.

Lizzy: See what I mean?

Lizzy: But we were talking about stalkers.

Ben: Not really for me. I'm lucky. The other guys can't walk down the street without getting hassled. I'm less in the limelight. Not so recognizable.

Lizzy: U kidding? You're built like King Kong.

Ben: Ha. Jimmy had stalkers that got creepy. One broke into his place a few years back stole some shit.

Ben: Mal had one that ended in a restraining order.

Lizzy: Wow. What did the stalker do?

Ben: No, the stalker had to get a restraining order against Mal. He kept showing up at the guys work, trying to hug him and leaving weird phone messages etc.

Lizzy: Lol.

Ben: Gotta go. Music breaks over.

Lizzy: I make killer cheesy cornbread.

Ben: Do u?

Lizzy: I do. & I just so happen 2 be making some right now. My plans tonight r cheesy cornbread & bad zombie films. Tempted?

Ben: Like u wouldn't believe.

Lizzy: But ur busy w the guys?

Ben: No. Guys with their girlfriends. I'm busy killing people.

Lizzy: Online I trust?

Ben: Ha. Yes.

Lizzy: I'd better leave u 2 it then.

Ben: I can torpedo & talk to u. How was ur day?

Lizzy: Not bad. Classes mostly. How about u?

Ben: Recording. Fucking frustrating. Jim was in a mood. This is just between us, yeah?

Lizzy: Absolutely.

Ben: Good. Boring night. Portland is no LA.

Lizzy: Come over. We can throw cornbread at the undead on tv. I'll judge you on your aim.

Ben: Fuck I wish I could.

Lizzy: Me too
Ben: One day

Lizzy: U awake? I can't sleep.
Ben: Count sheep like a good girl.
Lizzy: Can't. Too busy thinking about u.
Ben: Shit, Liz. No.
Lizzy: No, what?
Ben: Don't tell me ur in bed at 2 in the morning thinking about me. OK? U cannot tell me that. Too fucking tempting.
Ben: What are you wearing?
Lizzy: U really want me to answer that?
Ben: Yes.
Ben: No.
Ben: Shit. You're killing me. You know that right?
Lizzy: You say the nicest things. Night, Ben.
Ben: Night, sweetheart.

Lizzy: Sorry I missed your call earlier. Good luck with ur date with Lena tonight.
Lizzy: Actually, that was a lie. I didn't mean that at all.
Lizzy: About ur date. Not about missing ur call.
Lizzy: Now I feel guilty because Lena is so damn nice. I'm going to stop acting crazy & go meet a friend at Steel. Over & out.
Ben: The dive bar downtown? It's a fucking meat market.
Lizzy: Just arrived. Guess I'll see for myself.
Ben: That place is a pit. Get ur ass in a cab & go home. Ur not old enough to b drinking.
Lizzy: I have fake ID. Don't worry. I'll be fine.
Ben: I'm fucking serious. U are not going in there. Full of fucking creeps.

Lizzy: Have a nice night w Lena. U deserve someone
      great like her. Really.

Still no answer from Ben on my last text.

Emo indie music wailed out of the speakers, as Christy,
my ex-roommate, bopped as best she could on the spot
beside me.

"Great place, huh?" she yelled.

"Yeah. Great."

The place sucked. I mean literally—my shoes stuck to
the floor. The bar was grossly lacking in hygiene. Also, it
was overcrowded and reeked of decades of spilled drinks,
questionable hookups, and broken hearts. Pretty much in
that order. My clothes were going to stink for days. And if
one more person trod on my toes, exposed care of my
sweet '50s-style black heels, I'd scream. When I'd chosen
them I'd needed a pick-me-up, I'd wanted to feel pretty. But
now all around us people pressed in. Sweat raced down
my spine, dampening the back of my black T-shirt and the
band of my jeans.

Yuck.

I pretty much wanted to call in one of those toxic hazard teams to hose me down, decontaminate me from this
pit of beer and despair. Ben might have had a point about
the place being shit. Damned if I'd ever admit it to him,
though. Nope, I was going to have fun if it killed me. I slid
my cell out of my pocket just for fun, taking a peek at the
glowing green screen. Nothing. What a surprise. Time to
saddle up ye olde horse of hopelessness and move on.

"He answer yet?" asked Christy, leaning in and yelling
to be heard over the music.

I shook my head.

My former dorm roommate sucked back some beer.
"Fuck him."

"I'm trying."

"What?"

"Yes," I hollered, giving her a brave smile. "Fuck him."

"You can do better." Little lines appeared between her brows. "You can."

"Thank you." I highly doubted that. Nice of her to say so, though. I drank a hefty mouthful of my third Moscow Mule. Vodka was the only way I'd get through this. My feelings for Ben were just a weird obsessive-compulsive disorder or something. Or no, posttraumatic stress from meeting manic Mal. I'd inadvertently attached my affections to the first sane and single hot bearded man in the room. A totally plausible analysis. Freud with his own hairy face would be impressed.

Not that I'd be volunteering that analysis for my finals.

Actually, my psych books had been less than helpful in working out exactly what this love thing was about. To be fair, I did learn some fun facts. Turns out a boy rat and a girl rat, both virgins meeting for the first time, can fornicate immediately in a proficient fashion. No messing around working out the mechanics, they're just into it. But not so with the higher primates like monkeys. They bumble and fumble their way through initial attempts, working out the relationship and requirements. So it was a relief to know it wasn't just me. Or even just humans. Apes screw up first dates too. And they don't even have condoms or bra straps to deal with.

Anyhoo, the point is, the books were big on weird facts about animals getting it on but short on the particulars regarding the type of love or lust at first sight that was plaguing my every waking moment—and a good majority of my nonwaking moments too.

Christy's new roommate, Imelda, glared at me over the edge of her bright blue drink. Lord knows what was in there to make it that color. I'd only moved into Anne's old apartment two weeks ago. Apparently, however, these

two had already bonded to the point of creepy posses-
siveness.

The bar had been Imelda's choice.

"Chris says you know the guys from Stage Dive," she
said.

My ex-roommate shifted nervously.

I just shrugged. Photos of Anne and Mal together had
done the rounds of the Internet a couple of times. It was
pretty much an open secret in Portland these days. Though
me talking about my sister's business didn't need to happen. Ever. And Christy was well aware of that policy.

"I think it's bullshit," the girl continued, standing so
close her hot breath hit my ear.

I resisted the urge to recoil. "Think what you like."

Her eyes narrowed.

"Why don't we dance?" Christy suggested, sounding
as fake peppy as could be. "Quick, drink up!"

We did as told. Then, all of a sudden, Imelda was all
hands up in the air waving them about without a care. She
snagged Christy's hand and started dragging her through
the crowd. Christy in turn caught my wrist, towing me
along. Alrighty then. Our progression through the throng
was not gentle. Elbows and assorted other body bits
bumped into me, sending me reeling this way and that. A
hand grabbed my ass.

"Hey!" I growled, spinning around. In the dark sea of
people surrounding us it could have been anyone. "Asshole."

When I turned back, Christy and her new BF had disappeared. Strobe lights blinded me. I could barely see for
shit. Crowds have always made me nervy, and this place
was a crush. It wasn't a phobia, exactly, just a distinct dislike I'd been working hard on overcoming.

Surely Christy would realize she'd lost me and come

back. Surely. Waiting. Still waiting. Some chick trod good and hard on my toe, bringing actual tears to my eyes. I tried to hop on one foot to give the other a rub and almost landed on my butt in the process. Yeah, Christy wasn't coming back. Furthermore, I might have never loved crowds, but right now I was deep in the land of hate.

God, screw this.

It was ridiculous. I was a hairsbreadth away from being twenty-one and over the whole scene already. Guess I'd just go back to my lonely girl apartment. As nice as it was to have some space, I'd never actually lived on my own before. I wasn't lonely, exactly, it was just that the absence of other people made for a definite adjustment. Bet Ben and Lena were getting on like a house on fire. How could they not, what with Lena being all funny and gorgeous and Ben being Ben.

Another body in the near-dark knocked into me, sending me staggering sideways. Since when did you need to wear full body armor to be in a bar? Perhaps I should head back to the bar, where we'd been standing before. But surely I was better staying here, where Christy last saw me. I looked back and forth in indecision. Neither option appealed. Hell, being here no longer appealed.

I blinked furiously. Not crying, just . . . you know, my toe stung.

It might be time to go catch a cab. I'm pretty sure at home I had all of the ingredients required for emergency mood-enhancing nachos. The bonus being not having to share it with anyone. Call me greedy, I don't care, and bring on the melted cheese, baby.

Suddenly, two huge hands descended upon my shoulders and I was forcibly turned around. Some sort of mountain stood before me. A man mountain.

"Ben!" I cried happily, throwing myself at him (which

of course didn't move the man an inch). His big hot body felt divine, heavenly. I wrapped my arms tight around his waist and clung ever so slightly. "I'm so glad to see you."

His hands tensed on my shoulders, fingers rubbing. "I told you not to come in here."

"I know." I sniffed, then set my chin on his chest and gazed up adoringly at him. "But have you noticed how I actually make my own choices like a real live adult?"

"You don't say?" He gave me a dour look and tucked an errant strand of hair behind my ear. Such a simple, sweet move; it worked for me big-time. Of course, anything involving him touching me would.

"How was your date with Lena?"

No reply.

"That good, huh? Oh well."

"I can see you're real cut up about it," he said with a smile.

"Yeah. The pain goes deep. It's really good to see you."

He looked at me for a long moment. "Yeah, you too. Still, kinda pissed you came in here, though."

What a silly statement. I gave him both brows up and *Oh really* in the eyes. Start out as you mean to go on and all that. Because at no stage would I be answering to the man for where I went and what I did. Trust and respect, etcetera.

He shrugged, unimpressed. "You didn't like me going out with Lena. I didn't like you coming here."

"Both of these things are true," I said, relenting just a little. "What are we going to do about them, though? That's the question."

"Hmm." He grabbed hold of my hand, giving it a squeeze. "C'mon, I'll drive you home."

"I'd like that."

Without another word he led me through the crowd, clearing the way with his body. In his plain jeans and plaid shirt, no one seemed to recognize him. In Portland, he was just one more bearded, tattooed dude among many. Attached to Ben, no one messed with me. I was neither bumped nor groped, thank god. Ah, togetherness. What a rare and beautiful thing. No wonder Anne was so wacky about Mal if this was how he made her feel. Walking beside Ben, my heart seemed so light I might hit my head on the ceiling.

"Later," the very pierced bouncer said, opening the door to let us through.

"Thanks, Marc."

Outside, the air was crisp, decidedly cool. I bundled myself up in my coat. Ben didn't seem to have brought one. He just shoved his hands in his pockets and hunched his shoulders. A beaten-up Chevy truck, from the '80s at best, sat at the corner. It might once have been pale blue. With all the fading and the couple of spots of rust, it was hard to say.

"This is your ride?" I asked, surprised.

In lieu of a response, Ben unlocked the passenger side door, holding it open.

"Huh."

I climbed up and in, sitting carefully on the cold, cracked vinyl seating. Cassettes spilled out of the glove box. Actual cassettes. "Stunned" kind of fit the situation. The man had money, lots of it.

He swung the door shut, then strode around to the driver's side. Soon enough the engine was roaring to life with minimal splutter. Clearly the car was kept in good condition.

"Expecting a Porsche?" he asked.

"No. Just something slightly less older than me."

He snorted.

We pulled out into the traffic, the low hum of some old Pearl Jam song playing. Cassettes. Christ.

"It belonged to my grandfather," he said. "He taught me how to fix it, handed over the keys when I got my license."

"Nice."

He gave me side eyes.

"I mean it, Ben. I didn't have much in the way of family myself. So I get that's nice."

A faint smile. "Yeah. We didn't have a lot of money so . . . I thought so."

The shadows of his face were frankly fascinating beneath the passing street lights, the sudden brightness of oncoming traffic, everything. He had perfect cheekbones. You could almost miss them above the beard, but the lines of his face were both sharp and beautiful. His lips, for instance. I could have stared at them for hours.

"Will you tell me about your home?" I asked.

"Not much to tell," he said, eventually. "Mom and Dad owned a cleaning business so they were gone most of the time. They were real hard workers. The business was everything to 'em. My grandparents lived next door and they fed us and kept an eye on things."

"Must have been wonderful to have them around. A stable influence like that can mean all the difference to a kid."

"You diagnosing me or something, Miss Psychology Student?"

"No. Sorry." I groaned. "Please continue. You mentioned an 'us'?"

"Me and my sister."

"You have a sister? What's she like?"

He squinted, little lines appearing beside his eyes. "Martha's . . . Martha. She's living over in New York these days, enjoys the party scene."

"That's pretty far." I couldn't imagine being on the opposite side of the country from Anne, living without my last bit of real family close by. "You must miss her."

"It's probably for the best," he said. "She caused some shit a while back. I didn't help much either."

I stayed silent, waiting for him to go on. People usually would feel compelled to fill a silence, you just had to be patient.

"Martha and David went out all through high school, and after, when the band started to take off. Then she did something stupid." He shook his head. "So fucking dumb."

"What did she do?"

He raised a brow. "You haven't heard?"

"No."

"Huh. Thought Ev might have talked about it."

"I've only met her a couple of times."

"Yeah, I guess." His fingers tapped out a beat against the steering wheel. "Martha didn't like Dave being away so much. We were working hard, touring when we weren't recording. Thought she understood. . . ."

A fire engine roared past with sirens blazing, distracting us for a moment.

"We were finally getting somewhere, really starting to make it, playing to bigger crowds, and getting some decent publicity." He exhaled noisily. "Anyway, she must have figured with him being on the road all the time that he had to be messing around on her. She got pissed one night and cheated on him."

"Oh."

"Guy couldn't have been more crazy in love with her if he tried. Never even saw him look at another woman. They'd been so tight for years. I tried to tell her, but she got this stupid idea into her head, and . . . yeah." His low laugh was bitter, horrible to hear. "She took something beautiful and shit on it. Everything went to hell after that."

"I'm sorry."

"Me too. Really thought they'd make it, get married, have kids and everything. Live the dream. She worked as an assistant for the band for a while, but when Dave and Ev got married she didn't take it too well."

"That's when she moved?"

"That's when she moved." He said nothing for a moment. "Tried one last time to get him back, and I was stupid enough to help. It didn't turn out so well. Things were tense between me and Dave for a while, and it wasn't good for the band."

"I'm sorry." I took a big breath, choosing my words with care. This had obviously hurt him. It was in the tone of his voice, the shadows on his face. Also, I didn't want to treat him like a patient or a subject. He mattered to me much deeper than that.

"It seems you guys are closer to brothers than friends, even though he and your sister didn't wind up staying together," I said. "But I'm sorry you got caught in the middle of it. That must have been hard."

"Yeah. Don't know why I'm telling you all this." He gave me a look out of the corner of his eye. "You're too easy to talk to, you know?"

I smiled. "So are you."

"You haven't told me anything yet."

"Ah, all right." I rubbed my palms against the sides of my jeans, warming them up. What to tell him? His honesty and openness meant I could give him no less. Might as well just lay it all out. "My parents divorced when I was fourteen. It messed me up for a while. But Anne helped me get back on track, helped me graduate and get into college."

"Pretty good sister."

"She's an amazing sister."

His gaze switched back and forth between me and the road. "You work hard too, though."

"Yes. But college is expensive and she sacrificed a lot to get me there, so she deserves the bulk of the credit."

"Sounds like you both hauled ass to get out of a bad situation."

"Hmm." I rested my head against the back of the car seat. The man was far too easy to talk to. I liked it. "That's it really. I work part time at the same bookstore as Anne."

He half smiled, and sadly even that made me giddy. God, he was beautiful. I never wanted this car ride to end. We could drive to Wisconsin for all I cared. Just point the hood east and keep going until we ran out of gas.

"Messed you up in what way?" he asked.

That stopped the happy. "Not a topic I like to talk about."

He just waited, drawing me out, playing me at my own game. Sneaky.

"I hung out with some losers. Drank, did drugs. Speed and pot, nothing too hard-core. I ditched school and did things I shouldn't have. Dangerous things. Dated the wrong guy for a while." My fingernails dug into me through the fabric of my jeans. All of those memories were ugly. I'd been so young and idiotic. "Then I got busted stealing. The guy who owned the shop kept saying he was going to call the police, but Anne managed to talk him out of it. That scared the shit out of me. Plus, seeing how upset Anne got about it. It finally got through to me that I wasn't the only one hurting. I stopped sneaking out at night and messing around, started going to school again. I was just so angry that they couldn't keep their shit together and be like a normal mom and dad."

"I bet."

"Though what even is normal? Seems like everyone's parents are divorced these days."

"Yeah. Just about."

"Doesn't make for much of an example, does it?"

He made a humming noise of agreement.

"So that's why I'm into psychology. One day I hope to be able to help other kids ride out the rough patches."

He smiled.

"Anyway, enough of me and my early-teen angst." I crossed my legs, turning toward him in the seat. "When did you start playing bass?"

"Fourteen or so. Dave was always crazy about guitars, and then Mal's mom got him the kit. Jimmy'd already decided he was gonna be the singer. I had an uncle who owned an old bass guitar. Grandpa talked him into giving it to me."

"The same Grandpa who gave you the truck? He sounds awesome."

"He was, Lizzy. He really was."

We pulled up outside my apartment building. Funny, I'd never hated the sight of it before, but I didn't want the trip to end. Time alone with Ben, talking, was special. I clasped my hands in my lap, studying the lines of his face. A moment later, he turned off the engine.

"Thank you for the lift home," I said.

"Any time. I mean that." He rested a hand on the steering wheel, shifting slightly to look my way.

Happy chemicals stirred inside of me. Lustful, crazy things telling me to jump him, to climb all over him and cover his gorgeous face in kisses. To rub my jaw against his beard and see if it felt soft or not. To let him see exactly how he affected me, how adored he could be.

"Kills me when you look at me like that," he murmured.

I just smiled. My tongue was too tangled for any attempt at wit. Thing was, I couldn't *not* look at him like that. It just wasn't in me to be any other way, not with him.

He exhaled hard, staring out the windshield. "I go to that club a couple of times a week to pick up. Place like that? Easy as hell. Pretty much the only reason people go there is to get drunk and get laid."

"I see."

"I'm serious."

"Okay, Ben. You're not a virgin. Duly noted. Me neither, by the way."

Dreamy dark eyes pinned me in place, owning me. He licked his lips. Every time he did that my hormones erupted into the song of joy, a full orchestra plus heavenly choir accompanying. The whole shebang. It was ridiculous.

"Fuck, you're pretty," he sighed. "Make me wish for all sorts of shit I shouldn't."

"Who says you shouldn't?" I asked, leaning closer.

"Mal. Your sister."

"This isn't about them. It's about you and me."

"Sweetheart. Liz . . ." The deep, dirty way he said my name, holy shit. His voice rumbled through me, lighting fires and causing chaos everywhere it went. I'd never be the same.

"Yeah?" I leaned closer, and then closer still, heart thundering and lips at the ready. Never in my life had kissing someone seemed so important. I needed his mouth on mine. His breath and his body, all of him.

Nothing else mattered.

I turned, propping a knee beneath me to help with the height difference. Hesitant but hopeful smile in place, I put my hand on his shoulder, getting closer. Fuck waiting on him to make the first move. Time to go after what I wanted.

"Liz."

"Yeah?"

That's when it registered. Ben's body language was all wrong. The man wasn't moving into me, wanting me back. I was alone in this.

"You don't . . ." Words caught in my dry throat, sticking. I withdrew my hand.

"I can't."

"What?"

He stared straight ahead. "You should go in."

Whatever face I had on, it wasn't happy. "You want me to go?"

"It's for the best."

"It's for the best," I parroted, staring perplexed at the dogged shadows on his face.

"I can't do this, Liz. I can't do it to the band."

"And you answer to the band for who you date?"

"We're not dating."

I cleared my throat. "No, we're not dating. But god, we spent hours talking and texting to each other."

The look he gave me was tortured. "I'm sorry. I can't."

"Right." All of the emotion inside me felt huge, over-whelming. Still my mind worked, turning all of the evidence over, trying to figure out where I'd lost the track. How the fuck I came to be flailing in the woods. "I think you were a little bored, a little lonely maybe, so you played with me."

With a grimace he turned away.

"Tell me I'm wrong."

Nothing.

At least now I knew where I stood. As if that was any real consolation. I pushed open the passenger's side door, climbing down.

"Liz—"

I slammed the truck door shut, cold metal stinging the palms of my hands. Done with him. I was so damn done with him. The bitter night air slapped me in the face, waking me right the hell up. How fucking embarrassing. I'd felt so much and been so sure. Went to show you how much I knew.

Nothing.

Not a single fucking thing.

Time to put my heart and hopes back on ice.

CHAPTER THREE

Ben: Hey, how you going?

Ben: You doing okay? Studies all good and everything?

Ben: C'mon, Liz. Talk to me. I'm still your friend.

Ben: So I guess you'll be at the wedding?

"He's not really going to wear one of those white satin Elvis jumpsuits, is he?"

My sister shrugged. "Whatever makes him happy."

"Yeah, but this is your wedding."

"*Our* wedding," she corrected, applying a final coat of lipstick then blotting it carefully on a tissue.

"God, Anne. You look amazing."

She really did. The vintage lace dress was divine. With her bright-red hair artfully drawn back from her face, she looked so elegant. I had to blink a time or two, my eyes actually getting a little misty. Given how long the makeup artist had labored over my face, I didn't dare mess up her hard work.

"Thank you." She reached out, giving my hand a squeeze. "You're looking pretty awesome yourself, birthday girl."

My birthday had actually been yesterday. Anne had insisted on waiting until I was old enough to legally join in the wedding celebrations in Vegas. Rather an unexpected delight, since treating me like a full-fledged grown-up wasn't really her thing.

Ev, Lena, Anne, and I had spent my birthday hanging out in this Bellagio villa's personal hot tub, nibbling yummy things and sipping cocktails while being waited on hand and foot. Because of course the villa came with a personal butler. Oh, and the outdoor fireplace had been roaring because during December in the desert it actually does cool right down at night. Last but not least, we had cake pops, because nothing could possibly be better than cake on a stick covered in candy.

That shit owned my soul.

I smoothed down the skirt of my own vintage dress, a knee-length ink-blue Dior number we'd found during a Saturday market hunt a few weeks back. It was beautiful. Feminine without being froufrou. My hair too had been pulled back into a simple but classy style.

Wonder what Ben would think.

Not that it mattered. I felt good about how I looked and that was that. My world didn't stop or spin based purely on his or any other male's validation. Until my feelings for Ben simmered down some, however, I'd just keep doing my best to avoid him—or at least eye contact with him. Even a stubborn heart like mine had to give up eventually. School had been busy and work much the same. What with Anne occupied with wedding arrangements, Rhys had given me extra hours in the bookstore, so there'd been plenty to keep me occupied. Ben Nicholson had been little more than a stray thought. Mostly. It would be nice later tonight to get out and let my hair down a little. See what Vegas was all about.

Sam stood, giving me a nod. It was time. Any lingering

thoughts about the man gave way to squeeful excitement. Muted conversation could be heard coming from the living room, the faint sounds of music.

"Okay, future Mrs. Ericson. Everyone's arrived so—"

"Pumpkin!" an overly familiar voice wailed. "Pumpkin, where are you?"

A picture of perfect calm, Anne turned to face the doorway and hollered back, "In here."

The doors crashed inward and Mal appeared, turned out in a truly amazing slick black suit with matching Converse on his feet. What a sight. His golden hair shone, falling over his shoulders. Left undone at the bride's request. Already he felt more like a brother. But even I had to admit, the man had it going on and then some.

"You're not meant to see me before the ceremony," said Anne.

"I don't like rules."

"I noticed."

He ambled up to Anne with a faint smile on his face. "You know, I look pretty fucking awesome. But, Pumpkin, you look even better."

My sister smiled back at him. "Thank you."

"Gonna marry me?"

"You better believe it."

He buried his face in her neck. A moment later Anne squeaked and beat him on the back. "Do not give me a hickey before the wedding, Mal, or I will kill you."

Maniacal laughter filled the room.

"I'm serious!"

"I love you. Let's wed it on." Like something out of a movie, he swooped her up into his arms and carried her out, pausing briefly at the door. "You don't look too bad either, Lizzy. C'mon, let's do this!"

I picked up both mine and Anne's bouquets and followed with a smile. This was going to be awesome.

Out in the super fancy living room, the furniture had been set aside, leaving plenty of space for the ceremony. And the Santa Elvis performing it. The big bewigged guy wore a belt bearing so many sparkly stones it was a wonder his pants stayed up. That thing had to weigh a ton. Vases full of red roses covered every available surface, the heady scent filling the room. A roaring fire burned in the corner. It was perfect, beautiful, and there were so many happy, familiar faces all gathered around, waiting to share the moment. Anne finally had the family she deserved.

In the corner, a string quartet started playing, and Santa Elvis opened his mouth. His rendition of "Love Me Tender" was wonderful. Or so I was later told.

Ben stood to the side with Jimmy and David, all of them dressed in similar dark suits. Only Ben had actually ditched his jacket and tie. He'd rolled up the sleeves of his white dress shirt, leaving the ink on his thick arms exposed. God, he was glorious. So . . . manly, for want of a better word. Everyone else faded into the background. He looked so damn fine. It hurt, and angry or not I'd have told him as much, had I been able to find my tongue.

He looked up and found me staring. There was no censure in his eyes. Just the same, embarrassment threatened to flood me, turning my face to red. But he stopped and stared at me too. If our breathing and hearts were beating in exactly the same rhythm, it wouldn't have surprised me. It was crazy. I should have known better by now.

There was just me and him.

Things were said and I heard my sister's laughter.

His gaze strayed down over my dress then back up again. Little lines appeared beside his eyes, his face tensing. As for me, my jaw ached from all the things I was holding in, all the words left unsaid. Or maybe it was just more of the same, the urge to convince him that there was something real between us that was worth the risk. Some jumble of sex and friendship and I don't know what. The fabled connection.

In all likelihood, he still wouldn't want to hear it. The man made my head and my heart hurt.

"No, you're not doing it right." The pronouncement split my focus, my gaze darting to the front of the room. Something was wrong in wedding town.

"*I'll* do it," Mal told Santa Elvis.

The King just shrugged. Guess he got paid either way.

"Of course you, Anne, take me, Mal," he proceeded, my sister still held high in his arms. "You're my Pumpkin, my whole damn world. You get my music and all my weird moods, and you think I'm funny when other people are just shaking their heads wondering what the fuck I'm on about. I think it's cute when you have your little hissy fits, but if you need me to listen and take shit serious, I promise I will. Good times or bad, you're with me and I'm with you. No matter what, we'll always work stuff out together, okay?"

"Okay," said my sister, raising a hand to wipe a tear from her face.

"You're the only woman I want or need, and no way are you into any other guy, 'cause you got me and I'm awesome. We good?"

"We're good."

"Right," said Mal. "We're married."

"They're married!" shouted Santa Elvis, throwing in a hip swivel just for fun.

Music started up again and the room filled with the sounds of clapping and cheering. Mal's and Anne's mouths were melded together. I wanted that, what they had together, and without a doubt it would be worth waiting for. After spending seven years believing love had to be just so much bullshit, I couldn't give up on it again now. That was the truth. One day I'd find someone else who made me feel like Ben did.

I just had to wait it out.

Santa Elvis started beating out "Viva Las Vegas" while those assembled went wild. Everyone apart from me and Ben. Shit. I'd pretty much missed the entire ceremony. Thank goodness, Mal's dad appeared to be taping it. Worst sister ever. I went to start clapping, like everyone else, then remembered the posies of flowers still gripped tight in my hands. Whoops, better not.

So many happy smiling faces—except for one. Oh great, my mom was here. From the other side of the room, her mouth wrinkled, brows drawn in tight. Seemed my initial lack of attention on the bride and groom hadn't escaped everyone's notice. Her gaze darted between me and Ben, her frown deepening. Might be best if I avoided dear mama for the rest of the night. Possibly the next decade too, just to be safe. The last thing I needed was for Jan to decide to start sticking her nose back into my life now.

No, thank you.

"Little sister," Mal cried, bearing down on me with arms wide open.

He'd obviously finally set Anne down, because she was busy being tag-team squeezed by David and Ev. My new brother-in-law basically tackle-hugged me, picking me up around the waist and squeezing me crazytown tight. Breathing . . . so passé.

"This is going to be great. I always wanted a little sister," he said. "Older sisters are okay, I mean, don't get me wrong. But little sisters are way more fun, right?"

I just kind of wheezed.

"And you wait until you see what I got you for your birthday. Best. Present. Ever."

"Dude, put her down before you fucking break her," said Ben with some urgency.

"What?" Mal deposited me back on my feet. Thank god.

I gave my sore ribs a rub, taking nice deep breaths. "There was a touch too much love in that hug."

"Oops. Sorry, little sis."

"All good." I grinned, still catching my breath. "Congratulations."

"Yeah. Congrats, man," said Ben. They shook hands vigorously, followed by some shoulder slapping.

"Thanks, dude."

Without missing a beat, the drummer moved on to his next love hug victim. Which left me and Ben staring at each other again. Not awkward at all.

"You look great, Lizzy."

"You too." I couldn't meet his dark eyes any longer, so instead I studied his shoes. A nice safe target. The big black boots made for quite a dramatic contrast against the cream marble floor.

He said nothing.

And yeah, okay, I was done. "Have a nice night."

"Liz, wait—"

"Must mingle."

His hand hooked my arm. "Wait. I want to talk to you."

"I don't think that's a good idea." I pulled my elbow free.

"Please."

That one simple word did it, made me hesitate. Stupid soft me. "Okay. Maybe later."

"Later."

It was good to want things in life. Didn't mean you were necessarily going to get them. Already, the thought of hearing whatever he had to say brought anxiety rushing to the surface. Bridesmaids are busy people; I had shit to do. Ben Nicholson could just wait. Tonight wasn't about me or him or the lingering mess between us. Not even a little. There were about twenty-five or so people present, excluding Santa Elvis and the string quartet. Mal's family, his dad and sisters, husbands and kids. Mine and Anne's mom (henceforth known as She Who Must Be Avoided). The Stage Dive members and their partners, plus Lauren and Nate, of course. Lots of people to meet and greet and mingle up a storm with.

But first I wanted to hug my sister. To hold her tight and know that good things happened to good people, and that she was every bit as happy as she'd always deserved to be.

So that's what I did.

After I spent almost five hours chatting and being the best bridesmaid possible, the wedding reception finally began to wind down. Hand to god, I'd more than earned my night out on the town. I'd avoided both Ben and my mom by never standing still for long. My attempts to keep Mal's clutter of nephews and nieces under control went a long way toward helping.

Mental note to never, ever have children. Working with them would be fine, but I wanted to be able to clock out at the end of the day, thank you very much. They might be cute, but they could also be total maniacs. I was pretty damn certain Mal would be getting hit up for the replacement of at least one of the fancy jacquard-covered chairs. I'd tried to get the pâté finger art out, but with little luck. The perpetrator of that particular crime remained hidden under a hallway table.

Couples were beginning to get overly amorous, what with the late hour, rich food, and expensive booze. As for me, I was ready to par-tay!

"We're about to slip away," reported Anne, hooking my elbow with a hand. Her other arm was occupied resting around her husband's neck.

"I guessed." I nodded. "The dude attached to the side of your head kind of gave it away."

Mal didn't bother coming up for air. Instead, he kept right on nibbling at Anne's ear. But he did say something. Some muttered string of words I didn't have a hope in hell of understanding.

"What did he say?" I asked.

"He said we have to go consummate our marriage," said Anne.

"Of course he did. Have fun with that."

"We will."

More incoherent mumbling from the guy attached to her ear.

"I thought that was meant to be a surprise for when she got back?" replied Anne.

Mal finally surfaced. "But it's just so cool. I am just so cool. I think she deserves to know this."

"It's your present, it's up to you. Tell her if you like." Anne laughed.

The smile Mal gave me was megawatt, blinding. "I got you a baby blue 1967 Mustang GT for your birthday."

"You did?" I shrieked in glee.

"Exactly. Aren't I just the best? Ohmigod I'm fucking amazing! My own mind is just blown by me. Put it there, little sis." He held up his hand for a high five.

I slapped palms with him with much zest. "That's awesome, Mal!"

"I know, right?"

"Thank you so much."

"It's nothing." A careless hand waved my gratitude away. "Sheesh."

Only Anne seemed unenthused. "You got Liz a muscle car? You bought me a Prius."

With pouty lips, Mal framed her face with his hands.

"Because you're my Pumpkin Prius princess. Girls like you don't drive muscle cars."

"Girls like me?"

"Beautiful, clever, good girls with lots of respect for traffic lights and shit like that. Besides, you've got me. You don't need any more muscle in your life."

I wouldn't say Anne looked appeased, exactly. But she did drop the subject after yet another lingering kiss.

"What are you up to tonight?" she asked me eventually.

"I thought I might go dancing or something," I said, rocking back on my heels in excitement. Vegas, here I come. "Put my legal ID to good use."

Anne's grin faltered. "Right, yeah. Listen, Sam was thinking of going around to a couple of clubs too. You mind if he tags along?"

Ruh-roh. "Sam the security man?"

"Yeah." Her gaze wandered around the room for a moment, avoiding mine. "He won't get in the way, I promise. He's a really great guy and going out on your own in Vegas isn't the smartest idea. You don't mind do you? I promise he won't get in your way or anything."

"No, I guess not."

"Good." She visibly relaxed, leaning against Mal. "I think they took your stuff up to the penthouse suite already, by the way. You've got the key, right?"

"Yep. All set."

"And if you go anywhere on your own, don't get lost in the hotel. That place is huge."

"I'll be fine. Go make merry with your husband." I smacked a light kiss on her cheek. "Congratulations. It was a wonderful night. You looked beautiful."

"What 'bout me?" came from Mal.

"Very pretty." I gave him a pat on the head. "Later!"

I had a man to forget and a town to explore.

CHAPTER FOUR

"What'd you say your name was again?"

"Liz."

"Lisa?"

"Close enough." I gave the drunken blond a smile and took another sip of my margarita. He might be cute, but cute didn't make up for rampant stupidity or a blood alcohol level sky-high, such as he had to have. He gave me his version of a pantie-wetting grin and I had no doubt it worked when the dude was sober. Or when the object of his lustful affections was in the same state of inebriation.

Sadly, my two-and-a-half-margarita happy buzz didn't even begin to qualify.

We'd been dancing for an hour or so, having fun. There'd been no real touching or grinding or anything to lead him on.

Because I knew limits, didn't I? Yes I did.

The hotel had a large selection of bars and nightclubs. Not to mention the plethora of nearby ones. We'd started at a place across the road before heading back closer to home. Good music, lots of dancing, and a couple of drinks. My fun had been found, my hair let down.

Anyway, a pity he had to go and wreck it now by trying

to score. Over my shoulder, Sam the security man (who most definitely didn't dance) kept the same position he had for the past three hours, holding up the bar with a glass of whiskey in hand. He'd wanted to check out a couple of clubs, my ass. The man had been sicced onto me for certain. For not the first time tonight, he narrowed his eyes at my dance partner and shook his head in disbelief. I just smiled back at him. Tonight wasn't about serious. It was about laughing, dancing, having a few drinks, and celebrating being young and single.

My drunken companion slipped an arm around my waist, licking his lips. "So, Lila."

"Yeah, Mike?"

A frown. "Mark. My name's Mark."

"Oh, gosh, sorry, Mark. My bad."

"No worries, babe." A hazy grin slipped across his face once more as he leaned forward, moving in for the kill.

I think not.

I turned my face away and took a hasty side step, escaping his attempt at any mouth-on-mouth behavior. Once my last half of salty, tequila-infused heaven on ice was finished, I was out of there. Sam and I could find somewhere else to hang. If it wasn't guaranteed to give me a brain freeze I'd have just downed it. "Well, this has been great."

"Party's just starting," he slurred.

In what was no doubt planned to be a smooth move, the douche stumbled into me, knocking my back into the bar. Worse yet, my god damn drink spilled all over the floor. Those things were not cheap, and I sure as hell hadn't been willing to let Mark buy me any. He'd started getting enough ideas as it was. Idiot.

"Shit." I shoved at the drunken twit's chest, trying to get him off of me. "Move it."

Like my words had suddenly grown superpowers, the dickhead flew backward into the crowd, landing sprawled

on his ass several yards away. Whoa. How about that. I
gazed in slack-jawed surprise. Then, into the wide-open
space in front of me stepped Ben.

Crap.

"Hey," I said, setting my now empty glass on the bar.
"Hi."

His forehead was furrowed, his mouth a severely straight,
unimpressed line. Goodness, did he look angry. Between the
beard and the expression on his face, he looked downright
barbaric. He might as well be dressed in furs and carrying
a spear, presenting me with the boar he'd caught for dinner.
Ah, good old-fashioned Stone Age romance.

"How you doing?" I asked.

Still nothing from him.

"Did you want something to drink? I was just about to
move on to another club, but if you'd like to hang here for
a while, that's fine with me."

He set a hand on the bar either side of me, fencing
me in. Huh.

"Having a good night?" I asked.

"Not really. Been looking for you."

"That's sweet. But you didn't need to do that."

"You knew I wanted to talk to you."

"Yes, I knew."

"You said we'd talk later."

"I know. But here's the thing: maybe I didn't want to
talk to you after all, Ben. Maybe I just want to forget what
happened and move on with my life."

Behind him, two of the bar's bulky security guys ever
so gently escorted my former drunken dance partner from
the premises.

"Bye, Mike." I finger waved.

"And what the fuck were you doing with that guy?"
he growled.

"Dancing, until he got a wee bit too inebriated. My

safety isn't the issue here. I have my friend Sam with me, should I run into any trouble." I nodded to where the man stood by the bar.

If anything, his presence just seemed to make Ben crankier. "Then why wasn't he doing something about that idiot crawling all over you?"

"Probably because he knew I had it covered."

He cocked his head. "You had it covered?"

"Yep."

"Funny, sweetheart. Cause I could have sworn I walked in here to find some *drunken asshole trying to maul you*." The man, he fumed, his cheeks turning red and eyes blazing. It was kind of impressive.

"I realize it looked bad, but I had it under control."

"You did, huh?" His laughter, it didn't really sound the smallest bit amused. "Christ. You're done here."

"Ah, no. I'm actually not. Now see, this is where we have a problem." I folded my arms. Then unfolded them because like fuck I'd look defensive. He was the one in the wrong, not me. "You're not prepared to take me, or my feelings, seriously. What you want is to hide away in Mr. Too Cool for Commitment land and just play with my affections when it suits you. Okay, I've accepted that. But none of that means it's okay for you to come in here and act like you're the boss of me. None of it."

"That so?" he asked, leaning down so that we were almost nose to nose.

"That's so, baby." I play-punched him in the shoulder, which it should be noted, I barely came up to. Okay, so maybe the alcohol on a mostly empty stomach had made me slightly/lots braver/sillier. "So why don't you take your little caveman jealous tantrum bullshit somewhere else. See, I do this funny thing I like to refer to as whatever the fuck I want. Understand?"

He just stared.

"And as pretty as you are with your beard and your muscles, you are too damn tricky and . . . complicated and shit for me."

"I am?"

"Yes, you are. Are you finally seeing my point here?"

"You bet."

"Excellent. So take your hotness elsewhere, kind sir. I want no part of it!" Huh. I had so told him. Drunken bravado was the best.

He nodded once, not so much at my words but as if he'd decided something. It didn't take me long to find out what. The man grabbed my hips tight and bent, setting his shoulder to my middle.

"Don't—"

And up I went. Then down went the front half of me. Down, over his shoulder in a fireman's hold.

"Ben, put me down."

His arm went around my knees, a hand holding onto the back of one thigh. Almost at a not cool height. Though not a single little damn thing about this actually was cool. Then the ground started moving beneath us.

"Ben!"

He didn't even slow down.

"I take it you're finished for the night, Miss Rollins," asked Sam.

"Make him put me down," I screeched.

"I'm afraid I can't interfere. You see, Mr. Nicholson also contributes to my wages."

"You have to be kidding me."

"Puts me in kind of a difficult situation. You understand."

I had nothing.

"To be fair, he texted me asking where you were, hours ago," said Sam. "I didn't tell him."

"Oh yeah, you're a peach."

Sam grinned. The jerk.

"I've got this," grumbled the prehistoric asshole carrying me.

"Right," said the incredibly useless security man. "Might go lose some money on a card game, then. Night-night."

Ben just grunted.

So I smacked him on the ass. "You're being absolutely ridiculous. Put me down."

"Nope."

"Do you have any idea how insane this must look?"

"Don't care."

"I do. God, Ben. You drive me nuts."

Another grunt. How original.

My laughter came out slightly too high-pitched, too crazy. What a night.

So tempting to lose my shit, but no. Conflict resolution. I was a professional to the last. "Ben, why don't you put me down and we can talk about whatever you want over a drink. You've obviously got my attention now."

"I don't think so."

"Look, I'm sorry I didn't take your request to talk seriously before. Let me make it up to you."

He ignored me.

Pity those around us didn't. They giggled and pointed and carried on like we were a damn comedy act. But did anyone think to try and help me? No.

People.

"I'm trying to be reasonable here!"

"I know."

"Which is pretty fucking mature of me, given I'm upside down talking to your ass, Ben!" I growled in frustration, slapping at his rear one more time just for fun. Had ever a man been born so bone of head and firm of butt? I think not.

"Keep that up, I'm going to start giving it back to you," he warned. "And my hands are a hell of a lot bigger than yours, Liz."

"You are such an asshole."

"You know, you act all cute, but you've got a mouth on you when you get riled up."

"Bite me."

"It's late, Lizzy. Time for bad girls to go to bed," he said.

"Aw, Ben. If you were having trouble scoring, you should have just said so. We could have worked something out."

His laughter was low-down and dirty. "That's real accommodating of you, sweetheart."

"No worries. I think it's a damn shame a big strong hairy rock star such as yourself has to take to kidnapping women out of bars to get any."

Cool air hit the back of my thighs as the skirt of my dress was raised. Teeth grazed over my soft skin in warning, his breath coming dangerously close to warming pertinent areas. Or maybe that was just my imagination. Either way, time to freak right out.

"Don't you fucking dare," I screeched, wriggling around.

Arms tightened around me and the sharp teeth were replaced with his lips. "Stop squirming."

"Stop being such a bastard and put me down."

"You said to bite you." The idiot tittered.

Whatever. Simple people are often easily amused.

Hell I was a long way up. It was a little scary. Down a fancy hallway we ventured, the sound of slot machines and the faint stink of cigarettes indicating the massive gaming room had to be somewhere near. Next, a glossy elevator with an ad for some show, playing on repeat. The foolish man had left his wallet sitting in his back pocket. At last, some entertainment. Why not, since I was along for the ride?

"Who's Meli? And . . ." I held the next scrawled-on piece of paper up to my face. "Crap. I think it says Karen. I don't think you should call Karen for a good time. The poor girl can barely spell her own name. Hey, mind if I borrow your credit card?"

The Neanderthal dipped and my feet once more met the ground. He held onto my elbow with a strong hand. A good thing because, whoa, my head spun around and around as the world slowly righted itself.

"Give me that," he growled, snatching the wallet out of my hands and stuffing it back into his pocket. "Stop acting like a brat."

"I'm acting like a brat? Are you serious?"

"Saying you'll talk to me later, then disappearing."

I snorted. "Because hearing more of your excuses sounds like such a good time."

"It's not like that."

"Bullshit," I said, hands on hips. "Go find someone who wants to play your games, Ben."

"Fuck." He turned away, mouth all scrunched up. "I wanted to apologize, okay?"

I watched and waited.

"I miss you, Liz. I didn't mean to hurt you." He seemed sincere, eyes all tortured. "I'm sorry."

"Okay. But I still can't do it."

His gaze searched my face. "You can't what?"

"Be friends with you."

He said nothing.

"I'm sorry. I know you're lonely and you miss L.A., but I can't. I have feelings for you and I can't just put them away because you're not prepared to go there."

He pressed his lips tight together, hard enough to turn them white. Then he turned his back on me.

"Ben?"

Silence.

"For what it's worth, I missed you too."

The elevator pinged and the doors slid smoothly open.

"Thanks for the lift." I wandered out, fishing my room key out of my bra ever so subtly. He'd been right. It probably was time to call it a night. At least I'd gotten some dancing and a drink or two in. I'd seen some of Vegas for myself and Anne and Mal were happily married. All in all, a highly successful trip. So why did it feel like I was being broken open because of him one more time?

Ben trudged along behind me, saying nothing. He could do as he pleased. Obviously. It was around midnight, give or take. Today had been long, with all the wedding preparations, and last night had been a late one, with my birthday celebration. Fact was, bed sounded like a damn fine idea actually.

I opened the door to my penthouse suite and stepped inside. Everything was marble and mirrors and splendor. The curtains were drawn back, displaying the Strip all lit up. A thing of beauty.

"Wow."

The moody man mountain leaned his butt against the table, legs spread wide and muscular arms crossed over his chest. What he did to me. I never stood a chance. My heart went *boom* and my body woke right the hell up. The temptation to go climb him, to touch him and taste him, was too strong. He needed to leave.

"Shouldn't you be off hitting up Karen or Meli or whoever else passed you their number?" I asked.

"You jealous?"

I tried to smile. I'm pretty sure I failed. "What would be the point?"

He just gazed at me, his blank face a mystery. Hell, all of him a mystery. One I would never solve.

"You can leave," I said. "I won't be going out again."

The man crashed down on the couch. "Give me a break. I've been chasing you all over town for the last few hours."

Again and again. Whatever.

Beyond the open living and dining room lay the bedroom. A mother of a bed. You'd pretty much want to pack a lunch if you were going to try and cross the thing. More flower arrangements and fancy furniture. The bathroom was equally huge and majestic. Two baths, for some reason. Wild. I wandered up to one of the basins, studying the girl in the mirror. Not bad. Pretty enough, if not beautiful. Hopefully the bulk of the time she had half a brain in her head and a promising future ahead of her.

But in the meantime the updo needed dealing with. Then I could get down to scrubbing all the makeup off my face. Maybe I'd even test-drive one of the tubs.

Ben appeared in the doorway with an open beer in his hand. Another of the buttons of his white shirt had been undone. Such a bull of a neck. No god damn idea why that worked for me.

"I take it you've decided you're staying?" I reached back, searching for the first of what would no doubt be many, many hairpins.

"You mind?"

"No, I give up. But what would Mal say?"

"I'll crash on the couch," he said, ignoring my question entirely.

I continued duking it out with the do.

"Let me help." He stepped closer, setting his beer down. Dark brows drew in a ways as he gave my hair a good glaring at. Then, with careful fingers, he gently tugged free his first pin and tossed it onto the counter.

"Thanks."

Without comment, he kept on with the job while I

watched. Weird. I barely came up to the guy's shoulder, even in my high heels. The width of him dwarfed me. I wasn't particularly tiny or petite, being basically average everything. But with him standing behind me I looked like some small, dainty thing. The guy could crush me one-handed. Hell, he'd done a pretty good job on my heart from afar.

"Don't know why you do all this," he said. "It looks just as good down."

My eyebrows rose right up. "I didn't know you noticed."

Nothing.

I stole a sip of his beer. A fancy German one in a big shiny green bottle. Hoppy. Nice.

"Don't need all that shit on your face, either." He took the beer off me and had another swig before returning to tending my hair. Our gazes met ever so briefly in the mirror, then his darted away. He took a deep breath, got busy.

"Thanks. I think."

A shrug.

My fingers toyed with the edge of the counter, nails flicking back and forth. A nervous habit. He shifted slightly, moving a little closer. I could feel the heat of him at my back, the solidity of him.

"Maybe I should do this myself," I said.

"You'll be here all fucking night you try to do it by yourself. How many pins did they stick in this thing?"

"I lost count after the first dozen or so."

He worked for a while in silence. Yeah. Awesome. Not awkward at all.

"Happy Birthday for yesterday," he mumbled in a rough low voice. More pins were tossed onto the counter.

"Thanks."

Carefully, he started pulling sections of my hair free, letting them fall down my back. The intent look in his eyes, the absolute focus as he did it, nearly killed me. What the hell was going on here? Talk about mixed signals. Maybe I'd have a cold bath, ice, the whole works. It would take at least that to put out the fire in my pants.

"Happy Twenty-Ninth Birthday for before Christmas," I said, voice wavering. "I, um . . . I know I was there for the dinner, but . . ."

"But you were avoiding me." The edges of his mouth slid into a smile. It seemed self-deprecating somehow. Definitely unfunny.

"Yeah."

He stared at me in the mirror. And then he stared at me some more. God, I wish I could read him. Just for a moment even. I wished I could touch him even more.

"Funny," he said. "We were only texting, but I got used to it."

"Me too."

"What do you want for your birthday?" he asked, changing the topic abruptly.

"Ah, nothing. You don't need to buy me anything."

"I want to get you something. So what do you want? What do you need?"

Him and him with his heart on his sleeve. "The handle on my canvas satchel broke the other day. Guess I could do with a new one of those, if you wanted to get me something. But Ben, it's really not necessary."

"A satchel. Okay. What else?"

"Nothing else. Thank you. Just a new satchel would be great."

He shook his head. "Most women would be asking for diamonds."

"Ben, I don't like you because you have money. I like you because you're you."

His thumb stroked over the back of my neck, there and gone in an instant. Perhaps it was an accident. "Thank you."

I plucked a pin from my hair, taking over the job. "We better get this done. It's late."

"I got it," he said, focusing on my hair once more.

"Okay." God he was beautiful. Why did I have to go nuts every time he came near? Just once it would be nice if I could not play the fool where this man was concerned. "I think maybe you should leave. I think I need you to."

Thick fingers removed another pin, like I hadn't said a word.

"Why are you here?" I reached back behind my head and grabbed his wrists, stilling him. "Ben?"

"Because apparently I'm shit at staying away from you."

"Then I guess we have a problem." Our fingers meshed, holding on tight.

"That's putting it fucking mildly."

My eyelids started blinking like crazy for some reason. "I warned you not to flirt with me again unless you meant it."

He didn't answer, just released my fingers and went back to playing with my hair, running it over the back of his hand, laying it over my shoulder. Such a stern look on his face, the frown embedded on his sharp features. My hands fell back to my sides.

And call me a blundering fool, but I was going there again. Apparently I would never learn. Hair half up, half down, and the buzz from the margaritas fading much too fast to help fuel such bravery. Damn it. I looked crazy—and hell, I probably was. Who are we kidding?

"Hey." I turned, cupping his cheek with my hand. The bristle of his beard felt amazing, sort of soft and yet not quite. Even more amazing, he wasn't stopping me or drawing back.

"Talk to me," I repeated.

"Fucking hated seeing that guy all over you."

"What? In the bar?"

A jut of the chin and he went back to examining my hair, carefully extracting another pin.

My hand slipped down, fingers skating over the side of his warm neck. The skin was so soft and smooth. "If it makes you feel any better, I pretty much want to scratch Karen and Meli's eyes out with my bare hands. But that doesn't change the situation here."

The edges of his mouth turned down.

Fuck it. I edged forward, getting closer, leaning into his broad chest.

No.

No.

Apparently the dude seriously liked my hair. Because something in his pants was definitely making its presence felt against my stomach. The fire in my pants turned into a blazing inferno. I'm surprised we weren't both incinerated on the spot. Everything low in me tensed, my thighs getting weak and strung out all at once. So this was what being really and truly fuck-me-now-or-I'll-die turned on felt like. And yet, leaning into the heat and strength of him, I also felt perfectly safe.

Just not from rejection.

"Ben?"

"Hmm?"

"What is this? Do you know what you're doing?"

"What I shouldn't be doing."

He slid his hand down my back, drawing me in firmly against his erection. Oh yeah. I dug my fingers nails into his neck, holding on tight. If he tried to ditch me now, I'd kill him. No joke. Death by hairpins. It would be messy but highly necessary.

Lucky for him, he didn't.

"I mean it," he said, voice devastatingly low but certain. So beautifully, perfectly certain.

"Okay."

He covered my hand with his, holding it against his skin. The small acceptance of me touching him turned me on almost as much as the heat of his body. I rocked against him, rubbing myself against his erection.

The man swore up a storm. "Fuck, Lizzy."

"What a good idea." My heavy head lolled to the side and his hot mouth was there, sucking, licking, and biting. My blood ran hot, racing through me at the speed of light. His teeth sunk just a little into my skin, making me moan. Then his hand slid down, cupping my ass through the silk of my dress, fingers digging in. And this was all nice, really nice. But I wanted to kiss him so bad.

"Let me . . ." I stretched up, looping my arms around his neck, dragging his mouth down to mine. Once, twice, he grazed my lips with his. The fucking tease. And I had no control over him at all because, "You're too tall!"

He laughed deep and dirty, hands sliding over my ass to lift me up. Genius. The man was a fucking gorgeous, bearded, bass-playing, oversize genius. My legs went around his waist and the smile on his face—shit. It was a total smirk. Just this once, he could have it, and for the record, it looked damn good on him too.

"Better?" he asked.

"Yes." I attached my lips to his and shoved my tongue into his mouth and kissed the man stupid. Just like I'd been dying to do for so long.

He groaned, one hand cupping my ass, the other rubbing and caressing the back of my neck. Encouraging me or holding me in place, I don't know. Either way, it felt sublime. What was going on between my legs, meanwhile, the hard length of his cock rubbing just so, pretty much drove me out of my mind. When had sex gotten so good? My six-or-so-year abstinence had a lot to answer for, and yet I was damn glad I'd waited.

I kissed him deep, tasting and exploring. The feel of his beard brushing against my face, the soft slip of his hair through my hands. In lieu of actual fucking, I'd done a lot of making out over the years. No one kissed like Ben, though. Though I'd started out in charge of the mouth-to-mouth, the battle was more of a draw now. His tongue slipped into my mouth, teasing and tantalizing me, turning me on even more.

I hadn't even realized we were moving until my back hit the wall. The bathroom wall. We wouldn't be making it to the bedroom this time, and all right, fair enough. His hand moved from my neck to fumble with his zipper, knuckles brushing against the damp crotch of my panties. Ratcheting up my excitement levels just that much more. Then his finger hooked the satin material of my panties aside and his cock was rubbing against me there. Right fucking there. Yes, yes, yes.

"Ben."

"Lizzy. Shit. Stay still."

"I'm trying."

He pressed into me, the lips of my pussy giving, opening to take him. And there was a lot of him. His hips flexed and I squeaked in surprise. But it wasn't long before we were both groaning, in both the good and the bad ways. The thick head of his cock was lodged inside of me, but going no further. Not without some serious pain, at least on my part. How damn wide was the guy?

Ben rested his damp forehead against mine, panting. "This isn't working."

"I'm not a virgin, it's just been a while. It should fit!" I clung to him tighter, hiding my face in his neck. No way would I burst into tears, despite the current uncertainty of the situation within my actual tear ducts, fueled by both pain and need. How ridiculous. A hand rubbed my back in big, soothing circles.

"Shouldn't have rushed," he said.

I sniffed.

"Easy." He lifted me off of him, and even that did not feel good. " 's okay."

"I really wanted this." I confessed into his neck. "You."

"And you'll have me. Shh."

We moved again, this time into the bedroom.

"I had no fucking business being inside you without protection anyway."

"It felt good. Until it felt bad."

"I know."

A hand searched for the zip on the back of my dress, tugging it down. The air-conditioning hit my skin, sending a shiver down my spine. Or maybe it was just the way he looked at me, all aggressive and tender at once. I was laid out on the mattress, Ben working busily to get me bare.

"We're really not stopping?" I asked, lust burning bright once again. Not that it had ever really disappeared. How could it, with him around? My girl parts were sadly predictable like that.

"Fuck no."

I smiled, wiggling and rolling this way and that, according to what would be most helpful. No hesitation. Off came my bra, the slick pointy-toed heels and thigh-high stockings, then he hovered over my fancy silk panties.

"What?" I asked, panting just a little.

Fingers stroked over the curves of my hips, my thighs. The man was probably used to models and starlets, women in no way normal. Of all times to get an attack of the nerves. I crossed my arms demurely over my bare breasts, biting at the inside of my cheek.

"Ben, what's the problem?"

"No problem." His gaze met mine. Then he noticed the crossed arms, covering my chest. "Don't."

My hands fluttered, unsure what to do.

He took hold of both wrists, bending over me to press them into the bed above my head.

"Keep 'em there," he said, voice gruff, clipped, and eyes deadly serious. "'kay?"

"Okay."

His hands traced down the length of my arms, over my armpits, then down my sides. The tension inside me seemed unbearable. My mind was whirling in circles, befuddled and aroused both. What was he going to do?

Thumbs hooked into the sides of my sole remaining piece of clothing and slowly dragged them down my legs. While his tickly bearded chin trailed down over my breastbone, between my pert breasts, and over my belly. Softly, he placed a kiss on my belly button, then dropped my underwear onto the floor.

"All good?" he asked.

"Y-yes."

The man sank to his knees by the side of the bed, the palms of his hands stroking over my thighs. "Good."

Without further preamble, he grabbed my hips, dragging me to the edge of the mattress to meet his waiting mouth. And yes, my legs were spread, they were wide open. With his head in the way, they had few other options. The feeling of his hot, eager mouth on my pussy . . . . there were no words. Or at least, none sufficient to sum this up.

"Fuck. Ben."

My back bowed, head pushing into the mattress. The pleasure was bigger than my body could contain. Every ounce of my consciousness was focused on the fast-building buzz between my legs. My heels pressed against his back through the fine material of his fancy dress shirt. He wrapped his arms around my thighs, holding me to him. As if I wanted to get away. His tongue dragged through my sex, lips sucking and teeth almost biting. Everywhere he went his facial hair followed, making my nerve endings tingle and my tummy tighten. Too much and not enough and give me more. Every now and then he'd give me a warning nip somewhere, such as the sensitive join of body and thigh, like I needed a reminder regarding who was in charge.

Who was doing what to whom.

He ground his face into me, eating me, going wild, and it felt fucking amazing. Mind-blowing, breath-stealing. Everything. I got it now. Beards were the best. His tongue was like a lick of heat, his lips silken smooth and so damn strong. That beard, however. Holy shit. Too many sensations, too much, and all I could do was take it. The man was damn skilled, but I didn't want to think about how many women he'd practiced on. Forget that. Only now mattered.

I was so damn wet. He slid two thick fingers into me, working me inside and out. My whole body tensed unbearably tight, until it seemed like I might shatter. Just explode into chaos and love-struck confusion. Then he flicked his tongue back and forth across my clit, stopping to suck at it every other time, lips encasing my swollen, completely overexcited sex.

I couldn't take it any longer. My whole body went *boom*.

I came with a shout, eyes open wide but unseeing. He'd colored my world in sparkles. Multitudes of little flashy lights, filling my mind and lighting me up. I just floated, lost in the feel-good chemical haze he'd induced. The mediocre to bad sex I'd had during my juvenile, idiotic, wild phase didn't even begin to compare. Nothing in common with how Ben worked my body. The pleasure he gave me. Damn he was good at oral. Scarily so.

When the haze of blinky lights faded, he was busy pulling his shirt off over his head. Apparently undoing the buttons would have taken too long. He wiped off his mouth, dark gaze glued to me all the while. Next he toed off his boots and ripped into the pants—belt, button, and zip. Plain black boxer briefs outlined a monster of a hard-on. No wonder it wouldn't fit. And the way he looked at me, like he wasn't sure if he wanted to take a bite out of me or what. I don't know. But his gaze slipped over me so warmly, belying the hunger in his eyes.

Then the boxers went down and he was climbing over me, hooking an arm around my waist to drag me back into the middle of the bed.

"Are we going to—"

"Yeah," he said, then tore open a condom wrapper with his teeth. One-handed he rolled it on, the slippery, smooth latex rubbing against me between my legs.

"Good. That's . . . that's good."

His moist lips covered mine, kissing me hard.

"Trust me," he said, positioning the broad blunt head of his cock against my opening.

I nodded.

"Legs and arms around me."

"Yes." I did as told, wrapping him up tight.

"That's it, sweetheart," he murmured, flexing his hips. His lips played with mine, tongue licking my jaw, my neck, as he worked his cock inside of me. Arms encircled my head and his beautiful face was so close, bristly cheek resting against mine, teeth nipping my ear. Now that I was plenty wet, things went smoother. But still, he was not a small man. He felt good, but . . . substantial. Thick. It might take me a while to get used to him.

And there weren't enough words to explain how I wanted to get used to him, in all the ways.

"Wait." I squirmed beneath him, tilting my hips to take him deeper. "Oh god, yeah. Like that."

"There?" He surged forward, filling me, his hips pressing me deep into the mattress. I sighed and he moaned, his pelvis shifting restlessly against me.

"Yeah."

"Fuck you feel good," he said, face buried in my hair. "So fucking good."

I flexed my thigh muscles, tightening my hold on him. Given half a chance, I'd never let him go. In return, he groaned, easing back to thrust forward again, slow and easy. The motion smooth and precise. Ben fucked me so sweetly, working himself deep into me in sure, steady strokes. Accustoming me to his presence. His body trembled with the effort, sweat dripping off his brow. I'd never experienced anything more perfect than being in bed with him. Being the focus of all his attention.

It was like we were each other's whole world. Nothing else existed beyond the bed.

His mouth took mine, his hand slipping down between us to explore where we were joined. Fingers caressing the stretched lips of my sex, just above my still sensitive clit. I gasped and he smiled, adjusting his angle slightly so he rubbed against it. He fucked me harder then, pushing me up and up toward climax once more.

"Ben," I panted.

His arms tightened, caging me in, keeping me safe. A hand slipped beneath my ass cheek then traveled up my leg, sliding over my sweaty skin. He grabbed ahold of my thigh, hard, fingers digging in. The familiar ecstatic tension spread through me, completing me. It was out of control. Everything about sex with Ben was out of control. The way his hard chest rubbed against my breasts and the single-mindedness in the way he watched me, gauging every response. His big body covered me, his cock filling me. Pleasure was the only possible response.

I came, shuddering, biting into his shoulder. I shook

and shook, and he held onto me even tighter. He drove himself deep and came, one hand in my hair and the other still wrapped around my thigh.

Nothing could ever compare.

Ben collapsed beside me. He hit the mattress so hard I bounced into his side and stayed there, curling up against him. It took a while for the world to stop spinning, for us both to catch our breath.

My insides buzzed. Hell, my whole body buzzed. I hid my face in his skin, grinning like a fool. How incredible for me and him to be in the same bed doing the postcoital bliss thing. I'd been this happy, this certain of something, precisely never in my life. It wouldn't be easy but it would be worth it. Mal and Anne would adjust, because eight years was nothing, really.

I rolled onto my side and snuggled into him. The dude had more than enough body warmth for both of us in the cool air-conditioning. Then, from somewhere close, came a buzzing.

Ben stirred, reaching down to snag his cell from the pocket of his jeans before tossing them aside. When he saw the name on the screen his whole body stiffened. The buzzing went on. His thumb slid across the front of the cell and he held it to his ear.

"Hey."

A faint voice from the phone.

"No, no. I dropped her back at her room."

More from the caller.

"For fuck's sake, man. When will you get it through your head nothing's going on? Girl's not my kind."

My heart stuttered. It hurt.

"Ha-ha. Yeah, fuck off. Go back to your bride. I'm heading to a bar uptown. Shilly's playing. Said I'd join for a while."

More talk.

"Yeah, I'll tell him you said hi. Later."

Above me, the ceiling swam blurrily, my vision wavering. Silly me, always so surprised. When would I learn?

"Were you ever going to tell him?" I asked quietly.

"What?" Ben sat at the side of the bed, head in his hands. He was just having a moment, the sex had been intense and so on. All of us processed emotional moments in our own sweet way. "You want a drink or something?"

"No. I want the truth." Strangely calm, I sat up, tugging the sheet with me. All of a sudden being naked didn't seem like such a smart idea. "Were you ever planning on telling Mal about us?"

"We only just finished having sex. The man's on his honeymoon. It's his wedding night. You really want me to get into it with him right now?"

"No. What I'm asking is if you're planning on getting into it with him ever."

Ben looked away, wiping his face with a hand. "It's complicated."

"Yeah. But I'm not sure you lying to him helps."

"And I'm not sure me telling him I just banged his little-sister-in-law would help, either," he snapped. "Shit. Liz, I didn't mean it like that."

"I know. It's complicated." My voice seemed so small.

He looked back over his shoulder at me, face guarded. "Wait . . ."

"It was an accident. You got jealous when you saw that guy with me in the bar, overheated. I get it."

"I didn't mean—"

"You never do." Without further ado I rolled off the bed, taking the sheet with me. "I'd like you to leave."

"Lizzy." It was right there on his face and in his eyes. The set of his shoulders shouted it, and those curled fingers just reinforced everything. Regret.

"Leave, please. You know you want to."

Jeans lay abandoned just inside the bathroom door. I halfheartedly kicked them aside, locking myself in.

"Sweetheart." A timid knock or two. "C'mon, open up."

My back to the door, I slumped down, not stopping until the hard marble chilled my ass. Egyptian cotton didn't have such great thermal properties, apparently. Tears fell, but I just ignored them. Whatever.

"Let me explain."

I don't think so.

"I just . . . I panicked when I saw it was him. Fuck, Lizzy." An angry thump on the door. "You don't get how hard this is. I like you, but . . ."

But. But me no buts. Fuck.

"I'm not saying I wouldn't have told him in time."

Huh. Nor was he saying he would have.

"Christ, can I at least have my pants?" he grumbled.

No, actually. No he couldn't. From me, he couldn't have a single thing more. I'd given all I would.

More tears fell unchecked. My body still buzzing but my heart breaking open. How confusing. So much good with the bad. It really was complicated. Everything went quiet out there; he said no more. I guess, at the end of the day, I just wasn't the kind of girl that "complicated" worked for. I wasn't in search of drama. I wasn't only happy when it rained. So instead I sat on the cold bathroom floor and cried and cried.

Eventually, dimly, I heard the front door slam shut.

Over and out.

CHAPTER FIVE

NOW

"No."

"What do you mean, no?" asked Anne, face incredulous.

"No. I'm not going to explain what went on between me and Ben to you."

She just blinked.

"It's personal." I stood tall, despite feeling about two inches off the floor. "I just wanted you to know that I chased him, not the other way around. I had feelings for him and I acted on them. End of story."

So I guess I would explain what happened between us. At least a little of one side of the sorry tale. Hopefully enough to save the band. Good god, did my pride lay in tatters on the floor.

Mal wouldn't meet my eyes, and Ben's nose was still bleeding. Awesome. What a mess. The entire dinner party had denigrated into some blood-splattered, rock 'n' roll wrestling, multiple-surprise-baby-announcement mess. My fault. I should have handled it differently. Not that I had any idea how I could have done better just yet, but whatever. Doubtless some genius ideas would taunt me at two in the morning.

There were a lot of judgy eyes in the room. All of my new friends and family gathered around to watch the explosion. Shit.

"I'm sorry," I said and bolted for the door. I grabbed my coat and left.

A banging noise.

I cracked open an eyelid. In the darkness the alarm clock shone 3:18 a.m. in brilliant green. What in the everloving hell? The banging continued, followed by the muffled sound of voices. One was loud and belligerent, the other far calmer. I got up and flicked on the living room light, stumbled over to the front door. Whoever it was would just have to take me in socks, old sweatpants, and an oversize T-shirt. Away from the warmth of my bed, goose bumps covered my arms.

"Liz?" a familiar rough voice demanded. "Open up."

I did as asked, yawning and rubbing the sleep from my eyes all the while. "Wow. You look a mess."

"Yeah," said Ben, swaying slightly.

He stood upright mostly due to the aid of David, one big arm thrown over the other man's shoulders. Hair hung in his face, combining with the beard for a cross between a yeti and a Cousin It kind of feel. From between the dark strands, red eyes peered out at me. Oh, and lest I forget, he also stank like he'd recently bathed in a keg of beer, using Scotch-scented soap. Lovely.

"Sorry 'bout this," said the guitarist, half dragging Ben into my apartment. "He insisted on coming over."

"It's fine."

"On the couch?" David asked, face lined with strain.

"Ah, have to be the bed, please. He's too big to fit on the couch."

"Serve his stupid ass right if he woke up on the floor." David sighed.

"Let me help." I slid beneath Ben's other arm, trying to take some of the weight. Christ, the man could put a bear to shame in the sheer bulk department.

"Hey, sweetheart," said the giant drunken sod.

"Hey there, Ben." I grabbed hold of his hand, hanging on tight. "How you feeling?"

"Great." He chuckled.

"I'll go first," said David, directing the three of us sideways so we'd fit through my bedroom door.

"Okay. Go slow."

"Yep."

Operation Haul the Drunken Baby Daddy into Bed was going well. Except when Ben kind of stumbled halfway through. He surged forward, his forehead cracking into the doorjamb. I swear I felt the building shudder. There was definitely an indent in the wooden frame.

"Ow," he said, sort of contemplatively.

David just laughed.

"Crap. Are you all right?" I asked, trying to push the hair back from his face to see, while keeping him upright and hopefully safe from further harm. "Ben?"

"He's fine. Dude has the hardest head I've ever seen. One time when we were kids we got stoned up on the roof of my house. Ben walked straight off the edge. We were all freaking out, but by the time we got down there he'd already gotten on his bike and headed home. The big idiot's basically indestructible." David directed us toward the side of the bed. "Okay, let him go."

I did so, and the father of my unborn child toppled face-first onto the mattress. At least that had to be a soft landing. Still, he lay there completely unmoving, apart from the rebound of the springs. God, I hoped we hadn't accidentally killed him. If we had, at least the neglect wasn't willful.

I grabbed one of his sneakers and gave it a shake. "Ben, are you still breathing?"

A groan from the man on the bed. Not too bad, as signs of life went.

"Don't worry," said David. "He's fine. Just let him sleep it off."

I nodded, still frowning just the same.

"You right with him?" asked David, hands on his hips. "I can send Sam over if you like. He's finished babysitting Mal from what I hear."

"No need, thanks. Is he all right? Mal?"

He gaze softened. "Passed out just like this one, apparently."

Seriously, such a mess. Anne and Mal would probably never talk to me again. Well, Anne would, but she was my sister, so she had to forgive me eventually. Mal was another situation entirely. The thought of losing his high opinion and easy affection bit deep. Consequences were a bitch. Realistically, however, I couldn't imagine myself having done any differently even if I'd known Mal and Anne would be pissed. I mean, I'd already known that and it didn't even make me pause. Fewer star-crossed lovers and more adults should be allowed to date who they wanted.

Maybe if I'd known the night would result in the bean . . . I don't know. There was only one thing I was sure of: sex equaled nothing but chaos and confusion. It was official.

I squeezed my eyes shut. "You must hate me."

David's brow wrinkled up. "What? Why?"

"For causing all this trouble." The urge to flail was huge, but I restrained it. For now. Instead, I got busy wriggling Ben's shoes off his feet. No way were they making contact with my sheets.

"I'm assuming you didn't have to hold a gun to Ben's head to get him to fuck you?" The guy watched me unblinking, face dead serious.

"Um, no."

David shrugged. "There you go."

"Isn't that taking a slightly overly simplistic view of the situation?"

He smiled. "In my experience, shit usually is pretty simple when you get right down to it. When it comes to matters of the heart, you decide where you belong and you go be there. Simple. Ben wanted to be here. Don't think I didn't try to talk him out of it, either. The bastard insisted."

Maybe. "Wonder what his new girlfriend would make of your theory."

"Yeah." He winced, his mouth widening in imagined pain. "I'll leave that one up to you two to sort out. But try not to stress. Can't be good for Ben junior."

"Right." I rolled my eyes and dropped Ben's shoe on the floor. "But how is this going to affect the band, the two of them fighting?"

It took him a long time to answer. "I honestly don't know."

Fuck.

"Night. I'll lock the door on my way out." He raised a hand in salute. "Call Ev if you need anything."

"Thanks, David."

The front door clicked closed behind him, leaving me alone with Ben. He lay passed out sideways across my queen-size bed. Ben was in my actual bed. Holy hell. I didn't quite know what to do with that information. A pity there was nothing but boxes and junk in the spare room. Not that I didn't want him near. My heart wasn't so sensible. It was just time for me to start taking the safer option when it came to him. Past time even.

"Hey." I leaned over the mattress, giving his leg a shake. "Roll over."

A moan.

"Come on, big boy. Move it. You're taking up all the bed."

Incoherent muttering.

This was not working, and like hell I'd be sleeping on the love seat. I pulled off a sock and tugged on his big toe. "Ben. Wake up."

In slow motion, he stirred, lifting his shaggy head and looking around.

"Roll over."

"Wha—" He turned, easing himself up and over, as requested. He blinked and grimaced and looked generally displeased with the world. A lumpy red line bisected his forehead. Whatever David said, that had to hurt. "Lizzy?"

"Got it in one."

"How'd I get here?"

"David just dropped you off, remember?"

He scratched at his beard. "Uh. Okay."

"You need to move, you're taking up all of the room."

Bewildered, he rose up on his elbows and took a look around. "This your bed?"

"Yes."

"Did we . . ." He raised an eyebrow suggestively.

"No, I already learned my lesson, thank you very much."

"You sure?" He gave me a wonky smile. "It could be fun."

"Yeah, you look like you've had enough fun for the both of us for one night, buddy."

"Maybe." He contemplated the thin cotton of my shirt for a good long while, one corner of his mouth moving upward. "Hey, you're not wearing a bra."

"Shut up and move, Ben."

A groan. "All right."

It took him about forever to wriggle and roll and finally get his big fat head up on the pillow. On my favored side, damn it. Whatever. I lie down on my back beside him, keeping a nice, fun, celibate distance between our two bodies just in case he decided to try and get some. More sleep would be so great. To grow the bean, I really needed rest. My limbs were weighed down with lethargy, my head full of blergh.

"We could cuddle," he suggested, the words slurred, blurring together into one dumb drunken idea. Man, if he'd been even one inch sober I'd be all over him. A hug right now, letting me know everything would be okay, sounded sublime. A silly, childish wish, I know. Things were complicated enough. "I wouldn't try nothing, swear."

"Nice double negative. No, Ben."

A grunt of dismay.

"Go to sleep."

The world seemed still, almost perfectly quiet. A car passed by outside and the wind blew around the building. Everyone else would be fast asleep at this hour. I studied the water mark on the ceiling, the shadows cast by the dodgy old lamp on my bedside table. For some reason, being alone with him in the dark seemed too dangerous. The light could stay on.

"I'm gonna be a father," he said, eyes closed.

My whole body tensed instantly. "So I heard."

"Wasn't planning on having kids."

"You weren't?"

"No."

Drunk or not, he sounded so definite, so sure. It was like a dagger to my heart, the pain overwhelming. It hurt to breathe. "Not even when you were a little older?"

A sharp shake of the head in the negative.

Well.

I didn't know what to say. My throat constricted and my eyes stung. He'd had little more choice in becoming a parent than I had. We were both being thrown into this, and there were plans more than mine being disrupted. Still, he wasn't the one whose body was being hijacked, for all intents and purposes. Not that I hadn't had the option to end the pregnancy. I did, but I hadn't taken it. My heart had made its decision and there was no going back. Still, it was hard not to be all bitter and betrayed over his announcement. I didn't even have the luxury of being able to get blind rotten drunk. And believe me, dealing with all this sober sucked. My rational mind coughed up so many plausible, reasonable excuses for him—he was surprised, he was drunk, give him a chance to think things over, blah blah blah.

But fuck them all. Fuck him.

I'd kind of already been expecting the worst, to be in this alone. Now I knew. Twice he'd disappointed me; this couldn't be a surprise. Nothing had changed, not really. I slid a hand over my stomach, spread my fingers over the ever so slight bulge there. It might have just been my imagination, but I could feel her already getting busy in there, growing away. We'd be fine. We'd manage.

"Didn't want to settle down," he continued. "And kids, they need stability and shit. Time, energy, all those things."

"True." My voice sounded hollow, an emotionless echo.

At least I had the apartment paid up for the foreseeable future. Reece could no doubt use me more in the shop. I was fortunate there. Probably be best if I dropped out of school and started saving. Given how many days I'd been missing due to the puke-o-rama of morning sickness, my grades wouldn't be rocking this term anyway.

I swallowed hard.

"Like my life the way it is," he said, voice slurring at the edges.

"Yeah, I did too." I gave my stomach a pat. "Sorry, Bean."

"Like my freedom. Being able to jump on a plane and

go jam with a friend or play on their album. Things were perfect the way they were."

"Hmm."

"Couldn't stay away from you."

"Why not?" I asked, honestly curious.

"Don't know. You just . . . you stayed on my mind."

"And other women didn't?"

"Not like you."

"No?" Perhaps booze boy was back to wanting sex. Given my heart got stupid the minute he appeared, it was hard to tell.

He exhaled hard. "Wanted you, but . . . you were my friend too. I mean, really my friend. You didn't want nothing but me. To talk to me, to spend time . . ."

Silence.

"I knew you wanted more, but you didn't push. Missed you when you were gone and I couldn't tell you shit, talk to you about stuff."

My turn to sigh.

"Liz?"

"Yeah?"

"What are we gonna do?" He sounded almost afraid.

I gave in and rolled onto my side, all the better to watch him. If only he looked worse in profile. Instead, the dominant nose and plush lips seemed almost majestic somehow. The bastard. I inched closer, studying him. Eyelids closed, lips sealed shut. His forehead had smoothed out in repose, the curve of his cheekbones so obvious. I'd never really gotten to stare at him to my heart's content. All the same old feelings rushed up inside, only now there was more. So much more. A tiny bit of him and me was growing inside my body, making a permanent connection between us. It was kind of terrifying. I wondered if she'd have his mouth or his eyes.

The room stayed silent.

"Ben?"

I waited, but he said no more, his breathing falling into a deep, even pattern. Then the snoring started. I reared back in surprise. Holy fucking hell. He had to be kidding me. I covered my head with the pillow, resisting the urge to smother him with his. A chain saw duel to the death would be quieter than the commotion currently going down in his nasal region.

"Ben," I cried into the pillow, throwing in a scream or two of frustration for good measure, and more than a couple of tears.

This guy and me, we were doomed from the start.

"Time to wake up." I ever so gently kicked the bed.

The man sprawled out spread-eagle across it didn't even move. Sadly for him, Sleeping Beauty's time had come.

"Ben!"

His head shot up, eyes dazed and confused. "Huh?"

"Wake up. It's nearly eleven."

I set his coffee on the bedside table, then wandered over to the other side of the room to sip my own. Also to throw back the curtains, because I'm mean on broken dreams and limited sleep.

He blinked, yawned, and shied back from the light of day like a vampire. The dude definitely didn't sparkle, however. Nor did he smell particularly fresh.

Out of all the many fantasies I'd had about him, his waking up in my room looking like roadkill hadn't featured strongly. Yet, even with his clothes and hair all askew, and stinking of sweat and beer, there was just something about him. Something magnetic, urging me to get closer, and closer still.

Stupid me. Probably just pregnancy hormones or something running rife.

"Lizzy."

"Yeah?"

"Ah, shit," he groaned. "Davie listened to me. He should have just dumped me back at my hotel."

No comment. "Coffee's there beside you."

"Thanks." Slowly, he sat up, rubbing at his head. Then he looked around the room, taking it all in as if for the first time. Which it pretty much was. His eyes lingered on the cheap Japanese woodblock prints I'd picked up at the markets, and my stuffed bookcase. The stack of laundry waiting for a day when I wasn't busy feeling like I was about to start yet again puking my guts up. No doubt the scene was a dramatic comedown compared to what he had to be used to. I'd imagine chandeliers, marble, lots of splendor. Glamorous models in the place of one pasty-faced girl with wet hair and old jeans and an equally worn sweater that'd shrunk in the wash.

Whatever.

"We need to talk," I said.

He froze, and fair enough. Honestly, those four words had to be the most loathed between two people, ever. They were basically a death knell, right up there with *we can still be friends*. Except he and I had never gotten that far.

"Yeah, we do." He took a gulp of hot coffee, watching me over the rim of his cup the entire time. "Why you hiding over there? Scared I'm going to get physical or something?"

"No." I sat on the edge of the bed. "Just wanted to keep out of your way in case you felt the need to bolt again."

He coughed out a laugh. "Ouch."

I shrugged. Then I felt guilty. Then I remembered the snoring and stood tall once more.

"Look," he said, turning his head my way. "Whatever you need from me, okay?"

My mouth opened, shut. "Thank you."

His fingers flexed around the cup of coffee. "You want to keep it, right?"

"Yes."

A nod.

I took a deep breath, reaching deep inside for some strength. Time to get on with the business of letting him off the hook and out of my life. No tears or tantrums. We were beyond that now. "I know you didn't want to have children, Ben. That you like your life as it is. So if you—"

"I never said that," he bit out.

"Yes, you did. Last night."

"Lizzy." Dark eyes pinned me in place. "Hold up. What I say when I'm drunk off my ass doesn't mean a damn thing, all right?"

Given how many interesting things he'd said, I wasn't so sure about that. "All right."

"Do not use that against me." His nostrils flared as he took a big breath. "Last night . . . you kind of caught me off guard with this."

"It kind of caught me off guard too," I said, struggling to keep my voice from going all fishwife on his ass. "I didn't want to tell you under those conditions, Ben. It just happened. You can thank your new girlfriend for being so discreet."

He flinched. Direct hit, ten points.

"Look, what I'm trying to say here is that it's my decision to have this baby. And if you decide that you don't want us impacting on your life, then I understand." I curled an arm around my middle, hunching in on myself. "That's all."

Slowly, Ben rose to his feet, setting the coffee cup aside. "You think I would do that to you?"

"In this situation, I honestly have no idea how you're going to react."

"You're just expecting the worst."

"Last night—"

His hand cut through the air. "Do not repeat what I said last night."

I said nothing.

Then he must have realized how bad it all looked and sounded. The anger in his eyes calmed, his stance relaxing. "Shit. Sorry. I didn't mean to raise my voice."

"What do you want me to do here, Ben?" I threw my hands in the air. "Give me a clue. I'm pregnant. Neither of us planned it. We've barely even talked since that night in Vegas, and now you're seeing someone new. What do I do?"

"Give me a chance to catch up."

I just stared at him, trying to keep my cool. Took two to tango, yada yada.

"I'm serious." His shoulders heaved up and down. "Just give me a chance to catch up and I promise, Lizzy, I will have your back."

It sounded so promising. Honest to god, it really did. "What about your girlfriend?"

"She's got nothing to do with this." He didn't even hesitate. "This is just between you and me."

"Right." Any issues I had with the woman and her place in his life were mine. Sucked to be me. "Okay."

He picked up his coffee, his Adam's apple bobbing as he drank deep. "I'll, ah, get the lawyers to start drawing up some papers."

"Lawyers?"

A sharp nod.

"You're going to need money—living expenses, whatever. They'll get that all sorted out. Make sure you're looked after."

"Oh." I stared at the rumpled bed, my mind in a whirl.

"That okay?"

"I guess I was hoping we could keep this just between you and me. But you're right. You need to protect yourself."

"Lizzy, I don't mean I think you're going to try and rip me off or something."

"I'd hope not, considering I haven't asked you for a single thing."

Wow. Talk about looking uncomfortable. His tongue worked behind his cheek as he glared at the view out my bedroom window. Guess the tree out there really had done him wrong.

"The rent on this place is paid and I have a job, so I'm fine for now. But you get your lawyers to do whatever." I rubbed at the sudden pain between my eyes. This conversation was enough to give anyone a headache. "Guess I better get one too."

He pushed his hands into the back pockets of his jeans. Then he changed his mind, sat, and started putting on his shoes. "It's best if we get all that official stuff sorted up front, you know?"

No, in all honesty, I really didn't know. He'd just clearly demonstrated as much. My stomach performed a particularly nauseating somersault maneuver and I swallowed hard, fighting back the urge to puke. Gah. What I needed was a cracker. A cracker would solve everything. With all due haste, I hustled ass into the tiny kitchen and got busy feeding my face. This at least I had under control. Nothing I could do about Ben and his lawyers and whatever. But fetching a cracker? Now that was within my command.

Bean and I would be fine.

Fuck the world and all the rest.

"I gotta go," he said, now avoiding my eyes from the

all-new position of the living room. Awesome. Once he left, he'd have to get a new hobby. Maybe he could work at forgetting my name or something. "There's a practice session I need to get to. Tour kicks off soon, so things are really busy right now. Thanks for being cool about me crashing here. It won't happen again."

"Sure," I said.

"And don't worry about money or working extra hours. I'll get that all sorted out."

"Great." And it was great, but it was also cold and businesslike. "Thanks."

He mumbled some other stuff, but I just kind of tuned out. It was nothing I wanted to hear. How depressing this day had turned. I hated everything and everyone and anything else I could possibly think of. Apart from Bean. She was the innocent one in all of this mess.

God, sex sucked.

Never, ever would I do it again. Not even a little.

Also, there was a sad lack of cake at this pity party. Enough. I needed to shake this shit off. Get my mojo back. I'm positive pregnant women are supposed to glow or something. I just needed to find my light. Perhaps I'd go for a drive, get some fresh air. A solid idea. Right now, getting as far away from here as I possibly could sounded delightful, and my car was something special. It'd been waiting for me at the airport upon our return from Vegas. Mal had, as promised, gotten me a baby blue 1967 Mustang GT for my birthday. Best present ever. It was the prettiest heavy metal beast on the block. Ben looked vaguely panicked every time he laid eyes on the vehicle.

But yeah, my car was awesome.

A pity it wouldn't be suitable for transporting a baby around in, having only two doors. I'd just have to make the most of my beauty while I still could. Given that I had a whole day to myself, that meant driving out to the coast.

"Later, Liz."

"Later." I raised a cracker in salute, but he was already gone. And, for once, my heart couldn't quite bring itself to care.

CHAPTER SIX

Voices hit me as soon as I stepped through the apartment building's front door. Loud voices, and lots of them. Odd. Lauren hadn't mentioned anything about throwing a party tonight. Wait. My mistake. Those weren't party time voices. No, these were pissed in the nonalcoholic way.

I jogged up the steps, unbuttoning my coat. For a car that predated me, the Mustang ran spectacularly well. Its heating could be a little iffy, however, especially if you liked to crack open the window now and then to feel the ice-cold wind on your face. Silly, I know. It was just something I felt the need to indulge in every once in a while.

The hallway was brighter than usual, a light from the second floor shining out. I hastened up my steps.

Holy shit. My front door had been smashed off its hinges.

". . . expect a twenty-one-year-old girl to manage with a baby—" That was my sister's voice.

"Like I said before, she won't be doing it alone." And that was Ben's.

"Because you'll get your shit sorted and get married to her. Right, baby daddy?" Crap. That was Mal, and he sounded even angrier than he'd been the night before.

"You'll do the right thing and give up the single lifestyle with a different woman every night, won't you? 'Cause you're so fucking known for seeing shit through."

"Man, we've been over this already—"

"Yeah. And you're still not saying the right things. Do you get that?"

The living room was certainly crowded, that's for sure. Ben, Anne, and Mal were facing off in the middle. Clearly, two against one. While Sam the security guy and Lauren watched on from the sidelines, for some reason.

"Guys," I said.

They argued on.

"Guys!"

Still nothing.

Finally, I put two fingers in my mouth and let loose with an earsplitting whistle. A talent I'd perfected in my younger years. Useful for annoying the living shit out of my sister, if nothing else. The noise even rattled my own head.

Nothing but silence followed.

"Hi. How are you all?" I stood in what remained of the splintered frame. "I'd really like to know what happened to my door."

"Lizzy," said Ben, exhaling hard. "Thank fuck. Been worried sick about you."

"Where have you been?" My sister rushed forward, catching me up in a tight hug. "I've been trying to call you all day. We checked everywhere and couldn't find you."

"Sorry. I just needed some alone time." I squeezed her back, unable to stop from smiling. The thought of Anne turning her back on me had scared me more than I liked to admit.

"Well, I get you might want that." She stepped back. "But you could have told someone."

"You can't just disappear like that." And Ben kept right on frowning. "Shit, Liz, you're pregnant."

"Don't upset her," snapped Anne.

Ben ignored her. "I don't know what the hell's going on in your head. But you need to let me know where you are."

My eyebrows went up and my mouth opened, ready to rip him a new one.

"She doesn't answer to you. She'll let you know if and when she decides to let you know," said Mal, laying down the law to his bandmate before turning my way. "You will text your sister next time you decide to go wandering for a day, understood?"

My mouth, it still hung open.

"Christ, man." Over and over, Ben's hands rolled into tight fists before releasing again. "Can you cut the shit and get off my back for a fucking minute?"

"Don't swear at him." My usually sensible and staid sister poked a finger dead center in Ben's broad chest. "You're the one that caused this mess, thank you very much. She might still be a little young and naive, but you're definitely old enough to know better."

"That's right." Standing about as tall as a skyscraper, despite only coming up to Ben's nose, Mal stared him down. Or up. Whatever. "This is a family matter. You can leave, thanks."

The battle for control played out plainly on Ben's face. He forced out, through gritted teeth, "I can leave?"

"Yes."

This was insane.

Someone had to step up and be the voice of reason. Sadly, that someone was me. "Okay. Hold up, everybody. Why don't we all just calm down for a minute."

With all the skill and speed of a seasoned male stripper,

Mal turned on his heel. "And you, young lady! You are grounded until further notice."

"I'm grounded?"

"Babe." Anne winced. "That's not going to fly."

"And you are never to talk to Ben again. He is clearly a very bad influence on you." The drummer continued, oblivious, sneering at his former friend. "Is that understood, Elizabeth?"

Lauren snickered.

"Yeah. Okay," I said.

"Good."

"Get out," I said, my voice quite cool, quite calm. A little tired, but hey, it'd been a long day.

"What?" asked Anne.

"I love you both very much," I said. "But I'd like you both to leave now, please."

Her face fell and she took a step closer. "You don't have to handle this on your own. I get that things were stressed last night, but we do need to talk about this. I'm worried about you."

"I know, and we will."

A heavy sigh. "Will you call me tomorrow so we can talk?"

"Yes."

Anne gave me a slow nod. "Okay."

With a faint smile, Sam rose from his position on the couch and squeezed past me, out the door. Or what remained of the door. I still needed a *what the hell* on that count.

"Someone'll be by to fix it shortly, Miss Rollins," Sam said.

"Thank you."

"Holler if you need anything." Lauren left too.

"Thanks."

"But I don't want to leave," hissed Mal. Heated whispers

continued on between him and my sister. He even brushed her hand off of his tensed, folded arms. "She doesn't know what's best for her. Not like we do. Me in particular."

More whispers.

"Well, doesn't Ben have to go too? I'm not leaving unless he is."

"Mal," I groaned. "Please? If I promise to come over tomorrow and talk to you both about it all, please will you go for now?"

His eyes and mouth narrowed.

"Pretty please?"

"Fine." He slung an arm around Anne's neck, dragging her in against his body. "We know when we're not wanted. Don't we, Pumpkin?"

"Eventually, yes." My sister gave me a small smile.

"Thank you," I said, giving her free hand a squeeze before turning back to Mal. "And I need to know I haven't broken up the band."

Mal scowled and snarled.

Actions had consequences. I'd learned the lesson well. "Please."

"Fine. But only because you asked so nicely. Outside of band business, he is dead to me," Mal said to Ben, motioning a finger across his throat.

"Dude." Ben sighed.

"I mean it. I'm really pissed at you, bro. You knocked up my new little-sister-in-law. This is way worse than the time you broke my bike trying to take that jump in middle school. And that was *bad*." The newlyweds headed for the door. "See you tomorrow at rehearsal."

"Yep," said Ben, collapsing onto the love seat. His head fell back against the wall and he eyed me tiredly. "You gonna throw me out too?"

"I probably should. Are you what happened to my door?"

He wiped a hand over his face. "Yeah. Sorry about that."

"I couldn't help but notice that it's kind of no longer attached."

"I kind of broke it down."

"Right." I wandered over and planted my butt in the black leather wingback chair opposite him. Mal and Anne had left me some seriously sweet furniture when they vacated the apartment. "Why, may I ask?"

"Anne called, said she couldn't find you and you weren't answering your phone." He set one ankle on the opposite knee, his sneaker jiggling, constantly moving. "I got worried you were in here alone, freaking out about shit after this morning or something and refusing to talk to me."

"Ah."

"I overreacted." He wore his usual blue jeans and a T-shirt. Damn he wore them well. You'd think with my being pregnant that the hormones would settle down a little. But the silly things still burst into a happy dance every time he came near. It was ridiculous. I needed to gird my foolish loins, invest in a chastity belt or something.

Instead, I stuffed my hands between my legs, squeezing my thighs tightly together.

"We've got a problem," he said.

"Yeah."

"No, I mean a new one."

"What?"

He sat up, putting both feet on the floor. "Sasha didn't take my breaking up with her too well. Threatened to go to the media about you."

"You broke up with her?" My heart beat double time.

He paused. "Well, yeah."

"Why?" Oh, hell. My mouth. I blurted out the question

before I even stopped to think. "I mean. Okay, none of my business. I don't want to know."

It wasn't hope firing to life in my belly. No way could I be that stupid. Again. It had to be something else. Maybe Bean had taken up water aerobics or something.

Ben just kind of stared at me, stuck on pause for the longest moment. "Anyway."

"Yes?"

"You staying here on your own probably isn't a good idea. Especially now that the door needs fixing."

"True."

"Security is pretty shitty here anyway. So, I was thinking maybe it would be best if . . ."

"If?" I sat perched on the edge of my seat, literally waiting with bated breath. He couldn't be about to ask me to move in with him. Into his actual personal space. No one ever hung out at his hotel room or wherever the hell he lived. I had to admit, I'd been curious. Plus, the thought of living with him made me break out in a cold sweat. "If what?"

"If you moved in with Lena and Jim until we went on tour." His dark eyes never left my face. "I mean, I'm just assuming you'll come on tour now. You might not want to."

"You want me on tour?" But he didn't want me in his place. How confusing and disappointing both. Or maybe he wanted me on tour to keep an eye on me, the old silly-young-Lizzy-can't-look-after-herself standard. Christ, it hit me: I was going to be a mother. Apparently, I was going to be a single parent, no matter what soothing noises he was making. Come what may, I could only depend on myself.

"Figured with Anne planning on going, and Lena being pregnant too, that you might come," he said. "People will pack you up, all you'll have to do is get on and off a private jet every couple of days and then relax. These places have masseuses and whatever. There'll be doctors available to keep a check on you. I'll make sure you're looked after."

"I don't know. . . ."

To stay behind with Anne and the other girls gone wouldn't make me happy. I guess making friends wasn't really my forte. After the early-teen nutso period, I'd pretty much kept to myself. Anne and I had perfected the art of putting on a normal home front. Anyone looking beyond it would not have been good, because clearly mom wasn't functioning as the responsible adult. When Anne left to go on tour, I'd basically be alone. But there was more than me and my lonely girl ways to consider. There'd been so many dubious tales about what happened on tour. Him and other women. I didn't need to see that. Not this year, or the next. The Sasha thing had hurt enough. Wonder why he'd dumped her?

"I don't want to be in your way," I said, hands twining in my lap. "It might get awkward if we were in each other's faces every day."

I got a caveman grunt. It sounded serious, of the deep thoughts variety. Didn't clue me into shit, however.

"What do you think?" I asked.

The face he gave me was complicated, brows drawn together but lips slightly apart. It seemed he was on the verge of saying something.

Waiting.

"Speak, Ben."

He tensed. "I want you to come."

"Why?"

"To make sure you're okay, so I can keep an eye on you, so you're not here dealing with all this on your own. Lots of reasons."

As reasons went, they weren't bad ones. But as Mal had pointed out, Ben had issues with follow-through. History dictated he would eventually change his mind and leave me high and dry. What sort of father would he be? Lord help him if he ever pulled that shit with my child. No matter his size, my rage would be epic.

"Come on," he said, voice firmer. "We need to start figuring this out together. How to get along and be parents and everything. I don't want to be the guy Mal's accusing me of being. Give me a chance here, Liz."

"I honestly don't know what's best."

He hung his head. "Look, if you want to stay here, finish up school for the semester, I'll organize security for you. Take care of everything. It's your choice. I don't want to push you into anything."

"Security?"

"Yeah."

"Wow." I patted my stomach, my smile not quite staying in place. "I keep forgetting I'm carrying a famous person's baby. The next-generation Stage Dive."

He spread out his hands, a helpless kind of look in his eyes. At least he was here trying.

It was up to me. "All right, I'll come. I was thinking of dropping out of school. I've missed so much, with morning sickness, and days can still be hit or miss. I don't like my chances of catching up with everything going on."

A nod and a smile. His thick shoulders slumped like he'd finished fighting a war.

"You want me to stay with Lena and Jimmy?"

"I want you and the baby safe and looked after. Not that I'm not willing to be the one looking after you. It's just—"

"It's fine. It's complicated with us not actually being a couple and everything. I get it." I leaned back in my seat, turning it all over inside my head. "Not that I don't appreciate the offer."

His serious gaze revealed nothing. "Liz . . ."

"Mm?"

I waited, but he didn't continue. Thank goodness Bean would be a girl. (I could just feel it. Mother's intuition, et cetera.) Men were such a mystery. Not one I particularly cared to figure out at this point in time. Life had become busy enough. At least there'd been no further mention of lawyers. Baby steps—all puns intended.

"I'll sort things out for myself. I'll go to Mal and Anne's," I said. "It's not long before the tour starts. He shouldn't be able to drive me crazy that fast."

His brow furrowed. "You sure?"

"Yes." I nodded.

"'kay. But you'll let me support you financially, right?"

"Look, I ran some figures through my head today. Given that the rent on this place is paid up, and with my work at the—"

"Wherever you're going with this, the answer is no." The man leveled me with a look. Or tried to.

"Excuse me?"

"No, you can't go it on your own. More important, you don't have to. You've got me."

"But I haven't got you, Ben. That's the whole point." I sat forward in the seat, willing him to understand. He opened his mouth, but mine was faster. "Please, just listen. I'm going to have a baby, and that is huge. It's so big, when I try to think about it I feel like my head is going to explode. But I'll deal with it all because I have to, because this baby is relying on me to. What I can't think about or deal with is you—you and your life and how this all affects it. Because I know, no matter what you say, that having this baby is never going to be your first choice. So then I feel guilty, and then I feel angry because I feel guilty, and then it's just a big ugly mess that I don't know how to deal with."

"Liz." He scrubbed at his face with his hands. "Shit. It

doesn't have to be my first choice. Having a baby now wasn't your first choice either—"

"But—"

"No," he said, hands gripping his thighs tight. "My go to talk. Your turn to listen. Please."

I stopped, then nodded because fair enough.

"Okay." His thick shoulders rose and fell on a deep breath. "This is our baby. You and me, we made it together, whether we meant to or not. Those are the facts. No matter how I might have liked my life to play out, this is what's happening. No fucking way am I going to be some douchebag absentee dad missing from my kid's life or letting another man raise him."

"Or her."

"Or her." He gave me a meaningful look. "Yes."

I pretended to zip my lips closed.

"Thank you." Yeah, his tone wasn't sarcastic at all. "And I'm not letting you do this alone, either. No matter what Anne and Mal think of me right now, I am sticking by you however I can. We're not together, but we'll figure it out. The best way I can help you right now is to make sure you don't have to worry about money."

I took a deep breath, turning it all over inside my head. The man had a point. It would be nice to cross monetary concerns off the list. How many strings and complications the funds came with, however, concerned me. But he was Bean's father. If he did mean to be present, as stated, then I had to accept that, embrace it even.

Give him the requested chance.

"Worrying about you today, not knowing where you were or what was going on with you . . . it got me thinking. This'll fuck with your life every bit, if not more, than it will with mine. We don't need to add lawyers to the mix, what with your connection to Mal and everything. We can keep this simple."

"Hmm."

"Stop frowning." He frowned.

"I'm thinking."

"There's nothing to think about. It's already done."

"What?"

He scratched at his beard. "Transferred money into your account today. It's all done."

"How did you get my account number?"

"Anne gave it to me. I think she meant it as a dare."

My eyes felt wide as wide could be. "How much money?"

"Enough that you don't have to worry for a while."

"How long a while?"

He just stared at me.

Oh, whoa. Something told me a millionaire rock star's version of *a while* was a whole lot longer than mine. The thought made me panicky, my fingers twisting together in my lap. Legal documents were scary, but the thought of him giving me masses of his money seemed even worse. "But lawyers and contracts and stuff. What you talked about this morning."

"We'll sort it out between us, like you wanted." He seemed so calm, while I was anything but. "It'll be okay, Liz."

"That's a lot of trust you're putting in me."

"We're having a kid. We gotta start somewhere, right?"

There were scuff marks on my favorite boots. Quite a few of them. At least I wouldn't be growing out of my shoes. My clothes, on the other hand, would probably need replacing before long. Most of my things were a little worn or were bought secondhand. Not as if I'd have been willing to ask Mal or Anne for a handout to fund a flashy new maternity wardrobe. They did so much for me already. It would be bizarre to not have to worry about money. We hadn't grown up with much. I couldn't really remember a time when money hadn't been an issue.

"Right," I mused.

"No big deal."

I wasn't so sure about that.

"I appreciate you being willing to monetarily support us. That's going to make a huge difference." I told the floor, because looking at him seemed too hard just then. "It's a real weight off my shoulders."

"Listen," he said. "I'm sorry about last night. And this morning. I'm just . . . I'm doing the best I can here."

"Of course." I smiled as bright as bright could be. "We'll be friends for Bean's sake."

"Bean?"

My smile grew more genuine. "In the early stages they're kind of bean shaped and sized."

"Oh. Right." His fingers lay laced in front of him, jiggling yet again. For a second, his gaze landed in the region of my belly before darting away again. "Give me a chance to catch up, get used to the idea. Then we'll talk some more."

"Okay."

"And of course we'll be friends," he said. "We *are* friends."

"Of course."

He smiled back at me. But I don't think either of us was feeling anything but fear just yet.

CHAPTER SEVEN

While the guys were down at the Chateau Marmont in L.A. being interviewed by *Rolling Stone* magazine, up in Portland a complete stranger was checking out my girl bits. The fancily framed medical degrees hanging on her office wall did nothing to detract from the awkwardness of where she put her gloved fingers.

Yep, going to the OB/GYN was just the best.

Everything with Bean was fine, by the way. And hearing her heartbeat for the first time rocked my world. She was real. This was real. I was actually going to be a mother. Amazing.

With the band touring and Ben's ban from Mal and Anne's apartment (also, I'm pretty sure he was avoiding me, despite all his fine words), it was a full four weeks after he filled my humble bank account to bursting before we laid eyes on each other again. It took that long for me to stop constantly barfing and to be given the go-ahead to travel. Due to having my head in the toilet, I'd missed out on Vancouver, Seattle, Portland, San Francisco, and L.A. Anne and I met up with the band in Phoenix. We arrived near the end of their concert, having been delayed by a storm.

Sam met us and took us to the side of the stage to watch

the encore. It was cool to see Stage Dive play live again. I was sitting on an empty box behind a massive screen that projected the happenings out to the stadium audience. I couldn't see the people, but I could hear them. Roadies, set construction workers, and similar were also hanging out, waiting.

The minute the show was done, Mal attacked Anne. The man was all over her like a rash, rubbing his sweaty self against her and basically dry-humping in public. She didn't seem to mind. We didn't hang around, everyone heading straight to the hotel. Apparently any interviews and meet-and-greets were done before the show.

I got a welcoming chin tip from Ben, but that was it in the rush.

The line of luxury black Lexuses crawled to a stop as we neared the swanky hotel's back entrance. Hands battered at the windows, people struggling to get close enough to press their faces up against the darkened glass.

It was freaky.

Dave and Ev were already inside, having been in the first vehicle. Ben, Lena, and Jimmy jumped out of the vehicle in front of us. Immediately, Lena and Jimmy hurried through the corridor made by security, into the safety of the hotel. But Ben delayed, signing autographs and shaking hands.

There were so many people out there. A veritable sea of women and men both, crying, screaming, and carrying on. I'd known how big the guys were, but knowing it and seeing it were two entirely different things. There were even TV crews among the mix, cameras catching it all.

"Shit," I whispered, hunching down.

"Someone can't keep a secret," said Anne, sitting between Mal and me on the backseat.

Mal just shrugged. "Where we're staying always gets out. This is the norm. Get used to it, ladies."

A black-clad security person opened the door and the clamor hit me. It was staggering. A wall of mindless, maximum-volume, gray noise. Sweat wet my back but my mouth dried to nothing. Anne nudged me gently, nodding toward the door and the batshit-crazy crowd beyond. I swallowed hard and nodded back. Like it or not (*not!*), we were going out there. Generally, agoraphobia wasn't much of an issue (or enochlophobia, if you want to get technical about it). It didn't stop me from doing anything. Get me anywhere near a loud swarming mass of people, however, and I'm rarely at my best.

I cautiously stepped down, feeling my way across the concrete. All of the flashes from the cameras were dazzling my eyes.

Crap.

The crowd surged forward, closing in, and the line of security struggled to hold them back. People were yelling shit, none of it decipherable over the sound of my heartbeat pounding behind my ears. They were chanting a name, and from the shape of their lips, I'm pretty sure it was Mal's.

I stood frozen, gaping, totally immobile. Fuck. Nope. Couldn't do it. What if I somehow tripped or got trod on or misstepped and accidentally hurt Bean?

Before I could turn tail and run back to the car, however, a strong arm wrapped around me, pulling my body in against the safety of his.

"I've gotcha," he said, his breath warming my ear.

I wasn't up to speaking.

Ben hustled me down the narrow corridor formed by security and into the building. Both of his arms were around me, holding me tight until he had to remove one to punch the button for the elevator. Cool air soothed my hot face while I concentrated on getting back my breath. God, what an idiot I was, losing it like that. Some great mother or psychologist I'd make.

Behind us, Mal and Anne were still out there, barely visible among the crowd.

"Let's go." Ben's hand slid down to mine, grabbing hold to tow me into the elevator.

"Aren't they coming? What are they doing?"

The elevator doors slid closed.

"With Mal, it could be anything. Don't worry, they're fine."

I craned my neck, necessary for viewing him at close range. His hair was a little longer, tied back in a tiny man bun, his beard neatly trimmed. Still beautiful, damn it. His T-shirt, plain black with an Arizona postcard printed on the front, fit just right, being neither too big nor too small. The tang of salty sweat lingered in the air around him. I wanted to bury my face in his chest and breathe deep, over and over again, despite the scent of booze. I just wanted to get as close to him as physically possible. One day those feelings would fade. Hopefully one day soon.

He looked down at me with a tight smile, still holding on to my hand. The smile definitely didn't make it to his eyes. If anything, I'd say the man looked nervous.

"Sorry about wigging out," I said.

With a low digital tone, the doors slid open.

"Don't worry about it," he said, and let go of my hand, instead applying gentle pressure low on my back to guide me forward. His motions were sure, his steps steady. However much he'd had to drink, he was clearly still coherent. "C'mon."

Cream carpet shushed our steps, baby chandeliers lighting our way. It wasn't very different from Vegas, with the same pricey, luxurious appearance. Another couple of security guys prowled about up here, keeping an eye on things.

"Doesn't that bother other customers?" I asked, nodding in their direction.

"Band's got this floor. You're two doors down in Mal and Anne's suite." Ben held up a card to the swipe thing. The little light turned green and he pushed the door open. "Might as well come on in for a minute."

"Okay." Not exactly a warm welcome. Man, this was all so hatefully awkward.

Inside, his suite was big, with a nice view and lots of comfy-looking couches in shades of beige. Quite a collection of liquor bottles covered the side table, the only visible trace of any rock 'n' roll lifestyle in the otherwise pristine room.

None of my business what he'd been up to the night before. None at all.

"You okay?" he asked.

"Yes." We sat down opposite each other. "The morning sickness has eased up."

"Great."

"Yeah."

A nod.

"Thanks for the texts," I said. "That was good of you."

"No big deal."

Morning and night, he'd sent me the same brief almost impersonal question: *U ok?* I'd responded in kind: *Fine! Great! Terrific!* A smiley face now and then. It wasn't as if I could tell him I'd spent the morning hurling, feeling three days dead, with my emotions all over the place, my breasts aching, and my brain slowly being pickled by hormones. Things were too weird between us for such brutal honesty. Besides, he had a lot on his mind, with the concert and all. So instead I'd whined to Anne, and she'd been good enough not to tell me it was my own damn fault. The look lingered in her eyes now and then, but I could ignore it. No point feeling sorry for myself. Onward and upward—or outward as the case with my womb might be.

My hand strayed to my tiny baby bump, barely visible

beneath my blue tank top, and Ben's gaze followed. He rubbed the side of his hand against his lips, eyes stark. The look he gave my abdomen was one of great fear. I couldn't take it.

"Do you have a juice?" I asked.

"Sure." The man leapt out of his seat, obviously eager to be gone. He moved to the side cabinet where the bar fridge was cunningly concealed. The room was so silent. When he opened the small juice bottle, the pop of the air seal being broken made me jump.

"Maybe I should get going," I said, rising to my feet. "Leave you to it."

"But your juice . . ."

All of a sudden, the front door crashed open and a party walked in. There could be no other description. Laughter, beer, men and women, they all poured into the expensive suite until the room was close to capacity.

"Epic show," yelled a lanky guy with long black hair and a woman attached to his hip.

He and Ben smacked palms. "It was good."

Their talk got drowned out by Metallica. A tall guy covered in tats broke a beer off from his six-pack and thrust it into my hand. I took it out of sheer instinct, the wet can chilling my skin.

"Hey," he said, giving me a grin. Pale red hair sat spiked up, and you really had to give it to him, he had a nice face. "I'm Vaughan."

"Lizzy. Hi."

"Didn't see you here last night. I'd have definitely remembered you."

What a flirt. Must have been the boobs. I'd done okay in the past, but I wouldn't call myself a man magnet. Especially not in a room where half the women looked and dressed like lingerie models.

"Ah, no," I said. "I only got in this evening."

Vaughan opened a beer for himself, setting down the six-pack on the coffee table. "A fan, or attached to the band somehow?"

"Both, I guess."

"Both?" His eyes lit with interest. "Well, you're in Ben's room, so I'll assume you're a friend of his."

I just smiled. "How about you? How do you fit in here?"

"I play bass for the warm-up band, Down Fourth."

"Hey, wow! I've heard of you guys. You're great," I said, clapping my hands all enthused. You'd think I'd never met a famous musician before.

His grin grew broader. Way to be cool, me.

"I really love that song you do . . . Shit . . ."

He laughed while my face slowly started to burn.

"No, I know the name." How embarrassing and frustrating. "I do. I had it on repeat just the other day."

"It's fine."

"Don't tell me." I closed my eyes, searching for the information inside my head. To have my own body rebelling against me, turning me into one big giant, idiotic walking baby-making machine. It wasn't fair. "Just give me a minute."

He laughed at me some more.

"Gah. Stupid pregnancy hormones." I stopped dead.

The whites of Vaughan's eyes suddenly seemed huge and glaringly bright. Yet again I faced down man fear. I don't know why. It's not like there could be any possible chance it was his kid I carried. The irony of a guy who got down to death metal being scared of a pregnant girl was not lost on me.

Way to keep a secret. The minute I said it, I wanted to slap myself silly. Either that or buy myself a muzzle. My pregnancy had been kept under the general populace's radar, and I really wanted to keep it that way.

"I'd prefer that information didn't get repeated," I said, dropping my voice and moving a little closer to the man. "It's just that it's early days, and—"

"Vaughan." Ben stuck his hand out to the man with an excessive amount of male zest. "How you doing?"

"Yeah, good, Ben."

"See you met Liz." He pushed the long since requested juice into my spare hand, liberating the beer from my other. Then he cracked the ale open and drank deep.

"Yeah, we were just talking," said Vaughan, the fear of babies happily gone from his face, replaced once more with his friendly smile. Thank goodness. Maybe he wouldn't say anything. "Turns out she's a fan."

"She is?"

"I am," I confirmed. "I had 'Stop' on repeat all last week." Nailed it.

"How about that." Ben's smile looked about as natural, and as comfortable, as a polyester pantsuit in June. Whatever he was up to, it wasn't good. Then, just to confirm my thoughts, he slid his arm around my neck, pulling me in close. Only not as you would a girlfriend or a lover. Nope, nothing like that at all. "Liz is Mal's new sister-in-law. Aren't you, sweetheart?"

"Yep." Funny, I'd always loved it when he called me that. This time, however, was different. I took a sip of the apple juice to try to cool myself down.

Brows drawn in, Vaughan looked back and forth between the two of us, obviously confused. "Didn't realize."

"Yeah. Sorry to put the fear of Mal into you, but she's out of bounds. Okay, man?" Ben planted a kiss on top of my head, then went that last irrevocable step too far and actually ruffled my hair like I was snotty-nosed kid. "Word with you in the bedroom, Liz?"

"Sure thing, Ben," I said through gritted teeth.

He ushered me through the crowd, with a hand to the small of my back once more. The door to the main bedroom was closed—probably the only reason it too hadn't filled up with people.

I didn't say a word until he'd closed us in. Then I still didn't say a word.

Instead, I threw my drink in his face.

"What the fuck?!" he roared, wiping apple juice out of his eyes.

"How dare you ruffle my hair like I'm your kid sister or something." I dropped my empty glass onto the carpet. "How dare you?"

"I was doing you a favor."

"Like hell you were."

The man set aside his beer aside and stormed forward, towering over me. "The guy is a fucking man-whore, Liz. Nearly every night on tour he's had a different woman."

"What utter crap."

"I'm not lying to you. He was flirting with you, trying to get into your pants. It's what he does."

"I'm not talking about him."

Ben blinked.

"You and I, we are not together, remember? If I want to flirt with a guy, I will. It is none of your business."

"You're pregnant with my child." The anger in his eyes—a smarter woman would have stepped back. Screw that. I went nose to nose with him. Well, as close as I could get to it, with the height difference. Next time we fought I was definitely bringing a ladder.

"That's right, Ben, I'm carrying *our* child," I said, breathing hard. "And I'm on tour to help us to figure out how to get along and be parents. Something that involves us having mutual respect for one another."

"I got respect for you, Liz. What I haven't got is the ability to stand by while some player tries to chat you up."

"Oh yeah? Tell me you haven't had sex with one of those wonderfully liberated, barely dressed ladies out there. Let me know this isn't just some messed-up double standard you're trying on me."

He couldn't do it. His lips slammed shut and he shifted, edging back, putting room between us. It shouldn't have hurt, but it did. Hearts are dumb like that. At least he didn't try to give me excuses.

"No?" I asked.

Still nothing.

"We're not together. You have no right to try and warn a guy off me. And treating me like you did—like a child, ruffling my hair, calling me 'sweetheart' that way. . . ." My eyes were itchy, turning liquid. Like hell. "How fucking dare you."

I should have stormed out. I wanted to. The thought of losing it in front of the cool party crowd, however, stopped me cold. There had to be an alternative. Just a few minutes and I could pull myself together, go find my room. "I need to use the bathroom."

My dignity was small, about the same size as my bladder since the invention of Bean. I pretty much had to pee constantly, so it wasn't a complete lie, despite the sudden rising damp in my eyes. Dumb hormones. Idiot men and their god damn sperm. I strode into the grandiose bathroom and slammed the door shut. A tear trickled down my cheek, followed fast by another.

And the girl in the mirror, she still wasn't glowing. How fucking unfair.

I went and did my business in the toilet, scrubbed my hands and then my face. All of the emotions inside of me kept building up, threatening to leak out again. This situation with Ben was doing my head in. So I did what any sensible knocked-up twenty-one-year-old college drop-out would do and climbed into the massive, empty sunken tub to cool down and reassess my life. It was actually quite comfortable. In the distance I could hear the party carrying on with chatter and music. You'd think an up-market hotel such as this would have thicker walls.

For a good five, ten minutes I sat in there, calming myself, coming to grips with the situation. Perhaps Ben and I shouldn't talk for a while. We didn't have to be friends to raise a child together, if indeed that's what was going to happen. Him changing his mind on being involved would surprise approximately no one. Harsh but true.

Whatever. Come what may, I'd manage.

"Where's Lizzy?" asked a muffled voice in the next room, male and abrupt. Jimmy Ferris. Why he'd be interested in me I had no idea.

"In the john," said Ben. "What do you want with her?"

"Take it Mal and Anne are busy making up for lost time. Lena thought she might like to come hang with her."

"We're in the middle of something right now. I'll ask her in a few."

Jimmy snorted. "You're having a nice chat, huh? That why you're dripping wet and there's an empty glass on the floor? Try again, Ben."

"None of your fucking business."

"You're right about that. It's not. But oh well . . ."

For a moment there was nothing, during which I strained to hear something, anything.

"Man, you are fucking shit up with her so damn bad," said Jimmy, breaking the silence. "One way or another, this girl's going to be in your life from now on. Way you're playing it, won't be in a good way."

"What do you know about it?" growled Ben.

"What do I know about fucking up things with girls? You serious?"

No reply.

"How many times you talk to Lizzy in the last month?"

"We talk."

"Not face-to-face or I'd have heard about it from Mal. Another fucking mess you've failed to fix."

"I'm working on it," said Ben, his voice full of anger. "I'll smooth shit over with him."

"Believe it when I see it."

"Don't lecture me on messing with the band. Where the fuck were you that last practice session before Seattle, huh?"

Jimmy scoffed. "Taking Lena to see her obstetrician. Do you even know what the hell one of them is?"

"Of course I fucking do."

"Yeah? You taking Liz to her visits? Looking after her? 'Course not. Because if you were, every other member of this band would have a shitload more respect for you than they got right now."

"We were heading on tour," said Ben.

"Some things are more important, man. Take looking after the woman carrying your child, for example."

"Jim—"

"How many times have you even called that girl since we've been on tour?"

"What the fuck? You a relationship counselor now?"

Jimmy laughed. "My woman isn't throwing drinks in my face, so as far as you're concerned, I might as well be."

"She's not my woman."

"She's the girl you put a baby in, asshole. And if she's been going through half the shit Lena's been dealing with, then you are just about the lowest cunt I've come across in a long time for making her do it alone."

Guess Ben had no answer to that.

Have to admit, I felt bad for him. He loved these guys like brothers, and I'd been coping okay on my own, give or take. And yes, I did feel a little guilty for listening in on the conversation. Given that I was the topic, however . . .

"The baby's got her moods bouncing all over the place. One minute she's depressed as hell, worrying how we'll deal with this, sure things are gonna go to shit and I'll leave her. As if. Then the next, everything's great and she's excited again about becoming a mom."

A pause.

"It's hard on her, man, all the changes. And it's scary as hell to be facing, I know."

"Jim—"

"No. Just shut up and listen. I'm nearly finished." Jimmy exhaled roughly. "None of us planned this. But you need to drop out of the running for dickhead of the year and get yourself sorted out before it's too late."

"Okay. I'll talk to her."

"Think, Ben. Just think. How the hell are you going to explain this to your kid in five or ten years' time, hmm? That your baby momma doesn't talk to you because you spent her entire pregnancy hiding behind a bottle and getting blown by groupies?"

My stomach contracted sharply. There we go. I knew he'd been with other women, of course. It still hurt, however.

"It's not like that," yelled Ben.

"It's exactly like that. Give me a fucking break, dude. Just because I don't come to your nightly soirees doesn't mean I don't know what's going on here. Hell, anyone can see it."

Silence again from Ben.

"I don't know if you want her or not. But I'm telling you now, you're gonna lose her, and you're gonna lose your kid, and any shred of self-respect you might still have along with them. Your parents were useless, same as mine, so you know what it's like. Get your shit together."

The bedroom door opened, the noise from the party coming in clearer.

"Lizzy wants to hang with Lena, just bring her on over. She's welcome any time."

Ben didn't reply.

Noise from the party dropped in volume once again as the bedroom door closed. Then there came the *boom*. Once, twice, three times. I stared at the bathroom door in surprise, with just a small dash of fear. It'd been damn loud.

Might be time for me to go.

"Liz, can I come in?"

"It's not locked," I told the door.

Ever so slowly the handle turned. Then Ben stuck his head in as if he was expecting more projectiles, liquid or otherwise, to be lobbed his way.

"It's safe," I said.

"Hey."

"Hi."

He said no more, instead turning to the sink to wash off his face and neck. Guess I'd done a good job of juicing him, because he stripped off the Arizona T-shirt and tossed it aside. Next, he spent some time washing his hands.

Only then did he approach. "Mind if I join you?"

I shrugged. "It's your bath."

With a sigh, he climbed in and sat down opposite me at the other end of the tub. I tucked my legs up, ensuring he had plenty of room without us being required to touch. He stretched out his long legs on either side of mine, gaze glued to my face. What a sight we must have made, me fully dressed in the dry tub and him in his jeans and big black boots. Man, he had a nice chest. I did my best not to notice, but some things are beyond my control. A half-naked Ben was most definitely one of them. The fight with Jim, however, concerned me. As did the raw pink knuckles of his right hand. These guys obviously enjoyed

hitting walls when they got testy. I could remember Mal
once doing the same. Males. So violent.

Because of course I hadn't thrown anything at anybody
lately.

"Take it you heard me and Jim fighting," he said.

"Hard not to."

A nod.

"He was right about one thing: it's been a while since
we talked. I mean really talked."

"Yeah."

No one spoke for a moment. I sure as hell wasn't going
first. Right in that moment, I just wasn't that brave.

"I, um . . . shit's been busy with the tour." He stretched
his arms out around the edge of the tub, obviously getting
as comfortable as hard ceramic and the situation would allow. A small line of blood down his right hand, ignored.
"Weeks leading up to it, Adrian had us talking to every
damn reporter in the country. It was insane."

"Oh."

"The producers think the music just makes itself. Once
Dave's written the songs, they think it's a round or two in
the studio and we're done. But that's bullshit. Takes hours,
sometimes days, to get the sound right." Fervor shone
bright in his eyes, beyond the booze and whatever. His passion for the music. "Dave used to be a perfectionist about
it too, but all of the guys are distracted now, eyes on the
clock, wanting to get home to their women. I'm the one
sitting there with Dean and Tyler till four in the fucking
morning, getting it perfect."

"Sounds like a lot of work."

"It is. Jimmy and Mal go off onstage and Dave's still
the poet writing the songs. In the band, it's all down to me
now, though, to work the sound." He scratched at his chin.
"Know it makes me sound like a self-congratulating art

geek, but it's important, you know? Whatever we put out there, I need to know in my gut it's the best we've got."

"I can understand that."

"Wasn't avoiding you, Liz, but I wasn't putting any effort into seeing you, either. You might have noticed."

"Right."

"Thought I'd let things with Mal and Anne calm down. That's just another excuse, though." Dark eyes bored into me, as if he could see my soul. Who knows, maybe he could. I always felt too open, too exposed, around him. He made me so messy with all these wants and needs. I don't know if it was love that I felt for him or lust. But whatever it was, it sucked.

"I'm sorry, Liz," he said, his soft, deep voice filling the room. "I said I'd have your back and I didn't. I disappeared on you again, and this time you were actually going through shit. Serious shit."

Huh.

"Jimmy was right. You shouldn't have had to go through it alone."

"It wasn't so bad." I turned away. A lot of emotion for one day. "I had Anne."

"Yeah, but this is our baby, and Anne isn't me."

I breathed in through my nose and out through my mouth, nice and slow, trying to calm my racing heart. It was true. His absence had left a bruise, and no amount of go-girl lectures delivered in the bathroom mirror could alter the fact.

"Is she?" he asked.

"No, Ben, she's not."

He slowly nodded, like something had been decided.

"So what now?" I asked.

"Talk to me." The fingers of his left hand flicked and fiddled with the hard upper rim of the bathtub. Nerves or what, I had no idea. At least the blood from the knuckles on his right hand had dried.

"About what?"

"All the stuff I should have been hearing the past month." The man was serious. Very much so. "No more of this useless fucking texting, Liz. Talk to me. Right now, face-to-face. Help me prove Jim wrong."

Give him another chance.

I stared at him, lost, my brain searching for the words. Any easily retrieved information lacked in either dignity or strength. Ah, man. Could I trust him with my weaknesses and issues? That was the question.

"C'mon. How have you been, really? What's been going on with you?" he pushed. I frowned at him and he frowned right back. "Liz, please."

I groaned in defeat. "All right, I suck."

"Why do you suck?"

"So very many reasons." I pushed my hair back from my face—no more hiding. "Pregnancy sucks. It's natural, my ass. I finally stop throwing up, but I'm tired all the time. Giving up coffee was horrendous. None of my clothes fit right because of these stupid breasts, and they ache constantly. I have to pee like every thirty seconds, and then to top it off, I cry every time the Healthy Hound ad comes on. It's ridiculous."

Little wrinkles appeared either side of his nose. "You cry at a dog food ad?"

"Yes. The puppies jump all over each other to get to their mother and it's just so beautiful, with their cute little tails wagging and everything."

He just stared at me.

"I know it's psycho, Ben. Believe me, I'm well aware of this."

"Hey, it's fine." He covered a smile with his hand. Too late, the bastard.

"You try dealing with all these hormones going apeshit. Crap. Apeshoot."

"Apeshoot?"

"I'm trying not to swear," I explained. "You want the first word our child comes out with to be something bad?"

"No. Gotcha." The man was incredibly bad at hiding a grin. "No swearing."

Jerk. I narrowed my eyes on him, holding back my own smile.

"I'm taking you seriously. I am." He flat-out lied. Though it was rather nice to see him smile and to hear his low laugh. At least the bad mood was gone.

"And my ankles are all fat and gross," I said. "It's ridiculous."

"What? Show me." A giant paw grabbed hold of my limb, dragging it onto his lap. Without preamble he pushed up the leg of my jeans and wrestled off my sandal, dropping it out onto the floor. "It looks fine. There's nothing wrong with it."

"I'm retaining fluid. It's disgusting."

One-handed, he flipped back his long, dark fringe, giving me a look most dubious.

"Let go of my foot, please. I don't want you to see it."

He slowly shook his head. "This what you've been doing the last month? Talking yourself into crazy shit and crying at dog food ads?"

"My ankle is distinctly thicker, Ben. And I explained about the dog food ad. Give me my foot back."

"No." He tucked one leg underneath the other and rested my foot atop it before proceeding to rub my toes. Damn, that felt good. The man had incredibly strong fingers. Must have been a result of all that bass playing. Thumbs dug in deep to the arch of my foot and my spine basically melted. Heaven, nirvana—I had it all within my grasp so long as he kept doing his thing.

"God, that's so nice," I happy-sighed, sinking further into the tub.

He made a gruff noise. It could have almost been construed as the word *good*.

"Is your hand all right?" I asked eventually.

He looked up at me from beneath dark brows, lips shut. His magic fingers paused for a moment, then kept right on kneading. "I might have put a hole or two in the wall after Jim left."

"Oh."

"He was right. You've been dealing with this on your own from the start and all I've done is throw money at the problem, hoping it would go away." He moved down to rubbing at my heel, taking care with the swollen ankle. "I didn't want to know, Liz. That's why I kept my distance. I just wanted to go on like normal, pretend none of it was happening."

"Me too. But my body keeps messing things up for me." I laughed, despite the topic being distinctly unfunny. "We're not that different, Ben. This situation has thrown us both for a loop, and that's putting it mildly."

"Don't make excuses for me," he grumped.

"All right, you're an asshole and you let me down. Again. Feel better?"

The smile was much wider this time. "Thought we weren't swearing."

"Oops." It was amazing what a foot rub did for my mood. Right then, I pretty much loved the whole world. Real anger lay beyond my reach. He grasped my other foot, again rolling up my jeans, and tossed aside the sandal. I did not fight him—no sir, no way.

"Can I ask you a question?" I said.

"Shoot."

"Why didn't you ever want children?"

"Because this is me, Liz. What you see is what you get.

I like things calm, easy. But you and me, we've never been easy. Minute I saw you, it's been complicated. First with Mal, and you being a little younger, more serious, and now with the pregnancy." He shook his head. "Some women don't give a shit if I come and go. It's all good. But with you and the baby, you need more from me than that. And you deserve more."

"We're messing with your lifestyle."

He looked up at me from beneath drawn brows. "It's more than that. Shit. Never tried to explain this to someone before. When you were a kid, did you ever have some game you played that just rocked your world? And you'd wake up in the morning and realize today was the day you got to do nothing but play that game all day, and it was like life could never get better? That's what my life is like. Every day I get to get up and play music, I get to create something."

I nodded sadly, finally understanding. Ben was a man living his dream. As if anyone could compete with that. Maybe he'd liked the idea of me. Reality was, however, there'd never been room for me in his life.

"When the guys are busy, I can hop on a plane and go mix things up with another band," he continued. "Fill in or be a guest on their album. Even jamming with strangers in some shitty little bar where no one knows my name. That's my life, every day. I get to make something new, learn something. And it's fucking amazing. There's nothing like it."

"Sounds great."

"It is," he said. "And that's why I never thought about kids. Even a girlfriend seemed too much of a distraction. Don't get me wrong, I like women. But it was always easier to find someone for the night than to commit to something that stops me from being who I am, doing what I love."

I nodded. What was there to say? To go into a relationship expecting the other person to change was stupid. Ben and I had been over before we began, I just hadn't known it, understood, until now. No doubt he liked me just fine, but not enough.

"Doesn't mean I'm not going to be there for you and our kid. You said we could be friends," he said. "That offer still available?"

Friends was the right thing to do. I pushed aside my disappointment and put a smile on my face. "Absolutely."

"I'd like that."

It was me and Bean, and Bean and me. Come what may, I'd have my baby girl's back. Her daddy could do what he would. And the truth was, if he kept massaging my feet this way, I'd be his best damn friend, despite the break in my heart.

He kept his face down, his concentration on the task complete. Generally my feet were not that fascinating. Maybe he did have a foot fetish after all. Fingers drew soothing circles over my crappy ankle before digging in once more to the arch of my foot. Total and complete bliss. I could pretty much feel my crazy baby hormones rolling over and offering up their soft underbelly to him, preening and calling him Daddy, the dirty things. What this man's hands could do to me. Every part of me felt floaty and wonderful. Shivery good even.

Wait up. Crap, I was seriously turned on.

A wounded heart was apparently no competition for an overeager vagina. The urge for sperm made no sense. I already had a baby on board. My tarty, attention-seeking nipples stood out loud and proud beneath my top, just begging for his lips. The situation between my legs wasn't any better. Since when had my feet become such hardcore, triple X–rated erogenous zones? His able hands made sweet pornographic love to my toes, and my muscles turned to jelly. My legs just fell open in invitation. Beyond my control, I swear. It all just felt so impossibly damn good.

Holy god damn hell. No one had warned me pregnancy could send you into heat.

Despite the ecstasy, I couldn't help but notice there was only like three . . . four inches between the pad of my foot and the bulge behind the fly of his jeans. It wouldn't take much to touch. Why, little more than a flex would be more than sufficient. I could just brush my toes against the poor man's crotch and then gasp, pretending it was all some silly (wonderful) accident. Oops, clumsy me, fondling the innocent, unsuspecting man's genitals with my foot. How embarrassing—though really it could happen to anyone.

Not.

And really this is partly why, in my experience, friends don't rub friends' feet unless there's more going on. I got easily enough confused about the man, no need to make it worse.

A small moan slipped my lips, echoing in the tiled room.

"You okay?" he asked.

"Fine."

"You made a noise."

"No, I didn't."

A little line appeared above his nose. "Okay."

"That's great," I said, drawing my now slutty limbs back to the safe side of the tub. "Thanks. Very kind of you. I think we'll make great friends."

He gave me a long look. "Any time. If you need something, I want you to tell me. That's the only way this is going to work."

"Okay." I needed his naked body at my disposal. Now.

"I want total honesty from you, okay?"

"Total honesty." So help me, I'd ride him all the way home and back again.

"From now on, we talk," he said. "All the fucking time. Yap, yap, yap. That's us."

"Got it."

"Great." The way his tongue and lips played with that simple little word, it meant much, much more than it was ever meant to. And it might have been my imagination, but I'm pretty damn sure his pupils were about twice their normal size. They were like twin pools of black rock 'n' roll sexiness and desire just inviting me to jump on in and get all wet and wild and wanton. All of a sudden, breathing seemed to be an issue for me. Same with thinking, clearly. I don't know what it was about the man that made me attempt to get poetic. But it really needed to stop.

"I better go," I said.

"Fucking crazy . . ." he muttered.

"What?"

"You."

I groaned in embarrassment. "Come on, give me a break. I explained about the dog food ad. And hey, I told you that in confidence too. Don't you dare repeat it."

"Not talking about that," he said, the hint of a curve in the corner of his mouth doing dreadful things to me.

"What then?" I asked, both wanting and dreading knowing.

He hesitated, hiding another smile behind his hurt hand.

"Total honesty. Come on."

"Pretty sure you don't want to hear me talking about my dick."

"Your, um, your dick?"

"Yeah."

"Huh. How much have you had to drink?"

"Not nearly enough for this." The smile he gave me, I nearly came on the spot. The fact that it came framed in his particularly sleek-looking beard almost did me in. I knew exactly how his facial hair felt against me. So stimulating. Never had I wanted to rub my cheek and other pertinent parts against someone's face more. When it came to that night in Vegas, my memory was way too good.

"You asked if I'd had sex since I found out about the baby," he said. "Answer's no."

"Yeah right." I laughed.

"I'm serious. Nothing since that night. Haven't even come close."

Wow. "Why?"

"I don't know. Guess I lost my libido." He scratched at his chin. "Wasn't even interested. Just . . . nothing."

"You couldn't get it up?" I asked, mildly horrified, and much too curious. Ben always seemed so virile.

"I didn't want to get it up," he said. "There's a difference."

"Huh. But Jimmy said—"

"Jimmy doesn't know everything." He cracked his neck, irritation in his gaze. "Wish you hadn't heard all that."

I couldn't truthfully say the same. Their conversation had been most enlightening.

"I couldn't get interested in screwing anyone because I was worried about you and the baby," he said. "Dealing with all this has been big, you know?"

"Yeah. Sex having consequences is kind of a bummer." I smiled. "I guess I've been pretty sheltered, really. Anne always dealt with the serious stuff. But this time she can't. It's all on me."

"And me."

"Yes." Time would tell.

"Anyway," he said. "Just thought you'd find it funny."

"That you were suffering from erectile dysfunction? Ben, there's no way I'd find that funny."

"It's wasn't erectile dysfunction, Liz," he said with a wounded gaze. "Don't say that."

"Okay, okay. Sorry."

"I was just numb. Lost my interest in sex for a while."

"Right. Numb."

"Anyway," he said, still frowning. Male egos. So touchy. "Soon as I'm around you again, my dick decides to come out of hibernation. Thank fuck. Was worried I'd have to wait till you'd had the baby to get it back."

"Yeah. Phew." I thought the information over for a while. Not necessarily good news—for me, at least. The other women of the world would probably benefit greatly by it, however. "Well, we did talk out some of our issues, so it's entirely natural that you'd be feeling better about the situation, I suppose."

He screwed up his face. "Sweetheart, I'm not talking about us being friends, though that's nice and all. I'm talking about the fact that you turn me on. Have since the minute I met you. Physically, you get to me."

"I do?"

"Yeah, you do. I'm just going to have to channel that interest elsewhere."

My mouth worked, though nothing came out for a while. I got to him. God, if only he knew how much he still got to me. Hope was well out of my price range, however. I couldn't afford to get physical with him. My emotions were far too involved, and clearly the man was only out for some fun. Without a doubt, I knew that now.

"Ben, are you sure this isn't some mental block you were having," I asked. "All the worry about the pregnancy and how it was going to affect things, as opposed to me physically?"

He raised a brow.

"Hey, I've seen some of those women out there," I said. "They're stunning. And if they've been hanging around you night after night, then it seems unlikely that me with my beginner's baby bump and fat ankles suddenly lights up your life."

His tongue played behind his cheek and he said nothing. There was definitely laughter in his eyes, however.

"I'm just trying to be rational," I added.

"Problem is, rational doesn't come into it."

Hmm.

"Dicks don't have brains. It's why men get into trouble."

The man had a point. Dicks obviously didn't have emotions, either, the annoying things.

"The point I'm messing up here is, Liz, you're right. I was jealous. I want you. I'm not going to act on that because shit's complicated enough and we're working on being friends here. It's what's best for the baby."

"Right." What he said was no less than the truth. Still, my vagina went into a deep depression. My heart wasn't too happy about it, either.

"The business is hell on relationships—all the separations and everything. Couples don't last. Seen it time and time again. I don't want to put our kid through some messy split and neither do you."

"What?" I cocked my head. "You really mean that. But what about David and Ev?"

"Time'll tell."

My eyes were wide. "I think that's sad, Ben."

"Trust me, Liz. What's best for our kid right now is you and me working on having a long-term relationship we can both live with. That means us being friends and figuring out how to be parents together, right?"

"Right. I guess."

"I know I'm not the psychology student here, but I also

think it would really help if you didn't get with any of my friends or people I work with. Ever. I think that would, ah, complicate things."

"Yes. Fair enough."

"And I won't hook up with any of your friends, either. Ever."

"Thanks."

He tipped his chin in acknowledgment.

"Wow, we're really going great, setting up the friendship boundaries," I said.

A smile.

"This should all work perfectly." Heartbreakingly so.

"I hope so," he said.

"Might be best if we didn't talk about your penis and sex between us again in the future, though. Maybe we should tone back the total honesty just a little."

He winced. "You're right. My bad. No need to confuse shit."

"No problem."

He held out his right hand to me, knuckles pink and large fingers calloused. "Friends?"

"You bet. Being friends will be great."

CHAPTER EIGHT

Being friends sucked.

All told, there were thirty-five stops on the tour—seventeen in this first leg, before we headed over to Europe, then back home again to tour the northern states. The band played a new city pretty much every second night without break. Ben had been right, though, everything that could be done for me was done. All I had to worry about was walking on and off private jets and gestating, while room service catered to my every whim.

The routine went roughly like this: We arrived in a new place and settled into our hotel while fans screamed and fainted out front. Sometimes the guys got the rest of the day off, usually spending time with their significant others. Or, in Ben's case, jamming with the warm-up act, Down Fourth, and a case or two of beer.

Not to say that the guys didn't hang out together.

It seemed, though, that couples in their first year together spent the bulk of their time bonking. Noisily. Jim and Ben often hit the gym, and they'd all get together for an occasional early or late-night dinner. Since Mal still refused to talk to Ben outside of band business, however, those were difficult, to say the least.

The bulk of their time went toward publicity. TV shows, radio stations, news reporters—you name it, they talked to them. Then there'd be sound checks and rehearsals and meetings. Stage Dive might have toured the country a time or two, but the amount of the country they'd actually gotten to see was likely small. When it wasn't about the sexing, it seemed to be all business, all the time. Gave me plenty of opportunities to catch up on my reading and get a jump start on next year's classes, when I wasn't with Ben, trying to figure out how he and I could be friends. That the mere sight of him set off my horny hormonalness didn't help. The hours I spent amusing myself with my hand after one of our visits was plain sad. Pregnancy was crazy.

In Albuquerque we had a drink together one morning. Herbal tea for me and about a gallon of black coffee for him. Conversation was stilted, largely due to Ben having had only three hours' sleep.

No, I didn't ask for the exact details.

In Oklahoma we attempted lunch in his room. Problem was, an overly zealous fan managed to get onto the floor and handcuff himself to the emergency evacuation stairs door handle, opposite Ben's suite. Between his yelling and the fire alarm he managed to set off, lunch got canceled and the building was temporarily evacuated.

In Wichita we tried going for a walk, but then Ben nearly got mobbed and we had to make a run for it back to the hotel. He might not stick out back home in Portland, but in other cities, on Stage Dive–sighting alert, we weren't so lucky.

I hate to admit it, but by Atlanta I think we were both starting to give up. No plans were made. Plus I had the sniffles.

In Charlotte my cold decided to get more serious and a doctor was called in, doubtless at great expense. I could have told me to rest up and keep taking the prenatal vitamins for a whole lot less. My nose gleamed bright red and flowed like a river. It was beautiful. Anne was the only one permitted to come see me. No one else could afford to share in my germy state. Her having Mal stick his tongue in her mouth every chance he got didn't seem to matter. Adrian, the band's manager, immediately slapped a quarantine order on me. I wasn't permitted to stick my head outside my bedroom door, or else.

Asshole. As if I would.

Ben: U ok? Lena said you can't have visitors.

Lizzy: Fine. Just a cold.

Ben: Shitty. How bad? U c Dr?

Lizzy: Yes. Morning sickness & growing bean got me run down. Gotta drink more juice etc. Keep up the prenatal vitamins. Immune system is looking after her more than me apparently.

Ben: Ok. Need anything?

Lizzy: No thanks. Heard her heart again. Beating strong.

Ben: U can hear her heart already? Fuck. Amazing.

Lizzy: I know right?

Ben: Could be him.

Lizzy: Don't mess with mother's intuition.

Ben: Wouldn't dare.

Lizzy: I never realized there so many different types of juice. Thank you.

Ben: Think of anything u need tell me.

Lizzy: Will do. Thanks again.

Lizzy: Thanks for the flowers.

Ben: No problem. Feeling better?

Lizzy: Nope. All hail the Queen of Phlegm. They put me on antibiotics. Should be better soon.

Ben: Good. Can I get u anything?

Lizzy: No thanks. Have a good concert. Break a leg or whatever.

Ben: Take it easy. Rest.

Lizzy: Did Mal tell u I was staying here?

Ben: Ur not coming to Nashville?

Lizzy: No. They don't want me flying. Mal didn't tell u?

Ben: No.

Lizzy: Crap. Sorry.

Ben: Never mind. Ur still sick? How sick?

Lizzy: Nothing serious. They're just being careful. Plus u guys can't get sick.

Ben: Calling.

Lizzy: Losing voice. Hurts to speak.

Ben: Shit. U sure?

Ben: What did Dr say exactly?

Lizzy: It's common cold. Headaches & blocked nose. No high fevers which might b dangerous. All normal.

Ben: Mayb we should get 2nd opinion.

Lizzy: Don't worry. Anne will b w me. I'll be fine in a few days. C u in Memphis.

Ben: Keep me up to date. Need anything?

Lizzy: Will do. Just sleep. Later.

Ben: How u feeling today?

Lizzy: Nose running less green.

Ben: Good. Been worried about you.

Lizzy: I'm getting there. Sleeping and catching up on lots on day time tv.

Ben: Great. Take it easy.

Lizzy: With Anne in Nurse Ratched mode I have no other choice.

Ben: Haha. Family.

Lizzy: Exactly.

Ben: Can I get u anything?

Lizzy: I'm ok.

Ben: Sorry I missed ur call. What's happening?

Lizzy: Just wanted to wish u luck w the concert. How is Memphis? Any sightings of the King?

Ben: Not yet. But he's here somewhere. How u doing?

Lizzy: Much better. Bored. Want out of bed. Dr said a day or 2. Blood pressure was a little low, made me light headed. But no big deal.

Ben: You fainted? What happened?

Lizzy: No, just felt off. It's fine. Taking extra iron.

Ben: Christ, u sure?

Lizzy: Yes. Please don't worry. It's all getting worked out.

Ben: Shit. Ok. Be good to see you.

Lizzy: You too. So sick of being sick. Meet me in St Louis?

Ben: Deal.

Lizzy: Anne said u rang her. Brave.

Ben: Wanted to make sure u were ok.

Lizzy: I know. But I am telling u everything.

Ben: Yeah. Just worried.

Lizzy: Dr's good. If anything changes I'll let u know straight away. See u soon.

Lizzy: I am now the proud of owner of a wide selection of super comfy pjs and the worlds most extensive collection of zombie films.

Ben: :)

Lizzy: You rock in all the ways.

Ben: Pjs were Lena's idea. Zombies were mine.
Lizzy: They both made my day. Thank you.
Ben: What movie u watching?
Lizzy: Dawn of the Dead.
Ben: Original or remake?
Lizzy: Remake. Love the actors in it.
Ben: Cool. Never seen it.
Lizzy: It's not Romero, but its fun.
Ben: Show it to me sometime.
Lizzy: You got it.

Lizzy: Arrived. Going to sleep.
Ben: Ok?
Lizzy: Yes. Just tired. Have a good concert.
Ben: Thanks. C u in the morning.

Yes, the sad fact was, Ben and I were probably better at texting one another than we'd ever been communicating face-to-face. Apart from that one night in Vegas. Oh, and the time in his truck. And in his hotel suite tub after his argument with Jimmy, though he'd been somewhat under the influence that night.

Anyway, the flight wore me out. I went straight to bed when Anne and I hit Saint Louis. But I didn't exactly get much sleep.

"Fuck off, dude!" was my wake-up call. "You don't come in here."

"Out of my way," said someone in a distinctly deep and pissed off tone.

"Easy." Another male voice. A different one this time.

"Ben, be reasonable. She's still sleeping." That was Anne, her voice placating.

"It's one o'clock in the afternoon. She said she was better, why the fuck is she still sleeping?"

I sure as hell wasn't anymore.

"Anne, he's got a point. Has anyone checked on her lately?" I think that was Lena, but what she was doing here, I had no idea.

"Something's wrong. I want a doctor here now," said Ben.

"Just a minute. We're all worried about her." Ev, perhaps?

Hell, it sounded like everyone was visiting.

"Told you, man," said Mal. "You don't come into my rooms. I may have to work with you. But I don't want a fucking thing to do with you outside of that."

"For Christ's sake . . ."

"You fucked with my trust."

"I know," sighed Ben. "And I'm sorry. Right now, though, I need to know she's okay."

"I'm fine," I said, stepping out of my room. "Hey, you're really all here."

And I do mean everyone. David and Ev, Lena and Jimmy, and of course my sister and Mal, what with me still sharing their suite. Thank goodness I was wearing a pair of the spanking new blue lounge pants and matching striped tank top, tiny bare baby bulge poking out in between.

"Liz." Ben rushed me, engulfing me in his big strong arms.

"Hi." I mumbled into his T-shirt-covered pec. Yeah, I'd kind of frozen. Generally, we didn't do this, but also it felt far too good. My poor, tired body got shivery in the best way. The man was just asking for me to hump his leg or something. Desperate really wasn't pretty.

"Are you okay?" he asked, studying my face.

"I'm fine. I just overslept. Sorry to worry everyone."

He frowned, big hands cupping my face, gently turning it this way and that for his inspection. "You don't look okay. You look tired."

"I couldn't get to sleep last night. I'm bouncing back

from the cold just fine, though. No more Queen of the Phlegm or any of that."

"You sure?" He gave me a dubious look.

"Screw you, bud. I'm glowing."

The big jerk gave me a sheepish look. "Sorry. Just been worried about you."

"Apparently my iron levels were a little low. I'm taking supplements now, eating more. I'll be back to normal in no time. And really, I feel fine. I feel great! Being up and around is awesome."

"Why couldn't you sleep?"

My mouth worked fine, but really my brain was too sleep-addled just yet to invent a plausible lie on demand. Worse, my face began to fire up. Crap. Out of all the questions in all the world, I particularly did not want to answer that one. Not even a little.

"Why?"

"I don't know, I just couldn't."

"Liz."

"Ben."

"Tell me why," he barked.

"Because the walls here are thin, okay? It was too noisy. Now enough with the questions. I'm hungry."

"Ha," shouted Mal triumphantly, hands on hips. "Your nightly fun-time party boy bullshit kept her awake."

"I'm on the other side of the fucking building," said Ben. "How the hell could I be keeping her awake?"

"But then, if it wasn't you . . ." Anne's brows slowly rose and she covered her mouth with her hand. "Oh dear. Sorry, Liz."

I nodded, unable to face her just yet.

"What," asked Mal, eyes full of confusion. "What are you two talking about?"

Jimmy snorted. A moment later, his brother did much

the same. At least Ev and Lena managed to keep the bulk of their reaction on the inside. They were nice girls.

I'd never needed to know that my sister was a screamer. Never. That Mal was a screamer too just kind of confused me. If only you could have memories bleached from your brain. What an extraordinarily useful thing it would be.

"Pumpkin? Explain."

Anne pulled Mal in close and whispered in his ear. Then Mal started snickering.

"It's not funny," said Anne.

"It kind of is."

She shook her head, arms crossed over her chest.

"Lord of the Sex strikes again!"

"Shuddup."

Huge grin in place, Mal smacked a kiss on her lips.

"So you got caught up on sleep okay?" Ben asked, ignoring their carrying on.

"Yes. Thanks."

"We better get some breakfast into you. What do you feel like?"

"Hmm." My tummy grumbled audibly. Me no care. "I want the biggest omelet known to mankind."

"You got it."

His gaze fell to my waist, then his hand followed, tentatively covering my bump. It was still early days in Bean world. The bump might have been caused as much by bad posture as anything. But I knew she was in there, growing and doing her thing. Magic.

"You mind if I . . ." he asked.

"It's fine."

The palm of his hand warmed my skin, his calloused fingers softly tracing over me, tickling ever so slightly (Turning me on, of course. Gah.) The side of his thumb rubbed gently back and forth, the callus giving me goose bumps.

Actually, I'm pretty certain he himself gave me goose bumps. It didn't even seem to matter what his hands were up to. And I had the worse feeling that I'd missed him this last week. His voice, his presence, all of him. I stared up at his face, spellbound. It came as naturally as breathing, feeling for Ben. Whatever he'd been up to while I was away didn't even seem to matter just then. How dumb was my heart?

Meanwhile, the silence was starting to make me nervous.

"Fifteen weeks," I said.

"Wow." He smiled and I smiled back at him, lost. Same as always.

"Guess I should get dressed."

"Nah," he said. "Don't worry. Come to my room and we'll order your omelet. You can fill me in on everything over late breakfast."

"Okay. I'd like that."

We turned to face the assembled crowd. Every eye was on us—apparently our little conversation had held them enthralled. I'd kind of forgotten we had an audience at all, caught up in the moment.

"Man," said David, his hand clapping down on Mal's shoulder. "C'mon."

"What?" Mal scowled.

"This is getting sorted out," announced Jimmy. "Now. Time to kiss and make up, you two idiots."

"Fuck off, Jimbo."

Ben let go of my hand, taking a step forward. "They're right. What's it going to take?"

With the air of one greatly wounded, Mal turned to Anne. She too nodded, giving him a small smile.

"What I did was wrong. I gave you my word and I should have kept it." Hands to his sides, Ben faced Mal. "We've been friends since we were kids. Never should've given you reason to doubt me. I'm sorry."

"And you got her pregnant," bit out Mal.

"Yeah. But I'm not saying sorry for that. Never giving my kid cause to think they're not wanted."

Mal's eyes narrowed as he appraised Ben anew.

"This ain't good for Liz," Ben said, "getting caught in the shit between us. She doesn't need the stress." With a deep breath, Ben held his chin high. "What's it going to take?"

"Three," said Mal.

"Not the face." David moved in closer to the pair. "Agreed?"

"Gotta keep him pretty for the pictures," said Jimmy.

"Fine." Mal flexed his wrists, curling his right hand into a fist. "Don't want to damage these precious hands anyway."

"Wait!" I rushed forward, comprehension finally dawning. "You are not talking about hitting him. Over my dead body."

The other women looked resigned, concerned, combinations of both. None of them would interfere, however. It was there in their eyes. Fuck them.

Ben turned, grabbing hold of my arm and setting me back a pace. "Stay over there. Just in case."

"Ben. No."

"We need it done with."

"You are not letting him hit you."

"Liz—"

"I'm serious!"

"Sweetheart, it's okay," he said, eyes gentle but face set. "Calm down. We've been friends a long time. You got to let us work this one out our own way."

Like hell. "Anne, help me!"

My sister just grimaced. "Maybe he's right. Maybe we need to stay out of it."

"If this was Mal, would you stay out of it?" The thought

of Ben getting hurt, of Mal doing the hurting, and me being the cause . . . I basically wanted to vomit. "Mal, you lay one finger on him and I swear I am never talking to you again."

The idiot just rolled his eyes. "Please. I saw the sappy-ass way you just looked at him. He'll talk you 'round."

Then, before Ben was ready for it, Mal smashed his fist into the man's stomach. The breath whooshed out of Ben audibly and I winced. He bent forward, instinctively pro-tecting himself. Without pause, Mal delivered the second blow, a sharp jab to Ben's side. Ben grunted, rearing back, and Mal slammed him once more in the belly. My own belly contracted in empathy. He'd done it, Mal had really done it.

The silence that followed was stunning. Ben's harsh breathing filled the room as Mal held his hand out for shaking. It was over.

I'd seen a couple of fights in my life. One particularly nasty one in a backstreet during my wild period. Then of course there was the night my pregnancy had been an-nounced. At least the scent of blood didn't feature this time. Violence never fixed anything. Mal not waiting un-til Ben was ready, hitting him before he'd had a chance to brace for the blow, hurting the man I cared (too much) about. . . . Emotion tangled me up, turning me inside out. I didn't know whether to burst into tears or to start beat-ing on things myself.

Stupid hormones. Stupider boys.

"All good?" asked Mal.

"Yeah. Nice one with that opening hit." Ben slowly straightened, pain flashing across his face. Then he shook his bandmate's hand. The guys slapped each other's backs and the women wore relieved smiles. These people were fucking insane.

"Float like a butterfly, sting like a bee." With his fists held high, Mal jumped around. "Lizzy, babe, c'mon. It's manly man's business. You wouldn't understand, kid. You just gotta go with it."

"You . . ." I searched my mind but there wasn't a word harsh enough, an insult vile enough. Violence it was. I'd wipe that smile off his face. Top lip raised in a snarl, I stalked toward him, my bitch-slapping hand at the ready.

Unfortunately, Ben was at the ready too.

"No you don't." He swung me up into his arms, cradling me against him. "It's over."

"Put me down."

"Time for breakfast, remember? Let's go."

I swore up a storm, the whole no foul language thing long forgotten. What can I say? It was a heated moment.

"Whoa," said Mal, eyes wide with surprise. "She's a fierce critter."

On the other side of the room, Ev opened the door and we made straight for it. Involuntarily on my part. "No. Ben—"

"What did you want in your omelet?"

"Put me down."

"And how about some juice? You want juice too?"

"Do not patronize me. I am not a child."

"Believe me, sweetheart, I know. Despite the tantrum you're throwing right now."

"This is not a tantrum! This is me being outraged at Mal hitting you."

The door closed shut behind us and we stood in yet another long hotel hallway. Red carpet this time, with groovy art deco mirrors lining the walls. Ben's long-ass legs got us as far away from Mal and Anne's suite as fast as they could manage. Outside another doorway he paused, carefully setting me down while keeping one arm around my waist—in case of any escape attempts, no doubt. He slid a card through the lock and pushed open the door, giving me an encouraging nudge in the desired direction.

Inside, he sealed the door shut, slumped back against it. Then he just kind of stared at me.

"What?" I grouched, crossing my arms.

The corner of his mouth crept up.

"It's not funny. I can't believe you let him hurt you."

With a hearty sigh, Ben raised his arms, lacing his fingers on top of his head. Still staring.

"That should not have happened," I said. "And it was my fault. You got hurt by one of your oldest friends because of me."

He blinked, the hint of a smile disappearing. "No. I let Mal take a couple of shots at me *because* he's one of my oldest friends. Shit, he's more than that. He's my brother. When shit went bad between Dave and me last year, he's the one that talked Dave around, smoothed it over. Now, I gave Mal my word on you, and I broke it. I deserved him being pissed at me, and between us we just sorted that out. End of story."

"I don't like it."

"You don't have to like it. This is between me and Mal."

"So what I think doesn't matter?"

"Not about this, no," he said, looking me right in the eye.

Assholes. I turned my back on him for a minute, pulling myself together. Everything inside of me was in flux, a crazy mess.

"Never had a woman try to protect me like that before," he said softly. "Mal was right, you're fierce."

I raised my chin, turning back to face him.

"Stubborn. Loyal."

I shrugged. "Hungry."

He laughed, pushing off from the door with one foot, coming toward me. Once more he placed a kiss on the top of my head. Without thought I leaned into him. Ben had somehow come to represent warmth and safety. A kind of home for Bean and me, despite my best efforts to keep a safe distance between us. But maybe home wasn't about the heart, exactly, but about something deeper. We'd made a child together, it made sense there'd be a link. No need for me to get all carried away.

I don't know.

My feelings for him hadn't particularly made me any wiser. They constantly pushed and pulled me in different, confusing directions. I didn't know if I'd ever figure it out. What I felt for him, however, and what I felt for Bean, were so extraordinarily big. I'd never known there was room in me for so much emotion. If I could just attach myself to him, that would be great. Perhaps he'd like a pet limpet. Ha! It was all probably just another weirdo hormonal thing and in five minutes I'd be all whatever about him. A girl could hope.

"You okay?" he asked with a smile.

"Fine."

"Do me a favor?"

"What?"

"Stay out of fights. Keep our baby safe."

"Good point," I groaned. "I kind of lost it back there."

"Yeah, you kind of did."

"Sorry."

"I'm a big boy, Liz. You can trust me to look after myself, okay? I'm not going to be letting anyone else take a swing at me. I hit the gym just about every day with Jim. I'm no delicate little flower you need to protect."

"Okay."

He set his hands on my shoulders and gazed down. "And I understand. I do. Shit's complicated, but if anyone laid a finger on you, I'd lose it too. You're going to have to get over it and forgive Mal, though. I meant what I said. This isn't good. No more fighting within our family. I want it finished."

I gave him a nod. "I'll work on it. But there's no way I'm living with them anymore. For lots of reasons. Time to get my own room."

"Liz, you've just been sick enough to be on a week's bed rest. Anne said your blood pressure is still gonna be an issue for a while. I don't think now's the time to be alone. What if something happens?"

"What's my alternative? Jimmy and Lena need their alone time right now. I'm not going to inflict myself upon them."

Deep sigh. "Yeah, you're right. You better move in with me."

"With you?" I asked, surprised.

"Well, yeah." He spread his arms wide. "I get two-bedroom suites 'cause I like my space. Plenty of room for you."

"What about your nightly parties? I don't want to be a downer, but . . ."

"They'll go somewhere else. Fuck, Vaughan and Down Fourth can have 'em in their room for a change. Not a problem."

I slumped in relief. It also worked well to hide the excitement bolting through me. Me and Ben living together. Wow. What a notion. "Sounds great!"

"Cool." He clapped his hands, rubbed them together. "This'll work out great. We'll be meshing, working on being friends and all. Plus I won't have to worry about you being on your own."

"Friends. Awesome."

That word. I had to translate it to happy in my mind. Make it work. Ben and I would be friends. Friends friends friends.

He held up his big paw. "Give me five, friend."

I did so, smacking my palm against his with great zest. Fire-truck, that hurt.

CHAPTER NINE

After Saint Louis came Washington, DC, followed by Philadelphia. It took until then for me to fully get my bounce back and to forgive Mal. Well, to begin to forgive Mal. As much as everyone else liked to rationalize it, the memory of him driving his fist into Ben's gut still felt too fresh. My bitch-slapping hand started to twitch every time he came near. I couldn't help it.

Ben and I living together had not been the astronomical step toward a bright and beautiful romantic future I might have secretly, stupidly hoped for.

But that was my problem, not his.

There'd definitely been no more hugging. As a roommate, he was very polite—and frequently absent. Yep, Ben was a busy boy. He'd emerge from his room grizzly and bed-headed at nine and we'd have breakfast together, which was nice. For an hour or so we'd chat over pancakes or eggs Benedict or whatever. Conversation usually revolved around my health and the movie I'd watched the night before. Then he'd disappear to "do band shit." I don't quite know what he did, but apparently it took him all day and well into the night. So I'd taken to sitting up in front of the TV, hoping to catch him when he came in at whatever time. Instead, I'd wake up tucked into my own bed, come morning.

All very friendly. I just needed to adjust. Still. And damn it, tonight I would. Tonight, my crush on him came to an end. It had to. The man really was hell on my heart and loins.

"Remind me again why we're here," said Anne, slipping her arm around my shoulders.

"To party."

"We're here to party?"

"How could you doubt it?" I smoothed the big, flowy black T-shirt down over my small bump of a belly.

"So long as we're not here to spy on Ben."

I scoffed. "As if I'd do that."

"'Cause you're so over him."

"Big-time. Huge. We're friends."

Anne made a humming noise. "Friends don't let friends stalk their friends."

"You and I aren't friends, we're sisters. Totally different." My jaw cracked on a particularly large yawn. Ugh. This growing a baby stuff really took it out of you. "You have to suck it up and support me no matter what crackpot crap I do."

"You two still sharing the suite but not the bedroom, huh?"

"Do you really want to know?" I asked, curious.

She sighed. "You're pregnant with his baby. I give up. Of all the males I might have chosen for you, he's not even remotely on the list. But at the end of the day, it's your choice, not mine."

I nodded, pleased.

"I just want you to know, you have options." Just like when we were kids, Anne twirled a lock of my hair around a finger and gave it a tug. I slapped at her hand, same as I'd always done. She grabbed my fingers and held on tight.

"Mal and I have been talking. However you want to do this, we're happy to support you. Whether that's move in with us or whatever."

"I appreciate that."

"And on the off chance you and Ben can't work things out, you don't need to worry about money."

"Ben wouldn't leave me hanging like that, Anne."

"I'm just saying—"

"I know. But trust me, I don't need to worry about money."

"No. You don't."

"Yeah, I really don't," I said, turning to face her. "He put six figures in my account before the tour started."

"Huh." The whites of Anne's eyes were showing. "Good. This makes me think better of the bearded wonder."

"Mm." It was a step up from her calling him the Sperminator, at least.

We sat huddled together in a single large lounge chair, watching the postconcert party get going. When I'd moved into Ben's two-bedroom suite, the party had changed location to the room of Down Fourth's singer. He shared the smaller suite with his girlfriend, the band's drummer. She'd been more than welcoming, if a little surprised, when we knocked on the door.

I had the worst feeling that Anne was right, though, and I shouldn't have come. Not to this room, this tour, none of it. Also, apparently my mood currently registered around the shitty level. Shooty. No, that didn't work. Crappy. Yes, *crappy* made for a suitable non-sweary replacement.

"I hate that I have to be looked after, that all of a sudden I'm no longer me, I'm a condition, a baby-making machine." I leaned my head against Anne's with a *Poor me* sigh. "Should have stayed in Portland and worked in the bookstore. I don't belong here."

"Of course you belong here. Don't be a dolt."

I gave her a half smile. "I sound pathetic. Quick, slap me with a wet fish or something."

"If only I had one handy. This baby sure makes you an interesting person to be around. I never know what mood I'll get next."

"You have no idea. I need to get laid so bad . . . my dreams are just one endless stream of pornography."

"Oh-kay. So go on, talk to me about him. I'll try to be open-minded."

"There's not much to say."

"You two looked pretty cozy when he stormed the castle to rescue you from your evil sister and brother-in-law."

I raised my brows.

"Sorry," she said. "When he pushed his way in because he was worried about you—kudos to him for caring—you two looked like you were getting on well. I take it this is no longer the case, since you're clearly unhappy and we're lurking here, waiting for him to appear."

"We're very polite. We're always texting, he checks on me constantly, and if I need him he's there. But . . . I don't know. It's not like we're really saying anything. We share the same space but we're living at a distance. He does his thing, I do mine. He gets up and goes, comes back in the early hours after drinking here with these guys."

She frowned.

How to explain it? It was all such a mess. "Thing is, I can't get over him when I'm living with him. The proximity doesn't work. It just turns me into some perverted weirdo, hopped up on pregnancy hormones, sniffing his dirty laundry."

"You sniffed his dirty laundry?" Anne gave me a look of much judgment.

"It was only a shirt."

She cleared her throat. "Right. Okay."

"Anyway, it doesn't feel right, the way things are. I invaded his private space, taking up the offer of moving in. It was a bad move. So I've been thinking about either heading home or getting my own room."

"Don't leave. Move back in with me and Mal. I promise we'll keep the sex noises under control."

"No way. I still get these horrible flashbacks of that night and wake up crying, terrified that some sexed-up howler monkey is going to attack me." The sniggering— I couldn't contain it if I tried. So I didn't.

"Funny," she said drily.

"Thanks. I amuse me."

"I hate the thought of you being on your own."

"I know. But I'm going to be a single parent, Anne. I am on my own, it's a fact of life. Time I got used to it." I shrugged. "I know you and Mal want to do what you can, and I appreciate it. I do. Bean's lucky. She's going to have an awesome extended family with all of you guys."

"She really is."

I gave Anne's knee a friendly squeeze. "I'm glad we could talk about this. I've missed talking to you."

"Sorry I was so judgy. It was just hard, with all our plans for you to study and everything."

"Yeah, I know."

We just about sat in each other's laps we were so close. After the last few months, I think we needed it.

"I keep telling myself that he and I are just going to be friends," I said, letting it all out, dumping the whole sorry story on her. "There's a deeply stupid part of me that's still holding out hope, however, that doesn't quite want to accept it. I can't sit in his hotel room waiting for him to come home so we can have some magical moment together that'll fix everything and make it right. He and I are never going to be like that. I just have to accept it."

My sister just stared at me. "You have real feelings for him, don't you?"

I snorted. I don't know, it just seemed ridiculous that she was still in denial after everything.

"Sorry. I guess I just always thought this was some crush you'd get over," she said. "But it's not."

"No. But it's way past time for me to move on. You're right there. Hence we are here, waiting for him to make an appearance. I'll see him in action, schmoozing with sexy women, and hopefully realize the depth of my silliness. Then I'll tell him it's time for me to go big and get my own room or go home." I picked up my glass of lemonade from the coffee table and took a sip.

Anne cocked her head, studying me. "Are you in love with him?"

Good question.

"I just thought . . . maybe seeing him in action isn't what you need," she said. "Maybe taking a stand would work better."

"Demanding he love me? I don't think that would work."

"Hmm. But back to the original question. Do you love him?"

"I'm not sure I even know what love is."

"Does it hurt?"

Air was apparently in short supply. I stared at my sister, confused at the question and yet completely understanding. And that question—I didn't want to answer it. I needed to concentrate on my definites. Bean. Being a mom. Things like that.

"Well?" she asked.

"Yes." And god I hated it. The truth sucked.

Slowly Anne nodded, no smile on her face. "I'm sorry."

"Anyway." My smile felt so impossibly plastic. It was a wonder my face didn't crack. "When he gets here, I'll talk to him. In the meantime, party-party girl, that's me. And I've got a feeling this one's going to be an all-nighter."

"It's nearly midnight. I'm impressed you've managed to stay awake this long."

"You're only saying that because I've been asleep by eight o'clock every night this week."

She smiled.

"You wait. Later we'll go completely crazy and do shots of warm milk. It'll be awesome."

"Living on the edge."

"I know, right?" I turned to look over my shoulder at my new, ever-present shadow. "You can do the honors and pour, Sam."

"I'll look forward to that, Miss Rollins." The security man gave me an austere nod, never taking his eyes off the room. Damn it. He joked and smiled with the members of the band. I'd witnessed it with my own two eyes. Eventually I'd wear him down.

From out in the hall came the unmistakable wailing of He Who Shall Not Be Named. Stage Dive had finally arrived. Or some of them. Mal barreled into the room, searching for his mate, while Ben wandered in at a more sedate pace, chatting to a dude I didn't recognize. Ben's hair was slicked back, his beard neatly trimmed. I guessed he'd changed shirts after the show, because this one was a black button-down, neatly ironed. The cuffs were rolled up, the top few buttons undone.

He looked lovely. Hell, he looked like love. Harps, angels, all of it. God, I was a sap. I really had to get this under control, for my own sanity's sake if nothing else.

The crowd suddenly seemed at capacity. I guess a lot of people had been hanging out downstairs in the hotel bar, waiting for the important people to arrive.

The mad drummer went down on one knee before Anne, holding out a hand. With a grin, she placed her fingers in his.

"Who is this unearthly creature I see before me?" he

asked. "You dazzle my eyes, mysterious stranger. I must know who you are immediately."

"I'm your wife."

"Thought you looked familiar." He kissed the back of her hand, turning to rest his spine against the bottom of the lounge chair, between her legs. "Fuck that was a long night. Adrian lined up an interview after the show. Next time the little butt-weasel does that, remind me to kill him."

"You got it."

"Work my shoulders please, Pumpkin," he asked, cracking his neck. "I hurt."

Anne started rubbing him down. "Book you a massage tomorrow?"

"You're the best." He gave me a pat on the knee. "Lizzy, you talking to me today?"

"I haven't decided yet," I said.

"Isn't much of it left, baby momma. Better make up your mind." He smirked. "Benny-boy know you're here?"

"I don't have to report my whereabouts to him," I sputtered.

Mal laughed. "No? This should be interesting."

"Tell him, Sam." I chugged down my lemonade.

"Miss Rollins is a fully grown, independent adult," the security man reported dutifully.

"Puh-lease," said Mal. "Fifty says he hauls her ass out of here within the next five minutes."

"You're on." Sam shook his hand.

Screw them both. If I had to choose, however, Sam would get the win. With no grace but with great purpose I wriggled and lifted, maneuvering my way up and out of the chair. "I'm going to the ladies' room."

"Oh now, c'mon. You can't hide from him," cried Mal. "That's not fair."

I just smiled.

"Benny-boy, look who's here! Why, it's sweet little Liz, and she's up way past her bedtime. Don't you think you should do something about that?"

The asshat. With swearing ruled out, I flipped Mal the bird. No way was he winning the bet. I'd talk to Ben when I was damn well good and ready. With all due haste, I ducked my head and made for the bathroom. The great thing about pregnancy is the way you basically always need to pee. It makes for such an awesome hobby. Sam took up guard duty outside as I opened the door and slipped in, shutting and locking it.

And wow, how about that. The bathroom was occupied.

"Hi." I raised a hand.

"Liz, hey." Vaughan laughed, one hand going down to cover his abundant essentials. "Guess I forgot to lock the door."

My face was on fire. "Guess so. Sorry to barge in."

"My bad. But good to see you."

"Good to see you too." And to see so very much of him. I stared, stunned. Whoa, the man was built. What this did to my already hormonally needy-in-the-sexwise charged state was a worry. "Yeah. Ha."

"Been wanting to catch up with you. How are you?" he asked, running a spare hand through his wet hair, all relaxed-like.

"Good."

"Heard you were sick," he said.

"It was just a cold. I'm fine now. Feeling great." And horny. Wildly horny. The boy didn't understand how close to being attacked he was.

"That sucks. Glad you're better."

"Thanks." As long as my eyes stayed on his face I was fine. It'd just been a while since I'd seen any downstairs action. No need for my cheeks to go thermonuclear. How uncool to get all fussed. Clearly the man himself had no such hesitation about nudity. "How's the tour been going?"

"Great. Really good."

"Excellent." I studied the floor. "Yeah. Should I leave?"

"No, stay. Fuck knows when we'll get another chance to talk alone."

"Ah, okay, sure. You maybe want to wrap a towel around your waist or put on some pants?"

"In a minute. I want to ask you a question first," he said, dimple flashing in his cheek. The man was seriously cute. Also, nice to know he was a natural redhead. I didn't mean to look, it just happened. A bare, unintended glimpse when I first walked in. A real live naked man smiling at me invitingly—my body liked the notion all too much. Crazy-ass hormones.

"Shoot," I invited, my face firing up yet again at the thought of his groin. Holy crap.

"You really pregnant?"

"Yes, I am." I flattened the oversize shirt again over my belly. Soon there'd be no chance of hiding it.

"Damn. And I take it the daddy's Ben, huh?"

My mouth stayed shut.

"Not so hard to figure out." He reached for a towel off the rack, wrapping it around slim hips. "There's tension between him and Mal, but no one's saying why. Then you come on tour."

I shrugged. Not my business to admit to anything on Ben's behalf. It was only on the part of my big mouth that Vaughan knew anything was afoot. Or abelly. I guess it should really be abelly.

"Dude definitely didn't like it last time we talked," he said.

"True." But who could explain why Ben said and did half the things he did when it came to me? I highly doubted even he had a clue.

"Then the parties move to here because you're sharing his room, all of a sudden. Even I could figure that one out, and I'm apparently not the most perceptive."

I narrowed my eyes, outraged on his behalf. "Who said that? I think you're great."

"Thanks." He grinned, hands on hips. It might have been my imagination, but I'm pretty sure his towel was sliding down. Man, if I could just stop looking. Me and my hand needed some alone time. Again.

"I think you're great too," Vaughan said, his eyes going soft as he stared at me. "Sucks that the situation's the way it is."

"Yeah." Or did it? How often did I get a pass from a very nice man with such enviable assets? "I mean, he and I aren't *together* together. I'm single. But yeah, definitely pregnant."

We both jumped at the sudden knocking. Then Ben's deep voice boomed out from the other side of the door, "Liz, you in there?"

Vaughan and I looked at each other, something uneasy stirring deep inside of me. God, was that guilt? I had no reason to feel guilt. None at all. Though the idea of explaining how I accidentally stumbled in on a wet, naked Vaughan could probably wait for later. Forever would also be fine.

"Be out in a minute," I called back.

" 'kay."

"He treating you right?" asked Vaughan, his voice dropping in volume.

"I think he'll be a good father."

"Not what I'm asking." He took a step closer, studying my face intently. Outside, the music took a dramatic jump in volume. Good timing.

I didn't know what to say. Or think. "I, um, I'd appreciate you not saying anything about the baby to anyone yet."

"'Course."

"I better go."

"Sure," he said. "Ben's waiting."

"Right. Yes. Going." I fumbled behind me for the door handle, giving him a slightly dazed smile.

Vaughan stepped to the side, out of the line of sight. What a surprising encounter. Guess I'd finally started glowing. Of course, it might be the boobs. After I'd had the baby perhaps I'd consider implants, if this was the sort of attention they got me. Ha! Just joking. Mostly.

The minute I stepped outside, Ben was standing there, waiting, looming. Immediately my body went on high alert. I searched his face for his mood, read his body language (mildly impatient with a trace of don't-poke-the-bear cranky). There could be no denying that Vaughan was built and pretty. You'd have to be two days dead not to get turned on at the sight of him naked. But even then, Vaughan hadn't gotten to me like this. The moment I came into Ben Nicholson's orbit I was helpless, powerless to re-sist his pull. Foolish heart and vagina. The brain knew bet-ter but no one was listening.

People now filled the room and music was blasting out of the stereo. Ben bent, putting his mouth near my ear. "Anne said you wanted to talk. Let's head up to the room, yeah?"

I nodded.

"Everything okay?" he asked. And man, he'd asked me that question over and over again in so many different ways lately. I was tired of putting a smiley face on it.

"Let's talk upstairs."

He put an arm around me, safely guiding me out of the crowded room. People were dancing, drinking, who knows what. It was a regular rock 'n' roll hootenanny. We stayed silent, waiting for the elevator. When it arrived it was empty.

"Have a good night?" I asked, stepping inside.

"Explain something to me," he said, backing me up against the nearest wall.

"Ah, what?"

With muscular arms braced above my head, he narrowed his eyes on me. "I heard another voice in that bathroom. A man's voice."

I wasn't going to lie to him. I had no reason to. "Yes, I was talking to Vaughan."

"You were talking to Vaughan in the bathroom?" His head lowered, nose coming close to touching the tip of my own. The man had a raging fire in his dark eyes, I kid you not. Actual real live jealousy, burning bright.

"Are you serious?" I asked, deeply confused because I couldn't afford to be elated. Any minute now he'd do his usual thing and run. Just like in his truck that night. Just like in Vegas. I didn't really think I could handle it again. Not now. My life felt precarious enough as it was, so susceptible to sudden, extreme change.

"Very," he said, clearly cranky. "I already warned him off you."

"But you and I are just friends, remember?"

He blinked, outrage momentarily suspended by surprise.

"We already had this conversation and that's what you said you wanted," I said. "And now you're looking like you want to pee on my shoes to mark your territory." I shook my head. "What's going on here?"

"We need to talk."

"Yeah, good idea."

"Did he make a pass at you?"

"Not about that," I groaned. "Ben, I'm getting my own room. You do your thing and have your space, and I'll do the same. I think we'll get along a lot better long-term that way. That's what we decided, right? So that's what's happening. Decision made."

"Because of Vaughan?" he asked, his back teeth grinding.

"Vaughan has nothing to do with this. Because of us having a baby. Because of you and me and this crappy cycle we've got going on where I get my hopes up and then you run away or hide behind the *friends* thing. It's completely doing my head in. It's not healthy." I set my hands against his chest and pushed him back a step. "You know, you pretend to be this easy come, easy go, laid-back kind of guy. No ties or commitment, just living the rock 'n' roll lifestyle to the limit and all that. And hey, that's just awesome, Ben. Good for you. But if that's who you want to be, then don't go making a separate set of rules for me. Because that's as hypocritical as fuck."

Whoops. Another dollar for the swear jar.

His jaw shifted angrily. Or his beard did. Whatever.

"Good night." The elevator doors slid open and I slid out, walking so fast I was damn near running. Time to get my stuff packed. If there wasn't a spare room, I'd share with Anne and Mal for the night, make other arrangements in the morning. Man, I was so tired. Could have sworn my limbs weighed more than a mountain. If I was glowing, it sure as hell didn't feel like it at this time of night.

"I never wanted to be in a relationship," he yelled from back down the shiny hotel hallway.

"Congratulations. You're not." I gave him the bird too, because the bird was not swearing.

"Lizzy! Fuck. Wait."

I slid my key through the door lock and hustled my ass on in. Not locking him out, though it was tempting. But hell, one of us needed to be the adult. I charged on through the living room and into my room, grabbing a suitcase from out of the closet. It was already over half full. When you only ever stopped for two nights at a time, there never seemed much point in unpacking. A few items were hung up—a coat and a couple of dresses. The rest had gone to the laundry service. There was just my makeup and junk in the en suite, a couple of pairs of shoes strewn on the floor, and I was good to go. Vacating the premises, ahoy!

"You're leaving," he said, standing in the bedroom doorway.

"Yep."

"Liz . . ."

"Hmm?" I turned, waiting for whatever nonsense he'd try to sell me on next. The big man just stood there, though, face set in harsh lines.

And he had nothing.

"Probably for the best," I said. "I'm not sure there's anything either of us could say right now that would help. Let's take some time to calm down and talk about it tomorrow, okay?" Yeah. Toothbrush, hairbrushes, and all that crap got thrown into my toiletries bag, which was then shoved into the corner of the suitcase. Next went my Converse, Birks, and fancy sandals with a heel. Then everything out of the cabinet. "You know, I think if we have our own space we might actually be able to give the being friends thing a good shot."

No comment.

Over went the top of the suitcase and I started zipping it up. Better call someone up to help me carry it, since I doubted Ben was in the mood to be helpful. If I'd been warned once about lifting heavy objects "in my condition," I'd been warned a hundred times. I'd mosey on down to reception and—

Ben's hand slipped around to cup my jaw, his lips pressing firmly against mine. My mouth had been partially open already; no big deal for him to slide his tongue in and rub it against mine. He kissed me determinedly, taking me over. Christ, I could feel that down in my toes. They curled up tight, along with my eager insides. The edges of his beard brushed against my face and his other hand grabbed my ass, pulling me in tight against him. Already the man was thickening, getting hard. It felt so superlatively, unbelievably good. All of it.

And wrong.

"W-what are you doing?"

His reply was the lash of his hot, wet tongue against the side of my neck. Every nerve-ending in the vicinity went up in flames, while I went up on my toes, leaning into him, getting closer. No. Bad me. This wasn't what we were supposed to be doing at all.

"Oh god. Maybe we should talk now."

The man's hands, they were so clever. Beneath the skirt of my jersey and up and into the back of my panties before I had a clue where they were even heading. Strong fingers kneaded my butt cheeks while his teeth sank into the base of my neck. He groaned as my breath stuttered, my lungs contracting sharply.

"I'm supposed to be going."

If I could just keep my legs shut I might yet win this battle. It seemed an insurmountable task, given the array of his arsenal. The size of his artillery. One hand dived down further, stroking between my legs, while the other held the back of my head. I was helpless, the battle lost. God, I sucked. All right, so I was too turned on to think straight and my hormones were in open rebellion. Any attempt at coherent, rational thought was mercilessly slain upon the altar of my lust. Damn it.

"B-Ben."

In a move proving he was indeed one of the greats of rock 'n' roll, he kicked my suitcase clear off the queen bed with one big, black boot while dipping me back into his waiting arm, while moving his hand around to the front of my panties to apply pressure to my clit in the most amazing way. Holy hell. Stars danced before my eyes,

I was so ready to light up for him. Vegas had nothing on me.

Someone really needed to give him an award, though. Something to do with multitasking and hot sex moves and shit. Shoot.

My back hit the mattress and he climbed over me, situating himself between my legs. Fuck he was gorgeous. The strong, clean lines of his cheekbones and the moody-ass gonna-get-me-laid darkness of his eyes. I couldn't catch my breath, but it didn't matter. My breasts straining against his chest was its own reward. It was entirely possible I currently owned the hardest, happiest nipples in all of creation. They were so sensitive.

Who said pregnancy isn't fun?

He covered my mouth with his, kissing me stupid once more. Man, he tasted good. All the while he kept his weight on one elbow, putting no pressure on my belly. The things he could do with his free hand were delightful—running it up and down the outside of my thigh, slipping it up, up beneath my shirt to trace my ribs. But wait . . . I couldn't give up this easy. It was shameful. I'd been in the middle of making a point and everything.

"I was leaving. I was."

No answer from him. Instead, his hard cock rubbed back and forth between my legs, making my back bow. One pair of jeans and one pair of panties too many. That was the problem right there.

I gasped. "I don't think friends that are just friends are meant to do this."

Without comment he sat up, grabbing the back of his button-down shirt and pulling it off over his head. His chest was so pretty. So hard and big and stuff, it made my IQ drop to my shoe size. Everything about him did. The bearded sex machine turned me into a stuttering fool. Sad but true.

"Ben, I can't just spread for you the minute you decide you want some."

Sitting back on his heels, he grabbed both of my legs, holding them up against him. Off went my shoes, followed fast by my panties.

"Wait."

He didn't.

"Maybe I'm not interested in having sex with you." A blatant lie. But I was getting desperate for some kind of communication from him of the nonphysical sort. "Did you think of that?"

His gaze on mine, he held my underwear up to his nose.

"Oh my god, do not sniff my panties. Ben!"

A slow grin spread across his face.

"That's terrible. You don't see me going around doing stuff like that, do you? No." On account of me not wearing any pants, they couldn't catch on fire. Lucky.

He threw the innocent, soaked scrap of material aside.

"Anyway, my vagina is out of control. That proves nothing."

He placed a soft kiss against one of my fat ankles, giving it a good looking over.

"And don't look at my ankles. You know how I feel about them." I tried to retrieve my limbs, but he held on tight, wrapping both arms around them, holding them to his hot chest. "Why are you doing this?"

Slowly, he started one-handed massaging my toes. Nice, but beside the point.

"Say something."

"You said there wasn't anything I could say that would fix things," he mumbled, his warm, wet mouth kissing the side of my foot, his beard ticklish in just the right way. "Figured I'd just show you why you should stay."

"Sex?"

"Seems to be what you want right now."

I snorted. "You started it."

The bastard smirked. "Tell me more about your pussy being out of control. This interests me."

"No." Me and my idiot mouth. "Nothing to tell."

The lethal combination of his soft, warm lips and sleek beard was doing me in. The heat and strength of his body. Every time he touched me, I could have sworn there were sparkles inside of my skin. Little lights burning me up in the sweetest possible way. How the hell was a girl supposed to compete against that? The man had sexual superpowers and I was just me, dysfunctional at the best of times.

"Why do you want me to stay?" I asked, voice ever so slightly pleading. I didn't even know what for. Fingers wrapped around my ankles, rubbing gently. "Because of the baby?"

"No," he said. "Because of everything."

" 'Everything' being . . ."

His forehead went all wrinkly. "I don't know. I meant what I said. I never wanted to be in a relationship. But then you never wanted to be having a baby so young. Guess we're both just going to have to figure it out as we go along."

"Um, no." I shut my eyes tight. "Ben, we've been here before. You think you want something with me but then it's all too much and you run. And it's okay. It's okay for you to just concentrate on your music and living free and easy and to not want to be in a permanent relationship. What's not okay is for you to get my hopes up again, because honestly the comedown really sucks."

And that was my professional psychology student opinion, right there.

"Liz."

"No. I can't do this again."

He fell silent.

Too much emotion ran through me, my body at odds with my sensibilities. Damn, this was hard. I drew back from him and started crawling off the bed. A nice long cry in a hot shower, that's what I needed. Plus to get off. This hotel had an excellent showerhead and I'd be making the most of it, yessiree. And maybe some ice cream too. It really was an excellent remedy for a broken heart.

"Wait." A strong arm stopped me, drawing me back against his body. I just went. The man had the muscles to put me where he wanted—he'd already demonstrated it on numerous occasions. Me liking being in his arms would just have to be ignored.

"Why?" I cried. "C'mon, Ben. Give me a legitimate reason. Why should I stay?"

"Because of this." One oversize hand splayed across my belly, his tanned skin a stark contrast to my own. "Because of us. We made a baby, Liz. You and me."

"Ben . . ."

"Shh. Relax. Give me a minute here."

Easy for him to say; he wasn't having yet another emotional breakdown. Fire-trucking hormones. That I wanted him so bad didn't help at all. Sexual frustration seemed to own me. But the risk of emotional damage was too damn high.

"Didn't realize you'd gotten so big." His fingers gently stroked my bump. "It's only been a week."

"Yeah," I sniffled. "I kind of popped."

His nose nuzzled my neck, lips placing gentle kisses. "Have you ever seen anything more amazing in your life? Our baby growing inside of you."

I nodded, covering his hand with my own. "I know."

"Then share it with me. I want to see you every day. I want to know how you two are doing, and be a part of things." Despite his soothing words, I couldn't help but tense up in his arms. "You're beautiful. Relax."

"You try relaxing with a huge boner rubbing against your back. I'm trying to break up with you—not that we're even together—and your penis is not helping."

Next came soft laughter, but he made no move to remove said hard-on from the area surrounding my buttocks.

"You're going to have to get over being jealous," I said. "Eventually I'll meet someone else. You can't go caveman every time a guy speaks to me. Baby or no, you don't have the right, Ben."

"Then give me the right."

"So you can get scared and bolt? No."

"Shit. Look, I can't get over you, Liz. That's the problem." He rested his chin on my shoulder. "You're the only girl I want."

I stilled. Well, apart from the frown. "It this about your erectile issue? Because you don't seem to be having much of a problem right now."

"I don't have an erectile issue. I have a *you* issue. My dick thinks you own it, apparently. But there's more to it than that. . . ."

"Cocks don't think. We went over that."

"We were wrong."

"Huh. So I have a pet penis. Okay, keep talking." Curiosity had definitely gotten the better of me. "What more?"

Heat flooded the side of my neck as he pressed his face there. "Can't fucking stand the thought of someone else touching you."

I rolled my eyes. Such a Neanderthal. And while both were interesting points, neither constituted an occasion for any actual change from our status as friends.

"It's not just about the baby." He grunted.

"I'm not so sure about that," I said, resting my head

against his. Foolish of me, but it felt nice, cozying up to him. Besides, he'd grabbed me first.

"It's the truth."

"Prove it."

"Prove it? How the fuck am I supposed to do that?"

"I don't know."

"Christ. All right. I only used Sasha . . ." The rest was a mumbled mess. His warm mouth pressed against my neck, smothering the words.

"What did you say?"

More mumbling.

"Ben, speak clearly."

With a groan, he raised his head, leaning around to look me in the eyes. "I only used Sasha to get over you. Knew you couldn't be just a casual thing, and Mal kept asking what had happened in Vegas, if I'd gone out with you or what. Then he started saying you were seeing someone and he thought you were bringing them to the party."

"What?" I asked, screwing up my nose.

"Yeah."

"Why the hell would he do that?"

"Why do you think?"

"God that man is such a shit stirrer." Another coin for the swear jar. It'd be funding Bean's college education and first home at this rate. A gap year touring Europe, perhaps.

"Always has been, always will be. So I invited Sasha to that dinner to get him off my back. And I was missing you, and you wouldn't talk to me, and I thought you were bringing someone else."

I just shook my head.

"I don't know if it was just me trying to make you jealous or if a part of it was me trying to move on or what. She was a cool woman."

My chin jerked up. "You thought she was cool?"

"You didn't?"

"I didn't think she was that cool," I said in a voice without a trace of snobbery. Not even the merest hint.

"No?"

"I'm just saying, I thought she was a little bit know-it-all, really. Arrogant. And her hair was dumb. So . . . blue." Her hair was impossibly cool, but no way was I admitting to that.

The silence behind me was deafening.

"What?"

"Nothing," he said in a voice that implied anything but.

"Oh shut up." I sighed. "Fine, she was somewhat cool." At some point I'd started playing with his fingers, twining them with mine, touching and toying with them. This was the problem with Ben. For me, being intimate with him came far too easily.

"Anyway," he said. "That was all before I knew about the baby."

"That was a deeply crappy and immature thing to do to her."

"Yeah," he said solemnly.

"No wonder she was mad."

A nod.

Fingers caressed the side of my face tenderly.

"I'd have gone medieval on your man bits, if I was her," I said.

His brows descended in a fierce look.

I just shrugged. Reap what you sow, baby.

"Had to pay her off to keep quiet about you. Adrian and the lawyers sorted it out."

"No! The bitch."

"Hmm."

I huffed out a breath. "So we've established that we make each other behave like we're back in middle school. What does that prove?"

"That we need to figure this thing out between us."

"I thought that's what we've been trying to do."

A hand cupped my jaw. "I don't mean fight it. I'm done fighting it. I mean go slow and figure this thing out."

My forehead was a mass of wrinkles, I could feel it. I doubt my heart was much better.

"Sweetheart?"

"I don't trust you, Ben. I'm sorry. I wish I could feel differently. But I keep trying to do this with you, and thinking you want it too, and . . ."

"And I keep fucking it up."

"Yes."

I thought he'd let me go, run off back to the party to lick his wounds—or someone else maybe. But he didn't. Instead he settled on the bed with his back to the headboard, taking me with him, arranging me in his lap. I didn't fight him.

"Are you angry?" I asked, mystified.

"How do they say . . ." He made a low noise that was pure damn sex of the vocal chords, I tell you. "Lizzy, when you say you don't trust me it makes me feel like I want to tear shit up and go ballistic."

"That's an understandable if somewhat violent response."

"But with our history, shit's complicated," he said, rubbing his mouth and bristly beard against the back of my neck, sending shivers down my spine. Oh wow yeah. I needed to wear my hair up all the time. That felt divine.

"And as you said, we're having a baby," he said.

"True."

"But I'm not running away this time. Say what you want. Shred me. I'm staying."

"You are?"

"Yeah." Capable hands separated my legs, hot skin

soothing up my thighs. Christ, I loved it when he touched me. So damn much.

"What are you doing?" I asked, ever so slightly breathy.

"Nothing."

The backs of his fingers ran up my inner thighs, tracing a path with his knuckles. I nearly cried when he stopped short of my pussy and turned back.

"I do not believe you."

Neatly, he folded up my skirt, exposing it all. A sound of pure sex vibrated out of his chest, traveling through into my spine. "Fuck, Liz. Look at you. Love your pussy. Missed it."

"Mm." My shoulders tensed, rising higher. "Ben . . ."

"It's okay."

"This feels dangerous."

"No. This feels right," he murmured, teeth nipping at my ear. "You got my dick on a leash. Might as well have the rest of me."

"What does that mean?"

"Means I've given up getting over you and I'm focusing on getting into you instead."

"Neither of these statements are reassuring me, Ben." I leaned my head back, twisting to the side so I could see his face. Seemed sincere. But then, I'd made that mistake a time or two before. "Explain in non–rock 'n' roll speech please."

"And you said Sasha had an attitude." The corner of his lips twitched. "Means I'm going to get you to trust me again."

Me? I had nothing.

Staring at me all the while, he stuck two fingers in his mouth to wet them. Then he ever so slowly traced them back and forth over my labia, making me gasp. Everything down there spasmed in glee. Lord help me. If the man ever guessed to what degree he owned me, I'd be doomed.

"Fuck, sweetheart. You really are out of control. I've barely touched you."

"It's the baby hormones. They're psycho."

He smiled. That smile—I didn't trust it. But holy hell was it beautiful. My heart and my loins went into bloom. A rush of heat and emotion crashed through me. It was entirely possible I was in love with the bearded jerk, god help me. "You really want me to trust you?" I asked.

He drew slow circles around my clit before sliding the tip of a finger back and forth through me. The man slowly played with me. Pure, exquisite torture.

"Yeah," he said. "I really do."

"You're serious about this? Us?"

"I am." Still not breaking eye contact, he slid a finger into me. "You're very wet."

"Yeah. You know, it's kind of hard to focus on relationship talk when you're fingering me."

"We can talk all you want later. Promise."

"'kay." I made a pitiful noise in my throat, my muscles tightening on his thick digit. My own hands were claws, digging into his rock-hard, jean-clad thighs.

"I mean, you got hot for me in Vegas. But this . . . Sweetheart, Christ, this is fucking awesome."

"I masturbate. A lot."

"Not anymore," he rumbled. "Looking after you is my job. Trust me, Lizzy. I won't let you down again."

The finger inside me sought a sweet spot and proceeded to massage it with expert ease. Just that simply, he turned me inside out. It was a mercy my nipples didn't poke holes through the fabric of my shirt. They sure as hell felt hard enough. My shoulders pushed back against his solid chest as the side of his thumb brushed back and forth across my clit. Lightning and shooting stars and all of the good stuff. The whole world went to white.

I throttled the scream in my throat. Or at least part of it. Oh boy and damn. I lay panting in his lap, my skin over-sensitized, sweat beading on my forehead and back. How perfect.

He gently cupped my pussy with his hand. "I can still feel you throbbing."

I stretched and yawned, slowly coming back down to earth. All of the happy was mine.

"You really needed that."

"Yeah." I turned, cuddling against his chest. If I stayed sort of on my side, the bump was happy enough. And what a nice, big, comfortable man he was. Especially helpful when it came to orgasms too. His fingers were far superior to my own, I had to say.

"You going to sleep on me now?" he asked, incredulous.

I nodded, closing my eyes. Damn he smelled good. They should bottle his sweat. I'd buy it in bulk. Meanwhile his hard-on continued to press into my hip. Bad luck, bud. I was down and out for the count. No could do.

"You wanted to go slow," I said.

Disgruntled rumbling came from beneath me.

"You really want to be my boyfriend?" I asked, half opening one eye.

A hand smoothed down the fabric of my skirt and he shuffled us down the bed a little, getting comfortable.

"Boyfriend? Huh." His rough, deep voice rolled through me, lulling me further toward sleep. "Never been anyone's boyfriend before."

"No?"

"No."

Arms encircled me, the bristle of his beard brushing

against my forehead as he settled back against the cushions.

"Your boyfriend," he mused.

"It's a big decision. You should take your time, think about it. Let me know when you're ready to talk about it again."

His forehead creased. "You sure are playing it cool."

And about time, frankly. Lord knows, chasing after the man hadn't gotten me anywhere. A girl could only beat her brains against a brick wall for so long before it was time to rethink things.

I shrugged and slid my hand up his side, getting closer. His skin was so smooth, his smattering of chest hair delightful to the touch. Everything about him was delightful really. In all likelihood, even his toenails would thrill me. Didn't mean I'd be making it too easy on him.

"Liz?"

"Hmm?"

"This boyfriend position . . . it come with perks?"

"Maybe."

"Do I get to sleep with you and shower with you?"

"Yes."

He made a happy noise. "What about touching? Do I get to feel you up when I like?"

"Within reason."

"Got to say, sweetheart, your body was always gorgeous. But it's seriously off-the-fucking-charts beautiful right now."

"Really?" I asked, raising my head to give him a curious look. "Mostly I just feel leaky and lumpy."

A large hand cupped an ass cheek, rubbing. "Fuck no. You're all soft curves and you're carrying my baby. Never thought that'd be a big turn-on—never thought about it at all. But, sweetheart, it is."

"Huh."

"What else is involved in this boyfriend shit?" he asked, his voice rumbling through his chest and into my ear.

" 'This boyfriend shit'? Seriously?"

"Sorry. You know what I mean." He gave me a squeeze. "What else? C'mon."

"All right. Let me think." I trailed my fingers through his beard, sliding them back and forth through the soft whiskers. I could lie on him all night, happily, listening to his heart beating strong and steady within his chest. Feel the rhythmic rise and fall of his ribs with each breath. To lie there and know that this special man was alive and chose to be with me, here, right now. That sounded just like heaven.

"You know, I'm really not sure myself," I said in a quiet voice. "I've never had an official boyfriend before. But we have to be there for each other, and we have to talk. I don't see how it could work any other way."

"Hmm."

"And obviously, we'd be exclusive."

A grunt.

"If you decide it's what you want, then we take it slow and figure it out as we go, I guess."

"Yeah." He rubbed the heel of his hand gently up and down my back, smoothing out the tension.

"Ben, I don't want to take your freedom. I just want a place in your world. An important one."

He craned his neck, tipping my chin up to make me look at him at the same time. "Sweetheart, you've been important since day one. Only girl I kept coming back to. Didn't matter how far I ran, I couldn't get you off my mind. Never been this way about another woman."

"No?"

"No."

Fingers rubbed at my neck, working out the kinks. Silence fell between us for a while.

"I want to be your boyfriend, Liz."

I couldn't have held back the smile if I'd tried. "I'd like that."

He brushed the hair back from my face, gazing down at me. "Okay."

"Okay."

CHAPTER TEN

I slept well that night. Tattooed, bearded, bass-playing males easily outdid hotel pillows in terms of comfort. We slept in our underwear because of the whole taking it slow thing. I'd never spent the whole night with a man before, sexually active or no. But what could have been awkward, Ben made right. He fit himself into my life just like he belonged there.

My dreams were suitably pervy, though that was nothing new. The waking up with a man's head between my thighs, however, was a rather dramatic and welcome change. A hot, wet tongue dragged through the lips of my sex, startling the hell out of me. My hips bucked, eyes were suddenly wide open.

"Ben. What are you doing?" I gasped, the brain still in sleep mode.

"Licking my girlfriend's pussy," he said. "Perks, remember?"

Hands held my legs spread open, fingers digging into the flesh of my thighs. Then he did it again, the licking thing. I groaned and twisted, trying to get away, but not really, because holy shit. Nirvana.

"Go you," I happy-sighed.

The feeling of a man's beard brushing against your private parts cannot be adequately explained in words. It's a tactile delight. Soft and ticklish and amazing in all the ways. My muscles tensed, heels digging into the mattress. Where my panties had gotten to I had no idea. Nor any interest. What my boyfriend was up to, however, concerned me deeply. His tongue flicked back and forth over my clit, then his lips sucked at my labia. The man's oral skills were off the chart. Such attention to detail. And the enthusiasm—the man was starving and I was his meal. I shoved my pussy into his face, needing and getting everything he was giving.

But the raw energy between my hips, low in my spine—there wasn't enough me to contain it. The glorious sensation built and built, charging my whole being, lighting up my limbs. I came hard, calling his name. Pleasure tore me in two, my mind circling high. I was everything and nothing. Just floating around in the ether, enjoying the high.

But he wasn't finished.

He climbed up my body, shoving his boxer briefs down with a hand. Once, twice, three times he pumped his hard cock, spilling his hot seed on my breasts and belly. His forehead pressed against mine, warm breath on my lips.

"Hey," I mumbled, still trying to find my breath.

He kissed me, lips covering mine, tongue diving in. The rich taste filled my mouth as his fingers stroked over my belly, rubbing his cum into my skin.

"Morning," he whispered, still suspended above me on one elbow. Those perfect cheekbones, the wet curves of his lips, called to my fingers. I could happily touch him all day.

"Ben."

"Hmm?" Another kiss, this one softer, sweeter.

I lay beneath him, decimated. So many things I could

say, that I wanted to say. But *slow* was the key word here. What he did to my heart and mind couldn't be described. The way he filled my heart to overflowing scared the crap out of me. "Good morning."

"No touching yourself," he ordered in a low, gruff voice. "Getting you off is my job now. You need me, call. Get to you as soon as I can, okay?"

"Uh-huh."

He kissed me some more, making my head spin. "Things moving slow enough for you?"

"Sure."

He smiled, and good god, all I could do was stare. Had there ever been a more beautiful man in existence? I think not. His focus on me was complete, making for such a heady feeling. Dark eyes never strayed from my face, as if he was memorizing me.

"We're doing good, Liz." His hand covered my bump, lips brushing over my cheek.

"Yeah." I had no words. Not when he was like this.

The edge of his lips picked up some. "C'mon. Shower time."

I was still in the bathroom, fixing my hair and applying some concealer and mascara to up my glow factor, when I heard Ben and Sam chatting in the living room. No way did I mean to listen in. It just sort of happened.

"With Mal the way he is, the band's already on tenterhooks," said Ben. "I'm just not sure we should add her to the mix."

Wait, were they talking about me? But I was basically already living and touring with everyone. That made no sense.

"I love Martha, but we all know what she's like," Ben continued.

"Things are more stable now. It might be good for her,"

said Sam. "Besides, she's not going to get her shit together out there on her own, acting like the party queen of New York and burning through money."

"I don't know."

Sam made a *humph* sound. "She still makes the papers now and then. From a security perspective, it'd be easier having everyone in the same orbit, if not under one roof. News will hit about the pregnancies eventually. Be good to keep everyone close. That's my only point."

"Sure your concern about Martha isn't more personal than that?"

"Don't know what you're talking about, Mr. Nicholson."

I wandered in, curious, interrupting the very manly staring competition under way. "Hi, guys. Problem?"

Ben shook his head. "What are sisters for if not to fuck with your life now and then, right?"

"Just think about it." Sam clapped him on the shoulder, heading for the door. "Later, Miss Rollins."

"Bye." I turned to my boyfriend, gave his T-shirt an affectionate tug, drawing him in closer for a kiss. "Anything we need to talk about?"

"No." He gave me a gentle smile and an even gentler kiss. Followed by a hearty slap on the ass. "Go do your girl thing. I'm meeting Jim for a run."

I made a swipe at his butt but missed by about a mile. "Yeah, you better run, buddy."

He laughed all the way out the door. I held the dumb smile on my face for even longer.

"I guess you're wondering why I called you all here today," began Lena, a bottle of spring water balanced on her belly. Neat trick.

It was around midday. All four of us, Lena, Evelyn, Anne, and I, sat gathered in Lena and Jimmy's luxurious suite, just hanging out. A range of swanky sandwiches, pastries, fruits, and cheeses were laid out on the coffee table before us. No cake pops, but there were macaroons and madeleines, which you have to admit are almost as good.

Ev wiped a stray bread crumb from the corner of her mouth. "I thought we were just having lunch."

"She wouldn't have made that announcement if we were just having lunch," said Anne, stirring extra sugar into a cup of sweet tea.

"True."

Lena sat in a damask lounge chair, peering out through her groovy horn-rim glasses at each of us in turn. The woman was a good month ahead of my sixteen weeks. God help me when I got that big. Ben could just roll me places.

Pregnancy. So not natural.

"No, we are not here just to eat," she continued. "Though eat we will, and then some. What we are here to do is to meddle in Lizzy's life, because we love and care for her. Also, because being on tour gets boring after a while so I figured what the hell."

"Oh good." I took another sip of my decaf—read warm, beige milk.

"Did you notice she has a hickey on her shoulder?" asked Ev, wiggling her eyebrows.

"Nothing to see here." I pulled up my shirt collar. "Move along please."

"She does seem especially glowy this morning." Awesome. Even my own sister was getting in on the act. No loyalty.

"I noticed that." Lena tugged at a stray thread on the hem of her maternity Stage Dive T-shirt. It had to be pirated, what with it proudly proclaiming in fancy lettering, JIMMY FERRIS, I'D TAP THAT. I couldn't imagine the man ever okaying the design in this lifetime. "And get this.

When Ben stopped by to grab Jim to go work out earlier, the bearded dude was one happy, happy boy."

My brows descended. "No comment."

"About time," sighed Ev. "He's been so damn grumpy lately."

"Not anymore he isn't. She's got that boy walking on the sunshine."

"Thinking she used pussy magic on him?" asked Ev, eyeing me up in a dreadfully lewd fashion.

"That's my guess."

"You're not funny," I said, mostly unsmiling. "Anne, make them stop."

My sister tucked her bright-red hair neatly behind her ears and shook her head sadly. "Ah, hon. No can do. You're part of Stage Dive family now. Inner circle and all that. Best get used to it."

"Ben and I aren't married. We're not even together, exactly."

"Expound on 'exactly,'" said Anne, learning forward in her seat. "I haven't heard what happened last night after you two left the party to go talk."

"We talked. Nothing else to tell." Nothing else I was prepared to tell. The many changes were still too fresh. I hadn't quite turned all of the information over enough times in my head to make sense of it. Assuming I would in fact be able to make sense of it.

I was dubious.

My words were met with a chorus of boos and even some hissing. One individual who will remain unnamed (Lena) even went so far as to lob a Danish at my head. Pastries as projectiles . . . I never. Luckily I caught it before it could make contact. Cherry, yum.

"Okay, okay! Simmer down." Good lawd, these ladies. And I use the term *ladies* loosely. "The truth is I don't really know what's going on with us."

"Well, what do you think is going on with you two?" asked Anne, stealing half of my dessert. Girl was just lucky I loved her.

"Good question. Way I figure, there are several options." I paused to nibble. Oh such golden buttery flaky evil goodness—my third for the day. Seemed my self-control had gone weak in all sorts of interesting areas. I'd better watch it or my ass would be twice the size of my belly. On the other hand, golden buttery flaky goodness made me so-o-o happy, and really, isn't happiness what life is all about?

Bet they'd taste awesome with bacon on top.

"Continue," said Ev, clapping her hands together in a queenly fashion. "Tell us everything."

"Fine. One, I might be using him for sex," I confessed, a pronouncement met by several oohs and ahhs, and several sly grins. "I can't help it. The baby hormones have turned me into some sort of nympho and he's so beautiful and hot and I would like to point out that he started it. I did not go after him this time. And honestly, you have no idea how good that beard feels. The sensation of all that silky, bristly hair rubbing against your inner thighs and—"

"Whoa!" Anne covered her ears. "Stop."

"Sorry."

"Man. Wish that whole nympho thing had happened to me," said Lena. "I just got even more obsessed with pie. So unfair."

"Hmm."

"Lucky Jim's a breast man. He's like a kid at Christmas, playing with these cantaloupes. Can't keep his hands off them."

"They are damn impressive," I said, wiping my hands on a napkin. "Mine are annoying the hell out of me. I don't even usually bother with a bra, now that I suddenly have these apple-sized things hanging around. Not cool."

"What's option two in the you-and-Ben story?" asked Ev.

"Oh. Well, two, we might be going slow and trying to be boyfriend-girlfriend, but I don't know. He has a bad habit of changing his mind when it comes to me." I stared off into space, contemplating much but achieving little to no resolution. "Three, at the end of the day we're going to be parents, and that has to come first, whatever happens. So obviously, by putting this at three, I've been listing things in ascending order or something. Anyway, if he smashes my heart to smithereens yet again, we might well have a problem. Therefore, my question—seeing as you've all insisted on coming this far with me—is should I even be attempting anything beyond friendship with this man?"

"He smashed your heart to smithereens?" Ev's eyes got glossy. "That's terrible."

"I had . . . I have a lot of feelings for him. Each time he chose to not take things further with me, it hurt." I slumped back in my chair, relaxing, giving my full belly a chance to get with the digesting. "Ugh, boys suck. Such is life. What can you do?"

"Spoken like a true psychology student," said Ev with a smile.

"Thank you."

The blonde gave her ponytail a tug. A cute nervous trait. "I'm sorry you got hurt. I should probably never have given you his number. I knew he didn't date."

"Don't," I chided her. "I was a little obsessed with him, truth be told. One way or another I would have seen him again. He just gets to me. I didn't even think I had a type, but somehow he's it, from top to toe."

"He still should have thought of what he wanted, long before he came near you with his sperm." Anne's eyes narrowed in that deadly familiar way.

"Do you love him?" asked Lena, head tipping to the side.

I stared at the ceiling, my mind in a whirl. "Ah, like I said, I have feelings for him."

"Are those feelings love?"

"I don't want to answer that question."

"No?" Ev set her cup back on the table, setting her elbows on her knees.

I was surrounded. Encircled by well-meaning friends. Now I got it, why Anne was so taken with these girls. They were authentic, kind, and funny. And while it was nice, knowing their questions came from concern, I squirmed in my seat at the thought of airing mine and Ben's slightly soiled if not completely rank and feral laundry. I barely had a handle on the situation between us in my head, and by "barely" I mean not really at all.

"Because I'm not ready," I told the crystal chandelier hanging above our heads. Sunlight reflected on the walls, prisms splitting the white light into small slices of rainbows. Beautiful.

"No need to rush," said Anne, grabbing for my hand. "Slow."

"Slow," I agreed.

The suite's door pushed open and Jimmy and Ben strode in, both dripping sweat. Basketball shorts hung low on Ben's hips. He'd removed his T-shirt and was using it to mop his face.

"Hi, babe." Lena held a hand up and Jimmy grabbed it, leaning over the back of her chair to kiss her cheek.

"Cute T-shirt. How're my girls doing?" he asked, sliding a hand down to cover her belly.

"We're all good. Taking it easy, just like the doctor ordered."

"Girls?" Ev's eyes lit up like twin full moons.

"Oops. Secret's out," laughed Lena.

"A baby girl! That's so exciting."

No response from Lena, on account of her being busy trading spit with Jim. Whoa, they were really going for it. I wasn't so certain her obsession with pie was the only hormone enhancement.

"Hey." Ben kneeled beside my chair, sweaty shirt slung over one thick shoulder. His smile was all for me. It melted my insides, turning me to mush. What terrible power he had over me. The man should be ashamed of himself.

"Hi." I smiled. "Good workout?"

"Yeah, Dave even tagged along. It was fun."

Like a dinner bell had been rung, Ev jumped to her feet. Pavlov's dogs couldn't have been better trained. "Which means my hot husband's in the shower. Later guys."

And she was gone.

"Um, yeah. Meeting adjourned," Lena managed between kisses.

With a final evil-eyed look at my new boyfriend, Anne likewise got to her feet. "I should go see what mine's up to. Leaving him alone for long periods of time is dangerous. See you all on the flight to New York."

"Later." I waved.

"Am I going to have to let your sister take a swing at me too?" Ben grumbled in a gravelly voice.

"She'll come around."

"Thought letting Mal have his shots sorted all of this out."

"She worries about me." I tucked his long fringe aside, reveling in the freedom to touch as I liked. Sweaty or not, I'd take him and then some. "Give it time."

A scowl from the man.

"What? No." Jimmy barked tersely from the other side of the lounge chair.

"Just a little one," said Lena, stroking his face.

"I'm not growing a fucking beard. They itch."

"But—"

"Where the hell is this coming from, anyway?" Jimmy pierced me with a cranky look. "You been talking up beards or something?"

I gave him my best innocent face.

The broody lead singer shook his head. "You girls shouldn't be talking sex, for fuck's sake. We're all living on top of each other as it is."

"Liz just happened to mention the enhanced benefits of oral," said Lena, her face the picture of serenity. "You want me to be happy, don't you?"

"I keep you plenty happy," said Jim, rubbing the back of her neck.

"Of course you do, babe. I just thought you might want to think about growing one. You know, just to try something different."

Smirk in place, Ben took up the cause. Sort of. "Takes a real man to grow a beard. You're just not there yet, Jim. Don't feel bad."

"Go fuck yourself, sunshine." Jimmy hid a smile. "Both of you, out. I apparently have to prove my oral prowess to my girl, yet again."

"Sorry. My bad," said Lena, looking not the least bit sorry.

Ben snickered, rising to his feet, drawing me up by my hand on the way. Holding hands was nice. What was especially nice was how he didn't let go. Out we went, the suite's door locked soundly behind us.

"What've you been saying?" he asked, heading toward our own room. "Thought sex shit was private."

"Sorry. Girl talk. I got carried away."

"Hmm." His brows became one unhappy line.

"Are you really upset?" I asked, more than a smidgen

worried. Relationships were so tricky. Me and my mouth needed to take more care and do no expounding on him or his facial hair's sexy-times goodness.

"Nuh. Worth it to see the pissed off look on Jim's face." He chuckled.

"Oh good."

"We've got two hours before the flight," he said, dark eyes looking me over. "Plenty of time for some serious slow."

My pulse took up residence between my thighs. The man had my pussy's number and he used it with zero hesitation. Boyfriend-wise he was all over the sex, and I have to say, I really did respect him for that.

"Figure we've got some more getting to know each other to do," he said.

"You do, huh?"

He swiped the key through the lock, pushing open the door. "I gave you a hand job last night and my mouth this morning. If slow means we're doing no penetration for a while, then sweetheart, I need you to take mercy on me. I'm in desperate need of your fist wrapped around my cock."

"I'd like that."

"Trust me, I've been thinking about it all day. You sitting naked on my lap, jerking me off while I play with your gorgeous, sensitive tits. Bet I can make you come just from that. What do you say we do some experimenting and find out?"

My body buzzed, my breathing speeding. I swear I nearly came just from listening to him talking dirty. The man had hidden talents. "Okay."

"That's my girl. Who knows, maybe you could even write a paper on it."

I burst out laughing. "I don't know about that."

He grinned down at me, already lifting my oversize T-shirt off over my head.

"Your pants don't fit?" he asked, inspecting the hairband looped through my jeans' buttonhole. The sole means by which I could keep them up, since the zipper was completely out. And these were my loose low-cuts.

"Not much fits since I popped."

"You need some maternity gear like Lena. Jim said she found some real cute shit," he said. "You're spilling out of the bra too. Not that I don't like the look, but that can't be good."

"You and Jim talk about girls' clothes?"

He gave me a dour look. "Jim was just giving me some hints, what with Lena being further along than you and everything."

"The clothes aren't an issue. I can make do for a little while longer."

"You don't need to 'make do for a little while longer.' I want you comfortable."

"Weren't we going to have sex?" I asked, crossing my arms over my bountiful boobs and checking out the room. For some reason I just didn't feel like looking at him right then.

"Have you touched that money I put in your account?"

"Not yet. I haven't needed to."

"Clearly you need to." He crossed his arms too. No fair—his were so much bigger than mine. The fact that they were muscular and covered in tattoos pleased me just then. To be fair, Ben didn't seem so happy himself. "What's going on here, Liz?"

"Nothing. Which is the problem. I thought we were fooling around."

He just looked at me.

"What?" I asked.

A long-suffering sigh. Then his fingers dealt with the band on my pants in less than two seconds, the denim pooling at my feet.

"Up," he ordered, lifting me off the ground.

At last, sex. I wrapped my legs and arms around him, refinding my happy. "Were you really thinking about me all day?"

"Yeah, I was. And you're sure as shit on my mind now." Lines covered his high forehead. "So tell me, what's this bullshit about you not touching that money? It's yours for buying what you need, and clearly you need stuff."

"It's for Bean."

"It's for both of you."

"I don't like taking your money."

A grunt of disapproval. "You didn't take it, I gave it to you."

"It feels the same."

"Fine. Okay." His hands cupped my ass, fingers massaging. "I don't want you feeling weird about this. And relationships are about compromise, right?"

"Ri-i-ght." Suspicion was my middle name.

"Tomorrow we go shopping and put all the shit you need on my card."

"That's not compromise!"

"You don't like touching that money I put in your account, so don't. In fact, you don't have to touch any of my money at all. I'll deal with it."

"Ben."

"Liz. Fact is, you're probably never going to have the kind of money I've got. Since the band started earning, pretty much all I've done is invest it. I'm not like Jim with the flashy suits or Mal with the massive beach house and parties. I don't need much, live pretty simply. Drive the same old truck. I've got one expense, but it's under control." Dark eyes drew me in. "You've made your point. There's nothing in me thinking you're into me for the money, okay? Now, I'm not having this discussion with you every time you need something. You and Bean are mine, and I look after what's mine."

I took a deep breath.

"We good?" he asked.

"I'll try."

"Do more than try. Rely on me. It's what I'm here for."

"That was a really sweet thing to say." My eyes misted up. Crazy-ass hormones. "I guess because I didn't grow up with much it just . . . it feels weird even having it there but not having worked for it. Like I stole it or something."

"Sweetheart, you didn't steal the money. You stole me. The money comes with me. Okay?"

"Okay." A tear trickled down my cheek. "I really like you, Ben. So damn much."

"Christ, what are you crying for? Come here, give me that mouth."

I did as told. After that, there was more coming than crying that day.

CHAPTER ELEVEN

Ben was gone again when I woke up the next morning, in New York. Due to the three scheduled concerts, we'd be in the city for nearly a week. The thing about being on tour was the endless possibilities for late mornings. I'd be part sloth by the time we got home. There'd been a band dinner the night before, despite Jimmy's complaint about everyone living on top of each other. I think his eternal bad mood secretly hid one hell of a soft inside. And yes, that was my professional opinion. I'd caught him stroking his chin while giving Lena a thoughtful look, more than once. Wouldn't surprise me if we had another beard on board in the near future.

With my sloth side in mind, I met Anne at the gym and we took up residence on a pair of exercise bikes for half an hour. The last gyno I saw a few days back had said light exercise was fine and dandy. Despite the occasional fetish for some weird food, and Lena's pastry party yesterday, I hadn't been indulging too much. Lots of salad and vegetables and the occasional trip to the dark side of decadent desserts. Total denial didn't suit me. At the end of the day, a healthy Bean and happy me was more important than the size of my butt.

The menfolk had gone off for a sound check, followed by various TV appearances before they hit the stage. Maternity shopping could fall by the wayside for a while, no biggie. A reporter from some big-name music magazine had taken to tagging along with the band, adding to the busy. Apparently an in-depth Stage Dive on Tour: The Real Story Behind the Public Facade article was in the making. Ben had seemed singularly unimpressed with the whole thing. But then, little moved him. He tended to take the bulk of things in his stride.

Which was great.

I could, I know, become rather strung out at times. Overthink things a little. Though with the gene pool Anne and I came from, it was probably a wonder we hadn't both become crazy cat ladies at the age of eighteen or something. Not that I was making excuses or suggesting that passing on blame for a person's personal behavior was a go. But for me, I think Ben's aura of calm and direct was a good thing. People with low self-esteem fear love. (Yep. Psychology degree rears its head again.) They doubt another person's ability to appreciate them, because they don't see the worth in themselves. I knew I deserved good things. Or at the very least, I wouldn't settle for less than a good thing.

In my rolled-down yoga pants, tank top slightly too small to contain the boobs and belly, and sweaty ponytail, I wandered back into our suite. Charcoal gray with features of slate this time. Awesome view of Manhattan. Very nice.

What was waiting inside for me, not so much.

"You are fucking kidding me," the stranger snarled, glaring at my baby belly.

I put a hand to my middle, stopping cold.

The woman was tall, brunette, slick beyond belief. Around thirty maybe. It was hard to tell, the way her sneer warped her model-like face and cherry red lips. Guess she was Ben's hookup in New York or something. How awkward. Also, how the hell had she gotten in here?

"And you would be?" I asked, with an edge to my voice.

"If you think you're getting a fucking dime out of him without a paternity test you are dreaming. And even then, he will fight you for custody."

Interesting. She seemed to believe she knew a hell of a lot about my boyfriend without actually knowing anything at all.

"Your name, please?" I asked.

"You're not the first little cunt to try this shit with one of them, and you sure as hell won't be the last." The woman, henceforth known as "the bitch," stared down at me from her stiletto-aided superior height. "Why Adrian didn't let me know I have no idea."

She was pals with Adrian? Not a good sign. Everything I'd seen and heard about the band's manager led me to believe he was one of the great douches of our time.

"Was Ben expecting you?" He sure as hell hadn't mentioned any visitors to me.

"I'm welcome here."

"Yeah? How did you get in, just out of interest?"

"Security knows me." A defiant flip of the hair. Christ, the woman was just like every mean girl I had ever encountered in high school. Amazing how some people just stopped developing beyond a certain age and got stuck.

Outside I did my best to look calm and cool, but inside I was one riled-up, unhappy camper. What the hell was she doing in our room? I guess Ben hadn't had a chance to break it off with this chick. Awesome. "Would you like a juice? I'm dying for a juice."

"Let me guess: you're some trailer trash little gold-

digging whore who thought getting backstage and sucking one of the guys' dicks would get you somewhere."

Guess she didn't want a drink. But also, "You don't get
pregnant by sucking dick. I'm not majoring in biology or
anything, but pretty damn sure of that one."

The bitch just stared at me. Okay, so this was really not
going well.

"Sorry," I said. Not sorry. "Didn't mean to interrupt
your righteous rant. Please keep going. I honestly can't
wait to hear what you have to say next."

Beautiful face scrunched up all cat-asslike, the woman
actually had the audacity to stalk toward me, her hands
curled into fists. The girl was out of her god damn head.
My heart beat double time, every protective instinct in me
rising up in alarm. Do violence on me and my Bean? I
think not. Happily, the bar had a wide assortment of weapons at the ready. My personal favorite being a bottle of
Chivas. I hefted it from one hand to the other. Three quar-
ters full. It was weighty enough. No way was I playing
nice with this piece of work.

"Martha," shouted Sam the security man, saving the
day. Don't know when he'd snuck in, but I was mighty
damn glad to see him. Given half the chance, I'd cover his
craggy face in kisses. "Lay one fucking hand on her and
your brother will never forgive you. I guarantee it."

The bitch froze.

"Hey, Sam. You want some Chivas?" I asked, offering
the black-suited muscle man the bottle.

"Perfect. I'll take that, shall I, Miss Rollins?" He set the
bottle back in its place among the fine selection of booze.

"So you're Ben's sister," I said, sucking down my apple
juice once more. "Interesting."

Sam put his cell to his ear, eyes looking somewhat worried for once. The bulky bodyguard had never shown the

slightest hint of fear before that I'd seen. What a turn for the bizarre my day had taken. And what an almighty bitch on wheels Ben's sister was. I sent up a quick prayer that those particular genes skipped a generation or three. No wonder Dave had traded up for Ev. Yikes.

"No way can he be swallowing whatever shit she's peddling," spat Martha.

"Mr. Nicholson," said Sam into the cell. "Your sister has come to visit."

"Let me talk to him." Martha stuck out her hand.

The look Sam gave her. Whoa. It even made Martha pause again. Whatever the history was, there, I bet it was one hell of a tale.

"Yes, Miss Rollins and her have met," reported Sam into the cell. "I just interrupted them exchanging words. The situation was somewhat volatile."

He quieted, listening to whatever Ben was saying. Then he turned to me. "Miss Rollins, he'd like to know if you're okay."

"Best of health, Sam. All good." I grinned. It'd been a good six or so years since I'd gotten into any fights. The bulk of us grew up and cut out such nonsense. If Martha was hell-bent on meeting my protective mothering instincts, however, then so be it.

Ben and Sam chatted on. Mostly the conversation on Sam's side consisted of yes, sirs and so on. "Sir," said Sam eventually, "I wonder if it might help resolve the situation if I had a quiet talk with your sister?" One final "Yes, sir" and he disconnected the call.

"Miss Rollins, would you be so good as to give Martha and I a moment alone?"

"Sure, Sam." I wandered into my bedroom, juice in hand. My ear was pressed up against the closed door within two one-hundredths of a second. Listening in to others' conversations is a terrible flaw, I know. No way, however, could I miss this.

"What the hell is wrong with you?" Sam began, his voice low and deadly. "I watched you fuck up shit with your brother and Dave for years. To the point where you had to be sent to the other side of the country so you'd stop causing trouble."

"Who is she?"

"She's the girl your brother thinks the fucking world of, and she's carrying his kid. He was planning on introducing you to her tomorrow, after giving you a heads-up about the situation," said Sam. "He was hoping you could help her get some maternity clothes, since you know the city."

The bitch scoffed. "You must be joking."

"No. See here's the sad thing. Your brother actually believes in you, thinks you've just made a couple of mistakes but that you've learned from them and have grown up. He doesn't get what a bitter, self-centered bitch you are."

Apparently she had nothing to say to this.

"But then, love fucks with how people see things. And your brother, he does love you, despite all the shit you've pulled over the years."

"I only want to protect him," she said, voice trembling with fury. "She's conning him, she's got to be. Ben's never been the type to settle down, you know that as well as I do. He's basically a professional millionaire slacker. He can barely see beyond the next jam session and bottle of beer."

"People change."

"Well, if he's so into her then no way is he thinking clearly. He's soft, Sam. He's not like us. We see the world as it really is. People are just out to use the guys, they always have been. And this girl is no different, I can tell just by looking at her."

Like hell she could.

Sam swore fervently. "You're right that we see things as they really are. What are you really afraid of, Martha? Worried that if your brother's actually in a relationship for once, got a woman and a kid to look after, he won't be inclined to keep propping up your expensive lifestyle?"

Silence.

"You're the user here, Martha. You always were."

"Fuck you. He's my brother."

"Yeah, your brother, not your bank account. You might want to learn the difference between the two one day."

No way. Holy hell. So that's the expense Ben talked about last night—keeping his sister in the lifestyle she'd apparently become accustomed to while living with the band. The only real family he had was bleeding him dry. What an utter bitch. No matter what he'd said, I highly doubted that anything involving this money-sucking leech was under control. Man, did I want another chance to swing a nice hard object at her pretty little skull. But it was his money and family, not mine. Therefore, none of my business really. Not that I stopped listening or dreaming of ways to make this woman disappear. Odd, caring for Bean and Ben really brought out the violent side of me. I swear I was a pacifist usually.

"That girl—"

"Loves your brother. And he loves her. I've never seen him like this with anyone, and she's good for him. He's spending less time alone, talking more, interacting. He's happy, Martha."

"Please. What the hell would you know? You're just the hired help."

"Don't be naive. If you were really that stupid we wouldn't even be having this conversation."

"He can't be that hung up on her. I didn't see a ring on her finger."

"It'll happen. They're just both too thrown by the baby to get around to making shit official yet," said Sam, the hammering of my heart nearly drowning him out. "You do one thing to cause trouble for them and I will make sure you are never accepted back among the band ever again. Your exclusion will be permanent."

"They're my family," she said in a horrified tone.

"Then start acting like it. Stop taking your brother's money and stand on your own two feet. Treat Lizzy and all of the women with some respect."

No reply.

"You're never getting Dave back. Those days are gone. Accept it. If you don't want to lose your brother too, you'll take my advice."

A moment later the front door slammed shut.

Then the knocking on my bedroom door slammed through my head. Ouches. Eavesdropping was a dangerous pastime.

"You can come out now, Miss Rollins."

I emerged, sipping the last of my juice, doing my best to appear blasé about all the drama-rama.

Amusement shone in Sam's eyes. "It's rude to listen in on other people's conversations."

"I don't know what you're talking about," I said, my nose sky-high.

"Of course you don't."

I lowered my nose back to where it belonged before I got a crick in my neck. "You really think I make him happy?"

The black-suited dude smiled. It was the smallest of things. There and gone in an instant. "You're the psychology student. Think about it. Each of the guys plays a role in the band. Not just an instrument, but a piece of the puzzle that makes them work. Dave's the sensitive poet, Mal's the loudmouth clown, and Jimmy's the brooding bastard. But

Ben, he just goes on with the work, doing his thing. He's
the only one I don't have to flip out about if he goes out in
public. No interest in the limelight. The guy just pretty
much blends, you know?"

"Yeah. I guess so."

"The other guys all bought mansions and shit, but not
him. He just kept moving, living in hotels, playing his music." Sam looked at me down the length of his busted nose.
Lord knows how many times it'd been broken. "You're
giving him a place to belong, things to plan for, a life outside of all of this. Idiot didn't even realize he needed it, but
he does. You're grounding him. No one else has given him
that in a long time."

"You're kind of a philosopher, Sam."

"Nuh." Another millisecond smile. "I just use my eyes.
It's what I'm paid to do."

I smiled back at him. Mine lasted longer.

"Martha comes back, call me. I don't think she'll cause
any more trouble, but with her . . ."

"You got it."

Something woke me at around one in the morning. The
light from an e-reader, strangely enough.

"Ben?" I yawned, rolling over to hit warm, hard flesh.
"Hey. When did you get in?"

"Not long ago." He pushed my hair out of my face, proceeding to rub my neck. "Didn't mean to wake you. Want
me to go read out in the living room?"

"No." I mooshed my face against his ribs, breathing in
hot male. Divine. Even the soft, soap-scented hairs under
his arms worked for me. As for the treasure trail leading
from his belly button down into his boxer briefs . . . heaven.
Impossible to keep my fingers away from it.

"You are such a cuddler." He chuckled.

"Is that a problem?" The thought that my limpetlike

attachment to him might be annoying hadn't crossed my mind.

"Nope. I like having you close. Means I can keep you out of trouble."

I set my chin on his chest. "And what does that mean?"

"Heard about your showdown with Martha today. Were you really going to brain her with a bottle of twenty-five-year-old Scotch whisky?"

"If she'd come any closer to me and Bean with her hand raised, you betcha. Apparently I have a violent streak these days, which is a worry. But I'm not willing to stand by while me or mine get hurt."

"Hmm."

"I did not initiate it, Ben."

"I know." The corners of his gorgeous lips turned down. "I'm so fucking sorry that happened, sweetheart. Had no idea she'd react like that. I mean . . . I knew she'd think the worst. She's seen enough of the crap people have tried to pull with the band over the years. Just thought I'd be here to control shit."

I hid my face against his side. There weren't a great many polite ways to tell someone that their only real family was an asshole of the worst sort.

"Was hoping you and her would be friends," he added.

Not fire-trucking likely.

"What were you reading?" I asked, taking the safer option.

"Jim gave it to me. Loaded it up with baby books."

"He did?"

"Yeah." Ben smiled and raised the e-reader up to his face. "Did you know that contractions are like waves from the deepest sea, rolling pure natural energy through you? You must embrace them and open like a flower to the morning sun so your child can be born."

"That sounds like some fantastic crap."

"Yeah, don't know if this book's so worthwhile. Might try another."

"I haven't done a huge amount of research yet into the actual delivery process. But mostly I'm imagining pain, drugs, and yelling random abuse at anyone nearby."

A snort. "Also, babies need a shit-ton of stuff," he went on. "We better get cracking on that. Jim lined up a specialist for him and Lena, who'll work with them on decorating the nursery and putting in everything they need."

"Wow."

"Yeah. Might be worth thinking about, since we're still on tour for a while."

I rubbed my chin against his pec, thinking deep thoughts. "That all sounds great, but we've only just decided to try the girlfriend and boyfriend thing. We have no idea if we'll be living in my apartment or where."

"True." He tossed aside the e-reader and curved his hand around my hip. "Was thinking, some of the books said yoga was great through maternity and preparing to give birth and all. I remember you saying you liked doing it but didn't have a lot of time or money when you were studying. So—and don't get pissy at me here, 'cause you don't have to do if you don't want—but I thought it might be nice if you and Lena had a specialist instructor along, to work with you whenever you felt like it."

My mouth fell open. "You did?"

"Jim said Lena would be into it, and I thought you might enjoy it. But it's your call," he continued. "Oh, and Jim said to especially point out that in no way is this me worrying about the size of your ass or something, 'cause it's not. I think your ass is awesome. If it gets bigger, that just means there's more of it for me to play with. I just wanted to do something good for you, and I know being on tour gets a little bit boring sometimes. And I thought—"

I alleviated his concerns by straddling the man and

kissing him good and hard. And then I kissed him good and hard some more because he'd thought of me. No matter that he'd been off doing his thing, totally unrelated to me. At some stage of the day I'd been on his mind. I mattered to him. Proof of this was just about the sweetest thing ever.

Breathing heavy, my boyfriend gave me a slow grin. "You like the idea."

"I love the idea. Thank you."

"Tomorrow I'll take you shopping myself, okay? Promise."

"Okay." My chest filled to overflowing with warm and fuzzy feelings. Every last little bit of emotion inspired by him. We were going to make it. We were. Him, me, and Bean would be the best family ever. Our baby girl would never doubt she was loved and looked after.

"I really am sorry about my sister today, sweetheart," he said. "No fucking way should you have had to deal with that shit."

"I don't want to talk about her right now," I said, climbing down his long body.

"No?"

"Nope. I'm hungry." I buried my face in his neck, breathing in the scent of him. God help me, Sam was right. I was in love with this man. I could put off saying the words and deny it all I liked. The truth, however, wasn't going anywhere. Slow. If we just took it slow, this could really work.

"What do you feel like? I'll order you up some room service."

"You."

"Me?" His voice dropped by at least an octave.

I kissed first one flat brown nipple then the other, taking turns flicking my tongue across each. "Mm-hm."

With the aid of my feet, I pushed down the sheet,

shuffling slowly lower and lower. The line of each rib and the curve of each muscle. The indent of his belly button and those lines on either side, leading out to his hips. Soon enough I was face-to-face with his hard-on, which was straining the black cotton of his boxer briefs. I swear the man's eyes were on fire, watching me do my thing.

Nothing was said. But then, nothing needed saying.

A large candy skull tattoo decorated his left side, the detail and colors amazing. Lines from an old Led Zep song covered his right. The man was a walking work of art.

He ever so helpfully raised his hips so I could slide his underwear halfway down his muscular thighs. I'd never really stopped and reflected, really gotten up close and personal in this manner with his cock. A damn shame. He was thick and long and ridged with veins, the wide, flat head just calling to my tongue. For now, though, I ran the flat of my thumb over the silken skin, feeling out the ridge and indent where the sweet spot sat.

Ben inhaled hard when I massaged it, his rib cage standing out. Man, he was beautiful. His vibrant eyes and the lines of those cheekbones. His perfect mouth and that beard. Whoa, that beard. The things it could do. If the man ever shaved it, I wasn't putting out till it grew back.

"What are you thinking about?" he asked, voice barely above a rumble.

I tightened my grip on his dick, enjoying the feel of him so smooth and hot against my palm. I pumped him once, twice. "Nothing."

"You know, you act real nice, but you've got a bad girl streak in you. I like it."

"I don't know what you're talking about." Nice and slow I bent over, dragging my tongue across the flat head of his cock. Mm, salty pre-cum. Yummy.

"Playing with me like this, for starters."

"You don't like this?" I traced the ridge of his dick with

the tip of my tongue before digging in deep to his sweet spot. The head fit into my mouth just fine—all the better to suck at him.

"Fuck," he hissed, hips bucking, forcing himself further in.

I drew on him hard, sucking and slurping his thick cock, making a meal of him. There'd been no lie in me, I really was hungry. And pleasing my boyfriend was number one on the menu. I took him in as deep as I could go, trying to get my jaw slack. This would really require practice, given his size. Somehow, I doubt he'd mind.

On my hips above him, wearing only a thin tank top and panties, I gave him my all. If my technique was messy or somewhat technically lacking, Ben never mentioned it. I dragged my tongue back and forth up the length of him, tracing the veins and teasing the ridge. Then I opened wide and took him as deep as I could. Probably wasn't much, but what I could take I made count. It was definitely one of those occasions were suction equaled love. Lots of love. The salty taste on my tongue and his moaning and the words of praise filling my ears confirmed this.

Giving head to Ben was great.

The big, hairy man was completely at my mercy. His hips started churning, obviously unable to hold back much longer, and I drew on him hard. He shouted, hands tangled in my hair, tugging just the right amount to wake up my scalp. That slight sting worked for me, big-time. He held me in place to take all of his cum. I swallowed as fast as I could, cleaning up the rest with tongue and fingers. He was mine, and taking care of him was definitely its own reward.

Cheeks pinked and rib cage working hard, he stared down at me in awe. I don't know that what I'd done was so remarkable, but it was nice to be appreciated. The man certainly brought out my will to please. He looked cute right after he came. All dazed and befuddled, his face slack, at peace.

I climbed back up him, lying on my side on his chest. Immediately his arms came around me, holding on tight.

"Sorry I grabbed your hair, held you down," he said, still breathing heavy. "Never done that before."

"It was fine."

"It'll never happen again. Don't know what the fuck came over me."

"Hey," I said, getting up on one elbow to look him in the face. Some serious panicky eyes there. "Ben, I liked it. I like that you were so into it, that I could do that to you, make you lose control a little."

He just stared.

I gave him a smile and carefully rolled off. "I'm getting water. You need some?"

A nod. "You really didn't mind?"

"I like being soft with you. I do. But I think getting a little rough with you now and then is fun too. I know we're kind of limited with what we can do with baby on board." I gave my belly a pat. "After, though?"

Another nod, this one downright enthusiastic, to the point where I was worried he might give himself whiplash. Seemed my man really did like to play.

"Great," I said.

After all, what was the point of having a gorgeous, hulking big boyfriend if you weren't willing to play with him? It was all just another healthy exploration of the bounds of our relationship. Us meshing in bed gave me good feelings. It gave me hope.

"I'll look forward to it." I gave him a wink.

I so had this girlfriend thing down. Go, me.

CHAPTER TWELVE

"Lizzy!" Mal skipped over to me, dragging Anne by the hand.

"Hey, you two." I sat, kicking my heels, down in the hotel café. My iced chocolate loaded with ice cream and syrup had long since disappeared from the glass in front of me. Not that I was cranky at being left waiting. All good. He hadn't forgotten me, he'd just gotten held up with something. I trusted him.

"What're you doing hanging down here on your own?" asked Anne.

"Ben's taking me maternity clothes shopping."

"When?"

I gave her a half smile. "Soon."

"Shouldn't you have Sam or one of his goons with you?" asked Mal, tucking his long blond hair behind an ear.

"No need. Ben'll be here soon."

"When?"

"Soon."

"You keep saying that." Mal frowned. "Give me specifics."

My cell buzzed in my bag. "This'll probably be him."

But it wasn't. Weirdly enough, my ex-roommate Christy's name flashed up on the screen. We hadn't talked since the nightclub abandonment issue.

"Hello?"

"I'm really sorry. Is it true?" came at me in an almighty rush.

"Is what true?" I asked.

"That you're pregnant?" she said. "I didn't mean to give them the photo, but then Imelda said it would be okay. That everyone deserved their fifteen minutes of fame. They said they were just doing a piece about life on campus. I didn't think you'd mind. I had no idea they were going to use it like that."

"Who is 'they'?" I asked, my insides twisting as the dread rose and rose.

"A reporter from *The Daily*."

"Check *The Daily*," I said to Anne. She whipped out her cell and got busy. "Christy, what photo did you give them?"

She paused, gulped. "Well, they just asked if they could use my pics from Facebook. I hadn't really thought that much about what was on there. I was kind of hoping they'd use the one of the two of us at Crater Lake. You remember you always loved that shot. But they wound up using that one from the Hawaiian luau at one of the sororities last year. When you were talking to those guys from Economics. I'm really sorry."

I knew the picture. All the girls had been in bikinis and grass skirts or sarongs. I'd worn cutoff jeans, covering more than most because that's how I'd felt comfortable. Each to their own and all. Everyone was sinking red Solo cups of beer, decorated with those dumb little umbrellas and chunks of pineapple. An interesting taste sensation. A member of the football team had worn a bright yellow mankini on a dare. It'd been hilarious. Good music. A good night. So I'd had a few drinks at a party while talking to a couple of guys, one of whom had thrown his arm around me for the shot. We were all grinning big, just enjoying the party. Why the hell would that excite a reporter?

Anne's brows drew tight and she showed me her cell.

College dropout pregnant with Stage Dive baby. Reportedly continuing living the high life with her numerous male friends. Grave concerns for the fetus's health. Vicious tug-of-war over custody anticipated. Demands for millions of dollars in alimony expected. A person close to the band reports they are horrified. Ben Nicholson as yet refusing to comment.

With numb fingers I hung up on a still babbling Christy. *Reportedly. Anticipated. Expected.* It was all so brutally worded, the worst inferred to perfection by the photo. Assholes. They didn't have a clue who I was. Worse, they didn't even care. Whatever lies would sell. Thank god I didn't have a juvenile record for them to go poking around at, closed or open. Still, if they asked certain people about what I was up to during that misspent year of my youth . . . Nightmarish thoughts flooded my mind. If Ben and I did split, if something happened and things turned bad, would it be enough for him to claim full custody of Bean?

Christ.

And what about when I went for a job? Who the hell was going to trust their kid to a psychologist with a background like mine?

People were talking but I couldn't quite make out the words. It was like being underwater, the noises distant gibberish. The bubbles in my ears made hearing anything impossible.

Hands held my face, tipping it up. Then he was looking down at me, dark eyes intent. "Sweetheart?"

The bubbles burst, reality intruding, pushing the shock aside. "Ben?"

"Let's go up to the suite."

"Yes," I said, taking Ben's hand and letting him lead me, shelter me with his body.

There was yelling behind us. A sudden scuffle and the clicking of cameras. Security closed in. Everything happened so fast. I guess the paparazzi had been following Ben, figuring he'd lead them to me—knocked-up party girl, money-hungry whore extraordinaire in a bikini top.

Mal and Anne followed close behind, piling into the elevator. Soft pan flute music filled the air. No one said anything. Worse yet, no one even looked that surprised. Apart from me, that is. The whites of my eyes and pale face were perfectly reflected in the shiny metal doors. They slid open and Anne grabbed at my arm.

"Let me talk to her."

"Later," said Ben. "Right now she needs to lie down and chill out before she falls down."

"I'm not going to fall down." But I held on tight to his hand just in case. "I'm fine."

Anne let me go without further comment. Just as well. I couldn't dump all of this on her. She was still in blushing bride, newly married mode. No way should I be messing with that. Lately she'd taken on more than her share of big-sisterly duties, accompanying me on doctors' visits, staying behind with me in Portland.

The suite seemed eerily quiet after all of the commotion downstairs. All of the noise and thoughts continued rattling around in my head, however. Out beyond the floor-to-ceiling windows the city carried on. Christ, this was really happening.

"Come and sit down." He led me to the suede couch.

I disentangled my hand from his, shaking with some

emotion. I just wasn't sure which, yet. "No. I . . . I don't want to sit."

Ben collapsed on the couch, crossing his legs, ankle to knee. His arms spread out along the back of the couch, watching me pace back and forth. So many words were crammed inside me, fighting to get out. If I could just think straight. No point taking it personally, the journalists and photographers were just doing their jobs. Didn't make them any less of a bunch of gossip-mongering asshats, but there you go.

"I feel so . . . so powerless."

"I know," he said.

"They basically made me out to be some alcoholic who has orgies every night of the week ending in *Y*." I rubbed my hands against the sides of my jeans. Still staying up by virtue of a hairband. Though pants weren't much of a problem in the scale of things right now.

"You're not," he said, so certain.

"My *numerous* male friends," I sneered.

"It's bullshit."

"Why does it always come down to sex with women in the media? How many people have you slept with?" I asked, hands on hips. "Well?"

His tongue played behind his cheek. "I, ah, I didn't really keep count."

"They didn't infer you were some kind of slut, and you've probably slept with dozens more people than me."

He gave a careful nod.

"Hundreds?" I hazarded.

He cleared his throat, turning away and scratching at his beard.

"Right. Not that it matters. And yet I'm the slut because I'm the woman. Like it's anyone's fucking business how many either of us has slept with or if I enjoy going out for

a beer occasionally. I'm not getting behind the wheel of a
car and driving drunk. I'm having a few drinks with friends
at a party and organizing to get home safely. And if I'm
taking someone home, that is none of their business. Those
hypocritical motherfuckers, condemning me for these
things. What consenting adults do in private should not
be entertainment for the world at large. Nor is it in any
way a viable judge of a person's character."

"Liz."

"Mother-fire-truckers." I gave my belly a pat of apology. "Sorry, baby."

"Liz."

"That double standard between men and women drives
me insane."

"Yeah, I'm getting that." One side of his mouth tipped
up. "You want me to sue for defamation? I can get the lawyers onto it now, if you want. See what we can do. But they
probably can't do much. The press had a field day with
Jimmy, and we could never get a retraction on even the most
out-there stuff they wrote. But if that's what you want . . ."

With a sigh, I went back to pacing. "It's out there. No
matter what, it's out there now."

A slow nod. "Yeah, sweetheart. It is."

"I just . . . I never thought this would impact on my future this way. I knew studying would have to take a backseat for a few years to motherhood." I pulled my blond hair
back off my face, giving it a fierce tug. "I knew Bean would
have to come first, that's the reality of it. But I thought one
day . . ."

"You will get to finish your study and practice psychology. Don't you dare give into this shit." Ben sat forward,
elbows on his knees. "There will always be some fucknut
out there saying something, trying to bring you down just
to make a buck or because they can. Because their own
lives are shit. You cannot let them win."

"They're saying it to a potential audience of billions on the Internet, Ben."

"I do not care," he said, eyes blazing with anger. "You will not let these shitheads win. You're better than that. Stronger."

I stared at him, amazed. "You really believe that?"

"I know it. From the minute word got out you were pregnant, you weren't looking for someone to blame. You were pulling yourself together, planning ahead for your baby."

I stood taller, just looking at him. It was as if I could feel myself being stronger just because he believed it.

"Well?" he asked.

"To be honest, I was kind of upset with your penis and testes for a while. I may have called your sperm some bad names."

He chuckled. "Yeah? How you feel about my reproductive organs now?"

A sudden urge to burn up the panicky energy raced through me. "I feel that I'd very much like to fire-truck you."

Once more he sat back, arms spread out along the back of the couch. Such a slow, filthy smile on his handsome face. "Just so happens, I'd very much like to be fire-trucked by you."

"Child-appropriate dirty talk. There's something very wrong with that." I wandered over to him, kicking off my flats. Next came unhooking my hairband waist rigging so I could push down my jeans. My top and bra disappeared in a flash, leaving my panties for lucky last.

And all the while Ben sat there, taking me in, mouth slightly open in appreciation. "Fuck, you're pretty. And I love it when you get all riled up and righteous."

"My bearded beauty."

He laughed, hands reaching for my hips. "At your service, sweetheart."

"I'll hold you to that." I straddled his lap, bare-ass naked and perfectly content to be so. This was trust, giving him all of me, no holding back. "No more slow."

His nostrils flared as he inhaled hard. "Whatever you want."

"You. Just you."

Our mouths met, kisses hard and soft, sweet and greedy. Everything all at once. Perfect. I slid my hands up beneath his T-shirt, pulling it up over his head. How annoying, leaving his mouth for even a moment. But for skin on skin, these sacrifices must be made. And holy hell, Ben's skin. All of the art of his tattoos and the hard of his muscles. His hands covered my breasts, ever so gently massaging.

"More or less?" he asked.

"A little more." Fingers toyed with my nipples, turning me right the hell on. "That's it."

I rubbed my bare pussy against the ridge in his jeans. Who even invented clothes? What an idiot. My hormones ran rife, my skin alive with sensation. Calloused fingers slid down to my round belly, spreading out over it.

"You're fucking beautiful, carrying our baby."

"Glad you think so."

"Ah, sweetheart. You got no idea. You drive me out of my fucking mind."

A hand tangled in my hair, holding me in place for his mouth. He kissed me till my head spun. His tongue exploring my mouth, teasing and tantalizing. I could happily kiss him forever. If only my insides didn't feel so empty and needy. A thumb toyed with my clit, sliding back and forth through the ample wetness, raising my awareness of just how turned on I was. Like I needed reminding. Him in me now was the only beat running through my brain. The abrasive rub of his jeans felt . . . interesting good. For sure I'd left a hell of a wet patch to testify to that. But I seriously needed to get at what lay beneath, and I needed it now.

I raised up as high as I could on my knees, hands tugging at his belt buckle. "Off!"

"Where's the manners, sweetheart? What kind of example you setting, hmm?"

I groaned. "Please, Ben, will you take your pants off for me? It's kind of important."

"Sure thing, Liz. Thanks for asking so nicely." He wriggled down a little, dealing with his belt and jeans button and zipper far more effectively than I ever could. The thick head of his cock prodded at my slick opening. "Easy. It's been a while since we did this."

"I don't think we're going to have any problems this time." Wet as I was, my only fears were for staining the suede couch. No way, however, was I stopping. Expensive furniture be damned.

Slowly, I lowered myself onto him. The swollen lips of my pussy parting, my body opening, letting the thick length of him go deep where he belonged.

"Oh god, that feels good," I moaned.

"Yeah."

Teeth grazed my neck, nipping, sending a thrill racing down my spine. Finally, I sat on his bare thighs, the waist and zip of his jeans lightly scratching my ass. Next time we'd make it to the bedroom. Get all naked and go for it. Next time. Because there had to be more and it needed to be soon.

I threaded a hand through the longer hair on top of his head, fucking up his too-cool rock star do, tugging just a little. He opened his mouth wide, nipping at my lips, smiling. Two could tease.

"You want to play, Lizzy?"

"With you? Always."

"You're killin' me."

Despite my dare, he settled for licking my bottom lip, sucking on it. Then the strong hands beneath my ass took the lead, gently lifted me up, before letting me slide back down. We both moaned then. Holy hell, it all felt so good. His cock was a thing of pure man magic. Don't get me wrong, though, only this man would do. He made every piece of me light up with sensation, loving it. Loving him.

No matter his teasing, with his strength, he was so careful with me. Delicate even. No one had ever done that, made me feel like I was precious. Only him.

I got in on the action, raising and lowering myself with his help, riding him harder. Careful was all good and well, but a girl knows what she needs. I needed him. He filled my body in every way, gave me what I needed in a way my own nimble fingers never could. Also, emotionally, he left my hand way behind. No way could I wrap me up warm and safe like this. Fingers dug into my ass, his thick cock powering into my body. I wrapped my arms around his neck, holding on. His beard brushed against my cheek, then his mouth pressed into the corner of my lips.

"You're so fucking close, I can feel you," he said, breath hot on my skin.

"Ben," I panted. I'd be embarrassed at being so easy to please, but psycho baby hormones, etcetera. I needed it bad with him, no excuses. "I need to come."

"Get to it, sweetheart. Show me how it's done."

His slid further down, giving me more room to rise and fall on his lap, moving me into a better position without putting pressure on my belly. With one hand on his shoulder and the other between my legs, I got busy. Thighs working hard, keeping the sweet slide of him going in and out of me.

"Fuck me," he muttered. "Hottest thing ever."

His language truly was appalling during sex. Later, after I'd come, I'd definitely have stern words with him about it. In the meantime . . .

"Harder," I ordered/begged. One or the other. With all the panting it was a little hard to tell.

The grin on Ben's lips was its own reward. "That's my bad girl."

The hands on my hips slammed me down onto his cock. I centered my efforts around my clit. Close. So damn close. Felt like my body was about to go *bang*. Energy gathered at the base of my spine, all around where we were joined. I wanted that peak as bad as I never wanted it to end. Then his cock moved over something wonderful inside of me and I gasped. Bright light blinded me, my whole body tensing before releasing completely. My head fell forward onto his shoulder, all of me shaking and shuddering.

Ben held me down hard, his hips bucking, driving himself in as deep as could be. Amazing.

Then, I kind of died. Or did a very good impersonation of it, collapsing on top of him, totally limp. Maybe I'd just have a snooze right there, with him still lodged inside of me. Not an ounce of inclination to move. Hopefully there'd be no leakage of shared body fluids. Have to admit though, I didn't really care.

Hands soothed down my back, tracing each and every ridge of my spine, massaging my ass, stroking my thighs. It went on and on. Him just touching every part of me he could reach. Soothing or claiming me, I don't know. But I loved it. The scent of us lingering in the air, our sweaty bodies all but glued together. If I stayed sort of on my side there was plenty of room for the swell of my belly.

"Comfortable?" he asked. "Warm enough?"

I nodded.

"I'm sorry they came at you like this, saying that shit about you."

"It's okay." I sighed. "You're worth it to me."

"Sweetheart." He kissed the top of my head, the side of my face.

Nothing needed to be said, not right then. One day soon, I'd tell him. If he couldn't feel it, however, with me basically trying to climb beneath his skin, to get as close as I could to him . . . well then, the man was a dumbass. My feelings for Ben Nicholson were huge. Epic. As far as his were concerned, with his hands traveling over me, treasuring me, they had to be good and real. They had to be.

Soon enough we were going to be a family. Already we were each other's home.

Turned out Ben did get a somewhat hefty bill for the cleaning of the suede couch. The man swore it was worth every cent, bless him.

CHAPTER THIRTEEN

"Hell of a fucking coincidence," said Jim, adding more baked salmon and broccoli to Lena's plate.

"Thanks, babe." She dove right in.

It was beautiful, the way he way he paid such keen attention to her. The woman was clearly his world. Lena had no sooner looked at something than he was serving it up. She shifted in her seat and he ran for more cushions. A queen couldn't have been treated better. The love in her eyes and the soft smiles every time she looked at him made my heart ache. It was an intense love, so open and honest. Every love, every relationship, was different. And no way could anyone who wasn't on the inside understand how that couple worked. Let people judge. People didn't know shit. Shoot. At any rate, I didn't need to be the center of Ben's world. But I knew me. I did need to be up there, vying for top position with his music, having his trust.

One day Ben and I would get there. Without a doubt.

Each of the Stage Dive couples was pretty much variations of the same. Maybe that's the way musicians and artists loved, how they committed. All or nothing. They were in touch with their passions, so those passions tended to run large through their lives.

We'd all attended the concert tonight to hear the first performance of one of the band's new songs. Not a slow love song, though there'd been a lot of love in it. More of a hot, raw, rock 'n' roll, doing-my-girl-makes-me-pretty-damn-happy kind of thing. A little awkward when you knew the guy and girl in question. David did like to write songs about his wife, and damn he did it well. The crowd had gone wild.

Yesterday we'd had a day off. Given that the news of my whorish money-making scheme had hit the papers just the day before, Ben and I had stayed in. It'd been nice. We'd slept until ten and had a late breakfast in bed. I'd even bravely dealt with all the missed calls from my mom. There'd been some yelling and tears on her part. A fair amount of *what would the neighbors think*. Thing was, my mom checked out of my life a long time ago, to Anne's and my detriment. That I permitted her back in at all was sort of a miracle. Her opinion on my life was not required. I let her carry on for five minutes exactly and then told her I had to go and hung up. My life currently held enough drama without her getting involved. I didn't want to hurt her, but nor would I allow myself to be hurt by her. The end.

Ben and I watched movies and caught up on some sexing. In the afternoon a plethora of boxes and bags from places like A Pea in the Pod, Neiman Marcus, and some boutique called Veronique arrived. All the maternity wear and then some. I didn't dare ask what it cost. Ben gave me the Look. What with now being in a relationship and having my own Look, signifying a line which should not be crossed, I respected his need to support me and Bean and wisely let it go. At seventeen weeks, I looked rockin' good that night in my maternity jeans and black tunic, both of which actually fit for a change.

But back to the dinner conversation.

"Marty can definitely be rabid when she puts her mind to it," said Mal, his arm slung around the back of Anne's chair. "Wouldn't have thought she'd sic the press on someone, but like Jim said, hell of a coincidence, timingwise, for the story to break the day after her visit."

We sat gathered around a big mahogany dining table in David and Ev's suite, sharing an extravagant dinner. The chefs in these places knew their stuff. Foodgasms galore.

"I don't buy it." David sat back, fingers pinching his lips. "She knows that'd only lead to them being all over Ben too. For all her faults, she loves her brother. No way she'd do anything again to directly fuck with him."

"She didn't do it." Ben remained adamant. And rather peeved, if the furrows on his forehead and sliver-thin lips were any indication.

I put my hand on his leg, gave him a small smile. Frankly, I wouldn't put anything past the crazy-ass bitch. Right now, though, Ben needed me on his side. With next to no evidence, I'd be cautious but I wouldn't damn her just yet. Nor would I be letting her near me, however. "What does it even matter who did it? It's done."

My sister gave me a long, assessing look.

"It was bound to come out sooner or later, especially with us on tour," said Anne, taking my back. "God knows how many different people have seen her coming in and out of Ben's suite, or just seen them together in general. And she's showing now. It wouldn't take much to put two and two together. There'd be big money up for grabs for a story like that. Especially once they had the right pic to sell it."

"Exactly. I doubt the girl will be throwing me a baby shower anytime soon. But let's not assume the worst until we know more."

Ben gave my hand a squeeze of appreciation.

"Pumpkin's right. It was bound to get out. Fact is, we'll

probably never know who the helpful little shithead was who ratted Lizzy out." Mal swirled a glass of red wine before downing it in one fell swoop. "Let's just enjoy our night off."

Various nods and murmurs of agreement. Thank goodness.

"Hear Down Fourth are breaking up after the tour," said Ben, one hand holding mine and the other holding a beer.

"No shit?" Jim hand-fed Lena a chocolate-covered strawberry.

"Keep that up I'll be as big as a house," she said after swallowing it down.

"Making babies takes a lot of energy."

"Lead singer got offered a solo deal and their drummer's moving on to Ninety-Nine," continued Ben.

"Hard on Vaughan and Conn," said David.

"Nature of the business. Some bands are just pit stops on the way to other things. Surprising, though. They've been together a long time." Mal beat out a rhythm with thumb and forefinger on the table. "Vaughan's actually a damn good guitarist with not a bad voice. Heard him messing around the other night. Think he just got stuck playing bass for them. Might be a chance for him to trade up."

"Nothing wrong with bass," said Ben, giving the drummer a foul look.

"Be fair, Benny-boy. There's nothing right with it, either." Mal grinned. "Is it true bass players can't count past four?"

"Says the dickhead that can barely hold two sticks."

"Enough," said David, raising his chin. "The girls wanted a nice dinner, with no arguing for a change."

"A noble dream," chuckled Mal. "Seriously though, bands breaking up happens all the time. Takes a fair amount to put up with the same people day in, day out."

"This your way of saying you're out?" asked Jim, smirk in place.

"Damn, man," said Ben with a straight face. "We'll miss you and shit."

"Wait, what was your name again?" asked David, scratching his head.

Mal gave them all the bird. "Ha-ha. You useless fuckers. You'd be lost without me."

David lobbed a bread roll at the drummer's head.

"No," shouted Ev. "No food fights. We're behaving like adults for once. Stop it."

"Way to be the fun police, child bride," chided Mal, setting a profiterole back on his plate.

A waiter in a fancy suit stepped into the room, carrying a silver platter with a single white-frosted cupcake sitting in the middle. He stopped beside Lena and with great pomp and pageantry offered her the dessert.

"What is this?" she asked Jimmy, pointing at the cake like it was toxic. "We talked about this."

"Yeah, and I disagreed."

"You don't get to disagree." A distinct little line appeared above her nose. "You asked, I said no. End of discussion."

Clear blue eyes unimpressed, the man sat back in his seat, propping his ankle on his knee. "Sure I do. Put on the ring, Lena."

Crap, he was right. I don't know how I'd missed it. But there was an almighty chunk of bling sitting in pride of place on top of the cupcake. Holy hell, it would have made Liz Taylor weep with envy.

Lena narrowed her eyes on the man. "I said no. I still say no."

"No worries, babe. You don't want to get married, we won't get married. But you're still wearing the ring."

"Why? Why is this so important to you?" she asked,

mouth drawn in frustration. Or maybe she too was slightly astounded by the size of the rock. And I'd thought Anne's and Ev's rings were huge. This one bordered on accidental-eye-gouging ridiculousness.

"'Cause you're mine, and I'm yours. And I want that clear to everyone." Jimmy sat forward, staring her down. "I love you, Lena. Put on the fucking ring."

"Put on the fucking ring," she mumbled, doing an apt impersonation of the man. In a discreet show of emotion, the very pregnant brunette sniffed. "Honestly. You didn't even say 'please.'"

Jimmy rolled his eyes. "Please."

"Fine," she grouched, plucking the rock out of the cake and sucking off the icing. Then she slid the massive diamond onto her ring finger. "I'll wear the stupid thing. But we are not getting married. I don't care what you say. We've barely known each other half a year."

"Whatever you want, Lena."

She snorted. "Yeah right."

There was a stunned sort of silence around the table as Jimmy sucked down some mineral water and Lena got on with eating the little cake. Like nothing had happened.

Finally, David Ferris cleared his throat. "Did you two actually just get engaged?"

Lena shrugged.

"Yeah. Pretty much," said Jimmy.

Barely holding back a laugh, Ben raised his beer. "Congratulations, guys."

I, David, Mal, and Anne likewise raised drinks in salute. With a gasp, Ev clasped her hands to her mouth, eyes glossy with emotion.

"Don't make a big deal out of it," said Lena. "It's just a ring. The way I'm retaining fluid, it won't even fit me by next week."

Jimmy rolled up the cuffs on his fitted white shirt. "No

worries. I got you a nice matching chain necklace for you to wear it on."

"You do think of everything."

"Anything for you, Lena."

She gave him a dry look.

"What about you two?" asked Mal, tipping his freshly refilled glass of wine in Ben's and my direction.

"You're the only one left now," said David, his amused gaze on Ben.

My boyfriend shifted in his seat, letting go of my hand. He licked his lips and fussed some more, clearly uncomfortable with all of the attention. Fair enough. We'd been dating for like two of the seventeen weeks I'd been pregnant. We'd known each other for only a few months before the miraculous conception. Now was definitely not the time to put on the pressure and rush into marriage.

"Don't know if I'm really the marrying kind," he said with a deep, not so humorous laugh.

Shit.

Every eye in the place apart from his turned to me, waiting on my reaction. Of all the things for him to say, the hundred and one ways to put off the question. God, laughing at it alone would have done the trick. I kept my gaze down, concentrating on my mostly empty plate. My stomach clenched, a weird, wiggling, vaguely nauseous sensation rising up inside. Meanwhile, you couldn't have found a more profound silence in a church.

The ringing of Ben's cell broke the quiet. He answered it with a manly grunt. Did I even want to marry someone who answered the phone with a grunt? I don't know. And apparently I'd never need to decide. He wasn't the marrying kind. All of a sudden the safety I'd found with him felt precarious indeed. The ledge that was our relationship had begun crumbling beneath my feet.

"Yeah . . . sure, send her in." He turned to me, sounding

relieved to change the subject. "Ah, Martha's here. She wants to apologize to you for the other day."

I just looked at him.

"That's all right, isn't it?" he asked, obviously referring to his sister. Sadly, I was still stuck back on his awesome announcement.

The door opened and the woman herself walked in, head held high and a big black patent leather handbag slung over one shoulder. A brief flash of pain crossed her face at the sight of David, her nose wrinkled at Ev.

Ben pushed back out of his chair and stood, going to her side.

"Make it good," he ordered in a low voice.

As if I had any interest in an apology, good or otherwise, from this woman.

Ben's words twirled around and around inside my head. We'd never even talked marriage, not really. I guess the fairy tales had been playing out in the back of my head, though, the usual fantasies of tulle, silk, and eternal love. The odd dove or two. Cake.

Yeah. Not so much, apparently. I needed to leave right now. Go be alone for a while until I had things figured out again, now that my bright shiny future had been flushed down the toilet.

Martha retrieved a couple of papers from her handbag and shoved them in my general direction. "You want me to believe you're not just using my brother and this child to make some money? Prove it to me. Sign this."

The whites of Ben's eyes were huge, massive. "Martha—"

"What is that?" I asked, the noise of my voice coming from far, far away.

"It's the contract he had drawn up, covering shared custody and a more than fair payment for maintenance— upon proof of paternity, of course," she answered.

"Of course."

"Shouldn't be a big deal for you to sign." She took another step forward, still holding out the papers. "Your own sister signed a prenup. Did you know that?"

"It's what Anne wanted. You've got no fucking business talking about that, Marty." Mal slowly got to his feet, a hand on my sister's shoulder. "And I am very unhappy at Adrian for discussing that shit with you."

"He didn't." The snake of a woman sneered. "But his new little secretary is very chatty. Not the brightest, though, unfortunately for her."

"Get the fuck out of here," said David. "Now, Martha."

"Doesn't concern you," she said without sparing him a glance. Still looking at me, she continued, "You want to prove to me that you love my brother? That you have his best interests at heart? Sign it."

I just stared at the papers, perplexed.

"Martha!" David kicked back his chair.

"When?" I asked Ben, doing my best to meet his eyes, but not quite managing. I stared off over his thick shoulder at the lights of the city below. It was all just too raw, too painful. "You agreed we'd handle this between us not twenty-four hours after you found out I was pregnant. So when exactly did you ask for this contract to be drawn up?"

He stared at me, unmoving.

"Let me guess. You had it drawn up 'just in case'?"

"Lizzy." His Adam's apple bobbed.

"Did you think I wouldn't understand your need to protect yourself?"

"You didn't like the idea when I first brought it up."

"I barely had a chance to get used to the idea," I cried. "Christ, Ben. Most people would be a little wary at the mention of having lawyers sicced on them, don't you think?"

"What's it matter?" he asked, jaw shifting angrily. "I haven't asked you to sign it."

"Don't play stupid with her, Ben," Martha sneered. "Adrian sent you a copy weeks ago. His little secretary said he asked her to double check that you still had it last week. He was wondering what the holdup is."

Ben glared furiously at Martha, but he didn't deny it.

"Just in case." I wrapped my arms around myself, holding on tight. "Why are we even doing this? I mean really. You lied to me, Ben. You're just waiting for this to fall to apart, aren't you? You're not the marrying kind? Honestly, I don't even know that you're the relationship kind. In a lot of ways you've avoided commitment at every step. I was just too stupid to see."

"Check it out, Ben," said Martha, voice low and hypnotic. "This is what happens when you threaten their money. The claws come out and you find out what they were up to all along." She turned on me. "So go on then. Storm out and lawyer up all you want—but everyone here has seen you for what you really are now."

"God, you . . ." There weren't words bad enough for this sort of bitch. I snatched the contract from her hands, slapping it down on the table. It was surprisingly slim, only three or so pages. "Pen!"

Martha hunted through her handbag for one.

"Don't," Ben said, pushing the word out through gritted teeth.

I grabbed the pen Martha was offering. Funny, there was none of the triumph or venom remaining on her face now. If anything, her gaze seemed confused, cautious. Like I could care. This had nothing do with her anymore.

I moved my dinner plate aside and flipped through the papers, finding the big, juicy number meant to buy me off. Fuck's sake, he'd already put half a million into my bank account. How ridiculous. Without hesitation I scribbled out the number and wrote in a big fat zero. Then I read through it, doing a check on the custody and other assorted details.

As promised, Bean would be shared evenly between the two of us. Any disputes would be sorted out in family court, in the event of mediation failing. Good. It all seemed standard.

There. Signed and done.

If they needed anything else they could catch up with me later. At a mutually beneficial time when I wasn't about to have a messy emotional breakdown, possibly involving puking my guts up.

His sister snatched up the contract, hurriedly examining it.

"I'd appreciate it if you'd give me an hour to remove my belongings from the room before returning to it," I told Ben, not even bothering with the pretense of facing him this time.

"We need to talk," he said. "Liz."

"You signed it," Martha said. "You even crossed out the money." The look on his bitch of a sister's face would have been hilarious had I not been in the middle of getting my heart broken. Her brows might never return to normal, they'd risen so high on her perfect forehead.

"I don't give a fuck about the contract," Ben snarled, grabbing hold of my arm.

"If you didn't give a fuck about the contract, then it wouldn't exist." I tugged my arm from his grasp. "You sure as hell wouldn't be carrying a copy of it around with you."

"Sweetheart—"

"No. Never again. I'm an never . . . ever . . . going through this with you again." I sucked in a sharp breath. "Don't feel too bad about it, Ben. You did warn me, after all. I was just stupid enough to believe that maybe I could matter to you as much as you do to me. My bad."

Still, Martha stared at the papers, stunned.

"You do matter to me," he said, breathing hard.

"But not enough. Not enough to be honest with me. Not

enough to talk to me about this, about your fears . . . God, did you really think I would be like her?" I pointed a thumb at his abomination of a sister. "That I would cheat? Lie? Use you for money time and again, messing with your life?"

"I love my brother," Martha shouted.

"You shut your god damn mouth!" Tears poured down my face. I was beyond caring, really. Beyond everything. I rested my hand on my belly, feeling that strange stirring sensation within again. Bean apparently didn't care for shouting. I lowered my voice accordingly. "I will deal with you when I am good and ready."

Martha shut it, face still stunned.

"I was never trying to change you," I said, finding my last ounce of bravery and staring Ben in the face. "I just wanted some of your time, your attention. I wanted to be a part of what you love."

Dark eyes gave me nothing but grief.

"You've got another six or so weeks on tour. I don't want to hear from you during that time," I said, turning away. "I'll make sure any medical updates are forwarded to you. Otherwise . . . I just . . . I need a break. From all of this."

"You're going back to Portland?" he asked, obviously unhappy. His man-feelings had been hurt. Too bad.

"Yes."

As expected, Anne opened her mouth, rising to her feet. She'd have my back, of course she would. But I halted her with a hand. "Later."

She nodded.

I turned toward Martha, tamping down the need to beat her with the nearest solid object. "I don't have much family, and sadly, your brother seems all too willing to tolerate your borderline personality disorder. But you will *never* treat my child in a way that is anything less than loving and supportive. Is that understood?"

Numbly, she nodded.

"Good."

Anne took my hand. Solidarity among sisters, etcetera, and thank god for it. I really needed her right then. Together, with Mal behind us, we left.

CHAPTER FOURTEEN

"Are you sure?" my sister asked, not for the first time. Not even for the hundredth, for that matter.

"I'm sure."

"I don't like you being sure."

"I get that." I sat on the bed in her suite's spare bedroom, watching as she meticulously packed my case. My underwear had basically been alphabetized. "And I love you for it."

She sighed, refolding one of my maternity tops for the third time. "I love you too. I'm just sorry it ended this way. He seemed so into you. I really thought he'd get his act together."

"I guess some people are just wandering souls. They really are better off alone. They need their freedom more than they need love and companionship. Better to find out now than to keep persevering at a relationship that's ultimately doomed because he's unable to trust and commit." I gave her the same brave, what-can-you-do smile I'd been wearing for the last twenty-four hours. My cheeks hurt. Much more and I'd have to ice my face.

"You're so full of shit," she sighed.

I smiled some more.

"Stop trying to appear so cool about it. I know full well the asshole has ripped your beating heart right out of your chest and stomped all over it with his huge black boots."

"Nice visual."

"I hate him. Next time we have a band dinner, I'm stabbing him with a fork."

"You are not stabbing him with a fork," I said, patting her hand. "You're going to be perfectly polite and carry on with business as usual."

Eyes narrowed, she gave me a stubborn look.

"For Mal's sake," I said. "I'll go home and get the nursery sorted. It'll be fine, Anne. Really."

"Let me come with you."

"No." I shook my head determinedly. "Absolutely not. You've never been to Europe. You've been looking forward to this trip for months. It's only six weeks. I'll manage. Besides, honestly, I need the space right now."

Her shoulders slumped in defeat. "You promise you'll call me if you need me."

I held up my hand. "I solemnly swear."

"Hmm."

"Killer and I are just going to hang out, take it easy."

"He's definitely going to be relieved to get out of the pet hotel. That's one silver lining at least. The last few times I've called, he's flat-out refused to speak to me."

"He's a dog, Anne. He can't talk."

More frowning. "But he used to make these little yipping noises and bark at me. You know what I mean. I'm worried this has given him abandonment issues. He's a very sensitive animal. He's like Mal, deep down, in a way."

"He's a lunatic who chases his own tail until he falls over," I said. "Actually, he kind of is like Mal, you're right."

"True." Anne nodded with a thoughtful look.

"Well, I promise to apply all of my psychology skills to resolving his issues before you return." In my experience,

Killer's happiness could be bought with a pack of Canadian bacon and the destruction of one of Mal's Converses. I'd already stolen a reasonably new-looking shoe out of Mal's closet for just this purpose. The dog would be back to his usual tail-wagging, gleeful, psycho self in no time.

My own abandonment issues might take a little longer to resolve.

Tomorrow, Stage Dive moved on to Montreal, then Europe. Slightly sooner, in secret, I'd return to Oregon. Everyone was going to the concert tonight for the first performance of yet another song. I guess it was a new tradition to have everyone there. Nice. Seemed David was in fine writing form these days—touring agreed with him. While they were gone, I'd make my sneaky exit. Anne didn't know, she thought I was leaving in the morning. But she'd understand. There'd been enough drama. A big emotional good-bye wouldn't help anyone. Certainly not me. Staying in the same city as Ben, even for the last twenty-four hours, was grating on me. I ached to have his whole world behind me. I wasn't being naive and pretending my grief wouldn't be boarding that plane right along with me. It was more a feeling that I couldn't even begin to move on until I could see this city recede into nothing through the little airline window. It would be all the closure I'd get.

Besides, the town of Seaside on the Oregon coast was beautiful this time of year. It also wouldn't be where the press would expect me to turn up. I'd drive out there in the Mustang and get a room, something overlooking the ocean. A pretty view to help me pull myself together, to get over my disappointment and get myself in the right frame of mind for single motherhood. Me and Bean would be fine. Killer too, for that matter.

"You're just going to go to sleep?" Anne asked, zipping up my case and lugging it off the bed.

"Yeah. I'll take a shower and then crash. Thanks for

helping me pack," I said. "You better get going. The guys
will be taking to the stage soon. And you know what traffic is like in New York."

She dropped a kiss on top of my head. Then went crazy
with both hands, messing up my hair like we were all of
fourteen again or something.

"God, grow up, would you?" I groused, pushing my
long locks back off my face.

"'Night." She grinned. Marriage to Mal had apparently
given her the childhood she'd missed out on the first time
around, what with our parents' selfishness. It was nice, if
occasionally somewhat annoying. I really needed to remember to give her a wedgie in retribution, next time I
saw her.

"'Night."

She walked out with a final wave.

I sat perfectly still, waiting for the click of the outer
door closing. Then, just to be certain, I waited another
ten minutes. And . . . yes. Operation Make a Run for It
was a go.

I slipped on my black flats and stuffed my blond hair
up under a plain black baseball cap, raising the handle on
my case. Done. My one-way ticket home had been booked
earlier, during a particularly long stint in the john. It
seemed the only place some concerned soul wouldn't interrupt me every two minutes: Was I hungry? Nope. What
about a drink? Nuh. How about a rehashing of the god-
awful events of the night before, followed by a good long
cry on concerned soul's shoulder, with excessive hugging
thrown in? No way. But thanks for asking.

I loved the girls. Honest to god I did. But right then
I needed space from everyone.

I peeked my head out. Nada. Not a sign of security in
sight. To be expected, given I'd promised to stay in my
room and you could only access the floor with the special

key. Down I went in the shiny elevator. Across the bright, busy ground floor I all but ran, towing my case behind me. My plane left in a little over two hours. Even with the hellish New York traffic, it should be plenty of time to reach the airport and get through security.

Outside, the night air was warm, alive with light and color. New York really was the city that never slept.

"Can I help you, miss?" a nice doorman asked me, holding out a gloved hand for my case.

"Yes, thank you. I'd like a cab to JFK, please."

"Of course, miss." He held up a hand, summoning a taxi like magic.

In no time at all my case was in the trunk and I was safely buckled in the back. That was when things went kind of wrong.

The car door opened and a large, smelly male slid in beside me. It's a reality of these types of men, not often discussed. In the same way that cowboys stink of horse and cow crap, after a concert, rock stars reek of sweat—and lots of it. Kind of bursts the bubble somewhat, doesn't it? But the stink alone narrowed down the cab-stealing stranger's identity.

"Hey, Liz."

"Vaughan?"

"How's it going?"

I blinked. And then I blinked again, because he was still there, messing with my escape plan, damn it. "What are you doing here?"

Without so much as an as-you-please, he directed the cab driver to the stadium where Stage Dive was playing. The hundred-dollar bill he passed along with the instructions meant he got the driver's attention. Not little old me.

"Any particular reason you're hijacking my cab?" I asked.

"It was going to be Conn, but then, you haven't really met him. We figured it'd freak you out less if it was me."

"Right . . . right." I nodded. "Doesn't really answer the question."

"Well, all of the other guys are busy playing, so it had to be one of us." He slicked back his sweat-dampened hair with a hand and flashed me a smile. "Need you to see something."

"What?"

"You'll see." He chuckled.

I chuckled along with him. "Wow. Yeah. I'm really going to miss you after I kill you and throw your body off the Brooklyn Bridge."

"C'mon, don't be like that. You don't like what you see, I'll make sure you still get to the airport with plenty of time to make your flight."

"How do you know about that?" I leaned an elbow on the window ledge, trying to keep my cool. Not really succeeding. Outside the city lights sped by.

"Same way I was waiting for you to make your escape," he said. "Sam."

"Ah." Trust the superspy security guy to be a step ahead of me. Jerk.

"Anyway, they figured I'd have a better chance at sweet talking you into coming along."

"Did they now?" I showed him my teeth. It could have been misconstrued as a smile, but as previously noted, Vaughan was no dummy.

"Liz, please. If I didn't think it'd be worth your while, no fucking chance I'd have let them talk me into this. I got no desire to have you hate me."

I sighed determinedly. "Look," I said, putting on my best laying-down-the-law voice, "all I want right now is to get all of this behind me as fast as I possibly can. I'm sick of being here. I'm sick of the band, and rock 'n' roll, and most of all I'm sick of smiling through it all. I do think you're sweet, and kudos to you for trying whatever you're trying. But I am officially over it. I am so past over it."

"Huh," he said, sitting back in his seat and smiling out the window at the Manhattan lights. "I guess I'm the opposite, aren't I? It's all over for you and you can't wait to get away. It's all over for me too, and I just keep trying to squeeze out another few seconds from my fifteen minutes of fame. Your strategy does sound better. Figures, what with your psychiatry degree and all."

"Psychology," I corrected absently. I'd forgotten I wasn't the only one who was dealing with a breakup of sorts. "I heard you guys were finishing, but it's hardly all over for you, is it? I've seen you up onstage. You've got it going on just fine."

Vaughan smiled sadly. "You've never really seen the rock 'n' roll life, have you?" he asked. "You just got vaulted into the penthouse without getting a taste of the industry. For every Stage Dive there's a hundred Down Fourths. A thousand. We had one or two hits. We backed up a major band. If we'd held on to that and managed to score a major label contract, who knows? Maybe it all would have happened. Rock superstars, platinum albums, and the cover of *Rolling Stone*. But we couldn't keep it together. Too many egos and pissy little arguments, to the point we're barely fucking talking to each other. Luke's off to bigger and better things, sure. But for the rest of us it's back to square one. At the end of the day, the last ten years don't mean shit. I'm tired, Liz. Tired of sleeping in shitty hotels and always traveling and playing shows, trying to make enough to pay for just a little more studio time. I want to go home and see my family, wake up and actually know what town I'm in. I want to see if there's a better way to do this that doesn't cost me my sanity and fuck with my liver every night of the week."

"You're right, I never thought of any of it like that."

He scrubbed at his face with his hands, gave me that same sad smile again. "I love the music. Always have, always will. But maybe the constant push to get big enough to play stadiums isn't for me."

"Maybe not."

"Maybe I'll find a girl like you who isn't already pregnant and is all over finding me bare-ass naked. A girl who won't even think about asking me to cover up."

I laughed, covering my face with my hands. "I really hope you find her, Vaughan. You're a great guy. You deserve the best."

"Thanks. Anyway, enough of my shit. Come with me to the concert," he said, his voice quiet. "Maybe it can be the last crazy thing you do with a rock star. Maybe it can be the last crazy thing I do as a rock star." He smiled, but his eyes looked sad.

Resigned.

Slowly, also resigned, I breathed in through my nose and out through my mouth. "I better not miss that flight, Vaughan."

"You come along with me and don't like what you see or hear . . . the minute you say so, I'll get you out of there and it's a Stage Dive limo straight to the airport. Deal?"

"You know, you should get out of rock 'n' roll and do psychology," I grumbled. "Deal."

Backstage hadn't changed any. Lots of busy people and equipment on the go.

With no fuss we made our way through security, one of Sam's men appearing at my back. No one questioned us further once he was there. Vaughan took control of my luggage—more in case I tried to make a run for it than to be helpful, I think. I'd never imagined being in this position again—access to all areas, escorted down hallways and up stairs to the side of the stage. I wasn't a girlfriend anymore. I wasn't anything.

So what the hell was this all about?

The band were playing "Last Back," a hit off the previous album. Anne, Ev, and Lena were over on the other side of the stage, weirdly enough. I was pretty much on my own, apart from some sound guys and Pam, the tour photographer. She was a nice woman, married to Tyler, one of the favored sound engineers. They'd both been with the band for ages.

When Anne saw me, she cocked her head curiously, giving me a wave.

I waved back but stayed put.

The song came to an earsplitting crescendo, finishing with a staccato frenzy of belted chords. At point-blank range the noise shuddered up through my ankles and quivered my spine. The fans went wild.

"Ladies and gentlemen," purred Jimmy, in full leading-man mode, standing front and center on the stage. Clad in black pants with a black button-down shirt, the cuffs rolled back to reveal some of his ink. "Got something special for you tonight."

Lots of screaming from out in the stadium. I covered my ears, but too late. Holy hell. Inside my belly, the squirmy sensation came again.

Huh.

"Benny-boy, our bass player here, has a little something he'd like to say."

And I'd been trying so hard not to look at him. My face felt brittle, my eyes hot and hard. He handed over his favorite bass, the Gibson Thunderbird, to a roadie. His gaze strayed over to me as he walked up to the microphone. He knew I was there. Even in the darkness outside the foot-lights, he saw me.

Jimmy gave his shoulder a squeeze and then stepped back. Ben moved a hand up to cradle the microphone, but his eyes stayed on mine, his face sideways to the crowd. I shouldn't have come. Sweat poured out of my palms, from within my clenched fists. Far more than the night air could account for.

It would be okay. This was nothing special, surely. Just some weird variation on a rock star good-bye. These guys, they always did things big. Maybe there'd be a sorry-it-all-went-to-shit song just for me. How sweet.

Ben wore the typical black boots, blue jeans, and a faded gray T-shirt with some band name on it. His usual uniform. Man, if only he'd stop staring at me. It was like he held me immobile. I couldn't move, couldn't breathe.

"Hey," he said, his voice filling the night air, magni-fied however many thousand times. Once again the crowd went wild. Some started chanting his name, screaming out I love yous and the like. Who the hell could ever compete with this? The mass adulation. The worship of a crowd of this magnitude. I'd never stood a chance.

"Know there's been a lot of shit in the papers lately, gossip about my becoming a father." The long dark hair on top of his head had escaped whatever styling product they'd used. It fell around his face, strands catching on his beard. "I wanted to set things straight tonight."

More mania from the crowd. General confusion from me. This all could have been done without my presence. Easily. Hell, he could have held a press conference tomor-row, when I'd be on the other side of the country, licking my wounds and rebuilding my life. Why this? My emo-tions had been through the mill enough already.

I turned to leave but Vaughan caught my arm, halt-ing me.

"Give it one more minute," he said.

"Oh for fuck's sake." I turned, not so barely holding in my temper. Not even sorry I'd sworn. Fucking Ben fucking Nicholson. Well he could just fuck right off, couldn't he? Yes he fucking could. Not a single fucking fire truck needed to be involved in the entire process.

I looked back to find him staring straight back at me, dark eyes searing into me, despite the distance. One fucking minute, that's all he had. And I'm pretty damn certain by the set of my lips he knew it too.

"I love you, Lizzy," he said.

Everything stopped. It was like the world held its breath. I know I did, stunned.

"I was a fucking idiot not to say it to you sooner." His hand tightened on the microphone, the lines of tension embedded deep in his face. "Shit was just changing so fast and I . . . I got scared."

Talk about making a public statement. Holy hell. The beat of silence dissolved, and the screaming and cat-whistling of the crowd came close to drowning out his words. As for me, I could barely believe my ears.

"You can have my time, and you can have my attention," he said, words slow and deliberate. "Sweetheart, you can have whatever the fuck you want, I promise. Whatever you need. No more holding back, no more fear. And if you still feel you have to get on that plane tonight, then we're doing it together."

I sucked in a deep breath, what with my body urgently needing it and all. White dots receded and I saw him clearly once again, standing before me, offering everything. I swayed slightly, the squirming sensation inside stronger this time, more definite. Vaughan and the security guy each grabbed an arm, keeping me upright.

Ben bolted across the stage toward me, grabbing me carefully around the waist and shifting me onto the stage, beneath the heat of the bright lights. I could hear the crowd screaming, but they sounded distant, otherworldly.

"What's wrong?" asked Ben, eyes panicked.

"She's moving," I said, one hand on his shoulder and the other on my belly. "She's moving, Ben. I felt her move. Our baby."

He buried his face in my hair, keeping me close, taking my weight.

"I didn't know what it was before, but it's her. Isn't that amazing?"

"Yeah, that's wild."

"Your voice was so loud, she must have heard it and recognized it." I smiled at him in amazement.

He swept me off my feet, holding me high and striding toward the center of the stage. "That's great, Liz. It really is. But, sweetheart, I need to know if you heard me too."

Slowly, I nodded, putting my palm to his face, against the bristle of his beard. "I heard you."

"What do you say?"

I took a moment, thinking it through. Big, life-changing decisions deserve at least a second of contemplation. "We don't have to get on that plane."

"Okay," he exhaled hard, smiling.

"And I love you too."

His smile stretched his beard wide. "I know I'm going to fuck up now and then, but just stick with me, okay? I don't want to do shit without you. I don't want to be places where you're not. That's not who I am anymore."

"We'll work it out."

"Yeah. We will." He covered my lips with his, kissing me stupid.

"Everybody," Ben said into the microphone, his voice once more filling the stadium. "This is my girl, Liz. Say hi. We're going to be having a baby."

And that was that.

EPILOGUE

"Get! It! Out!"

"Okay, sweetheart," said Ben, holding my sweaty, straining hand. "Just breathe."

"Don't you *sweetheart* me. It was your penis that did this."

Dr. Peer, the obstetrician, looked at me over the rim of her face mask thingy, eyes singularly unimpressed with the drama. Asshole. She wasn't the one lying on a bed with her legs up in stirrups, vagina exposed for the whole fucking world to see, was she? No. No, she wasn't. I was. And this whole labor thing had been going on for twenty-one fucking hours now, so really something needed to be done sooner rather than later. At fifteen hours I'd given in and asked for an epidural. Best thing ever. But now my high was fading. My happy was long gone.

"You can do this, I know you can," said the amazing maternity nurse, Amy.

"Have you done it?" I snarled.

"Well . . . no."

I let my eyes do the talking.

The woman took a step back.

"Easy," said Anne, bravely holding on to my other hand.

"Liz, your baby's head seems to be lodged in the birth canal," said Dr. Peer. "She isn't showing any signs of distress yet. So we can continue on as we're doing, and hopefully push her out the old-fashioned way, or you could let us help things along with a suction extraction."

"I read about those." My eyes stayed on the blip-blip-blip of the baby heart monitor screen beside me.

"Is it dangerous?" asked Ben.

"With any procedure there's a risk, but it's very minimal. Generally the child's head will just display a small bump, something like a blood blister, on the crown of her head for a couple of days. Nothing more."

"What do you want to do, sweetheart? Keep going a little longer?" He picked up a wet cloth and wiped my sweat-soaked face with it.

"I'm so tired," I cried. "Why is your head so big? If your head wasn't so big this wouldn't be happening."

"Sorry," he mumbled. At around fourteen hours, Ben had stopped trying to defend himself. Probably for the best. I wasn't to be reasoned with.

"I feel very bad for me." I cried some more.

"Another contraction coming soon," Anne announced, watching the monitor.

"Miss Rollins, why don't we set up for the extraction, just in case?" asked the ever-calm Dr. Peer.

"Okay." Some weeping.

"Oh my fucking god," said the voice of about the last person on earth I had any interest in dealing with just then. "What is the holdup in here? Do you have any idea how boring it is, waiting around for this kid to appear?"

"Martha, you cannot be in here," said Ben through gritted teeth, giving his sister a foul look.

"Get out, bitch," said Anne, ever so eloquently.

The woman swanned on over to my bedside, avoiding the sight of my girl bits so proudly on display, with a look of distaste on her perfect face. "Liz. Christ you're a mess."

Ben cracked his jaw. "Martha—"

She placed a hand on her brother's arm, gave him a look. "Relax. I have an important role here that everyone can agree I am well placed to perform. I'm here to take the abuse. Figure by now you must be running out of energy for it. And given I could hear her screams from the waiting room . . ."

"Contraction coming," warned Anne again.

"Get that uptight fucking bitch out of my sight," I said.

"Is that the best you've got?" Martha yawned oh so delicately. "I thought you'd be getting to be a seriously cranky little girl by now."

"You are the worst person to be in here."

"Oh please," she said, sitting down beside me and patting my shoulder. "You were handing out worse abuse to Ben and Anne, and they're saints compared to me. Let it all out."

"God you suck."

"You know, I've been sitting out there for hours, putting up with the stinky diapers and crying from Jimmy's little twin angel girls. And if your kid is anything like them, count me out for babysitting." Hand on hip, she faced me down.

"As if I'd allow my child anywhere near you unchaperoned," I snarled.

"Cute names, though. Lori and Jean. Much nicer than what you've got picked out. I really do pity that child during her school years."

"Fuck I hate you!" I screamed, every inch of me straining, bearing down with my very last reserves of energy, giving it my all.

"Gibson Thunderbird Rollins-Nicholson." I stroked a finger across his soft, sweet little cheek. "You are loved."

"Truer words were never spoken," said Anne, giving my shoulder a squeeze. "We'll give you two guys some time alone."

"Right. Later. Nice baby." Martha followed my sister, brows drawn down and a thoughtful look on her face.

The good doctor and nurse had likewise made themselves scarce. Thank goodness for the quiet. To think, after all those months of being careful with my language, all he'd heard upon entering the world was profanity. Oh well. Win some, lose some.

"I love you," said Ben, nuzzling my face.

"I love you too." I turned, kissing the tip of his nose. "We're a family now."

He smiled. "Lizzy, you've been my family since the day I met you. My best friend. My lover. You going to make it official now and be my wife too?"

Gibson started to cry, little head trying to turn this way and that—seeking out something to suck, most likely. God, he was amazing. So beautiful.

"Here." Ben helped me rearrange him, opening the neckline on my gown to give my bubba access. "Guess I'm going to have to share those for a while."

"A noble sacrifice."

One hand rubbing his son's back, and the other smoothing back my messy hair, Ben stared down at me. "You didn't answer my question. Will you marry me?"

I smiled through the happy tears. "Oh yeah. I'd really like that."